MORE THAN
IT HURTS YOU

MORE THAN IT HURTS YOU

ALSO BY DARIN STRAUSS

Chang and Eng
The Real McCoy

MORE THAN IT HURTS YOU

A NOVEL

DARIN STRAUSS

DUTTON

DUTTON
Published by Penguin Group (USA) Inc.
375 Hudson Street, New York, New York 10014, U.S.A.
Penguin Group (Canada), 90 Eglinton Avenue East, Suite 700, Toronto, Ontario M4P 2Y3,
Canada (a division of Pearson Penguin Canada Inc.); Penguin Books Ltd, 80 Strand,
London WC2R 0RL, England; Penguin Ireland, 25 St Stephen's Green, Dublin 2, Ireland
(a division of Penguin Books Ltd); Penguin Group (Australia), 250 Camberwell Road,
Camberwell, Victoria 3124, Australia (a division of Pearson Australia Group Pty Ltd);
Penguin Books India Pvt Ltd, 11 Community Centre, Panchsheel Park, New Delhi – 110 017,
India; Penguin Group (NZ), 67 Apollo Drive, Rosedale, North Shore 0632, New Zealand
(a division of Pearson New Zealand Ltd); Penguin Books (South Africa) (Pty) Ltd,
24 Sturdee Avenue, Rosebank, Johannesburg 2196, South Africa

Penguin Books Ltd, Registered Offices: 80 Strand, London WC2R 0RL, England

Published by Dutton, a member of Penguin Group (USA) Inc.

First printing, June 2008
1   3   5   7   9   10   8   6   4   2

 REGISTERED TRADEMARK—MARCA REGISTRADA

LIBRARY OF CONGRESS CATALOGING-IN-PUBLICATION DATA
Strauss, Darin.
More than it hurts you / by Darin Strauss.
p. cm.
ISBN 978-0-525-95070-7 (hardcover)
I. Title.
PS3569.T692245M67 2008
813'.54—dc22   2007043742

Printed in the United States of America
Set in Granjon with Serlio Display
Designed by Elke Sigal

To Sus—Without whom, zilch.

The old woman called her husband to her side. "Do you remember?" she asked him. "Do you remember how fifty years ago God gave us a little baby with curly golden hair? Do you remember how you and I used to sit on the bank of the river and sing songs under the willow tree?" Then with a bitter smile she added: "The baby died."

The husband racked his brains, but for the life of him he could not recall the child or the willow tree.

"You are dreaming," he said.

*— A*NTON C*HEKHOV*

Fifteen minutes before happiness left him, Josh Goldin led his summer intern by the elbow to share in the hallelujah of a Friday afternoon.

Work was petering out across Sales. The butter smell off somebody's microwave popcorn settled on the cubicles and teased even the far offices—the first hint of weekend, and eloquent in its way: *You are a bored and hungry creature; why screw around on the 'net when there's fun in the coffee room?* But that summer intern with her frown like shark gills at the corners of her mouth—Trisha? Alyssa?—lacked what Josh believed all of us are made for: knowing when to work hard and when to let up.

"You don't think you can outrun the long arm of the weekend, do you?" Josh said.

He got familiar with people right away; he had that puppy quality, of never being a stranger to anyone. He acted cheerfully and blessed and it's hard to believe that what happened, happened.

"The weekend? But it's still Friday," Trisha/Alyssa said, laughing, smiling—in other words acting unlike herself. She was a mumbler whose temperament was a kind of infirmity.

"You know, work," said Josh, squeezing her elbow lightly, "isn't only for work."

They were walking really close. Josh moved quickly; each long stride was effortless. Alyssa/Trisha could barely keep up, her heart gasping for circulation. Yet she felt the usual pleasure, looking Josh in the face: his dimples, the constant wattage of his smile, his air of couldn't-be-better. Very few people met life with a face that free of grievance. Of course, it helped to be very handsome.

"Well, all righty, then," Trisha/Alyssa said. Her little laugh came as two hard breaths out her nostrils. "I never thought of it in that way, Mr. Goldin."

Like many women feeling the first cool drafts of spinsterhood, Alyssa/Trisha worried about bad breath. She'd forsworn coffee—and so the coffee room—since she'd begun working at Sparkplug TV.

"Wait, let me understand this," Josh said. "You haven't been on break the entire week, is what you're saying? That's downright un-American."

This was his specialty, teasing in feather touches. He never upset you at all.

"Well, Mr. Goldin. I'm really an Arab. Can't you tell?"

"No doubt."

She had goose pimples now, every little hair on her arms standing up. At the same time—despite the warm nudity of the boss's hand on her—she found herself more relaxed than she'd been this whole first week. That's the power of genuine attentiveness for you. The key was the tenure of that touch, the hand babying your elbow.

"I'm just kidding about being, you know," she said, "Arab."

"Yeah, sure, keep ululating—*Muhammad*."

His normal smile was a pleasant, subtle mocking. But for tough cases like Alyssa/Trisha his laughing eyes, out of courtesy, took on a nearly female gentility; his curved black lashes touched at the corners. Josh had enough social generosity to create his music even for someone this dreary.

She didn't pull her hair over her mouth now. She didn't stammer just because this handsome man was making talk with her. (Josh had been aware of instigating this sort of quick evolution before.)

He got her to the coffee room at the height of somebody's repartee.

Paul Damphouse, a young sales exec, roly-poly and bald too soon, was recapping a *Saturday Night Live* skit about the president. Office humor in a nutshell: impersonations of impersonations. For his size, Damphouse had a large head. For his sins, he had an ulcer.

"You bastards microwaving p-corn without me?" Josh said. With an athlete's liveliness he hurried in. A smallish lounge was all, three men and one woman in it, everyone idling near a surprisingly crappy sofa. These people were assistants or planners: beneath an account exec such as Josh.

"Shit, it's the boss. Hide the premium blends," said Doug Moscow. He was a young guy glittering with the importance of an intern made assistant.

"Not the boss, my friend," Josh said. "Just *your* boss."

Moscow ticked his head back, a breezy *wha's up*. At which point Alyssa/Trisha's throat shut like a chimney flue.

"Hello," she managed.

The light from the overhead fluorescents quivered. It jangled the nerves and gave everyone the appearance of being photocopied where they stood.

Josh gave Trisha/Alyssa a distinct nudge of a look.

But she just hovered there, frumped-out in a polyester skirt-suit. She was prim as Popeye's Olive Oyl, with the same shapeless frankfurter torso. In the uncomfortable quiet—the only sound the latte machine's revolving-door *whoosh*—everyone was waiting for Alyssa/Trisha to introduce herself. She didn't understand and just kept smiling. But once a smile becomes a decision it's no longer a smile.

Small talk abhors a vacuum. The other guy here, Mark Santella, started chatting about his teenaged daughters. Somehow a conversation got pieced together—Our kids, they're crazier than we were. Well, you were probably *never* that crazy. Yeah, and what were you, some kind of goddamn . . .

As Santella and Damphouse crunched through this faux argument—*Dude, you totally rock out for what are you, eighty? Well, you haven't been shitfaced since I'm guessing junior prom*—Moscow watched, like a cat following a Ping-Pong game. As the younger man, he needed to end up on the side that would win this crowd's approval. Then he'd know whom to ridicule, and whose side he'd been on all along.

But Josh—flaunting his charm and celebrity smile, raising a Clooney eyebrow—quickly ended it.

"Hate to say this, but I've seen both you guys pass out from one beer." He was a married man with a baby, and recently he seemed removed by half a degree from any childishness he might have joined in.

The coffee room was Josh's forté. He felt comfortable everywhere, this airtime salesman who was the reverse of the old joke: He had no acquaintances and many friends. But he could *really* open up his charms here, where your schedule lobbed you a mock day-off a couple times a day. Late Friday afternoons were the best, of course: the week already throttling down, relaxing into quoted movie lines, ribbing, more open flirting, and the anticipation of home. This newly refurnished lounge had been done up with imitation school pennants ("Sparkplug Spirit, '07"), an exhausted sofa, scuffed Led Zep stickers on the fridge; a perfectly balanced stalemate of Yankees and Mets paraphernalia; an injury-retardant Nerf dartboard (never used); some 1970s-vintage posters of Lee Majors. But somehow, all these theatrically dirtbag touches sort of didn't add up to anything. Prior to Sparkplug TV's new regime, the coffee room had been merely drab and impersonal. Now it was impersonal, drab, and wacky. (This residue of counterfeit wackiness having been the dot-com culture's dying gift to legit business.) Still, the lounge was alive—who wouldn't want to hang in the only break room? Or, at any rate, it seemed warmed a little by the joking that had accumulated there.

In fact, Josh probably felt more at home here than at home. No one nagged him here; people understood that a sales dinner wasn't *all* fun. It was work, too.

Josh took the first scalding gulp of his coffee. He didn't join the conversation, but—by giving confiding looks all around—he lent the break his unspoken clout and felt happy. He was the smartest guy in the room. Other afternoons, for fun, he might have charmed his co-workers into making little revelations, job qualms, misdemeanors, nothing *too* serious, just a flutter of anecdote to close out an afternoon. But he preferred this more humdrum kind of break, because then he could just unplug his brain (a sales rep named Kate Wilbur was telling everybody a story about a sales exec at MTV Networks, and Josh grabbed a few snacks from the Styrofoam cup without registering what kind of food it was)—really, what could be better than bullshitting with people who were more or less like you, nice, unpretentious guys, not perfect maybe, but good people at the end of a good, hard week. Guys like Moscow (Moscow who, with the helplessness of a boy stealing bites of cake, couldn't quit eyeing the sloping shelf of Kate Wilbur's breasts), and guys like Paul Damphouse (although Damphouse *was* a little weird, smiling when he talked and scowling when he didn't, as if rationing his anger so that in conversation he might be an average human being). Even Kate Wilbur here was basically cool. Except she hoarded stockpiles of gum and cookies. Her heavy mascara threw him, too; her eyelashes were clotted black like the tines of a muddy rake.

And she kept on hemorrhaging talk: The dude she knew at MTV had been a buyer at PHD Agency before jumping to the sales side for a buttload of money—MTV paid great—but the guy totally had carb face now. As Kate said this, her shrug added a postscript: It said, *All single men have carb face, at least the ones I meet.* Josh realized that the snack he was eating was Fruit Skittles.

So, anyhow, carb-face-guy replaced some dude who'd overestimated the market, holding inventory back. A huge fuckup. Then MTV ended up cutting spot prices in the non-upfront thingy— the scatter market; *that*'s what it's called, thank you—by as much as what? Fifty percent? Sixty? All right, so not everyone is good at telling a story. Kate was still pretty cool in Josh's book. Even Alyssa—that was her name—was almost cool. She was eyeing her knuckles, head down, her cheeks tomatoes of unease. But hadn't he shared kind of a good time with her walking over here? Josh lived his comfy life by having faith in people, faith that whoever he met was like him in some central way.

He happened to look out at the reception area, and saw some kind of fuss. His secretary, Damita Melendez, a phone on her ear, tensed, blinked—whatever she was hearing had her *ripped*.

Boyfriend dump her again? Josh leaned forward to peek.

Damita was putting a hand to her very emotional face. Her light brown cheeks had gained in color like steeping tea. And now she was hurrying to the break room—to Josh.

"I'm the type of guy, I had to cut prices fifty percent? I'd chop my own nuts off," Mark Santella said. He talked in that loud interrupting manner perfected on NFL pregame shows: language as a punch in the arm. "Really, I'm the type of guy I think I have that work ethic. I'm not saying that your friend's a loser necessarily but all I'm saying is if I could chop my own nuts off."

Damita Melendez reached the break room. Josh tried his paternal face, his squint of experience—because what is a boss but a nine-to-five father? But right away he felt there was some reversal. Somehow she had slipped past his preparations. Here was the beginning, the first mystery blip on the radar sceen.

"Uh, Mr. Goldin?" she said. She fidgeted and stared dumbly with a hot face. "Your wife left a voice message. It's, um, it's Zack," she said. Zack was Josh's eight-month-old. "Uh, he's—" Then she let out a noise streaked with tears.

It's one of those human quirks that no one can account for: but the first reports of horrifying news often cause giddiness. Josh gave a laugh, feeble and quick, that he'd regret forever. *"What?"*

Damita only said, "Something terrible—" and with these words snapped Josh's life into before and after.

In the sudden pressure drop, Josh said: "Zack is what?"

Everybody else looked at one another uneasily, furtively—the same way people in a crowd hearing of a pickpocket will unconsciously feel for their keys and money. Everybody but Josh had the passing thought: *Does this affect me? Am I all right?* Which got replaced right away with the soggy, recalibrated belief that, somehow or other, Josh might be at fault here—*It's a shame that his son is sick or might even die because he's a really good guy, at least on the surface he is, though maybe people have to do something to deserve stuff like this; maybe Josh is a bad parent or person, unlike me.* All this in half a second.

"Oh, God," Kate Wilbur said, with a promiscuous woman's special reverence for family. She was crying, ruining her mascara. "Oh, my God."

It seemed Josh was watching a movie. But the dialogue and the lips weren't quite synched up. Except for a few words—the words most people have the luck not to have much practice with: *intensive care, lost consciousness, blood*—he missed what she was saying.

Damita stopped talking anyway. She felt terrible: Probably she should've gotten Josh alone to tell him. *I never do anything right*, she thought.

Josh—as if he'd fallen from one movie into another—found himself outside, racing through the office park. He gripped his car keys without remembering having taken them. The office buildings he passed were geometrically simple and ugly in the tipped-over-refrigerator style. It was a world of tipped, ugly immensities.

What exactly had Damita said? Josh was now at the door to his Lexus. Zack couldn't have stopped *breathing*. That would mean he wasn't alive. The car's black roof was sequined with raindrops. Had it rained? What Josh became aware of next was the flap of the windshield wipers, that metronome. He was driving along the L.I.E. service road, it was raining again—he was aware of that.

Intensive care, lost consciousness, he thought. And then he let the associations drop there.

The word he didn't confront devastated him. It was like something heavy and leaning behind a door that he didn't want to open. Yet in what was this ongoing movie he still didn't feel the word's full power.

His life was coming as if through a sieve.

Coma, Josh thought—that was the word. He got slammed by a fist of panic and almost lost the wheel of the car.

In the days when she'd worked, Dori had been a blood taker, a phlebotomist (after the second Austin Powers came out, Josh called her his *phlem-bot*). Whatever was happening, she must have things under control. That was one benefit of having married into medicine. Just calm down here.

Josh was pinching and wriggling his cell phone out of his pocket.

"Hi, you've reached Dori's cell phone . . ." Voice mail. A fierce betrayal, that spirited hello, as if the bad news hadn't reached every shadow of her.

Josh realized his car radio was on. WFAN's 20/20 Sports Update: Derek Jeter had rolled an ankle and would have to go on the DL. This stole Josh's concentration—*Shit, right in midseason?* Immediately there was the firmer, canceling voice in his head, *Forget Jeter! What's wrong with you?* But maybe being distractible through a crisis is another way we protect ourselves, the body guarding against terror as against infection.

And then Josh's brain left the road again. He looked into the window of memory, a neat square cut into years. Right after the baby had come out—wrinkled head, scrunched E.T. face—Dr. Feldcamp had asked whether Josh wanted to hold his son. This had been right there in the delivery room, with all that blood and the thick salt smells. So he carefully rested the video camera on a flat, dry space by the birthing table. He took the twenty-inch-long purple thing into his hands, how do you hold it, all the while the creature squirming and howling. His son really *had* looked kind of freaky, too, if you thought about it. Not so! He'd had this solid, living *weight*, and I loved him right from the start. But what Josh actually meant was: *Had* I loved him right from the start?

His newborn son was the one person Josh had ever met without feeling an instant connection to.

"No no no"—Josh punched at the radio; turn that goddamn thing off—"Why think *that*?"

He exhaled. Rain had grayed over the world. The wipers

smoothed water away, waited, smoothed it away again. He wanted so desperately to be at that hospital already; he was also afraid to *get* there.

The first day of Zack's life Josh had watched the baby in a hospital bassinet, sleeping on the other side of a glass wall. Wrapped, cleaned, peaceful, and, somehow, but clearly, his. Is that not love?

White, tall St. Joseph's Medical Center, like a fort, had a windowless face and held the top of a smooth, mowed hill. He was so close now. Josh sat trapped at the red traffic light across the street. He thought, *My son is in that building.* It seemed to be an hour, just to gather air in through a nostril, feel it curl and unwind through his lungs, and then to let it out, all with his eye on that fixed red circle.

Josh would have given his house, his car, screw it—his own health, not that it'd ever come to that probably—to have this be a misunderstanding, an overreaction. Didn't the actressy part of Dori exaggerate sometimes? The baby wouldn't have had to be perfect, mind you, just alive and minimally damaged. Not brain-damaged, though. The typical American secular Jew's approach: backing into prayer. Not that the antique alphabet of devotion was anything but gibberish to him. But Josh's inner voice begged with his idea of God anyway, a sort of wily old solid midwesterner with a Kringle beard. In this negotiation, he could tell that the old campaigner saw through him—what did Josh really have to offer?—and so he found himself repeating "Please," over and over. "Please please pl—"

Green light.

Then the ridiculousness of trying to find parking when your kid might be dead. A black hulking Range Rover, swaggering into the last available spot, nearly crushed Josh's bumper. He hurled curses, orbited the lot again, and then raced to the red cross-hatching of a *no parking* zone. Then he was out in the rain again—his headlights on, screw the beeping—and sprinting to the glass door whose sliding open would allow him, at last, to apply his confidence to this disaster.

Inside the wide-open brightness of the emergency room, the sodium light handed out a little frazzle to everybody.

"Okey-dokey, let me just check," the admitting clerk said. She'd been on her headset phone before she'd noticed Josh. "Goldman, you said."

"Gold*in*."

A salesman is a professional noticer. The nurse wouldn't look him in the face—probably embarrassed by the rings under her eyes, which were brown: like where napkins have been stung by the coffee cup. Even now, Josh felt tuned in, awake to the human cues. And getting this woman to like him seemed the first step toward assuring Zack's health.

"The baby's eight months," he said. "Zack Goldin." His voice broke when it touched the familiarity of the name.

"Ooops," the nurse said. The far corner TV ran a sitcom at midvolume, *Everybody Loves Raymond*. "Sorry sorry sorry," said the nurse.

She squinted her eyes to slits of inattention. Josh even wondered if she might still have a friend connected to her through the earpiece. Nurses who seem to lack feeling must do it for two reasons. Either they have an epicurean's taste for blistering arguments, or they've got so much compassion it's a risk to reveal any emotion at all. Then again, only a saint would reflect, *Hey, this is life or death,* for every patient, every time.

Josh was leaning on the desk. Under his elbow, some waiting-room detritus: a *New York Post*, back page up, "Boston Comeback Sinks Yanks." He was kind of wet from the rain; his elbow print was a gray continent across the photo of Josh Beckett. It was amazing how distinct, how spotlit, everything in a hospital was.

"Here we go, Mr. Goldin," the nurse said. "Isaac, age thirty-five weeks."

Then her face had a nervous moment. "I'll—have to let you talk to the attending, okay? I'm sending an IM upstairs." (A lot of suspicious overblinking.)

Josh rummaged through his jacket pocket. His shirt was sticking to his chest in splatty flaps.

"Oh, sir, I'm *sorry*. We don't allow cell phones in the hospital. They'll be with you shortly, okay? I sent an IM." (Already back to tapping at the computer. Was this for show?)

He dialed anyway. And throughout the dialing he had this thought: *Four months.*

"Sir, the machines are very sensitive if you use your cell phone. It's a rule for a reason."

Josh's eyes went violent. "I'm trying to find out what's wrong with my son. I'm calling my wife. Do you want a scene here?"— Josh taking a stand, feeling as if he was at least doing something— " 'Cause I'll make a scene."

And it was pointless anyway: . . . *you've reached Dori's cell phone* . . . The hospital kept humming all around.

Many times when Josh sat at his desk alone at work, chatted with an E.V.P., or joked his way through a business lunch at some American Fusion restaurant—anytime he happened to find himself without his wife—he had a strange thought. He almost believed that Dori was at his side, a dark knockout with a high, old-fashioned forehead. For Josh, marriage was companionship that never stopped. But he felt entirely by himself in this emergency room. A hundred percent alone.

Four months, could that be? That was when Zack had first smiled—had first seemed actually to recognize his father. Josh hadn't felt genuine love for his son right away. He had to admit it—it had taken months!

Dori appeared in front of the elevator. Searching for Josh, standing in her queenly way, a frown tugging her soft pale lips. Even now, her particular beauty was the thing you noticed first— the sly width of her temples, the vivid throat, the mouth whose fleshier bottom lip obtruded like a drawer left partway open. Her skin took even this unflattering hospital light and did something dulcet with it.

Josh met her face across the waiting area—"Honey!"—and reached her in what seemed two floorless strides. From the television came recorded applause, as if endorsing his hopefulness. She was wearing his old Reggie Jackson shirt.

Right away, he came out with the panicky, high-pitched inevitables. She just took him into a hug. He had the soft of her body, at least.

"No, it's not good news," Dori said.

Somehow it was the girlish voice he'd heard each day for the past eight years—in bed; at parties; over morning coffee; in the cars they'd owned; on airplanes; a voice that so often delighted in the sunlight and in the dark, a voice that signified to him the assorted teeming sentiment of family itself—telling him, "It's not good news." She went on hugging.

"He's under observation, we don't know"—and her perfume (he'd smelled it just this morning) lifted into his nostrils again, there was sweet familiarity in it, everything's got to be okay. "Thank God you're here," she said. She didn't know a thing about Turkey, or even like to discuss it, but she was part Turkish, and that dissident splash gave Dori her proud, uncommon look.

She told all: that Zack had been fine, just sitting in the Baby-Björn, they'd been in Pathmark, but around noon he just started kind of throwing up. She wouldn't have worried, but there'd been blood in the throw-up. Not much, but any is some. It had been terrifying and awful. By the time they reached the hospital, this doctor had had to push on Zack's chest to get his heart going again—her voice staggered a bit here—because Zack "coded."

Jesus Christ, but was the baby going to be *okay*? This, finally, was the real terror, the trapdoor, the abrupt fall.

"Well, thank God he's breathing normally now, which is great," Dori said without histrionics. But her mouth, dry and pulpy with trembling corners, gave the game away. "No, I don't know. I think probably yes. They were actually going to send him home at first. But then he passed out—"

"Thank God?" Josh said, with a stringy feeling behind his knees. Using all his mental strength just to follow along. Thinking: *This is allowed to just happen to regular people?*

Two old ladies walked right at Dori and Josh. They parted around the Goldins and then closed ranks again—crying as they went. That was the thing: Everybody in this emergency room was draped in her own concern.

Dori showed Josh her gallant cheeks. He had an impulse to beg forgiveness. He couldn't think for what, but then realized it was for not having loved Zack quickly enough. There had also been that silly, mostly innocent thing he'd done that time. Dori never knew about it, and wasn't it stupid to think that *that* thing, that one worthless dangling thread on the steadfast embroidery of their marriage, was relevant now?

Josh was about to ask Dori to take him to Zack when she said, "Let's go there together."

THROUGH THE CORRIDORS of Pediatrics a disheartening smell floated in waves. It was composed of rubbing alcohol, plastic, and, very faintly, shit. You could taste that hospital mix on the back of your tongue. Dori hurried them past a statue of Big Bird. They followed a trail of paw tracks that had been painted on the wall. All this nullifying cheerfulness (smiley faces peeping Kilroy-style around corners; clouds painted by the light fixtures) was made even weirder because the rooms they passed were beeping. There was no way to soften or disguise life-or-death machines.

Josh believed he could get over it—that is, if, God forbid, it came to that. But how grindingly, obliteratingly sad that there were so many people in the world who would never meet his son.

And could she get over it? he wondered. Dori had started crying gently; her pale eyes had the lit-from-within color of nighttime swimming pools.

A long-faced black woman stood at the entrance of the Pediatric Intensive Care Unit.

"Excuse me." Josh peered over the woman's shoulder. "But we're looking for the supervising doctor."

"You're in luck, then." The woman laughed shyly and at the same time a bit touchily. She was two women, one of them offended.

Dori said, "This is Dr. Stokes."

Well, that was it, then: This black doctor would think he was racist. All through his body Josh felt his heart going, felt the great *thump!* of worry. The doctor would take it out on the baby. Maybe not in an overt way. He wanted to tell this black woman that, even if Dori didn't look it, she had some Turkish blood in her. So how racist could he be?

He didn't trust a thing about this doctor's looks. She wore her hair bullied straight back. Suddenly Josh was sure Zack was already dead. They were keeping it from him.

Meanwhile, Dr. Stokes moved ahead into a flash flood of confusing talk.

Something or other in vomit shows that gut obstruction could be a possible something. Gastric something lavage. AVM. Stool guaiac is the most common form of something occult blood test. When Josh pressed his closed eyes with his thumb and middle finger, it made fireworks in his lids. For this test the baby would have an NG tube up his nose, and then we inject saline, which we suck back up to look for blood. Josh opened his eyes. The doctor had a slumped-forward way of standing, which gave her lanky frame a false impression of weight. Some of her phrases, as they slipped by, did have a familiar grabbable part or two, and Josh made a collection of words he recognized: Checking for tumors. Possibly fatal.

Hospital was a language Dori spoke. "Okay," she said, "but all that is highly unlikely, right?" She was nodding, grilling the doctor, her voice flicking up into melancholy competence. Thank God for Dori. Josh always found it kind of a surprise, like a holiday whose calendar location you forgot, to remember she knew things he didn't.

"Dr. Stokes, we really appreciate it," Dori said. She let a gulp of hesitation pass. "Still, if Zack's vomit had blood in it, why did no one check his coags?" Even surrounded by makeup smudges her eyes, deeply open now, shed their bright blue. The effect was striking.

"Wait." Josh said, "There was a screw-up? Somebody made a mistake?"

The doctor's barricades withstood this; she had a tantrum-repelling calm. "I'll look into that, Mr. and Mrs. Goldin. I can tell you, however, that the ER note reads—"

"Can we see him?" Josh said, pleasantly but not without some starch in it. Even here, he wouldn't take on the lowercase life of an Alyssa. "Please, Dr. Stokes, I'm just his dad. Where's Zack?"

"Honey." Dori quietly took his arm. "They're running tests right now, Josh. All of us need to find out what's wrong, okay?"

"Right." Josh felt an uncried cry wedged in his throat. "Of course I understand that."

As with everything he'd said the last unthinkable hour, this really meant: *Please, I'm just looking for someone to tell me what's going to happen.*

Dr. Stokes tried a smile at Josh, tried to avoid the condescension that passes between doctors and those who need them. The professional face of physicians and prostitutes: the mouth getting the job done, the eyes belonging to somebody else. The presumption of Dori's "All of us" seemed to have annoyed her.

Dr. Stokes turned once more to Dori, whom she'd fixed on as the spouse in charge. According to the emergency-room note, there'd been no symptoms to indicate that someone named Dr. Weiss should have checked "coagulation factors."

That drab imitation warmth, the stiffness—*This is the best try this woman can give us?* Josh wondered.

"I mean, I know what I told that other doctor," Dori said. She drew herself up into a hallowed dignity—a mother guarding her cub. This was beyond the pettiness of who said what. She wristed her cheeks dry.

Did the hospital blow it? Josh thought. *Is that what happened? I have to find out if that's what happened.*

Dori brought her hand to Josh's damp face, which was the way he learned that he had started crying, too.

Dr. Stokes's eyebrows arched politely closer together. "I know it's very hard to process right now," she said. This was more than hospital consolation; it really did seem genuine. It must have been the result of Josh's crying. Men's tears, like any rare and glittering commodity, always get people's attention. Josh's son hadn't even spoken his first words yet.

Dr. Stokes had the edgy officious person's inclination to keep talking even after the point had been made. "I do understand, really. I'm a parent myself. I have a seven-year-old boy. Your child is in expert hands. I can promise you." Then she threw a glance at something or someone down the hallway.

"We'll have more solid information after his liver-function tests. Please. But you'll have to excuse me now."

An Asian nurse arrived at Josh's elbow wearing all pink. She told them in a quiet, candied voice that, pardon me, Mom and Dad, it's time to leave the ICU. "Let the doctors do what they do best."

The nurse's plastic name tag had a teddy bear sticker on it. They were marketing the hospital experience to toddlers. But what good did Josh's noticing do him now?

The nurse put her hand on Dori's elbow to move her gently along. They all saw a suburban mom in a Yankees shirt, another minivan panicker. Only Josh knew how trained his wife was.

When Josh leaned in to shake Dr. Stokes's hand good-bye, he realized he was still holding the *New York Post* he'd first seen in the Emergency Room. He didn't remember having taken it, but here it was. "Boston Comeback Sinks Yanks."

FEAR OF TRAGEDY prowls the margins of every decision to get married. In an emergency, companionship becomes essential where it had been only pleasurable, substantial where it had been light. The proverbial comfy old chair has to become a life raft. Everybody will need this someday; everybody knows it.

Whenever she'd come to Sparkplug get-togethers, Dori had gotten covered by that spouse-camouflage thing that happens: She'd blended in with furniture and other nonoffice people. Even worse, Josh had always been a prick about visiting Dori at her work. But now, as they rode the elevator downstairs, he looked into her confident face and thought, *What can I add here?* Dori spoke fluent hospital. His talent was fluffing people's mental pillows; he got others to open up, to share surface truths: to bullshit.

Five stories under Pediatrics, in St. Joe's cafeteria, the wall clock had an advertisement on its face: "Norvasc (amlodipine besylate) is the most prescribed branded anti-hypertensive agent in the *world*." The clock read 7:32 P.M.

Josh worked at figuring this whole thing out—the million-to-one of a sick child, the hospital's fuckup, his maybe sonless future, everything—but it made him tired. He felt numbly dismal. Dori would have to explain it all. She'd gone to the bathroom.

Josh bought two cellophane-wrapped apples, yogurts, a shivering Jell-O, and he waited for her in a padded booth. (The Goldins were healthy eaters.) These apples were deviously wrapped. Opening one, he lowered his head in concentration. He always found Dori a booth when he could; she liked them better than regular tables. Someone had scratched the initials "D.H.L." on the seat here.

A shy-mouthed Hispanic kid made his way past with limped, wary steps. He seemed to be moving in slow motion. It was a slow-motion world down here. People sluggish with contagion, with shitty luck. The kid wore the disbelieving face of misfortune—that sense of a promise broken. In the absence of wood, he was knocking on his head. Everyone with their stratagems, their God wooing; everyone with some kind of rabbit's foot against the worst.

Josh, a genius of optimism, had no talent for despair. How could he have? When Josh had been a kid his own father would lift him to the ceiling and goof: "Nothing bad can happen to a Superboy." He'd lived happily, he was coveted and appealing, he entertained, but Josh's imagination was limited. It didn't stretch far enough, that rickety bridge, to lead him to the unfamiliar. And yet, sitting in the cafeteria—he pictured Zack's funeral: shiny brown coffin, yellow bulldozer, sinister hole in the earth. (Were there special coffins for babies?) He imagined shoveling the dirt himself, everyone super-quiet, the only noises the earth scattering on the polished lid. And the crying. Josh even guessed how a baby's death might feel—an eternity of never being able to talk.

Now he felt his wife's stare on his cheek. And heard the familiar sound of her, the thumbprint her presence made in the air: "You all right, Mr. G.?"

Watching Dori usually showed Josh his own reactions happening across another face. Husband and wife had been that synched up, secret-sharing, when things were normal. So he expected to see his anxiety cast back at him. But Dori wasn't simply a reflection of his life, not now.

She stood before him with her steady chin and her steady breathing; the eyes were tensed, but in quick evaluation.

He asked if something else was going on, if the hospital screwed up.

"Just don't worry about it," she said. "It's not really anything."

There are shifts between husbands and wives that feel tectonic. She hadn't even sat down yet; they stayed there looking at each other, these two people who'd had so little practice in the crash tests of life. She'd meant, of course, that *she* would be the one to worry about it. Cheerful wall-posters added to the vibe (*Watch for Wellness and You! Menu Solutions; Better By Design Means . . . Healthier Cuisine*) of tragic tedium here.

"Tell me, honey," Josh said. "Tell me what they did."

Dori sat. She leaned her elbows on the Formica conspiratorially.

"Okay," she said, "I didn't say anything to you about it, because, well."

She was using the lively if hushed voice of risky collaboration. Some middle-aged eavesdropper at the next booth couldn't hide his gleam of curiosity. It was clear to him that the Goldins were sheltered in the force field of marriage. They were a team against something awful.

"It's just," Dori was saying, "they were sort of surprisingly dense and rude, these doctors. At least this guy Dr. Weiss from I guess Pediatrics was."

Just saying this relaxed Dori's face terrifically. " 'So, Mrs. Goldin, it's probably only a little stomach thing.' The doctor actually told me that at first. He just sent me and Zack on our way, like it was nothing."

"Is it possible that's all it is?" Josh said. "Stomach thing?"

"A child's brought in, there's blood in his throw-up, and *that's* the best they come up with? *No*"—Dori's voice was a near-laugh. There's a surprise invigoration in sharing even joyless confidences. " 'Oh, have some Pedialyte, Mrs. Goldin, we're done, go home now.' And then he codes."

Josh waited. He waited for the electric bolt of recognition. It never came. He sat there with his bewildered eyebrows.

"Okay, so," Dori said, gentling her husband out of his ignorance. "The first thing you're supposed to check, when a baby throws up blood, are his coagulation factors. You test coags when there's bleeding or bruising. Especially in a young kid. It's the way to determine like if you have vitamin deficiency, if you swallowed something you shouldn't have, or—"

She lopped off her explanation here and it was obvious why. There would be pain in getting specific. Coag testing can show liver disease, uremia, cancers, bone marrow disorder, horrors all.

"I just wish," he said, "I knew more about medicine."

Now and then, Josh would fail to understand things. This had been by choice as much as anything else. He'd let, say, a nothing detail at work elude him; or one of the problems of the female variety that husbands, through some osmosis of marriage, are expected to figure out. He was a skating-by expert. And he'd been this way ever since his terrific puberty. He could simply mimic comprehension, if he needed to. In a pinch, using his natural smarts he could eventually grasp most stuff. But even that little effort was generally unnecessary. He'd just play up the cool and enameled part of his personality—without even realizing he was doing it. And time and again, people seemed to admire that Josh Goldin didn't give them his full attention; they just wanted to be near him. And, if he had been genuinely warm and fun with them, they saw in him whatever he had needed them to see, whether that was different from the way he really was or not. But now he was in a hospital, failing to understand what had gone on with Zack—what was still going on with Zack. And so Josh saw his force of habit, his windup luster, for the social vocation it was.

"Hey," Dori said. "Hey."

She spoke in her softest voice. "I didn't say anything to you about it." She leaned closer. "I didn't want to worry you, is all."

Still, she wasn't done unloading. They'd also claimed, apparently, these stupid doctors, that she'd never alerted them that there'd been blood in Zack's vomit. But she *had* alerted them, as soon as she'd come in. So they'd sent her home. But then Zack passed out in the car, right outside the hospital. When she'd run back in minutes later, with Zack unconscious in her arms, they snatched him from her and hooked him up to a respirator and got his heart going again; they'd also called her a liar. They said that she'd never told them about the blood in his vomit. Crazy what these doctors you trust your kid with are capable of, but it's lucky that I, the truth is it never should've—

"Wait," Josh said. "You were here twice? Why didn't you call me right away? I mean like the first time?"

She chewed on her lip. "I didn't want to bother you," she said. "I know you don't like to be bothered at work with this kind of stuff. It's your crazy time, you said, with the scatter markets. You get so irritated when I interrupt you."

"You didn't want to *bother* me?" he said. "Oh, honey—"

He lifted his face that still had the clean look of shock and guilt on it. That shy-mouthed Hispanic kid passed their booth again, with his obliterated way of walking. Weren't there babies getting born somewhere nearby? Shouldn't some people in here be wearing good-news smiles? Then Josh realized: People with good news didn't stick around hospitals. So that's why the underwater stupor here looked unanimous. Except Dori—Dori didn't look that way. With a wife's determination, she was making her eyes call out to him.

"Josh," she said, retreating into professionalism and its associated comforts. "They didn't. They didn't check the coags until I'd brought in Zack again and made them. And then they pretended like I'd never asked them to in the first place."

He shifted in his seat. "If they fucked up," he said, crumpling a wisp of discarded cellophane, "we can't let that slide, honey." With something like a school bully's listless anger, he kept balling up that cellophane.

Josh's eyes, downward slanted, reminded Dori of something in his personality that she'd forgotten. The lids, small and creased, with faint red tendrils raking out above his lashes, may have been the only unappealing thing about him. And most people never noticed them.

"If they fucked up, honey," Josh said—all his focus keyholed around this single hard detail—"we can't let that slide."

"Hey, listen to me a second, Mr. Goldin," she said.

Her whole manner had lightened, had spread out. She was optimistic, kind of breathless, flushed, very beautiful. Her chin was up. "We're going to do this. We're going to get out of this okay. Sometimes babies just have kooky episodes."

She gave him her straight-on look, which stopped him from fiddling with the cellophane. "Listen. We need to make sure they don't get in the way of Zack getting better, is what we have to focus on." She was still showing Josh that look—her bright blue dignity. "If we can just stay really smart and watch them, okay?"

She quit talking, in case Josh had something to add.

"I'm going to get *on* these fucking people," he said.

Dori seemed about to grow brilliant with emotion again. But she tamped herself down.

"It broke my heart, seeing you cry like that," she said gently. "Up there, with the doctor, I mean. I never saw you cry before."

Josh pulled back. "Well," he said. He now imagined his few restrained tears as having looked much worse than they actually had looked: his nose wrinkling, his cheeks blimping out, totally unmanly. "I'm okay now."

In the conversation-reset that followed, Dori began silently arranging the contents of their food tray. Even her automatic little movements seemed to have the aptness of insight.

He had never known her quite like this. A year ago Josh had seen her become round with pregnancy; she'd grown taut as a grape, then dwindled back to herself. And now here they were.

"When you said babies just have kooky episodes sometimes," Josh said—gobbling up every bit of hope. Thoughts had started to take shape in his mind—in the way that discrete images begin rising from pages of squiggles in books of ocular gimmicks. But then they died away.

"I don't know what that means, episodes." He shook his head. He wasn't used to changing his self-assessments, but now he was apparently the kind of person who couldn't take care of himself.

He understood only that there existed a motherly power he didn't understand.

"Josh, if nothing else bad happens in the next few hours, and we watch him closely—the body is just a mystery sometimes—I really think he might be out of the woods. The next hours are really important. Think positive thoughts," she said, even as she began quietly to cry.

He reached across the table. The love that husbands declare at weddings is nothing more than a grainy snapshot compared to the vivid feeling, the full 3-D love in sitting opposite a wife who is saving your family. Maybe that motherly power even held absolution for whatever he'd done or was doing wrong. With prayerish appreciation, he put his hand deep into her heavy hair.

"Oh, Mr. Goldin," she said, and closed her eyes. This was her frequent nickname for him, less a joke than a message— together they'd traveled to the ends of intimacy and come full circle into pretend stiffness. He dried her cheek.

And she read his thoughts because she said, "Okay, let's go check on Zack." For years afterward, he'd remember the optimism that fired up even Dori's itch to hurry from her seat, and he'd feel destroyed.

Josh stared doggedly at the elevator buttons. The glass that covered each floor number was convex; the lighted buttons made perfect glowing domes. Josh started crying. He looked at his feet and swallowed back what he could. *You can hold it in,* he thought. *Come on.* But right then he got reduced to shuddery weeping. He turned his flushed wet face from Dori, to the wall, as if that would hide what he was feeling. Dori went to pat his neck—but then she thought maybe Josh didn't want his crying acknowledged. Men are weird about that stuff, she knew. Her hand lingered in the air like an awkward pause. She did understand her husband. Probably because she'd chosen not to caress him, he quit crying. The faucet had turned off and all that emotion shut up inside him again. Then she touched his face.

"Excuse me," Dori said to a skinny young male doctor as she and Josh reached the Peeds ICU. "I'm here to see my son."

"Oh, Dr. Stokes stepped away," said this kid physician, maybe having misheard. A stethoscope clasped his neck with its monkey arms. "Dr. Stokes is not here now, so."

"We're actually here to see Zack Goldin, the patient," Josh said, squinting. He held his big, attractive head at a slant. He was going eye-to-eye with the doctor. "Zack's our boy."

"I'm Dr. Weiss." Put at ease by Josh's manner, the young doctor smiled. "I met your wife, uh, earlier."

Josh felt more at ease, too. Even in this place of wires, of oscilloscope blips; even in this recondite nerve center. His storm winds had died down.

Part of it was the dorky and Jewish-looking doctor standing before him. Though Josh had never met the guy, Dr. Weiss was a totally familiar person: the bad posture, the bony nose with its hourglass bridge. Josh had known kids like this at sleepaway camp. Brillo-headed, delicate, bodyfatless nerds—guys who lived socially by the occasional, sidelong acquaintanceship with people like Josh. This Dr. Weiss was somebody you'd remember as having worn glasses, even though he hadn't.

Dr. Weiss spoke in that abstracted, tapering mumble of doctors and academics. He explained that, because the baby's "crit" was low, they couldn't see Zack right now. Josh thought he heard the doctor say that they would have to transfuse Zach's blood.

Josh looked to his wife for translation, but Weiss kept on.

"Zack has stabilized, though, is what's welcome. He's breathing on his own, and he's becoming alert—you know, interacting with his surroundings."

Stabilized. Crits, transfuse—those gave Josh that stalled feeling of noncomprehension—but everyone knew what stabilized meant. Josh was dying for moments spoken in the daylight language of health, when Zack's condition would peek out into the real world of words that he knew. Still, Josh turned to Dori, just making sure. *Stabilized*: the possibility of happiness, like one more signal noise pulsing in this hospital, cast its throbbing suspense.

Dori smiled. Sometimes, beauty springs from relief: crinkle-eyed, feminine head tilt, mouth half open. But what was all this medical-term bullshit, what about *transfuse*; what was that nag of doubt?

Dr. Weiss had long nervous lips that clearly registered self-reproach.

"I should tell you," Weiss said in a flat tone, "as a precaution." He swallowed. Amazing that he would have done this to them. "We have to rule out a source of upper GI bleeding that could return," he said.

His face went grim. He'd blown it; the parents' hopes were too high. "And there's still the, well, the issue of determining the source of the bleeding."

Then Weiss smoothed his green hospital smock; he regained his self-assurance by talking importantly: a monologue that Dori could follow, but that left Josh at the curb. It felt like being in Paris having only kindergarten French but being asked to negotiate a hostage situation. Esophageal varices; longitudinal; superficial venous; more terms and once in a while the clear words *satisfactory* and *life-threatening*—which made Josh's hands damp.

Weiss faced the Goldins with high-nosed brusqueness. He'd reached the one element of his job's stage business—the doctor polish, the doctor stability—that he felt he'd mastered: the quiet.

Dori said, "Are you a med student?"

Her voice came out mocking, dangerous—only Josh recognized it as the compromise result of clashing emotions. She withheld much nastier questions. "I mean, are you even a doctor?" she said.

Weiss rubbed his eyes, rubbing behind the lenses of those glasses he didn't have. "I'm a resident." He took a while to pacify himself. "Your training is as a phlebotomist, Mrs. Goldin. Isn't that what you told me?"

Josh felt something in himself snap shut against this person in a Venus flytrap way. He had a decision: to soothe this kid or to support his wife.

"A minute ago you tell us one thing," Josh said, "and now it's the lower end of the esophagus, which means what? Can we focus on how optimistic you were? You mentioned our son has stabilized. Right? Isn't that how optimistic?" His plaintive face seemed to ask a different question: *Hey, come on. We're all people here. What are you trying to put us through?*

"I'm sorry if I gave a more hopeful impression than the facts warrant," said Dr. Weiss, who on some basic level still really wanted to seem cool, more straightforward, more the guy he wanted himself to be around Josh: "I just—"

Dori did something Josh had only seen her do in private: a full-body interruption. She shut up Dr. Weiss by turning her back on him.

"Esophageal varices means Zack has chronic liver disease or something," she said. "It's a ridiculous thing for them to check for, Josh. He's an *eight*-month-old; we would have seen other signs."

She found the doctor's eyes again. "You're going overboard now, and you know it. It's just so you can say you tracked everything, is what I think."

To Josh she added: "No, they're doing tests because they screwed up before. I saw doctors do it all the time. Well, not with my son, doctor."

She had her shocked sensual look of having blurted out a dirty intimacy. This gave it the flavor of truth.

"We do have to test for these uncommon things, that's true," Dr. Weiss said. He sucked in his lower lip; his face got dimples around what had become an angry mouth. "Even what might strike all of us as highly improbable. Now, we have a Pediatrics waiting area, right down the corridor. We'll make sure to tell you when you can see him. . . ."

Josh kissed Dori as they sat down—to ease his wife's sadness, and his own. A little peck on her forehead. Her brow had a kind of burned smell, and seemed absolutely hard.

She didn't respond and Josh, as he sat back, stared at that almost-Elizabethan forehead of hers, which gave Dori her supermodel's-brainier-sister look. She'd been moody more often lately, sometimes dark moods that had confused him. But maybe that clouded over a memory of something else: Maybe Josh had once, a long time ago, understood that Dori possessed this kind of bravery and firmness; maybe, in the long years of marriage, it had become invisible to him—one of the vanishing acts that habit performs every day, to all familiar things.

WAITING, WAITING. PEOPLE say the Internet has made the world more convenient, but its real effect has been to turn everybody more restless; it's harder to wait when you're used to receiving the world

at high-speed connection. You feel all things—you feel life itself—
should be immediately searchable, quick as desire.

The Pediatrics waiting area was a half-circle of light-blue
couches, little desk, bronze reading lamp, plastic flowers in a
warmthless vase. All of it spotless, ecumenical, the set of a talk show
for two-year-olds.

Sitting with his wife, Josh rested his cheek on her hair, on the
pacifying warmth of it. She blew that hair dry every morning, each
day being a failed attempt to straighten her mermaid curls: one more
relic of their shared life.

He leaned on Dori for a while. He got up to stretch, ankles,
back, dismayed neck clicking; he saw, on top of the nearby table, a
piece of scrap paper—a printed-out e-mail someone had left *(what
up kid im so sorry im not around for you but U will beat it lookemia is
"BULLSHIT" I am here with marisa who thinks I am SO into nice
walks on the beach under the sunset lol . . . truthfully tho, juss wanted to
say hope you kick this thing. Hit me back when u can)*.

Josh thought of the idea of "vigil." A parent's job is to protect his
children, to do a vigil when the time comes.

Josh had always loved Dori a great deal. More than many of his
friends loved their wives, he thought. But like anything man-made,
the bond had had its flaws and tiny stress cracks. Even in a lucky relationship, an uncleaned dish may sometimes seem a thrown gauntlet, the sound of someone's loud-and-clear *fuck-you*. And of course,
in their eight years, the Goldins had not proved immune to parenthood's hibernal cycles of infrequent sex.

But sometimes the bummer had been smaller, more minor—for
instance, Josh's having to search for that Advil bottle he'd definitely
left on his nightstand (*Why's she always moving my shit?* he'd wonder).
Plus, there had been those recent moods of hers, which she'd only
recently started to overcome with the occasional shopping bender.

And yet, he wouldn't have traded his life and its cushy, glancing,
humdrum, fantastic pleasures. And here they were, doing a vigil.

If it was a Saturday with the baby napping, Josh might get a surprise afternoon peek at Dori as she walked, naked, into their bright astonished bedroom—her hips rosy, her hair dark and wet, all postshower sparkle—her breasts staring frankly in the film-set brightness, like two swollen eyes. That was nice: that unintended sex power. (And it turned out that he'd had the bottle of Advil in his pocket all along.) He had been happy, her moods weren't *that* bad—had he realized enough how lucky he was?

He leaned his head back to relax, just for a minute, and then he'd begin that vigil.

DORI WOKE HIM at three-thirty A.M. "I need you," she said.

Dori brushed past Dr. Weiss as she hurried into the Pediatrics ICU with Josh behind her.

"Um . . ." Dr. Weiss said, jogging to catch up—the way a salesperson would scoot to an intruding customer and tell her, sorry, the store's not quite open yet.

The baby—Josh had reached the baby—the baby lay squirming in a little elevated bed. He was attached to seven inconceivable wires and tubes, yellow, black, two see-through. The baby's face was pale and drenched in sweat. There were blue pouches under Zack's open blue eyes. *Why are you doing this to me? Is this the way things are, on this planet of yours?* said Zack's sleepy, trustful expression.

"Mr. and Mrs. Goldin, hello again"—a woman's voice. Josh didn't turn from the baby to see who this was. A year ago, he and Dori had stood watching an electric shadow on a sonogram, thrilled at a half-finished heart's little butterfly quiver.

"Hey, kiddo," Josh said now. He was always Jolly Dad, picking up his crying son, giving a calming Gentle Giant rub to the baby's back. "Show me a smile, buddy," the helpless giant said now.

Blue pouches under Zack's eyes were flecked with dried crud.

Last week, Josh had read in the *YouParent Book for Newbies,* "It's no big thing if your one-year-old doesn't speak yet, as long as s/he responds nonverbally to his/her name, and can follow supersimple instructions."

"Come on. Look at Daddy."

With his inadvertent Mohawk hair, his little horizontally creased wrists, Zack was still the same Zack—that perfect-circle head, the nub chin—still kicking his helpless feet; still a beautiful, personality-less aggregate of Josh and Dori's aspirations, and kind of chubby at twenty-one pounds. But could he follow super-simple instructions, was he responding nonverbally?

"Mrs. Goldin, I suppose I understand your point," that unfamiliar voice at Josh's back was saying. "But—"

Through all his baby watching, Josh had missed the on-ramp to the adult conversation. Dori was talking now: "What you're recommending sounds reasonable and on-the-safe-side, but all I'm saying is if you have to intubate my child for what isn't really a necessary test." Her voice, coming up against authority, was guarded: emotion taken by restraint. But neither was she backing down.

"You admitted to me that Zack seemed fine now, is what you just said, right?" She sounded exceptionally rational. "I don't want you to put him through any invasive procedure needlessly, is all I'm saying here."

Josh turned to see who his wife was talking to: the black doctor, Dr. Stokes. The woman stood hovering in the little purgatory of the doorway, holding a metal clipboard.

Stop thinking about this woman as black, Josh thought.

"Yes," Dr. Stokes said, "that's right"—plodding into the room with her heavy-shod, dogmatic step. "However—"

"You didn't check his coags," Josh said. The words just came to him. He had no idea what a coag was, he was mimicking—yes, this was his trait, his quality. This man who'd never considered the possibility of anyone being indifferent to him could add something here; he could gently turn up the bathwater's heat. "My son came in with bloody vomit. There it is—and you didn't check coags."

Dori rose a bit herself, on the uptick in Josh's confidence. She spoke louder: "Look, Dr. Stokes, I understand what the hospital thinks it's making up for. Beyond the coags test. This is unnecessary—all of it."

"I'll tell you straight," Josh said, "that's unforgivable. And we need to know things are happening to make our baby better, not things to make the hospital feel better."

"Mrs. Goldin, just hold on a minute," Dr. Weiss said. "What you told us, and you can look at the emergency-room note, the baby could still drink, had wet diapers, and that there was no blood, no yellow—"

"Dr. *Weiss*," Dr. Stokes said. Then she turned to Mr. Goldin. "The tests are intended to help us make your child better."

Dr. Stokes was in charge. Josh could see that; arguing with her would be as satisfying as shaking your fist at the Washington Monument. The businessman side of him couldn't help respecting this. She was holding her clipboard to her side so firmly it gave her shoulders a scoliotic tilt.

And now, that Asian nurse—the one from before—walked in, this time wheeling a stretcher.

Meanwhile, Dori had come over to peer in at her son, bending to him, her hands held primly and nunlike between her breasts. Her shadow went over the baby.

"Hi, sweet Zack," Dori singsonged. "Hi, there, sweet Zack. Hi."

Had the hospital damaged him? Josh wondered. *As long as s/he responds nonverbally to his/her name . . .*

"These people here," Dori said, still looking at the baby, "don't believe Mommy. Hi, there, Zackie. But she told them what really happened. And we're going to take you home—yes, we are. Home with Mommy."

"Again," Dr. Stokes, surprised, said, "I don't believe the hospital will allow that. Mrs. Goldin, your son must have been bleeding profusely. There are certain procedures we have to follow. Precautions must be taken. Also, I don't see why you won't let us do a few more tests."

"We're going to leave these people soon, Zackie." Dori's voice softened with a mother's endearment; it shimmered there without irony or, it seemed, anger toward anyone.

"We're not going to let them overdo the medical stuff on you," she said.

Dr. Weiss's eyes sharpened. "Dr. S., this woman never told me anything but that the baby had a stomachache; this is not the kind of blunder I would make. You and I have worked together for eighteen months."

Dr. Stokes, her eyes still fixed on Dori, said: "I know that, Arthur. Let's move on, please."

She'd kept that posture of command. "Nobody is saying you're lying, Mrs. Goldin. But I have faith in Dr. Weiss, and the emergency-room note says that you never told him. But perhaps you thought you told Dr. Weiss something that you didn't actually say. The relevant point here is, no one wants to 'overdo' anything. Zack really can't be allowed to leave the hospital tonight, Mrs. Goldin. He experienced respiratory failure."

"Didn't you all agree he's fine now?" Dori stood with hands fisted on her hips.

"Is that really what they said?" Josh said. He felt that racy impudent hope: Maybe he was getting his life back.

"Excuse me, Mom," said that Asian nurse. "Just have to get in here a second."

This woman leaned over with a perfunctory groan and she started removing the wires from Zack's chest. A machine next to the crib started beeping quickly in a tantrum. A horrifying sound.

"We actually have no guarantee if he's fine yet, Mrs. Goldin," Dr. Stokes said. "I simply don't understand why you wouldn't let us take more tests to determine that?"

"Here we go, Zack," said the nurse. "Upsy baby."

Those beeps, those undulating hops of noise, happened every time Zack moved one of his fingers that was still attached to wires.

"I didn't intend to give the impression I found you untruthful before, Mrs. Goldin," Weiss said, "if that's your takeaway from all this—"

And Zack was clawing the air with his hands as the nurse pulled at him: *Beep! Beep! Beep—!*

"*Arthur,* please," Dr. Stokes said.

It seemed to Josh that everyone was reciting lines and he'd forgotten his.

"I don't think you heard my wife," he said, finally, a stroke of overdue belligerence. Anger felt good, a stand-in for the more frightening emotions. "She told you what she said."

AFTER THEY FOLLOWED the baby down two floors to gastroenterology, and after some new doctors put out their hands to shake, Josh and Dori watched in the new green-and-oatmeal-colored GI lab—St. Joe's latest pride—as the anesthesiologist hooked Zack's arm to an IV. Then the gastro guy wedged what looked like the ruffled hose of a vacuum cleaner into the baby's mouth, through which, once he induced Zack to swallow the end of a camera-tipped wire, he snaked this internal peeping machine down the tiny unconscious throat, to the pharynx, the esophagus, stomach, finally to the duodenum, the opening of his small intestine; next, the Goldins saw something on the video monitor that no other generation of parents had ever seen: their child's working alimentary canal. Pink, gaping, round, and oddly adult-looking, it stared at them—an angry bloodshot monster eye.

It was easier for Josh to watch even those unreal, raw pictures on the screen than to look up and see the things that, ten yards away, were happening to his son. Little Zack was so outrageously vulnerable on the operating table. He appeared so small and dead-seeming under a light fixture that looked like a glowing UFO bottom. The baby had a sheet over his naked chest, and of course that tube in his mouth. An adult, even an older child, would know what was happening and what was expected of him. But how did the baby not gag while the gastro guy and the anesthesiologist bent over him, making small adjustments? Both men had the pale skin, the antisunburn, of hospital workers: pale in a good facsimile of the leaden skin of grief.

Dr. Stokes stood next to the Goldins. She maintained the calm of an implicit truce. And after a moment she explained the procedure.

An endoscope is an astonishing machine. It can be steered through the many turns of the gastrointestinal tract. It samples tissue with a little wire snare and a bolt of electric heat.

Josh, his head down, had just one question. "Does it hurt him?" The only safe thing he found to look at was the oceany swirls of floor wax.

"It's likely he'll be a little sore." Dr. Stokes delivered that everyday, hopeful phrase in a comforting voice. "He is sedated now, however, of course." But if her tone was friendly enough, her resolute eyes made a statement—the statement was: *Remember the ethics of professional distance and the inadvisability of forgetting them.*

Dori stood quietly shaking her head. "I don't think any of this is necessary." The Reggie Jackson shirt clung to her body with a particular tenderness.

Dr. Stokes pretended this hadn't been said. She explained the three categories of gastroduodenal mucosal something to look for in an endoscopy. The first was a superficial deterioration of the top something of the mucous membrane, which is the tissue lining all the body passages that come into contact with the body's internal air. The second kind is an acute erosion, but one where the wound is limited to the thin vascular layer of connective tissue. And finally— Josh's heart dropped as he watched her frown; this was the thicket— there was the harder result: deep, chronic ulcers, tumors, varices.

"But," Dr. Stokes added, "as you view the mucosa, it appears that—here, look—Zack is lesion-free." Hard to believe that Dr. Stokes could point out that sore pink tunnel on the screen and call it Zack. "Still, we have to keep him overnight, do some further tests."

So Dori was right; it was true. That field of salmon skin, his son's televised esophageal lining, wasn't broken at all.

Dori, unlooked-at, was still murmuring. "Ridiculous, ridiculous."

Dr. Stokes turned sharply to her. "The scope was more than a mere precaution, I would argue it was necessary. Even though I—we—did not expect that it would turn anything up. And now that we know this to be so, I'm sure we're all happy."

"Some of us thought this was bullshit, cover-your-ass stuff from the start."

"Dori," Josh said; you can't close such an important deal with this kind of hostility.

Off went the video monitor.

"That's it?" Josh said.

The gastroenterologist bent over Zack again, this time to pull the tube out.

"Does he have to *yank* that camera thing?" said Josh. "It looks really painful, tugging it."

A scowl had started to bunch on Dori's face. She stomped to her son. And someone called out, as an admonition: "Mrs. Goldin!" After an uncertain second Josh went with her. Is a husband required to follow the broad straight road of trust in these situations?

Zack, meanwhile, had been moved onto the wheeled stretcher. When Dori arrived, she said: "I think we're done here."

Josh said: "Honey?"—his voice full of *Are you sure?* (What had Dori meant before, babies just having "kooky episodes"?)

The nurse gave way to Dori. It was the gnashing jaw, and the greed of Dori's hands: Here, the decisive element was the inalienable rights of motherhood.

Dori picked up her son—the tendons of her longish neck raging. But as she leaned over the baby, she must have worried that someone might stop her. She shot back up straight, a volatile flush on her cheeks.

For a moment she and Dr. Weiss stood on either end of the stretcher, formally. Dr. Weiss seemed to waver—maybe he should just take up the baby himself?—and this led to a certain amount of his leaning and straightening, jerkily, like an American executive fumbling his first business meeting in Japan.

Josh had reached the scrum just as Dori bent again to scoop the baby into her arms a second time. If still a touch groggy, Zack looked, miraculously, beautifully, like himself—a twenty-one-pound baby of eight months, perfectly healthy.

"No," Dori said.

She had a searching look, a tone of cautious victory, her son in her arms. "No, I'll take my baby now, thank you." The eyes flashed; certainty arrived.

I think I get it, Josh thought (though he still couldn't put words to it). *I think—I mean, he's here, and he, I mean it seems . . .*

Dori threaded between the hospital people. That gastro guy still had lines in his naked cheeks, where the straps of the surgical mask had pinched. He backed away. It was only Dr. Stokes who stood in Dori's path now.

"We need to have the baby under observation for the night," said Dr. Stokes, really grinding the knuckle of her voice into the words. "We'd prefer, of course, to have parental consent."

"Yes, I'll bet," said Dori. That overhead UFO made a glinty aurora on top of her dark head. "I'll bet you would like to have our consent."

Stiff-backed, the two women had squared off—Dori's face blaring, Dr. Stokes holding her hands clasped, a hieroglyph of calm. They gazed at each other such a long, silent while that they'd slipped out of the rhythm of their argument. Everything felt very awkward.

Dori kept swaying on her toes, cradling her happiness close to her—against the clutches and bunglers of medicine. Each woman's gaze exclaimed its case in silence. *Yes, he is. No, he isn't.*

The baby had opened his round blue eyes and was looking around until he spotted, with a happy gurgle, his mother's face above his little own. It had been a very long night and two stray ringlets of Dori's sweaty hair were stuck to her forehead.

"Look at Zack," she said. Her own skin had turned red down past her chin, to the glowing throat. "And they're just going to hurt him *more*," she said.

"Mrs. Goldin," said Dr. Weiss. "You're being unreasonable. Just a few more tests and we'll know what's going on."

Dori shifted the way she held her son; she visored her eyes with her hand and something drew back in her expression.

"No," she said, "look at him. These tests are painful and unnecessary and you've hurt him already, you lost an hour when you could have been testing but you misdiagnosed, and I—"

Josh felt, in his brain, the moment when scattered iron filings snap to, in sudden magnetic order. Dori had the propensity to exaggerate now and then, but she'd been in the medicine business. Maybe this stuff *did* just happen to babies sometimes. He exhaled from his powerful chest. By giving him this chance to be her other half, Dori was also giving him permission to be himself—that is, lucky.

"You know what?" Josh said. "We are going home."

He put his hand on Dori's back, just above her tailbone: a gentle, husbandy nudge to start them moving.

Josh was the tallest one here. When a guy's the tallest person in a room, and he has a strong athletic chest, he's got the edge. "Come on, honey."

Dr. Weiss asked them to stop, in a voice that tripped all over itself. But the baby was doing one of his familiar nodding, openmouthed, tongue-out smiles. Once the Goldins had reached the hallway, Dori said to the doctors: "We're the parents, you know." And Josh, looking at his wife to make sure this was still the right thing to do, ignored the doctor as well.

He already started feeling breathless. And the baby kept on with his innocent baby smile. And they were all leaving together.

Yes, Josh thought. *Yes, this is the right thing.* A lucky man's hope is limitless. Josh had always known—even on this night—that the world was the best of all possible worlds. He kept his eyes on his wife as if she were a doctor herself, as if she were infallible.

We can always come hurrying back if something else happens again, he thought. *We'll stay up with him till morning. Tonight, and every night this week, every night this month, every night this year if we have to.*

He didn't want to look at anyone on the way out. Who wanted to see those staying behind in this shithole—where each patient was a sad rationalization unto himself, where everybody awaited science's Lazarus touch? If Josh could avoid noticing them, maybe he wouldn't feel he'd been one of them minutes before.

He had so wanted the doctors to say that the baby was definitely fine, and that it was okay for them to take Zack—it seemed now as if that had really happened. Maybe things had been going so quickly that Josh was forgetting some moments while they were happening?

The family with the second chance splashed into the lobby. "Thank you, honey," Josh said. Jitters, and respect for the fairness of the world, quivered his chin a little. He'd keep on being a good parent—maybe, somehow, an even better parent, because a new chance at life was starting. Not just for Zack but for him, too. This was the first time he really understood things, he told himself.

"Wow." He chuckled to himself, finding water in his eyes. "Wow." He forgot that he'd had similar "first" feelings of responsible adulthood before: at college graduation, starting his first good job, his wedding day, when feeling the lush sting of buying his first apartment. And while Zack was being born.

His son was bouncing in Dori's arms now, still smiling one of those tongue-out smiles—a tiny heavy-metal aficionado enjoying a guitar solo. The baby looked at Josh as if he knew exactly who his father was.

At the exit he deliberately let Dori step on the black-ribbed corduroy door-opener; she ought to be the one to leave this place first, she and Zack.

The word "love" seemed not enough. He saw what they had as something natural and perfected and self-sustaining, like a hundred-year-old tree.

Outside, Josh hurried to catch up, and touched his son's head gently on its front spongy part, the last lingering fontanel just over the hairline, where the skull bones weren't yet fully joined. His affection-flooded senses made him think he caught the smell of baby powder.

"He is going to be all right, though?" Josh said. "I mean, that stuff about babies having kooky episodes was—"

"No, I really think he's going to be fine, Mr. Goldin."

Josh's hand stole over to Zack's pudgy fist as they walked. A question came shyly into his heart, as if on tiptoe. But, no, forget it— And the nighttime humidity was adding to summer's whole aura of being lazily pleasant. Tonight was halo-around-the-streetlight weather.

"I love you, honey," Josh said.

Dori's elegant-boned face went to mush. But she recovered quickly.

"He's going to be okay—aren't you, Zack? Aren't you?" she said, cozying her nose into the baby's shoulder. The baby giggled, and the mother hid a few tears there.

Here Josh was, in the parking lot again, almost as if nothing at all had happened. The only difference being that it wasn't raining anymore, and it was dark. The lamps now gave out their yellowish stares. In that electric glow, only the moon was really seeable in the black sky, the moon and one star that shivered like a single tear anxious to drop. It was after four A.M. now—ten hours in that fortlike hospital. Maybe sick people need a fort to believe they can battle death?

Josh found himself saying, "Nothing bad can happen to a Superboy." It was a half-whisper to Zack.

Some car alarm started going, the annoying Indian war-whoop of it. But in the humid air the noise seemed to be under a blanket somewhere. And the God whom Josh had begged for help already vanished from his mind. That quickly, Josh's thoughtfulness had burned off.

His car wasn't where he'd parked it, with its front tire on top of the curb. Of course: towed. Which brought a trace element of annoyance into his happiness.

"Hey, don't," said Dori. "We'll just take my car." This little statement seemed, at that moment, an offering of indisputable assurance and understanding.

Josh was always the driver. The front passenger door of Dori's car had a lumbar-support pillow on it. After Dori strapped Zack into his child seat, she wedged the pillow behind her, did her thing with the safety belt, and Josh had them off.

Dori kept her hand on Josh's knee. She began saying something or other; Josh peeked in the rearview mirror at his son—who looked fine. Whenever Josh blinked, his son's alimentary canal, the red glaring eye, appeared pretty angry about having its photograph taken. Josh simply had to open his own eyes for the image to leave. But from that visualized alimentary stare, and with the memory of the doctors yelling at them down hallways, even an optimist couldn't shake the worry that something pretty terrible had happened—that they had made a mistake. And that they were still making a mistake in having taken the baby. It was so awful to think his son might be seriously sick and that his wife may be seriously wrong here; it was also difficult to imagine that true bad luck could happen to him. Above all, Josh so valued and needed his own lifelong sense of calm that he avoided thinking about it. He tried to convince himself that nothing *too* strange had happened—what did *he* know about this stuff?

Long Island on the map looks like a tailless crocodile with its mouth open. The island's far shore yawns into a pair of peninsulas a hundred miles east of New York City; meanwhile, the crocodile's hind-end asses right up against Manhattan. A quarter of the distance up the crocodile's back sits Glenwood Landing: the patch of low, sweet-smelling swampland where the Goldins made their home.

They'd made their way a mile uphill, downhill into town. Then the rearview pulsated red and white: the *one-two* hysterics of a police car's flashers. After that the siren, making its screeched demand.

Dori turned to Josh with the chaste expression women have in moments of bad trouble: a look of dreadful intensity, head high, throat bared, lips drawn tight over teeth.

The police had come to pull them over.

I

I trust you will recognize the disease.

—Isaac Bashevis Singer

1

WEEKDAYS, FIVE A.M., A BOWLING-PINNISH WOMAN FROM UNITED BAYside Methodist rose on tiptoes to kiss every freed inmate at his shoulder, his neck if she could reach. She grinned according to the tenets of belief, and this melted her fear as the devils stepped off the prison bus and into her orbit. Many of them burped or spat on little Methodist Connie's illdyed head.

She was aware of the presentation she made, the bad hair dye, the Abe Lincoln circles under her eyes; even these she loved as burdens of faith. " 'Accept, you woebegone who return!' " she said. "Corinthians nine sixteen!" (If she had been pretty once, slender and frisky, all that stuff belonged to that devil now, the past.)

For ex-cons, she was a hard first sight. Alone or in chorus, they found a lot to ridicule in this tired-looking woman who stood there open-armed and isolated as a scarecrow: the mole on her cheek from which gray feeler hairs shivered; her tight rayon pants; and the disdain she couldn't keep off her face (it fanned in arrows across her forehead). But above all, once the men realized that this dumpy lady puckering up in front of a housing complex was to be their first after-jail kiss, their bitterness about their own shit-filled lives returned.

But then why, in the early morning's sooty light, why did the reformed arsonist Javier Zabato crumple so gratefully in Connie's dishrag embrace? It was such a surprise for Connie that she failed to recite her Protestant pep talk, Come unto Him, you shall be saved, now please repeat it?

This Javier Zabato, wobbled by emotion, stood six two and wore a Japan-flag bandana. It was Connie's hug that kept him on his feet. He thought he'd walk off the bus to find nobody at all.

The guy owned *zilch* except the state's standard bequest of four dollars and a MetroCard. But to have been set free in Queens where his life and machismo began, and to find some forgotten familiars of his past (sneaker-fruit dangling from telephone wires; the local perfume of damp pavement and sewer), and to catch sight of tiara-like Manhattan rising like freedom's promise brought to glitter; and *then* to feel even this uninspiring lady's breath warm his throat—well, goddamn if he didn't feel like a lucky son of a bitch. Javier Zabato leaned into Connie, squeezing her for all she was worth. What a throne of joy Zabato saw all around in Jackson Avenue's elevated train-tracks, which had once been his tree house, his summer camp. The corners and sidewalks had been his adolescence; the bars and strip clubs—where he'd tried to work up a little business—had been his cocked-up luck.

"Okay, mister," Connie said, "that's just a little mucho for me, okay?" She couldn't help smelling Zabato's cologne—Brut or Old Spice, maybe a whole bottle when he'd dressed in his cell—even when she breathed through her mouth. Connie: the target of about fifty vicious jokes every morning. In addition to being irritated, she felt ashamed of being irritated. "The most important hug is between you and the Almighty," she said.

The sky to the east had a seashell look, opening out pink above white. And directly overhead was a darkness getting smaller, a melancholy dirge fading out slowly.

Connie started kissing Zabato's shoulder with pep—she often imagined Mary Magdalene as having pep when she applied the ointment on Christ's head. Now her mole whiskers bent like an ant's elbowed antennae against the fringes of Zabato's suede jacket. In Connie's imagination, the next guy off the bus was always another only begotten carpenter, the son in the three-part holy equation. And Zabato was blocking her from making his acquaintance. The one she was looking for would be an untouched innocent, who nobody else would have eyes to notice. He'd be called the Lamb because His beard was soft and curly but not the gross crinkled way that real lambs sometimes looked, almost like they were made of gray old men's pubic hair when she saw them on TV. In her mind, she knelt before His feet to whisper in the voice of altruism: "That ointment feels nice on your tootsies, I'll bet."

This was her vanity—even she saw that. Truth was, even the worst criminal off the bus was part of God the everlasting. All human devils were to be cautioned against, converted, resisted, soothed, censured, loved. Such knowledge girded her up; God was everywhere. Sometimes it was hard not to feel that if he was every-where, he wasn't *here* as much.

Anyway, this guy Javier Zabato was a nutjob. Violence insti-gated his every action. He felt loyal to violence, cultivated it, and, unsure how to deal with any tenderness at all, he started crushing Connie in a terrible bear hug.

"Please . . ." Connie's voice died into Zabato's shoulder.

Almost handsome, Zabato, devil-goatee'd like Snoop Dogg, was a Gulf War I vet who'd spent nine years in jail with only five visi-tors. With Connie's breasts smushing into his belly, his soul reached, briefly, a state of peace.

"No doubt," he sighed, moved by an exquisite brutality not un-like his thug's take on fucking. "Mmmm, no doubt, bitch," he said and slammed Connie into the bus door.

Something electrical from the elevated tracks made a noise that began as a *shhh* and ended as a pterodactyl-screak.

Behind Zabato, fifty-three released cons waited in place, anxious men jostling into one another like trapped marbles. Most of them carried everything they owned in plastic trash bags. Their grum-bling bespoke lives of dispossession and delayed satisfactions.

One of these released cons, a nasally sloucher, said: "M-move, partner." This was Carl Jefferson, a writer of bad checks. He chewed on his sunken mouth, his voice and body having been desiccated by the New York State prison system.

"M-move your ass," Jefferson said again. A tame guy, soft-shelled.

Someone else at the rear of the bus yelled out: "Y'all gonna fuck around up there and make me come up there?"

Zabato faced toward the inside of the bus now. Still squeezing, enjoying Connie's gasps and perspiry smell. *You fuckers keep talking*, was the message of his closed-eyed smile. *I don't even hear it.* The white sharps of his front teeth showed. Funny, he'd first thought to crush the religious lady as a quick joke. But if God Himself were to appear above the elevated tracks and demand in thunder that Zabato leave poor Connie alone, Zabato would have told God the same thing: to back the fuck up or he'd cut Him.

Behind Zabato, Carl Jefferson spoke again. His voice like a modest tap on the shoulder: "It ain't a m-man on this bus want to wait here." (Jefferson's thick tongue always slopped over the letter *m*, pronouncing it as if each hump made a separate sound.)

Another released con's voice came from deep inside the bus, comically high-pitched: *"Aaah!"*

Meanwhile Carl Jefferson, answering a reflex pang way back in his brain, opened his bag of personals for the sixteenth time (faux-switchblade comb, bible without its front cover, electric toothbrush minus batteries, huge old-style Walkman also minus batteries). Yes, everything he had was still here.

Outside the bus, the dawn was now a wraparound glow with no discernible source.

Cinching shut his property, Carl Jefferson puffed up to say: "It about to be some shit here, you don't get to stepping."

Carl's nephew Martin was supposed to have gotten him a job at T.G.I. Friday's, and Carl had defacto agreed to try it. But he'd been weighed down by that kind of bullshit all his life and who knew if his back would give out submitting to a little more?

As if against his will, Javier Zabato let Connie free. The former arsonist turned a smile. "Suck on my *dick,* all y'all!" he yelled—to Connie, Carl Jefferson, to everyone. He slapped at the bus's folding door. With the ungraceful head-lurch peculiar to him—and a half-moaned "Bring it"—he took off running, past the red-brickface Bagels Unlimited of USA and its dumpy neighbor the *Te-Amo* Deli, past a boarded-up warehouse, a neon-lit twenty-four-hour Check

Cashing that had a dismantled billboard's skeleton on its roof. The former arsonist made it across the loci of little traffic islands where six streets curved into one toward the Fifty-ninth Street Bridge.

"None of you ass-munches hit my door, got it?" said the bus driver.

Meanwhile, Connie hadn't moved from her spot on the corner. She blinked like a plane-crash survivor.

"Through that work of grace," she managed to recite, "Jesus' sheep know their terrible burden of sin, and come unto Him. Through that work . . ." But her voice, not to mention her faith, had gotten frayed. *Does the Lord in His wisdom*, she wondered, *really need all these devils?*

Carl Jefferson said: "You not gonna be the first kiss I get in three m-m-motherfucking years," and pushed right past her off the bus.

In forty minutes—though he'd promised his nephew he wouldn't do it—he'd get drunk, and give all he owned to Master-piece, a hooker in a straw cowboy hat who earned half her living from the daily Ginsberg State Penitentiary drop-off. Fast forward a few weeks and Carl Jefferson's ambitions and promises will have vanished into another four-year lap at Ginsberg: a crappy nearby restaurant, a botched robbery, a citizen's arrest. Fast forward a year and Carl Jefferson will be dead.

As for Bayside's four-foot-eleven Weeble of piety—Connie stood there having just about salvaged her Christian smile when the as-tonishing hit. Another of what she called her "thwacks": a glimpse, a brief suffusion of the divine spotted in some wretch's stormy, pass-ing face. Christ God's inexplicable brightness in this one's eye, or shadows forming a decisive cross over that one's jacket: the mun-dane providing sacred harmonies. This stretch of Jackson Avenue was full of evidence that He had forsaken the world—grandfatherly bums asleep on the sidewalk, the very sad graffito mural of a mur-dered neighborhood girl with the painted eyes scratched out, and finally just the sewer covers, with their infernal steam—but even among these men in whom Christian ethics had no more resonance than a snowflake, her mind went all at once free from doubt and worry. Of course the divine spark glowed *ex cathedra* in every last criminal off the bus. Of course she took in a breath, an "oh" of wonder. She was succumbing to religious transport, she was dazed past speaking, hoping that the awesome Lord might grant her to see, just for a moment, a combined incandescence of all the souls she had saved, all that supershine, while in the meanwhile fifty released cons shouldered by her, most not even acknowledging she was there—though this morning seven of them did give her the finger—as they pushed their way into this Jackson Avenue that was more real than any of them had imagined.

Now the general murmur of tough guy talk, with its bits of automythology: "No pizzle gonna hold *El Niño* forever, *adoquín*. . . ."

". . . the fuck out my way, bitch—we *out*."

"Call me Niggertine—'cause I'm smokin', and the Surgeon General say I'm dangerous to your health."

Storefronts were protected behind ribbed-metal curtains that shut at night to look like old-fashioned washboards. (This dinky semblance of lockdown demoralized many released cons, undermining their belief in advancement.) Some cars parked along the street were makes they'd never seen, a Volkswagen Passat, the latest Kia Rio, that weird Plymouth Prowler: cars that, in the plump of their taillights, looked both gently futuristic and nostalgic. Bubblegum spit out long ago decorated the sidewalk as black lily pads.

In their first and last conversation, a sex offender told a racketeer: "Need me some motherfucking smokes."

"Don't, yo. That stuff'll kill you."

Another man said, over and again: "I don't want to hurt nobody." His swastika neck tattoo, scabbed knuckles, even the teeth of his sneer made this seem a very literal truth: hurting nobody was the last thing on his mind. He wanted to hurt *every*body.

And there was one slouching middle-aged dude, apart from the others, who seemed to have trouble making his way.

Seventeenth off the bus, tall and plump in his Batman T-shirt and shorts, a man named Intelligent Muhammad—the once and future Charles Stokes, sixty-three, the bright spot of no one's morning—dawdled at the corner streetlamp. Some men can't bear their own happiness. One minute into freedom, under the calm of everything-is-possible, Intelligent Muhammad felt pessimistic. He had no way of knowing that, by the end of this morning, he would play the lead in what a frequent contributor to *The New York Times Magazine* would try to sell as an "incredible story of heroism."

Some pigeons at the curb jerked their heads, primly, spooked by the men who kept passing: criminals of all stripes, en route to the Jackson Avenue subway stop, the G train to Brooklyn, the 102 bus, the Pascack Valley Line of New Jersey Transit, or maybe they were just going in circles. Or their faces were brightening into thought: Maybe their big plot had, at that very moment, come together at last. Or maybe they were going merely to jerk off or take a shit in the sweet seclusion of an unsoiled bathroom, to borrow seven hundred dollars from a tightfisted cousin who was a dispatcher at UPS; or to listen with pleasure for that oily tumble when the lock of a favorite door unbolts. Or: They were hoping immediately to break probation at a craps table in Foxwoods; to go get on camera outside the *Today* show window; to buy a pair of new Prada shoes, to steal a used Oxford shirt that wasn't too stained at the armpits. Maybe they'd end the day in a homeless shelter, a Sutton Place duplex, a fistfight, an affordable computer class—maybe they'd find the men who dicked them in the first place. Maybe they just wanted to gulp down a suicidal measure of aspirin from the bottle.

One common thread: Few would deny their desires today. Some would live as goldfish live, taking whatever they were offered in lethal quantities.

Together, these released cons made less a frenzy out of Egypt than a straggling parade of stupid or luckless men. Some stepped into the lawful, snoring world with a loud roar. Others had mouths behind which shouts of joy turned out to be nothing but suppressed yawns. Twelve, including first-off-the-bus Javier Zabato, bought cocaine or guns from the dealers waiting under the bridge. Most charged ahead; Intelligent Muhammad kind of drag-assed. The November cold, the alleyways turned over to the rats, and the infinite cagework of the subway frames struck him as portions of the same insult: *You _know_ there's no way you'll make it, right?*

It was thirty-eight degrees out; his clothes were a pittance: shorts and a Batman T-shirt, a humiliation. The cold bit through his ribs.

What a fucked-up life! No woman, a daughter he'd never known. Now, if given the chance, he'd hand over every last thing just to have someone. *Not even pussy,* he thought, *just a lady who smelled nice who'd support my decisions.* But every last thing he had was not much at all. Who'd want it?

A voice from over his shoulder made him jump. "Yo, Intel—You ain't have to wait around, brother."

The voice belonged to the last of the released cons: With his fat face and shaved head, this guy resembled an oversize baby. He was wearing all red: a sweaty sweater, baggy red pants. Intelligent Muhammad had forgotten the man's name. Muhammad knew about *himself,* though—knew that people like this guy saw him as a loser. *Hey, who's that over there? Who, _that_ motherfucker?—just a dildo who call himself Intelligent Muhammad.*

"Sharif," Muhammad said, finding the man's name.

"We *out* now, Intel," Sharif said. "Free at last, free at last," he laughed, "thank God amighty, they freed your ass."

"Bet, bet," Muhammad said. He disliked having to talk con.

"Get me a decent meal, then a decent piece of 'tang, god*damn.*" Sharif gestured at a hooker who was bimboing toward them in stilt-heeled shoes that had made a thousand laps of Jackson Avenue. She wore shorts in the cold.

"Yo!" Sharif cried at her, "I'm a Pisces, shorty! I'm sensitive! What about me?" Then, to Muhammad: "Partner, I need me some of that."

The hooker crossed the street to jiggle her chaotic breasts at them. *"Mmm-hmm."*

"Don't be *doing* that to no Pisces," Sharif said, when the hooker reached them. "For real, though. A Pisces has sensi*tiv*ities. What, I look like a Virgo to you?" He hooked a thumb toward Muhammad. "And I know you ain't want to kill *this* middle-aged brother." Then he fell apart laughing.

The hooker's sensors weren't tuned to pick up joking, especially at five-thirty A.M. She exhaled through her mouth, narrowed her brown eyes.

"Are we talking, or are we doing?" she said.

"*You* talking. To two men of Allah—*word*. Can't tempt us. Right, Muhammad?"

The hooker's greasy face retreated into irritation. Irritation was her stasis. She fired a huff from the cannon of her nose, a woman beyond the reach of embarrassment. Her "Fuck you, *nigger*" brought the curtain down on this little farce of entrepreneurship. She stormed off: dimpled thighs, Jell-O for an ass.

"Poop-butt hood-rat," Sharif said, scratching at the shar-pei folds of his neck fat. "She *nasty*, partner." And then he walked away, too. Away and out of Muhammad's life forever. For the first time in years, Muhammad was physically alone.

He thought the hooker hadn't looked half-bad.

A garbage truck blustered past him now, clanging down the quiet street. Muhammad hadn't moved from the corner of Forty-third Avenue and Jackson.

Where to go, what to do? His criminal résumé had never been inspiring. He'd worked as a fence of stolen handguns for the Russian mob, then as a small-time crack dealer in the Bronx, then as muscle—sorry excuse for muscle—for a bunch of chump-change Dominicans, bookies in Washington Heights and the Bushwick section of Brooklyn. In every case, he'd been a weasel. He'd been a weasel everywhere. Muhammad weaseled friends and he weaseled enemies; he weaseled for money, drugs, sex, and occasionally for his own protection; he'd weaseled to avoid responsibility; for spite; at home, in jail (of course), in the navy (why not?); for affection gone astray; sometimes he weaseled just because. As a result, he had no one now to tell about his release. Not the mother of the daughter he never knew, not his brother, Willie, who hated him, not the zero friends to speak of, nobody.

Maybe he could call Charlene, his sister up in Inwood, who also hated him. The only money he had in the world was the $28.79 in his left shoe, and the $750 more at Charlene's house—if that cash was still where he'd left it before Ginsberg. He'd known this day was going to start tough. Probably that's why he hadn't planned it better—"release anxiety," he knew it was called. He was too hungry to think about it yet; he was living completely in the present, the way children and dogs do.

Just before he got to the door to Bagels Unlimited of USA, someone stopped him.

"Oh, *here* you are, man—where'd you run off to?" said a clean-shaven white guy. Muhammad hadn't ever seen him before. He jogged right up in his blue mock-turtleneck. "I thought you'd forgotten that coffee and bagel."

Muhammad's hands curled into fists before he was aware they were doing it. (This is what prison does to you; it makes you porcupine up like a cactus plant, and over nothing.)

"The fuck you want?" he said.

The white guy stopped short, letting his mouth fall open; he had all the *élan* of a substitute teacher wearing a taped Kick Me sign and wondering why the class won't listen to his calls for quiet.

"A minute ago, you said it?" The guy hand-combed his blond hair. "Not that you said coffee and bagels, *per se*. But, um."

The most noticeable qualities of this guy's handsome face were his thick mouth, and blue eyes that were now signaling just how nervous he was. " 'Member, man?" he said.

Muhammad unweaponed his hands.

"What you mean, coffee and a *bagel*, son?" Muhammad said. "I ain't eat no *bagels*."

The white guy laughed. It was the laugh of someone putting

faith in the power of shared levity to ease the separateness that he felt—that many white people feel—when hanging out with blacks.

The white guy apologized; his name was Ralph Dunn. He was "a reporter for the *Times Magazine*" (actually a freelancer), doing a story on the Ginsberg drop-off. Minutes back, he'd asked some ex-con out to breakfast; the ex-con had agreed, but had said that he'd needed to piss first, and they'd arranged to meet here. But maybe *that* ex-con had taken off on him, and so—well, anyway, would Muhammad like to be a part of the story, instead? It meant free breakfast, you know. Of course, not everyone likes bagels, that's completely understandable.

Muhammad hated dealing with the Ralph Dunns of the world. Some whites just had to use the word "man" when talking to black people.

Just the same. It was the media. Maybe not TV, but still. Celebrity, all that good stuff. "*Time* magazine?" Muhammad said. "*Trip.*"

"Excellent," said Ralph, opening the door.

"Talking 'bout, I ain't eat no bagels. Need to get me a decent meal. For real."

"That's fine," Ralph said. After deciding whether to break it to him, he added: "Not *Time* magazine, man. It's *The New York Times.*"

"The *news*paper? Hold up, you said magazine."

The interior of Bagels Unlimited of USA was wide, bright, and smelled of the morning's first powdery baking. Ralph Dunn and Intelligent Muhammad sat at the counter like two cartoon representations of incompatible aspirations. A line cook edged up to them, stout and floury, to ask their breakfast orders. The man's apron, gory with ketchup even at this hour, cupped around his belly like a bra.

"I gotta run you though the basic-question stuff first, okay, man? One, how long were you in for? And B, what crime? Also—you have any family?"

Back at Iceberg, guys were vain about what they were in for. That was the quickest path to cred—the worse the crime, the louder the message: *Back off, homes*. Outside, the instinct was embarrassment. Don't mention it at all, or else just accept the hard word "prison," nod, keep your mouth shut.

Not to mention, Muhammad always hated talking about that long-running disappointment, his past. But who gave a fuck now? Intelligent Muhammad figured that he was starting to *live*. There was growing ease in his posture. The calm of his sitting was a consolidation of recent gains. In prison you got seventeen minutes for your whole meal—just time enough to suffer through the cafeteria noise and mayhem into deep apathy, or into something worse. Muhammad found himself smiling. Never again would he have to sleep at the foot of a toilet while another man took a shit in his company. He let his attention drift out to the simple frame that Bagels Unlimited's plate-glass window made of the street. He looked a long time, and kept at it. The world from a diner stool.

"All right, *man*," said Muhammad finally. "I got a daughter I don't talk to. Suppose to be a doctor, you know."

Out the window, the Queensboro Bridge was seeable some twelve blocks away. Yeah, the world did indeed exist. Now Muhammad would—*trip*—live in it again. Among the humiliations of prison: Intelligent Muhammad had picked up the slang of a younger man. You had to. It was how everyone spoke.

"A medical doctor?" Ralph had his tape recorder out.

Since Muhammad had gotten off the bus, if he'd seen the bridge, it was as background. But if your life has been deprived, every new sight seems a hello. Bridges exist. Sexy whores exist. Bagel places, too.

"Talking 'bout, I don't really know her," Muhammad said, distractedly. From his angle, where you could see only the bridge's upper anatomy of arches and spans, the Queensboro's superstructure looked like a skeletal lion, stretched out on its belly.

"Wow. A medical doctor." It wasn't clear from Dunn's voice

whether this fact eliminated Muhammad from the kind of story he wanted to write. "What's her name?"

Muhammad resettled himself on his thighs. "Darlene," he said, lifting his chin.

"Dr. Darlene Muhammad." Dunn talked toward the recorder.

Muhammad laughed. "Darlene *Stokes*, son." Just above the bridge, the sun looked like a kernel of canned corn stuck to the sky. "I found Islam in prison, you know, the Koran, Ali, the caliphate, all that."

The line cook left two plates before them. *Here ya go, fellas. Couple egg sandwiches?*

Immediately, Muhammad took a few whamming bites. The first meal tasted in freedom: Nothing could ever meet those expectations. But this egg sandwich was delicious. "Mmmm. That's what I'm talking about. Ain't no *bagel*."

The prostitute Muhammad had seen earlier walked up to the window now, stopping in front of it. A familiar face: Christ, it felt like he was becoming part of a neighborhood. His eyes lapped up the sugar of her silhouette. Her face, hair, Jesus her motherfucking tits . . .

During his almost five years inside, Muhammad had gotten himself through a thousand bottomless nights by picturing chubby legs and sloppy breasts. A few times a week, when his cell mate slept, he'd reached down to confirm he was still alive. But now—damn, what he wouldn't do to *this* plump-and-lovely! Slide a cushion under her ass, bring her pussy up to the right height. She'd be on her back, ankles resting against his left shoulder—while he'd hug on her shins, free hand on her nipples. He bet she'd have pretty big-ass nipples, too, bouncing all over. Now he gave the hooker a smile that he'd mothballed for five years and eight months—no teeth showing, the least-threatening-black-man-in-New-York grin. She'd probably take up a whole jail-size bed by herself. Muhammad had a relentless, lonely boner. He used to consider himself a ladies' man; he'd fucked three hookers the night before his last trial. And what could he do now?

"Do you know her?" Dunn said, hopefully. When he saw Muhammad didn't, he went in for more fellowship. In these situations you always need to have something to say, something hip to say: "She looks all right to me, man."

The hooker bent forward to the window, her body touching the glass with the edges of her cupped hands. Those hands seemed lighted pink at their contact with the glass. Then she turned, just like that, and took off—gone.

The clock on the wall read 6:28. In jail, it's like a casino: A man rarely sees clocks, or wants to. It was time to stop wasting all this motherfucking time. "You got other questions?" Muhammad said.

"Well—yes, certainly. We just started?" Ralph ran a hand through his hair. He offered with a laugh, "One, how come African-Americans look good bald and white dudes don't?"

"What?"

Ralph's morale flickered, held on, but in the end it couldn't survive without nourishment.

"Little joke," he said. "I've been noticing I'm losing my hair." He blushed along his nose. Amazing there could be that much distance between two guys right next to each other. "So, really, man. One, what are your immediate plans now? How you going to make it from here?"

Ex-cons, even in the achievement and opportunity of new freedom, have a catechism. *When you out*, Muhammad thought sadly, *you alone*. He held this Iceberg wisdom. The former Charles Stokes kept thinking: *When you out, you all alone.*

"Cry two tears," he said, "shit in a bucket, fuck it." Back in Bushwick, his uncle Leon had used that expression in defeat: Leon who, except for the dark fish-foody grains across his cheeks, looked whitish—not unlike Colin Powell; Leon who'd spent half his years in jail and who died at fifty-seven. "Cry two tears," he said, "shit in a bucket, fuck it."

Ralph's voice put up a heroic battle not to register condescension. "That's great, but I don't think I can quote it." For the first time, he felt real sympathy for this guy. "So, does that mean you have no plans, as such?"

Muhammad dropped what was left of his sandwich onto his plate. It was easier to think of what he'd survived than where he was going. Hard times back there in prison, you know?—god*damn*. Motherfucking Ginsberg. They call that shit Iceberg for a reason. But also it's like—all right: jail, you know? Because, if you kept to yourself, you could only fall so far in Iceberg. There's immunity in the bottom. Not that he was homesick for prison. 'Course not, 'course not. But he wished he could have at least made his own presence here, on the outside, seem real to himself.

"Plans, yeah, I have plans," Muhammad lied.

Without warning he was occupied by memories: events laid down long ago taken up again, a sudden sensual unfolding. To the reporter Ralph Dunn, it looked as if his interviewee were merely gazing at the laminated Jerrold Nadler head shot taped over the slushy machine. But Intelligent Muhammad watched his own past spooling by, in gorgeous Technicolor: his ex-girlfriend Roberta's sad face just as it looked one afternoon in 1972, worry creases defining her smile, when his first jury's foreman had pronounced him guilty. Roberta's lipstick had been fresh and orange. Fossilized moments, voices not heard in years, drifted by like random kites on a single string, each in its turn. Nights spent at Mom's black-and-white TV, which always hurried the minutes toward bedtime: simple recollections, these relics of his long, too-quick-passing life. Many criminals, when they're in jail, they make an unspoken agreement with themselves—with their survival instinct—not to choke on scraps of the lives they lost. But who, during the unlived years of a long prison stretch, can shut down his own memory? It's going constantly. Still, if you're lucky, memories become like an old projector's flappy *whirr*, the muffled machine-gun noise that sometimes accompanies a movie but eventually fades; eventually it goes unnoticed after the credits come up—eventually you're able just to concentrate on the unfolding story. So, of course, freed men feel thunderstruck when the past intrudes like this, when twenty years happen in five seconds, when the ignored whirr now *becomes* the movie. The birth of his daughter, Darlene, for example: 1966. His daughter, from a woman he'd barely known. His thick, frowny baby had had dark skin and kinked "Egyptian" hair, a girl he'd *never* known, past that first day in the hospital.

"I'm a ask you something," Muhammad said to Dunn all of a sudden. "You got a job for me, something like that? Don't hold out."

"Sorry?"

"I'm serious now." Muhammad was addressing not Ralph but some invisible audience in the empty air next to Ralph. His attitude said: *Check me out, I'm beyond asking this fool for help*. It was part of that reaction to grievance that's called pride.

Muhammad said: "I'm chained to the game."

"Well, uh, let's just see how the interview goes," Ralph said. "I'm actually only a freelancer myself."

As soon as he'd asked for help, Muhammad realized it'd been stupid. He'd continued to ask only because he felt that creating an aura of violence was his best chance of making sure he got this breakfast for free. (His understanding was that meek compliance in small matters is what whites give blacks, instead of a real chance for improvement.)

"Don't hold out, now," he said. "Come on. Know what they call me, back in Iceberg? Niggertine. 'Cause I'm dangerous to your health, and I'm smoking."

That had been someone else on the bus's nickname. Muhammad didn't really feel fierce at the moment, but so what? Willed ferocity is a language you learn, a mandatory course you take upon your admission to Iceberg.

He took hold of Ralph Dunn's gaze. Dunn blinked, of course, but he worked to keep his eyes calm. He really was trying hard, but soon he looked away.

"Let's maybe do a few more questions? If that's all right?" Dunn said, looking at his tape recorder. "Back to the daughter, the doctor . . . ?" Muhammad's eyes fell to his plate, and Dunn read them correctly. "Oh, listen, *I'm* picking up this breakfast, don't worry about that. But—do you talk to her, the daughter? Any other friends or family?"

"A lot of people looking out for me, you understand? For *me*. I don't need help. You don't know, you better ask somebody."

"Well, that's something," Ralph said. He didn't understand what Muhammad was saying, not one iota, not a word. This was one of those waste-of-time interviews where the tape recorder might as well be a dried-out sponge—it would yield not a single helpful drop. He'd have to interview someone else. "I don't doubt it, Intelligent."

"You don't know, you better *ask* somebody."

Muhammad was about halfway to deciding that it was people like this fool who'd kept him down. To be alive for long enough is to blame other people.

"If you think about it, in a way you're lucky," Ralph was saying. "Or not totally unlucky. That you have friends, I mean. Seriously. I don't want to get corny, but I think we've all got blessings. Well, not *every*body has. I understand where you're coming from on *that* issue; we're all human."

"Fuck luck," said Muhammad. "You don't hear nobody from my neighborhood talking about blessings."

Dunn started talking again, talking, talking. He calmed into a half-minute of smiled advice about "the importance of taking risks but not unadvisable ones," about having "a support network."

And what happened next, happened very fast.

Out on Jackson Avenue, loping over from across the street, a man came up through the sunlight and kicked—*bam!*—the door of Bagels Unlimited open. This was Javier Zabato; Carl Jefferson hurried in on his heels.

They were here with a plot they'd just now conceived, out under the bridge, with Jefferson's newly purchased gun. Stick up the place, go 70–30 with the take, G-train it out of there: maybe not a plan as much as an itinerary.

The line cook took a step toward Zabato, and then—blinking—took a shuffle step back.

Zabato sounded very angry demanding the money in the register. As if the cash in there had been cheated from him.

"Not a lot," the line cook said. From the kitchen came a crashing noise—someone hiding, most likely.

"How m-much?" said Carl Jefferson, his tongue's clumsiness a real limitation on his menace. He was holding the gun inside his coat. Zabato had let him in on the deal because he'd agreed to be the "artillery" for this mission.

The line cook opened the drawer and groaned. Then he held out the contents of the register for his robber to see. Zabato ran over to the money and grabbed as many leafy handfuls as he could. The counting took no time at all.

Zabato said, "Seventy-eight dollars?"

"Hey, it's six-thirty in the fucking morning."

"All right," Zabato said. Then, to his partner: "Point the gun at this piece of shit."

Jefferson struggled even getting the .38 Special from his pocket, where he'd been flaunting it as a menacing lump, the way black-and-white gangsters did in bygone movies.

"How much you got on you?" Zabato asked the line cook.

"Personally?"

"Come on—how much?" he said. "What the fuck? Yeah, *personally*."

"I'm wearing an apron."

"How much! How much!" And then again, "Man, aim the fucking gun on him, I said!"

The line cook swallowed. "This doesn't even have, you know, a real pocket. Nothing. I have no cash on me."

Predictably, Zabato turned next to Ralph and Intelligent Muhammad. Zabato's lips glistened with rancor.

"Yo, hold up," Muhammad said, lifting his palm forward, traffic-cop style. "You know me, partner. I just got out myself. I sat like two seats behind you on the Iceberg Mobile, you understand?"

Ralph Dunn was already through his own wallet. "Forty-seven," he said. "I have forty-seven dollars." His eyes looked fluid and shaky, like uncooked eggs topped of half their shells.

"Tell him to get up," Zabato said.

The wall clock was humming. The slushy machine's inner mechanism churned around once.

"Why you want *m-me* to?" Carl said, then: "You mean the white guy, you talking about him?" They'd never worked a crime together before; they were an unpracticed team.

Without waiting for an answer, Carl said kind of softly to Ralph: "You, get up."

So Ralph rose, walked to Zabato, and handed him his money. After pocketing it, Zabato grabbed Ralph in a brutal half-Nelson.

"We're taking this asshole. Aim the gun on him. Jesus fucking Christ." Zabato rolled his eyes.

"Why?" Carl said. "Where we taking?"

"What you mean, *why?* A hundred-ten split two ways, that's why," Zabato said. "It's bullshit." He moved a step forward, and Ralph wavered in his grasp. But the two men took a second step together, already in synch like Siamese twins.

Zabato smiled gently, earnestly. "We're taking this asshole to his ATM machine," he said. "You ready, asshole?"

Next came an act that no one could explain. Real bravery or some element not unlike it brushed against Intelligent Muhammad. That was enough. He jumped to his feet, without a plan, without even thoughts of why: He acted. The strange thing was, the world in Bagels Unlimited of USA seemed to slow down as he bullrushed across the room, straight at Carl Jefferson.

Muhammad was trying to be a hero.

Carl Jefferson raised his .38 in a fast arc. The gunshot sounded in the air like the bark of an absolutely huge dog.

Just before Muhammad made it to Carl, he felt the gentle sensation of snow on his head. Carl's bullet had hit the asbestos ceiling.

Carl trained his gun at Muhammad this time—"Shoot!" Zabato was yelling; "shoot the motherfucker!"—but Muhammad grabbed Carl's weapon hand first.

Across the room Javier Zabato let go of Ralph. He ran in fury to Muhammad and Carl: to where his future was being determined.

Dunn could have come to help Muhammad.

Muhammad brought his knee up, hard, crunching into Carl's wrist. It sounded as if twigs had broken. And the gun clacked to the floor.

"Ow-*shit*!" Carl said, near to crying. "Why you *doing* this?"

If he'd thought about it, Muhammad wouldn't have been able to say why.

But as Zabato was about to reach this skirmish, Muhammad let fly a punch to the side of Carl Jefferson's head, a punch with the frightening *thud* of guaranteed pain, guaranteed injury. This was a more perfect blow than Muhammad had landed the whole time he'd been a bookie's hired muscle, had *ever* landed for that matter, a Tyson-in-his-prime kind of right hook, five years and eight months in the windup. Carl Jefferson went down as fast as water tossed out of a bucket. Even before he hit the ground unconscious (or maybe it had come when Muhammad bent to grab the revolver, or maybe when he stood up pointing the gun at Zabato and said, "We done now, you understand? We done"), the reporter Ralph Dunn had already started to first-draft his magazine story on Intelligent Muhammad, the rehabilitated man, hero ex-con, the father of Dr. Stokes. She was, he already understood, a woman somewhere in affluent, Sunday *Times*–buying Long Island.

2

Maybe the truest way to know a person is to learn what she's ashamed of.

Dr. Darlene Stokes, Chairperson, Pediatrics and Child Health Intensive Care Unit, wouldn't discuss her personal life—her childhood, especially. Even though by thirty-eight she had been the first black woman and the youngest person that St. Joseph's Hospital had ever selected to head an ICU section.

She'd grown up in Bushwick, Brooklyn, the child of an absent father and a mother who had to work what she called "shit jobs"; in the 1960s her mother, Alice Davis, began as a dishwasher in the high school from which she had dropped out a year earlier; then moved on to being a concession attendant for the Halsey Theatre movie house; after that, she became a receptionist at the Liebmann Brewery. She earned her high school equivalency, though, and then her associate's. (Night classes at Kingsborough Community College: not much homework, quick diploma, good luck to you.) Then Alice Davis, in 1979, got a paralegal job at Rothenberg & Rubinstein, a commercial firm in Brooklyn Heights. Six months in, she'd become Rothenberg & Rubinstein's only essential paralegal, analyzing statutes, preparing appeals, wills, and contracts, and even resolving simple legal matters without supervision or assistance. She could have been a Rothenberg or a Rubinstein herself.

But the law was a sideline, an avocation. From the moment of Darlene's birth, Alice Davis had made her daughter's success her life's central ambition.

Alice had never married; she'd had just the one child. Darlene's father had been the first man Alice had had sex with, and that had only happened one time, in 1966. ("One time, one kid," she used to joke. "God has a sense of humor on him, all right.") Charles Stokes had been a neighborly, neighborhood failure. He was years from being called Intelligent Muhammad.

Charles Stokes reminded Alice of her own father. She'd always disliked Charles Stokes—it was hard to like what you didn't respect—but the night before he left for the navy, Charles peacocked right up to her (she'd been idling on her front stoop, having just polished off an RC Cola) and he asked her, with a prepared voice, to walk him to the parking lot behind the brewery. That walk could mean only one thing. Alice, flat-chested at fifteen and sitting on her hands, considered the offer. To spite something she couldn't quite name, she said: "Sounds all right to me." ("Got me off the stoop, anyways," she'd say later. "And it got me *you*, baby girl.")

That was the end of a social life for Alice, a girl lifted straight into womanhood, with nausea and a growing belly and a pall of harsh comments; Alice to whose sass a few young men still had been attracted, men who were curious at first, later scared off, or unable to compete with the attention she eventually paid her daughter. And so they all withdrew, at last, to less troublesome situations, with less troublesome women.

Alice's mother was upset when Alice ended up pregnant, but her two brothers, and still more her father, seemed not really to mind. It gave them, at last, something to tease her about. "The little ghetto snob has a bun in the oven"—stuff like that.

As for Alice, she gave the impression of not caring one way or the other about what motherhood would mean to her own life. She did care, of course. But she cared mainly that her child should have, as she said, "advantages"—gratifications and chances, the things she herself hadn't ever known.

Darlene Stokes was born on the first of March 1968. Her mother had wanted a boy, for practical reasons, money-earning reasons. But all that didn't matter, not when Alice held her baby girl to her shoulder in the hospital bed. Alice was so roused by tenderness it felt like being wounded—by the child's warmth, the birth-slicked hair; by Darlene's puffy and closed "Chinese eyes," as Alice called them—each of these things, every detail about this person under her care forever, it all seemed unfathomable. "Just babies making babies," Alice's mother had said, *tsk*-ing. But right off, Darlene's little face looked to Alice as if it contained a certain emphasis, a certain wisdom—cramped and tense though the face may have been, looking like a swollen fist. Alice would stare at her daughter for hours on end. She tried to see all the different faces that Darlene might end up having—all the possible Darlenes that there might be. The baby cried loudly and uncontrollably. But she did so rarely, and never in front of strangers—as if little Darlene had already developed her public shyness. Maybe because Alice worked so hard, it seemed to her that Darlene grew out of babyhood extra fast. Alice was prepared to be strict. "Don't you backtalk me" was a line of her own mother's that she'd wanted to use herself, but Darlene rarely gave her the chance.

Darlene got teased sometimes for her peculiar lead-footed way of walking: her hips not moving at all and her heavy feet sucking back to earth, as if her heels were magnets.

The few times she got invited to another girl's apartment, she'd hang around near the father, if there happened to be a father. Darlene wasn't inclined to talk. But she wanted to see how these difficult-to-imagine creatures made their turbocharged way through the world: elusive, unpredictable, all over you, or just gone.

As she matured, she became more obviously self-confident, if more socially conservative; starting at about eight years old, Darlene had a clear understanding just how much her mother had sacrificed for her. It may have been her first mature thought. By nine, she'd already picked up a little of the musty, self-protective caution of an adult. If other kids provoked her, it was about this: They tried to restrict her, saying she "acted white." It hurt, but would have hurt more if they'd said she acted *old*. She didn't want to act, to seem, or even to be. She wanted only to become. She saw her future self: the bright, conscious black woman her mother was teaching her to grow into.

Adulthood couldn't come fast enough. Some classmates called her "Purple," because she was very dark-skinned, darker than her mother was, darker than almost anybody else in school, but she didn't care; she was just as dark as she wanted to be.

Pretty by eleven years old, chubby-cheeked, her glasses exaggerating her big dark soft eyes, Darlene found herself shocked by kids at her school, and by a few teachers, too.

But she wasn't shunned as much as discounted: Even by junior high she resided somewhere above above popularity concerns, above the pubescent obsession with categorizing. She certainly didn't get teased for not having a father. In her neighborhood lots of kids went without fathers.

"No one," she'd tell Alice, "knows how to behave." She was in the seventh grade.

"I know, baby," Alice would say. "It won't be us here forever."

But even difficult lives sometimes need an impetus, an occasion for change. On July 13, 1977, the Great Blackout came to make a lot of people's dissatisfactions concrete. Over two days Darlene's rioting neighbors burned down almost twenty percent of her neighborhood.

Darlene's mother had already been planning her application to Kingsborough. The day after the torching of Bushwick, she signed up for classes. As for Darlene, she'd remember for the rest of her life, but never mention, her fear and embarrassment over the old street's bitter ash smell. She felt it on her teeth whenever she left her apartment. So much ash everywhere—in streaks on the sidewalks, in Z shapes on boarded-up windows, in wide inky smudges on buildings, in the mire at every intersection. And when it rained, just when you were ready to forget it all, the ash ran in streamlets, giving the sense that the whole neighborhood was melting.

Four days straight that July, she passed the same bum, asleep or dead, lying at the corner of sour, neglected DeKalb Avenue. Maybe Darlene's father was a bum, too; or the kind of man who'd fight a kid over a stolen TV. DeKalb, bad as it all was, was better than all the vomit you always saw when you'd cut across a Sunday-morning alley.

The neighborhood kept up like that, long after the fires: For weeks, a parade of men in their tight-fitting, brassy '70s clothes stepped over unbagged garbage, carrying ovens, toasters; she saw a father beating up his son over that stolen TV right out on her street—that was what got her most, that father-son fight.

For the last two years of high school, Darlene moved with her mother to Gantwick, a humble, lower-middle-class black neighborhood with aluminum-sided, two-family row houses and birch trees on the sidewalks. What soothing visual music it became to see real live trees, however picayune and few, out the window.

Darlene started college. She was anxious not only to please her mother but also to justify the NIH Minority Access to Research Careers Grant she'd been given. She made sure to dazzle in her classes, most especially in organic chemistry, biology, physics, and calculus, as well as in English and philosophy. The latter two best suited her temperament. But she didn't know if she should work with greed among the materialists or wait on some higher purpose she couldn't identify yet. So she majored in premed/biology. Not only because she knew nothing would gratify her mother more than having a doctor in the family, but also because Darlene felt great pride at the idea of making so total a break from the deprivations of her own past. *Dr. Darlene Stokes:* had a ring to it, she could do some good, and be well-off, to boot.

She hadn't foreseen the loneliness of the young scholar at an American university, however.

Bookishness, hardheaded intellectualism, an affection for time-consuming study, the very qualities for which she'd thought she would've been, at last, rewarded—these things her classmates met with an amused ill will. Tufts placed her with a roommate who'd come from a malled-up Philadelphia suburb. Erin Parajanian was all smiles (fatuous) and baby fat. Just two weeks into school, Darlene overheard Erin saying into her pink Swatch phone: "My roommate is this black girl, from Brooklyn. You think she'd be cool, right? Totally faggy. She's driving me fucking crazy." What hurt most was the delighted laughter. Even Darlene's professors—or, more precisely, those professors who socialized with their students—seemed to prefer the less bookish kids. The cooler ones, the highflyers: the very type Darlene felt superior to.

Darlene wept all through the first half of freshman year; she missed her mother. Calling home often was an unaffordable indulgence—even with her job in the campus bookstore—and anyway, phoning Alice would have been an admission of weakness, of imperfection. Alice and Darlene didn't *do* imperfection.

After a friendless semester, Darlene worked out a plan: She made up her mind to meet people.

This having been 1986 at the most expensive non-Ivy in America, a large proportion of African-American students were part of the newly percolating black middle class. "Buppies," many of them called themselves with pride. The most fashionable belonged to what had been named the Melanin Society—which, unlike the more combative TPAA (Tufts Pan-African Association), was a more or less apolitical social group.

She attended the mandatory "The Souls of African-American Folks" seminar, she was present at all three of the Melanin Society's "Harlem Renaissance Dance Nights," she signed up for the African studies class "Power Violence in South Africa," and she published her own gloomy, high-minded short story called "The Forfeiture of One Mother" in the African-American lit journal called *Onyx*. But without, in fact, ever really assimilating the Melanin Society's way of talking beautifully about "blackness"—she still managed to win an invite to join the society. Screw Erin Parajanian and her endless laugh! Darlene, still in many ways that nine-year-old "Purple," believed that she had finally been delivered to real life. The dangerous undertow, for such former outcasts as Darlene, was peer pressure; how can you not get pulled in?

Her new friends nicknamed her "Bushwick," and later, taunting her studiousness, "Encyclopedia Bushwick." They seemed both impressed by and contemptuous of her Brooklyn pedigree. Being "street" was fine, more in theory than in practice, which involved her crummy clothes and student loan stuff; and she wasn't even street, at least not in the way she acted. Still, by fall midterms she had a close friend: Tiphanie Washington, an attractive young gadfly from Syosset, Long Island (vice president of the Kwanzaa Celebration Committee, president of her dormitory council, student member of the Higher Education Initiative Symposium); Tiphanie, whose clothes were always dry-cleaned and looked up-to-the-second.

Tiph often wore the scandalized face of the newly offended, as quite a few of Darlene's buppie friends did: They had just awakened to constraints of three hundred years of American favoritism, injustice, and gross improbity. By the second semester of sophomore year, Darlene had moved into the room next to Tiphanie's at Melanin House, which was open to scholarship kids because it was subsidized by the university. Tiph's room had a color TV, Betamax, a stereo, word processor, and an answering machine; Darlene's had only the bed and desk and a Walgreens phone. Though she and her mother were no longer poor, they hadn't the nerve yet to live as though they weren't.

Once in Melanin House (the group's name was a pun on the history of the house, which had been donated by Andrew Mellon some fifty thousand or so years before), Darlene settled into the society's clique the way she might have stepped into a very hot bath. It took her a while to accommodate herself, but once in she didn't want to get out. Not that she'd quit "studying like a madwoman." Most weeknights, well into the hours when everyone else was sleeping, she'd sit in the downstairs common room, doing her homework—ticking across some loose-leaf paper the equations for Chemistry 345 (Intermediate Organic), or arguing in an extra-credit paper that, if one accepts cultural relativism (and remains logically consistent), then one will have to accept certain other implausible propositions. She enjoyed the work and the monastery quiet. It was the loud nights she was less sure about, the nights when she would leave Melanin House's inevitable party at one A.M., and afterward lie in bed, awake for hours, her head lodged between two campus-issue pillows—her feeble defense against music that would rumble on until four, four-thirty.

"All you do is *study*, Bushwick," Tiphanie said categorically. "I'm not even talking about partying with us, which you don't. I'm talking about maybe we could use you on dorm council, or HEIS. But you never *ask* to help out. It's like you think, wow, but, you know, there's more to this house than Bushwick's grades." Her tone was so impressive that Darlene promised to join the following semester.

But, if she never quite felt like a phony with the Melanin Society kids, she also knew that she wasn't exactly herself around them. Whether it was impolitic of her to do so, Darlene grappled in private with her own anger at racism—an anger that certainly did exist, if perhaps *sub rosa*—whereas Tiphanie's indignation struck Darlene as faddish and performative.

After her chem lab partner sought her out, Darlene began socializing with white kids. Her mother had told her that white friends (Jews, particularly) might serve as "important business contacts" after college—long as you kept your eye on them. The happy surprise was this: Darlene found that whites, unlike "buppies," didn't make fun of her for having been born poor. At least not to her face.

She'd grown up knowing few whites, and so she'd never had to put an individual face to the racism that had always felt to her hopelessly, anonymously systemic, an all-pervading threat in the backdrop of every black person's life. (There had never been any truth to the charges, dating back to elementary school, that Darlene had wanted to act white; she just never understood why some intelligent, sheltered black kids needed to feel that an ongoing connection to "the street"—affecting bad grammar out of class; saying, "What's up?" to lingerers on street corners—was essential to their black pride.) Darlene did find it easier to make new white friends than, say, Tiphanie did; Tiphanie, who'd grown up alongside white kids whose long-standing friendship she now felt compelled to break off.

Another reason (a reason whose truth Darlene would admit to herself only twenty years later, when the whole Goldin family mess started, with all its attendant publicity) was that having white friends made the break that she'd undertaken from her own past seem complete. She always wondered about her dad, and worried that not having a father might have limited her social choices with suburban kids. He could be anywhere, in jail, on the streets, a janitor at this very college. But to her surprise, a good number of her new rich friends had absent fathers, too; cheating fathers; disappearing fathers; or at least sullen, *emotionally* distant fathers. She and her new friends passed entire nights in which the misbehavior of fathers was the binding topic.

Who in Bushwick had the sort of friends Darlene had, read the books she now did, or looked forward to the future that she would surely have?

A final benefit to hanging out with white kids: Though she had always been considered a gloomy nerd—and still was, by Melanin House—many whites at Tufts simply assumed she was cool, and pursued her friendship, because she was black.

She accepted this.

One evening in January Darlene went, with her bio/chem partner, to the "*Grease* Is the Word Mingle," a 1950s-themed party in the basement of one of the Jewish fraternities. She was a month from turning twenty.

By half-past ten, she stood alone, anchored to the corner opposite the "Rydell High" banner, as if removed from the drunken party, where she watched a game of beer pong and considered going home to *Ethics & Public Policy: The Omnibus Reader* and a cup of hot chocolate. A handsome white guy in a polo shirt came over, and asked her if she wanted a beer.

This was Leo Golovin—thinly built, a smiley if blushing sophomore with big dark eyes, very thin lips, and unkempt black hair.

"Awesome party, huh? Elvis and Sha Na Na," he said—overenunciating to suggest cynicism, the college-boy mode. But he was shy to face Darlene fully, and he had the wide-open eyes of a likably humble person.

"Do you hate it, too?" she said. "Frat parties like this?" She didn't know why she'd said that; it was so earnest.

For a second, his mouth quit the effort of its practiced grin. "Kinda."

He was very pale now that he'd stopped blushing, and he had a dark Marilyn Monroe dot on his cheek, a mite floating in a milk puddle, a companionless star in a negative-photograph sky. "Yeah, I do kinda."

"Me, too."

From this, Darlene and Leo edged into an increasingly unfrattish conversation for ten, twenty, then forty thrilling minutes.

Bathed in red party light and the doo-wop music of ironic nostalgia, Leo turned out to be surprisingly bookish. He charmed Darlene by sharing an anecdote he'd read about Emperor Caligula. (Caligula had thought himself a real-life god, and Roman senators would often find the Emperor conversing, arguing, and laughing alone with a statue of Jupiter in the Forum, his hand over the marble deity's shoulder.) Talking excitedly, with the blood pulsing in her temples, she returned the serve by describing a hilarious book called *Candide*—how it was funny but "still, its message resonates in today's world." Next, she went into the ways that her friend Tiphanie could be kind of silly. Then, without warning, oddly, and for the first time, she found herself confessing that her mother's life of sacrifice was both admirable and a real burden to her. She so powerfully felt the relief of having said this that she mistook it for romantic affection.

Leo, whose own family clung with white-knuckled tenacity to the upper middle class, told her seriously and not ungently:

"I bet it would be really hard growing up like that, and dealing with so much pressure or responsibility now." Leo knew some of his own failings, and one of them was that people took his kindnesses for their opposite, his attempts at sincerity for an acerbic mocking cynicism. "I mean, at this age when most people are fucking around. I'm sorry you have to go through it alone."

Darlene submitted the statement to Melanin House analysis. Was he making fun of her? Being smugly racist? Or inad*vertent*ly racist? She turned it over and over. Well, he hadn't shaken his head in fake compassion at her (that's what she'd expected). His dark eyes had in fact gone big with empathy. It was his look, his kind eyes, the slight flush back on his face that decided her, that got her to work on creating a notion of him right then.

All the same, she didn't yet mention that gaping hole in her life, her father.

Someone in a far corner of the party cut off the doo-wop. This left only the chatter, the shouted, drunken snippets of other people's nights. Still, Darlene's own night swirled ahead of her as if on delicate, continuous music. Leo gave her one beer after another—conscientiously, never enough to make her feel he was taking advantage of her.

"Our house blend," he said, handing her a drink. His grin showed the immaculate handiwork of his father, a Five Towns orthodontist. And: "Aged in wood casks for like five generations." And: "I trust you'll find the blend very much to your liking." And: "Oat soda, warm and watery. Unimpressive for first dates."

Leo's almost lipless mouth curled up at its edges. Something of the rogue in him, the wiseass; also something of the spoiled kid. But what charmed her was the suggestion of depth she believed she spotted underneath—some truth that he may not have known about himself, some inherent genuineness he wasn't aware of. He *did* keep blushing, didn't he?

The music started up again. Someone across the room had pressed play on Dan Hartman's "I Can Dream About You," a song she'd come to remember as emblematic of the schmaltz, timidity, and optimism of that time. (And itself the very crap that would become music of ironic nostalgia for the next generation of college partiers.)

"I'm not a beer connoisseur, Leo," she was saying. "I'm like the warm and watery blend."

Because she'd only read the word *connoisseur* and never heard it spoken, she mispronounced it: "con-oh-*see*-er."

"Confession is important on a first date."

His white shirt had lost its second button; in its place four little threads jabbed out like birthmark hairs. But Darlene would soon learn that, as with many of the Jewish boys of ΑΕΠ, the seeming carelessness of Leo's appearance wasn't all that careless.

She'd cocked her head. It'd taken her a minute to get the nerve up to ask: "Is this a first date?"

Darlene's mother had never had any romance lessons to pass on. (What little experience Alice Davis had known, she couldn't recommend.) But Tiphanie liked to say that if you can imagine enjoying taking care of a man when he twists his ankle playing sports, then you really like him. Darlene wanted Leo to break his legs so he'd need a wheelchair—and someone kindly to push him around.

"Call it a date," he said, smiling. "I will if you will."

The playful good cheer in his voice made his conversation erotic—his pronounced cheekbones didn't hurt, either. As she herself grew steadily more excited, she couldn't help remembering a line that had shocked her when she'd come across it in St. Augustine, something about "the hideous and involuntary erections in holy men." Was it possible that Leo had one, standing here talking with her?

He made a move to hold her hand and she let him.

That instant marked the happiest moment in Darlene's life, up to that time. Leo's hand in hers stirred her in a way that sex with him rarely would (and they were to have sex about four hours later). Not because she would fail to enjoy the fooling around—although the grunting inelegance of college sex did remind her of two people moving some unwieldy furniture. To her, *these* joys—the honesty of their conversation, the hand holding, and the ensuing sex—were of a piece. Darlene was alone among her friends in judging that what was best about sex was not the tingly physical stuff (though that was nice), but the implausible idea that two unrelated people would agree to get so embarrassingly naked in front of each other—and all for the reason (in her estimation) that by doing so they could grow more close, more sympathetic.

Later that night, in his T-shirty room that had a curtain for a door, on his single bed, under his ungraceful and gluttonous hands, his college-boy hands, Darlene spoke in a voice shaky with lust, as if she were light-headed. "Oh, this is fan*tas*tic," she said. "*Fantastic.*"

DARLENE STOKES, FATHERLESS and "goal-oriented" as she was, hadn't thought much about marriage.

But six weeks after she and Leo started dating—and right away she would have described theirs as a relationship of warmth, of a philosophical empathy, of gazing into eyes, of doodling pen-drawn hearts on bluejeans, at the campus center, on a museum bench, or in his single room, where he'd tell her that she was beautiful (which Darlene *was*, although she would only sometimes, bashfully as if against her will, allow herself to believe it)—he took her to *Nick's Beef and Beer Hall* and gave her an occasionless gift. She opened a black velvet box onto a pair of pearl drop earrings, jewelry much more expensive than anything she'd worn before. She turned contemplative. She leaned her forearms on the table so heavily that her head went low toward her shoulders. And she had this thought, which struck her as freshly as if never considered by anyone before: *I could spend my life with this person.*

A peculiar, grave happiness squeezed her throat; happiness, except it didn't feel so different from gloom. There was fear in it, fear that it could simply end. Across the restaurant, men's voices blared and then broke off. No, it wasn't gloom that Darlene felt, it was happiness. But it was overbearing and alarming. Her mouth went dry.

Until now it had been Leo who'd done the sweet-talking in their courtship. But now she needed to tell him about her feelings.

She arranged the sentence in her head first: "You are experiencing certain . . . forceful emotions, am I right? Well, Leo, I, *too,* am experience—" *No; don't be such a loser!* What about: "When young people our age perceive . . ." *No! Lord!*

She wasn't vain, but since dating Leo, Darlene had taken to staring at herself in the mirror quite a bit. Her face, her consequential legs, her breasts—weren't these really unrelated to her, just *things* paired up randomly with the self that took in so infinitely much?

Maybe she could say: "Have you noticed the intensity of emotion rising between us?" Come on, Darlene: say *something*!

Leo filled the pause with his wheezy laugh that meant he already knew her well.

I'm just going to tell him I love him, she thought. *Right now.* She said: "Thanks again for the earrings."

He laughed again. "No prob."

He felt he was being somewhat altruistic in liking her. He felt good and progressive. This feeling was all the more appetizing because it had a nice savory hint of self-pity to it. And, really, how many other girls had liked him this much?

AFTER HAVING BEEN the thousandth ultracompetitive kid from his ultracompetitive high school to use an exorbitant Kaplan SAT course, and after receiving a job-averting stipend from his father, Leo Golovin repudiated his own family in many subtle, unconscious ways. They were kindly, materialistic people.

His two sisters and his parents spoke with the flint vowels and sluggish diphthongs of the Long Island accent: slicing off the *r*'s with gusto, banishing their *g*'s into their throats. He'd never actually made a decision to reject their way of speaking—at least he couldn't remember having done so—but once in a great while, he'd pronounce certain words in that hated cadence. Especially if he was tired—"cwau-fee" instead of "coffee," say, as if he'd lowered some subliminal guard. It embarrassed him, as if he'd farted in public. *Where did that come from?*

But until he and Darlene Stokes agreed they were in love, Leo had few friends who weren't Jews. He never went to synagogue, but considered himself "culturally" Jewish: he belonged not just to ΑΕΠ, but—thanks to a hard-core Zionist ex-girlfriend—to the *Pioneers of Israel* club. He'd even auditioned for *Shir Appeal*, "Tufts's only coed, Jewish a cappella collective," though he did it merely because he thought that they might have been obliged to accept any Jew, even if he had a thin voice. (They were not.)

But once he fell in love with sober, precise, *black* Darlene Stokes, Leo Golovin recognized how unsophisticated his former attitudes had been. How did "the People of the Book" and their 5,745-year history link up with the Tufts chapter of ΑΕΠ, or with Lawrence, New York: that earthly-minded Jewish enclave of his shaping years? Leo didn't know, or want to learn, Hebrew. What did he feel beyond affiliation with a particular kind of nose, a certain shape to the eyes, and a tone of humorous complaint? So how was "cultural Judaism" divisible from a club or a nostalgia for the bad old times?

Leo and Darlene helped each other to see Tufts as the Toy UN it was. Everyone split into their little groups, their ethnic delegations, their sexual-orientation security councils. Who needed it?

His parents, sounding not one hundred percent at ease, said they didn't care that his girlfriend was "an illegitimate black girl from Brooklyn." It was Darlene's mother, Alice Davis, however, who stood against them.

"It's fine to have white-people friends, even good friends," Alice told Darlene. This was a planned lecture, delivered point by point in Rothenberg & Rubinstein style. "And some Jews are as good as people come. Mr. Rothenberg has always treated me in a humane manner. You know I *like* Joe Rothenberg. I've nothing against the man. But to raise your kids how? As Jews? Listen, my love, it's not that white people make me have some 'Go Tell It on the Mountain' thing. You know me. Don't you? I have nothing against Joe Rothenberg. Better a Jew than someone from Tulsa. It's just easier all around if they stay with their people and we stay with our people, when a level of seriousness becomes involved."

News of this shocked Leo. His white parents were cool with it, and it was whites who were usually the racist ones, right? So then, if the whites didn't mind, wasn't it kind of ridiculous for the *black* family—and let's be frank, a family with no father—to be against it? He would repeat that to himself, as if it were a joke: "Great Neck's covered. It's the *black* family that has an issue with it?"

Of course, he didn't phrase it that way to Darlene.

He was shocked that Darlene collapsed in the face of internal Stokes opposition. He didn't know that Alice had lost some distant family in Tulsa during the 1921 race riot that had killed hundreds: *The Tulsa Tribune* had printed a fabricated story that a black shoe-shine boy had raped a white elevator operator; the same paper ran an editorial called "To Lynch Negro Tonight in N—town"; Alice had heard tales of small airplanes having passed overhead to drop Molotov cocktails on Greenwood, the black Tulsa ghetto, the section that had gotten burned to nothing. Belulah Faye Winfield, Alice's great-aunt, had died from a gunshot wound to the thigh, of all places; no one had been able to take her to the hospital, and no one had ever gone to jail for Belulah Faye's, or any other, killing.

Darlene told Leo she needed to stop dating him. Then she gave up speaking to him altogether.

DARLENE BELIEVED, AT first, that nothing terribly derailing had happened. Months, a whole semester, wobbled by. She continued studying with the fervor of someone entered in a competition to better herself—though what "better" meant, specifically, she couldn't have said. "I won't talk to Leo. Or any other boys." And she believed that.

Sometimes she'd remember their first night together, the way he'd hopped out of his jeans as if he were in a sack race, and how her eyes had bounced over his shoulders, sped by his features in a terrible hot rush, all in their hurry to look at the fresh prow inside his tighty-whitey underpants. Sometimes she'd even laugh to herself about it, bringing her hand to cover her mouth, her cheeks blushing.

But by and large she kept her head buried in her new life.

She still lived at Melanin House, but if she hadn't been shunned, exactly, she'd become a bit player, an extra. Fine with her. Maybe loneliness was the cost of perfection. One member of the Melanin Society lighted a silly little controversy by circulating an imprecisely offensive, loosely antiwhite "Manifesto" in *The Tufts Daily,* suggesting that white scientists "may have invented HIV" as a way to "keep the black community down." Darlene stayed out of this ruckus, and—in private—let her mood darken out toward self-glorification.

No more foolishness.

She looked at student rallies with a haughty pragmatist's disdain. As Darlene understood it, demonstrations back in protesting's heyday—such as her hero MLK's March on Washington—lobbied for specific legislation, against particular, defeatable antagonists. This week, Tiphanie wanted Darlene to join the "Take Back the Night" rally. As a fellow-traveling leftist, Darlene enthusiastically agreed with that march's antirape message (who wouldn't?). But she saw the demonstration itself as an anodyne imitation of '60s protest-fun. What were the *goals* here—appealing to rapists to cut it out? Did the self congratulatory marchers think that opposing something as universally despised as rape meant they were taking an actual, heroic stand? *Maybe if they were marching on the security station to appeal for more campus cops on patrol, or if they were challenging the administration to get additional streetlights, it'd __mean__ something,* Darlene thought. But walking around a sheltered, innocent campus? Didn't it all seem just a way to feel righteous, to get attention? She looked out her window, at the rock-concert spectacle of flicky candles, the two hundred yellow dots held in protest of the existence of evil itself. Books, more books, classes taken, classes audited: Darlene was convinced that solitary endurance was the only answer to the world. It was the world she blamed for losing Leo, not her mother.

Everything changed one afternoon.

Darlene stepped in a puddle—her moist and heavy socks feeling like tongues on her feet—and after she'd cursed and wiped her outlet-mall Capezios, she lifted her eyes to see Leo Golovin not twenty yards off, by the Media Center. With a pretty blonde. *No!*— Darlene turned away, as if struck by something on the horizon. All across the paper-white sky, clouds looked like eraser smudges.

She forced herself to turn back. Leo's handsomeness was heightened by charisma and affection. Darlene had the odd thought: *Did he look this happy around me?* The blond girl was making him laugh, and he hadn't noticed that anyone was watching.

Her months of solitude disgusted her.

Shaking her head, but without crying, Darlene made her way across the treeless quad to chem lab.

Later, even the cool laboratory trappings that should have cleared Leo from her brain—a metal sink with twin swan-necked faucets, a beaker suspended over a Bunsen burner's hyacinth flame, all this indifferent apparatus—whispered in her ear: *Don't you remember the good times?*

Darlene loitered in front of the lab's big plate window as she daydreamed over the quad. And beyond it, to the far-off trees nodding in the dingy New England dusk, the squat library with its ATM stall and free-standing reinforced-concrete representation of a textbook; she felt overwhelmed by the campus's quiet, this stillness in which eccentricity was overprized, glamour rewarded, goof-offs lionized, and luckless hardworking Brooklyn girls were compelled to give up on their desires.

I've got to talk to somebody, she thought. But to whom? Her mother?

She wanted to go home and wriggle under her blankets; instead, assiduous as ever, she sighed, just once, and delved into the Nitrogen Rule, recrystallization, and characteristic bonds in IR spectra.

Later that week, a Thursday, Darlene's assignment for English 314 ("Making the Modernist Novel; or, Making the Novel Modernist") brought her, for the first time, to Joyce and his *Portrait of the Artist as a Young Man.* Late in the night, ignoring the noise of the Student of Color Outreach Program (SCOPE) fund-raiser beneath her—the laughs, drum machine, the furniture bumping—she read sentences of enough gravity to tug, and create, the tides by which her life would move. In a few paragraphs Joyce rejected family, custom, ethnicity—any net flung at the soul: *You talk to me of nationality, language, religion. I shall try to fly by those nets. . . . I will not serve that in which I no longer believe, whether it call itself my home, my fatherland, or my church: and I will try to express myself . . . using for my defense the only arms I allow myself to use—silence, exile, and cunning.*

It's just a book, she thought later, trying to sleep. But those words. Silence, exile, and cunning. Her eyes were tired and kept closing. But the rest of her body was awake. Silence. Exile. Cunning.

The next morning, Darlene called Leo. "I made a mistake," she said instantly. "I love you. Who was that white girl?"

She was pushing aside the curtain of her mother's influence, and seeing what was beyond it. What felt great, what felt liberating, what Joyce saw, was that there was nothing beyond it.

"Darlene?" Leo said. "S'that you? Uh, hello?"

Sitting alone in her austere room, with her back against the radiator, and hugging her knees to her chest, she imagined Leo's face. His pale, bony cheeks would be getting red around that Marilyn Monroe birthmark. She just knew he was about to hang up on her.

"There is no other girl. I'm glad you called. Really, really glad."

So Darlene and Leo got married.

How unlike her to jump into something like marriage right away, at City Hall (a sign read: "The throwing of rice, rose petals, or similar materials tends to cause sliding or slipping and is strictly prohibited"). In place of wedding rings, she and Leo each wore a twisted pipe cleaner.

In the Municipal Chapel, strangers' happy yelps at the altar and the machine-gun stutter of Super 8 cameras mixed with the faint, despondent noise of the nearby DMV and the occasional howl from Criminal Court. Darlene's resolve had beat out her inhibition. As she stood holding Leo's hand in line, waiting to go before a grinning justice of the peace, she was happy, not feeling at all the heavy way she usually did, as if she were carrying another person around. She and Leo were there without any friends or family.

"I do," she said—a fatherless momma's girl defying her mother. "Yes, yes yes I do."

Right away, having made herself dependent on Leo, she was dizzy with liberty. Chaining herself to this other person felt to Darlene like freedom. Not that she had the guts to tell her mother about the marriage. Silence, exile, and cunning. (Would the Student Aid Office blow the whistle? She had filed paperwork that requested they allow her to apply her housing scholarship money toward her new apartment with Leo on Powderhouse Avenue.)

Moving in with her adorable husband, sharing a bed and everything else, the long spasm of pleasurable adaptation, made it feel as if she and Leo had made themselves a very private club. Even her eyes became spunkier. She and Leo were the only married students on campus and people would come right out with it: "Why did you? No, really—why?" She could have gushed about the affectionate, groggy silences before morning coffee. Or the happiness of coming home to find dinner already prepared, no matter how unimpressive the meal—pasta, even an ordered-in pizza. Mainly, it was the delight in not having to worry over a huge future decision—marriage as one more insurance policy against prospective failure.

Love wasn't a thing you fell in, but rose to. It was what stopped you from falling.

Leo had a delicate hug, and his skin always smelled faintly and pleasantly of whatever he'd recently eaten.

Not that there was one hundred percent harmony. She'd have to restrain herself from pressing him about schoolwork. But marriage gave you new angles: Maybe he wasn't lazy; maybe *she* was overindustrious?

By the time Tufts had put on its sexy spring clothing, even students who didn't know Darlene—whites *and* blacks together, united, just the way the Student of Color Outreach Program wanted—looked at her with stares that asked, *What's it like to be crazy?* Tiphanie Washington's eyes put it another way: *What's it like to be a traitor?*

The joke was that Darlene didn't ever feel, nor want to be, white; the culture Darlene knew and treasured was her own. Whenever she felt entertained by Prince, or Miles Davis, or Otis Redding, or Richard Pryor, or Toni Morrison, or El DeBarge, even Eddie Murphy and Run-DMC (but never Niggaz with Attitude or Public Enemy, whose Professor Griff she now found anti-Semitic), she picked up some quality in these artists to which she might have said, "Yes, this is about, and for, and *with* me." The worst thing about spending time with Leo's friends—hell, about spending time with Leo—was that Darlene starved that indefinable black quality in herself. Sometimes she compared Leo's nearly lipless mouth to those of black kids and did feel, she had to admit, less attracted to him.

Still, in marriage she matured a year every week, intellectually and emotionally. This way, that way, in all kinds of ways, really—and she knew it to be happening. As a foreign tourist takes every local's idiosyncrasy for a clue into the national character, she investigated Leo for hints about manhood, that mysterious country. *Ah,* she'd think, *so I guess men don't watch TV news.*

Two months after the wedding, she phoned up a familiar number and said, "Momma, I got married." She waited. "And if you want me around you'll have to accept that."

She and Leo Amtraked down to New York for a weekend with Darlene's mother. None of Alice's world embarrassed Darlene as she'd fretted it might—not the mucusy gurgling sound when you pressed the buzzer to be let in, not the green-seam TV chair whose indented buttons were frayed black, not the carpeted toilet lid, and not Alice herself, shuffling across mornings in her pink slippers—these ancient particulars that hadn't changed while Darlene had.

Now an irritable oldish woman at just thirty-nine (pelvic myoneuropathy, obesity, a kaleidoscope of pills), Alice kept deferring to Leo. "Whatever you like," she'd say. "Scrambled or sunny side.

Whatever you like, Leo." No one argued the whole time, or actually talked. If Darlene had been blind she wouldn't have recognized her mother, so unusual was Alice's behavior, the weird smoothness of her voice. And so Darlene would say the trip "went well"—although it'd had, for her, the feel of a deindoctrination. After they left, Leo referred to his mother-in-law as "Chairman Ma." And Darlene laughed without guilt.

YEARS LATER, DURING a brief difficult stretch, when she'd find herself remembering the fever dream of her college days—when the hospital scandal, the defamation, *whatever* it could properly be called, pushed these memories upon her—Darlene realized that something about Leo reminded her of that Mr. Goldin. Not the Leo who was her husband, but Leo at the beginning: full of wit and confidence. The two men differed wildly in mannerism, but they alike had the unconscious assurance, the gently condescending vibe of someone raised to believe nothing bad was likely to happen to him, or was even possible. Could that have been related somehow to their being Long Island Jews? she would almost allow herself to wonder.

IN 1988, DARLENE Stokes finished college with a shining GPA and won six tuition-free years at NYU Med School.

Having grown up just outside Manhattan, Darlene as a teenager had suffered Cinderella frustrations. Living in the duller boroughs had felt like watching a royal ball from the far side of a moat. Now, with the giddiness of a party crasher, she moved with Leo to the fabled East Side—to Madison Avenue, that dapper eyeful.

They took one and a half bedrooms, high in a doorman building (Leo's uncle got them the deal; his father gave them "funds"). Leo got down to the ordering: Carolina Chair couch; projection-screen TV; king-size bed from the Door Store; Sharper Image exercise bike; massaging showerhead that looked like the blossom of a sunflower. He'd lived frugally in college as a self-prescribed trial; now he'd graduated, didn't he deserve the possessions his parents had?

(Although he tried to buy it all with a wink, to show he was cooler than his parents, who actually cared about this stuff.)

Leo's thrifty, serious wife wanted to be offended. But when she finally showed her mother the tricked-out apartment, Darlene couldn't stop grinning. The truth: It was nice to have nice things. Which, she thought, made as convincing a refutation of communism as she'd ever heard.

Still, for the rest of Leo's life, Darlene never allowed herself to see his money as half hers.

In October, NYU handed her a corpse for gross dissection. The dead body, bald, large, black, lay in a metal cistern, preserved with formaldehyde. In this unforeseen place, the silly thought scrolled across Darlene's mind, *Could this be my father?*

Of the three students filling out her dissection group, the first had gone to Harvard, the second to Princeton, and the last had made *cum laude* at Brown. All were white boys, drawn with feminine features. Sharing high fives, they named the dead black body Cosby.

Darlene took to calling her lab partners *rock-brains*. "Princeton's really freaked by the smell, that rock-brain," or "Today, Rock-Brain Harvard made a bigoted comment about Cosby's—I mean the corpse's—penis." One postgraduation reality: Campus victories against philistinism didn't carry over to the greater world. The Toy UN had no enforcement arm. Racism lived. It made her exhausting work even more exhausting. You try to debate with rocks all week, she'd complain.

And at home, at some point every day, her husband wore sweatpants.

Some people's minds just close for business after college. Once Leo graduated, he would never read a challenging book again, unless you counted the *Commercial Real Estate Career Education and Resource Prospectus.*

Leo, who'd majored in both history and classics, sneered at potential jobs, at entire careers. It wasn't laziness exactly. He understood that he really wanted something, and he could almost figure out what it was, could almost express it to himself, but his true ambition was forever just out of reach and needling him.

Leo felt guilty when he cashed his monthly check from Dad, but somehow he always found the strength of will to do it.

"Honey, we'll just live on your salary," he joked when his dad got tired of supporting his unemployed, healthy son. "Not forever. I do have savings in the meantime, though." Darlene shrugged at all this; it was like discovering a birthmark on Leo she'd almost forgotten about until now.

"All right," she said. She even smiled a little. In her way of killing the already slain, however, she added: "I know you'd never want to do nothing and just live off my salary." He nodded with a tight frown.

Because Darlene had cut herself off from her past, she didn't see that Leo's unwillingness to reach for even the bottom rung dishonored her own life story.

"Just one quick point I want to make, though," Leo said. "Office jobs never get you anywhere today. These are different times. You need something big to get ahead. A rich uncle, a venture capital idea. No one just climbs the ladder anymore."

They ended up talking for forty minutes and as often happened lately, their conversation moved from smallest specifics into the larger theater of their irreconcilable philosophies.

Soon, Leo was taking her work habits as a rebuke. Nights, he'd sit low in his Carolina Chair couch, a young man slumped under his dejection. At first, Darlene would make sure to ask her frowning husband about his job search; then, she made the same effort not to.

Whenever she put an ear to her marriage, she'd catch a faint heartbeat of Leo's disdain. What he held against her was the one problem she couldn't do anything to change. She'd worked her whole life to be who she was: the most inflexible doer of the right thing. Working, killing the engines just long enough to worry about Leo, and then getting back at it. If he had wanted something reason-

able of her, she could have done it. She was a past master of working things out, after all. She could have dressed sexier, she could
have planned a romantic vacation to Paris. But of all life's problems,
this—her diligent self—was the insoluble one.

So they separated.

He initiated it. "I'm not seeing anybody else," he said, though
she hadn't asked.

"What fan*tas*tic news," she said. *"Fantastic."* (She'd never used
sarcasm in her life before. That's what some marriages can do.)
Their relationship had the feel of a cracked pipeline—familiarity,
all their shared affection, just trickling out.

Leo said he was moving to his parents' house to "think about
some stuff, get my head together."

She tried to be sad, but it wasn't in her to grieve. She analyzed.
Why did Leo leave? Which turned into: *What had he liked about me
in the first place?* Experience had trained Darlene ever since she
was a girl to be a mom, a provider—but never much of a young
woman. She'd grown up with a family ethos whereby romantic
love had meant only blunders and absences. Mature but somehow
sort of bloodless, pretty in a haphazard way, somber even when she
laughed, Darlene saw herself as the choice men would make only to
offset their bad habits.

After she and Leo had been apart a few weeks, Darlene learned
she was pregnant. About a month before, the clouds had rolled back
for an hour near the end of what had become a very rainy marriage—
but that was all it had been, one final gleam of romance—and here
was this surprise pregnancy.

She'd been so vigilant. And yet this seemed the fate she'd almost
expected. "I *am* my mother," was her repeated psalm. "I'm going to
raise a kid by myself in a broken home."

If Alice was the only person to whom Darlene could appeal for
support, Alice was also the last person to whom she could complain,
or admit that single parenthood felt like abject failure. Darlene pretended that what seemed an injustice, was instead a joy.

Leo proved himself capable of obligatory politeness; he said: "I'll move back." (This after he'd gingerly sort of asked if she was open to abortion. She was not.)

Darlene was talking to Leo on the phone, sitting by herself in the room they'd shared, holding her knees to her chest. She felt the contours of a remembered conversation fall over this one.

She could picture his thin lips getting all pursed in deliberation, the movement of his mole when he added, "Okay, we'll just give it another shot, then."

"No," she said. "We won't."

Ever since graduation, Leo with a mocking look had brushed off the circumstances of his life, as if all of it had been merely warmup, with some great, creative project waiting patiently ahead. Now that false light had been snuffed out. He'd gotten a real estate job through his uncle, and would commute to Manhasset, Long Island, glumly, until the morning he died.

In 2001, she gave birth to a healthy boy named James. Having already specialized in pediatrics—peeds—she was wise to babies and the ways they came into this world. But how powerful these feelings were! The hugeness of affection, chest-filling warm terrifying supreme affection. Darlene hadn't loved enough before to prepare for this love. When she first gathered little James into her hug, when her son looked up at her with his smooshed face and puffy eyes, Darlene *ached* with love. Motherhood as luscious suffering. Oh, the tense wrinkles of his lids when he closed them, and the blotchy, half-fisted hands that padded at the tissue paper of her gown. As she held him, the baby scowled his cheeks red (the skin was lightish, a perfect halfway color); he had wispy eyelashes. He was beautiful.

Leo agreed not to fight Darlene about custody—as if he'd want *that* job—provided that Darlene would serve her residency at a hospital close to his new Long Island home. She picked St. Joe's Medical, the hospital that everyone said looked like a fort on top of its hill. She bought a two-story house in Washington Harbor, a lethargic village off the Long Island Sound.

Darlene found herself shy inside this hulking thing, her loose-fitting new home. Its bottom floor was larger than the entire apartment of her childhood, its basement having been rigged by people she'd never met with clanging basics she'd never considered—a dusty EnergyStar furnace; also the pipes, foam insulation, and heat tape that together reminded Darlene of ulnar bones membraned by their own soft tissue. Quaking guts, grunting pipes, creaky wood; she'd bought and would live in, it seemed, a giant arthritic whale. Darlene could look at a corpse, but she feared going to the dark basement.

It took a bucket brigade of stand-in moms—a Trinidadian nanny, an Irish exchange student from the local school, and frequently Alice—to hand cute little James back to Darlene at the end of a week. (Darlene even paid Alice a "salary" to allow Rothenberg & Rubinstein's favorite paralegal to go part-time.) For all that, Darlene managed to be a real—earnest, expert, and doting—mother. But even she wasn't capable of turning all this, all her efforts, all these people, into any kind of composite father.

Then Leo got into a car crash. He'd been turning into his office's parking lot when an SUV burned around a corner and into him. Darlene got the news from her answering machine, a summary message left by her onetime sister-in-law. Ex–sister-in-law; ex-husband; ex-person. Leo was dead.

After Darlene told her three-and-a-half-year-old son that his father had passed away—worrying when he didn't cry—she allowed herself a little nostalgia, lingering on a few remembered images: Leo's smile in front of the justice of the peace; and at the frat party where they'd met; her kissing his Monroeish mole the first time. But after unwrapping these private keepsakes, she folded them back away inside herself and looked up squarely into her life as it now was. She felt neither romantic nor bitter: Their time had been nothing special, just a love story. It was like the world—made of human kindness and cruelty. That was all it was. Over the next week everyone kept telling her how sad she must be about this event that wouldn't really change her life, at least not from a practical standpoint. She hadn't realized that she, too, had failed to cry.

Twenty months later when Darlene Stokes was thirty-eight, success clicked its heels again, gave a slight bow, and said: *Right this way, ma'am*. She was named head of the hospital's Peed's ICU, and first in line for the Chair of Pediatrics and Child Health. Still, she had to work at the practical math of being Darlene: how to remain a black woman while avoiding being thought of as black.

She had one friend, sort of: Jane Shepherd, chair of St. Joseph's Department of Obstetrics and Gynecology. But for all her victories, some administrators and other doctors (white, Asian, Indian, and even her black colleagues) presumed she'd been given a boost by affirmative action. Or, they presumed until they saw the distinction of her work. She kept faith in the rightness of that liberal rescue plan. It stung, though. It stung that anyone might think *she*'d needed that lifeline. It was complicated, this business of necessary evils.

All the same, the job was hers. Tall, austere-haired, invariably called "articulate" by her bosses, Darlene had been prized at St. Joe's (if not loved) when the Goldins had taken their baby to the hospital after Mrs. Goldin's son coded.

This changed Dr. Stokes's life forever.

II

*Tell me the truth, Doctor. I'd sooner know. But only if
the truth is what I want to hear.*

—Kingsley Amis

1

THE AFTERNOON ZACK WAS BROUGHT HOME FROM THE HOSPITAL marked the beginning of Josh Goldin's flawless father period.

It was simple. At six-thirty, he and Dori would handle Zack's dinner. But it was Josh alone who ran the boy's nighttime bath, that errand of splashes; Josh who then delivered the balance of Zack's bottle; and it was Josh who led his baby to sleep at seven-thirty: patting his small head, smoothing the feathery hair until Zack went down. Then Josh and Dori would eat whatever meal she'd cooked that day, in an atmosphere of epilogue, of afterthought, like roadies sneaking a meal on the tour bus. Zack was every night's headlining event.

In this way, the Goldins passed the summer in a riot of delusion.

It had been a month since St. Joseph's Hospital and its Dr. Stokes had sicced the police on the family. Josh and Dori's offense, as the couple saw it, had been loving the baby too much, and having been the only level heads in the GI lab that night. (As if the *parents* shouldn't be the ones who say where their kid goes and doesn't go?)

The whole deal was unpleasant to dredge up, like something you once vaguely dreamed, or a rumor you hear about yourself. What seemed certain was that the baby was entirely healthy now: Everything had worked out. Josh had never had more faith in Dori.

St. Joe's had maintained its suspicions for a little while, but in the grumpy *pro forma* way of a teacher, or a landlord who knew something troublesome had gone down but was willing to let it slide. The nerve of those people, though. It had been awful: Just when Dori and Josh thought they'd gotten Zack out of there, that police cruiser's siren had shattered their relief, had led them on a gloomy drive back to the hospital. They'd had to wait again in that dubious place, that hell's hotel lobby. A pack of medical exams went by—the first, verifying that Zack's red blood cells were the normal size; the second, that he had good reticulocytes; a third showed (a second time) that his crit had stabilized; they did a few other blood tests as well, which took forty hours to come back and, of course, doctors and nurses scrutinized and poked and stethoscoped Zack to make sure he hadn't bled or passed out again. Josh and Dori had no say over any of this. Dori was great, though. She'd told that kid Dr. Weiss: "You lost an hour when we could have done tests. He coded because none of you did anything when I told you about the bloody vomit."

And soon enough, Zack was home again; no charges had been filed. In the subsequent twice-weekly visits to the family pediatrician—smiling Dr. Keller with his Dum Dum lollipops— Zack showed no medical problems. Best of all, Dori was always so calm at Dr. Keller's office. Josh called her the Tower of Strength. They never discussed the incident at home, though. They didn't know why.

Still, Josh regained that social momentum that had benefited him since childhood. Or, he almost did.

The morning after the hospital, he'd retreated to the private back room where men give themselves pep talks before jogging back out to the playing fields of life. He promised himself: *I can do more to help.* Because he'd had to admit: Before the incident, he'd treated housework/parenting stuff/Dori's needs/etc. like mosquitoes. (Plus, there had been a different thing, a mistake, something else he didn't like to think about. Despite it, he still considered himself to have been one hundred percent faithful as a husband—if he was allowed to be technical about stuff. He never would have *really* cheated, so why think about it now?)

"I'll do more around the house," he told himself. His forehead veins flashed with emotion. "I will." And so, with its cooperations, its motley chores: the Flawless Father Period.

Sure, he worked hard at *Sparkplug*. No argument there. And in ad sales, that meant going out late, drinking with clients: getting paid, essentially, to be a *guy*. And it was true—he'd felt sometimes that his real homes were the coffee lounge and the conference room, where things ran smoothly and where he had real control.

But now he pictured marriage as some sales contest. Make your wife say to herself, *Holy shit, I can't believe how much I love this man:* that was his game now. He'd be the perfect dad, the great partner. He needed the Incident to convey some positive message, as the worst things in life always had to. And it would; it would do that for him. Plus, he could still be his old, cool self. He simply had to turn his personality, his whole character, an inch to the left and no more. And that would be that.

So every night when Josh came home, he studied the ease, the glint of self-satisfaction, Dori showed when stroking the baby's back—as if the kid were a genie's lamp you rubbed for luck. Watching became Josh's research. Dori would bounce Zack on the plump of her hip. Josh started doing this, too. Soon the levers of self-change warmed to his touch. And his life expanded.

He peeked around corners in socks, staring at his wife and son with a divine greed. He'd spy on Dori through the back-door screen, as she carried Zack across their deck ("*Shhh, shhh,* baby") with the sunlight passing through her legs. Dori would notice his watching, and smile.

Josh's added help (the baby baths, meals, diaper changes, the picking up after himself) endeared and thrilled. Dori's steep gratitude took the form of winks and embraces, constant compliments, love Post-its on the fridge, suggestive cell messages, spectacular foot massages.

Beyond that, Dori had no need to reciprocate; she'd *always* made the big effort for Josh. Their entire marriage, she'd worked—from the moment he got home—to be charming for him. (Not that it was easy lately: When you spend most of your time with an infant, you don't often have stuff to banter with your husband about.) Usually she prepared some tidbit: maybe a joke her witty friend Lisa told her, an interesting Oprah-gotten fact, local gossip, or even a squib off nytimes.com. But she wished she'd had an office job. Office jobs provide conversational ammo you can fire off later, at your loved ones.

The truth was, she wasn't always totally herself with Josh. She could admit that, she thought. Yes, there was some acting there, some always-joking-around part of her that wasn't altogether the real Dori. Some constituency in her always hung back, just a little, to see how her husband was taking her jokes or her announcements of love. But it wasn't that she didn't want to share all of herself with him. It's just that it's impossible, isn't it, to communicate every last bit of yourself?

All the same, since Josh had started the Flawless Father Period, those dark moods Dori had shown this past year lifted; her shopping benders had gone. But she didn't mention Josh's change, not outright. Maybe she was afraid the spell would break.

"Hi, honey," she'd say when she caught him studying her; not *What are you staring at me like that for?*

And he'd say, "Hey, honey," then return to lapping up her Zack know-how.

But every so often he'd find his eyes turning from his family back to the hospital room.

Even on pleasant nights, it had its special power to animate things—that instilled fear, that unspoken fear—in the same way background static makes you unconsciously talk louder.

"What a perfect son I have," he'd say to drown it out, holding Zack high over his head, grinning extra wide.

They had escaped two things at St. Joe's: the physicians, and the tragedy of a sick baby. Josh wondered if his luck could really be that good. But he kept reminding himself that it was all Dori—she had made it all possible. She was so confident and had been so consistently right, both at the hospital and during the visits to Dr. Keller's. Her poise reaffirmed his belief in his own winning streak. This well-intentioned if imperfect guy, a backward Yankees hat on his head, a lively color in his cheeks, his baby son now always near, again believed that his own expectations were the only forces that acted on his life. The world would yield to the reins of his luck, jump through the hoops of his desires, follow every pull of his strong, white hand. He had gotten off scot-free, hadn't he?

"Do you think Zack has jowls?" Josh said early one evening in their breakfast nook.

"*Zack?*"

"Yeah, *Señor* Jowls, here."

"No doubt." Dori laughed, using one of her husband's expressions.

It was a humid Tuesday—the baby's dinner hour. Dori had changed out of her sweats, having prettied herself as she always did for Josh's arrival, greeting him this time in Capri pants and makeup.

She was crinkling her grateful eyes at her baby in his high chair.

They'd lingered in front of him for almost twenty minutes, hypnotized by his ball-cheeked face, his short infant teeth.

"Isn't that right, Zack? Look at you," she said, smitten. "*Monsieur* Jowls." She spoke to Zack distinctly and patiently and wet-napped some gook off his mouth with love.

The baby had Josh's dark lashes, his mother's deep questioning stare, and a blunt chin that was his own.

"Got a little Mussolini chin there, don't you, Zackie?" Josh said.

"No, don't say that. People will think he's too, I don't know."

"That's only your being superstitious," Josh said. "People had to like Mussolini for him to seize power."

Under the FFP, Josh had started relishing this stuff, lingering before high chairs, slurping down the fulfillments that only a real adult—a parent—could ever know.

Dori wore a ponytail tonight. Josh gave her a kiss—the back of her naked neck. Their old romantic spot: not spice, not eros; possession. With a few loose curls of her hair mild under his mouth, he thought how nice it was that he still liked fooling around with her.

Josh's kisses moved toward her face now. The curve of her throat; the cream sweetness of the skin there; the buried necklace of her collarbone. She always looked her best, he thought—always. Not every marriage had this.

Young guys at the office always asked, Is it worth it having kids. They'd talk about does it totally change everything, can you still go out, does the sex stop, crap like that. Dudes, you don't know the half of it—that was his line now. He used to be more breezy, like, Well it does and it doesn't. (But now he'd flash on that aloof fucking Dr. Stokes; the sickness humidity in that hospital air, like the smell under a Band-Aid.) Ever seen someone you love plugged into IV tubes, endoscopes, into appliances meant for the old, the flawed, the dying? That is what he wanted to tell them.

Some days felt like when there are circles on the water from a rising fish that almost surfaces but never does, it never does. The action under the surface was: What if he and Dori had been wrong? The question would rise and fall, toward or away from awareness—as in some fourth dimension. What if they were wrong now?

There was another life that wouldn't leave their life.

"GOOD DINNER," HE said, already having forgotten what it had been.

"Wasn't it?"

Twenty minutes earlier Josh had carried his son off to bed, and now the Goldins relaxed into what must have been their five thousandth night together.

Lately, it occurred to him that in having underestimated her before the Incident, Josh hadn't known Dori as fully as he'd thought. So he'd begun cataloging things he loved about her. It was a reconnection to essential nourishments.

When Dori was young, she'd been a popular kid given to spontaneous handstands on kickball fields—even after she developed the bumps and curves that made doing so inappropriate. That topped his list, his inventory of entertaining Dori stuff.

Josh got under the covers now. He called to her: "So, a Netflix movie tonight, or just *Seinfeld*?"

If you really get someone, old stories can seem not just predictable but preknown; the *back then* appears to spring obviously from the *now*. That handstand—he felt as if he knew her even in those wide-open young days, even during the life she'd lived unimaginably without him.

"Which movies do we have?" Dori was saying now. "I'm sick of Netflix."

Things like that handstand were keepsakes, reminders to hold in his pocket: The giddy mellow life they had shared before the Incident wasn't a dream, or some fairy tale. It was still happening. Looking backward felt like part of the way forward. But Josh understood there were things about Dori that he didn't know, too.

"Honey," he said, "what you're saying makes no sense. Would you go, 'I'm sick of takeout'? Each Netflix is a different movie, so how can you be sick in general of it?"

"I just am, Josh." Dori had disappeared into the bathroom off their bedroom. "When you're at work, they just sit there on the table in the hall, those Netflix movies, and I know I can't watch them, because I have to wait for you to come home from work to watch them with, and by that time I don't even *want* to. It's like I don't have the energy."

Her Turkishness, for example—that seemed to him the one significant blank space in his knowledge of her. But then, even to Dori herself, Turkey was no more than what you see on postcards: giant-pencil minarets prodding a low night sky. Her father, who had left Istanbul as a twelve-year-old, never talked to her about his past. It had existed only for a young girl to be embarrassed about, the country with the goofiest bird as its name. She never bothered to learn more about it; there was no fun in remembering having been teased.

Now she was leaning back out into view. "Mr. Goldin, wouldn't it be great if I got pregnant again? I don't mean right this minute, but in a few months. No, what about just *Seinfeld* or something tonight—is that okay?" She was poking half in the room, torso and higher.

"It'd be fun, giving Zack a friend to play with," he said thoughtfully (forgetting the difficulties of pregnancy, Dori's terrible nausea, startling angers, and his own first-trimester irritation at the compulsory uxoriousness of being a pregnant woman's husband). "Boy or girl, do you think?"

"Which do I want, you mean?" She said, tipping fully back into the bathroom again. "Or which do I predict?"

"I guess both, honey." He couldn't see her anymore. "We have *Walk the Line* and *Babel*," he called out, "if you do want to do a movie after all."

He only half believed in the mystery stresses she attributed to her stay-at-home life—how could she fail to have the energy to watch a DVD when *he* worked all day? But it didn't really annoy him to hear her talk about it. He was glad to think of himself as a provider.

"We still have *Seinfeld* Season Eight on DVD, too, Dor, that we got at Hanukkah from your dad." He sat up, addressing the bathroom. "So we don't have to just watch it on TV. I really think another boy," he said.

"You always do, Mr. Goldin."

"He could be the first switch-pitcher," Josh said. "I'll teach him to throw righty *and* lefty. Revolutionize the sport." Josh's face gathered in thought. "I seriously can't figure why isn't there a switch-pitcher in all of baseball history."

"Wasn't it Zack you said who was going to be the first switch-whatever?"

"I got Zack down for playing wide receiver already, is why."

Dori came out of the bathroom, head tousled, cheeks a just-washed pink.

"No, maybe we just bag TV tonight, altogether?" she said, slipping off her white robe.

Since she'd begun nursing, Dori's breasts had gone pendulant and almost liquidy; in their downward prospect they suggested—when she was putting her arms up to get into her nightshirt—tears about to fall. He found this endearing. Her bra had left a tread mark on her skin.

"All right," Josh was saying. "Tonight, no TV"—with some mischief in his voice. "Hey, remember that first weekend, in the Hamptons?"

"Could I forget?"

He closed his eyes and smiled in anticipation. His heart was attached even to her knees, which were big and bony. Whenever Dori would open herself to Josh, she'd suck in her breath then whisper sexy or silly things, each one a surprise. ("Who's that knocking at my door?"; "Oooh, just like *that*.")

What would she say tonight?

When she got into bed now, Dori didn't give him a hug, as she always did. And her smile had turned. "Mr. Goldin," she said seriously.

Her kissable actressy playful mouth that had only just had a laugh on it was now biting at the skin of her thumb.

"There's something I've been thinking about," she said, reaching to put out the lamp. Dori got under the sheets, cozied up near him, her warmth outflowing. The house—dead quiet and lights off—had gone to sleep already.

"No," she said, "I hate to bring it up. I realize you don't want to talk about it, but."

He could probably guess what was coming. He was sort of sure what was coming. He knew what was coming.

"Well, I don't *not* want to talk about it," he lied.

Why think about all that now? They never talked about it. Out the bedroom window, the crowns of three trees—dark curly-heads in silhouette—looked graciously familiar and sent the bad thoughts away. His yard was a bulwark; his home, this bed, these sheets, were bulwarks.

A little more than a month before, they had slept (or failed to) in the Peeds ICU waiting area for half a week, where nobody ever turned down the lights. Her calming hand had reached for his cheek often. But Josh's life was no longer a movie. The terrors of moral and structure and story vanished. It was just life again.

He always hated shining any light on the bad thing—on the Incident. It was easy to make the actual become optimal, the way one excludes unhappy details on a résumé. And in their life's renewed constancy, there was, it seemed, a promise: They would never have to bring it up again. Because Dori had been the brave one, had stepped forward and put a stop to it.

But here, in the dark, her head was agitated on the pillow. She said she'd been thinking.

"We need to get a lawyer, Josh. I'm afraid it's not over."

"What?" Josh backed away on the mattress. How could she know a thing like that? It seemed Dori had sidestepped miles of maybe.

"I mean, no," Dori said quickly. "I'm not *sure*, it's just."

Josh thought she was trying, for his sake, not to sound overconcerned. There was another life that wouldn't leave their life.

But he felt a passion to jump to the baby's room, to bring Zack here, to say, *See? See?* He was a flawless father, and trouble didn't exist; there were no summer blizzards of shocking loss, not in this life.

"It has nothing to do with Zack's health," she said. She talked with the hurry of someone saying aloud what she'd pieced together in private. "Or in fact, it has everything to do with that. Because Zack is healthy, Mr. Goldin. Do you see what I'm getting at?"

Josh rustled his confusion in the sheets. He was a smart, attentive guy—why could he never follow this stuff? When did she get to be smarter than he was?

"Josh, I'm not saying it'll happen." Her voice came out gentle and hesitant. "These stupid places—hospitals. I just worry they could come after us." She was looking at him with her unavoidable face that he could just about make out in the dark, if not decipher. "A baby coded in their care. They don't like to be, you know."

"Humiliated?"

"Right." She sat up a little, marshaling half her weight on her elbows. "A big private hospital is like a corporation. What does a corporation want to do but cover up stuff? I mean like cover its ass?"

The crudeness of that term seemed a concession, a way to bring the talk to his level. "We need to be prepared, is all," she said.

"Okay, since Zack is fine, and they screwed up, wouldn't they want it *not* to come back?" he said.

The only thing he could seize upon was less an understanding than a feeling: that the rope by which he'd raised himself out of anxiety these last weeks might be frayed, might not be able to get him the whole way out, after all.

"Well," she was saying, "we know we did nothing wrong, right? And—"

"And is Zack is okay," he said, interrupting, making sure.

"And Zack is okay, yes," she said, kindly.

Once more her hand went to Josh, warm on the side of his face. He exhaled. He felt he'd managed to live through all this only because of what he didn't understand. Sometimes he'd clung to his ignorance.

Jesus, they couldn't make a grab at Zack again if he's healthy—could they?

"They didn't check what they were supposed to," Dori was saying.

Wait, she was on those tests again? *Enough* with the coags and the blood count, if Zack was fine.

She was clairvoyant when it came to Josh and so she said, "It's more than just checking his coags. What I mean is, they didn't listen to the mother. You know? I mean, they lost an hour. He coded because they acted like nothing was wrong even though I told them." She rose a little higher above him. "They care about the way that stuff looks. Also, that black doctor? She seems like one of those women you can't trust. The angry kind of woman that can't keep a man."

In a flash, he got it. "What they're primarily concerned with is are we planning to sue."

"I'm only saying when parents come into a place and then the doctors make a mistake."

"But we're not going to," he said.

"It's just, I heard stories back when I was working, they play defense by coming at you, these corporate hospitals. That's the sort of paranoia."

"So, if they pursue it."

"Exactly."

"Then we'll know they're worried that they fucked up," he said, mentally snapping his fingers. "They'd accuse us of something to cover their own mistake, right?"

"They get afraid and become aggressive, Mr. Goldin. And if they don't, well—but, no, I don't want to wait, you know? It's the question—do *we* prepare? Or just let the hospital?"

"Well, obviously not," he said.

A small excitement formed between them on the speed of this express conversation. He took his wife's hand under the blankets; he caressed it using mainly his thumb. It was legal stuff she was talking about, business—*his* purview, not hers, not life or death. Zack was fine; the idea of babies just having incidents had settled in again as part of the décor of his life.

"So, you see what I mean?" she said.

Her world was smaller than his. For Dori there was family, not just to be cherished but canonized, and there was the part of Long Island in which she grew up, and there were her limited number of friends, and the habits and patterns around which she'd arranged her life: the few things she loved, she loved fiercely; and what she didn't know, she didn't give a shit about. This was intoxicating, if you made the cut. But it made her more combative than he was.

"Talk to a lawyer, Josh. Not have them do anything, necessarily. Just to protect ourselves for the worst possibility. No, maybe I'm being silly. Listen, you *know* how I am," she said in her grateful voice.

He did know. Josh certainly did know. He had a thought. TV shows and movies can't really capture how married life is, nor even what a married conversation feels like—because a movie, say, can only give you the actual words going back and forth. But those convey so little. What's impossible to communicate, what you can't experience unless you're part of it, is the *sensation* of being in a real-life marriage. Even little chats seem to be floating in some kind of really vast liquid, and that vast liquid is the ocean of shared feelings and memories and shorthands, of understandings and *mis*understandings between the couple—their history ocean. More and more of their business tends to go underwater, and so even the important words feel only like individual waves popping up from that ocean. All that context, that history and those impressions from real life that the couple logs and drowns in, it all washes over everything.

He ran a hand over her arm, felt the warm give of her skin under his fingers. He and Dori were honest and good people in an ass-covering world.

In her worrying lay one reason she and Josh were a perfect match, complementary like the smile-and-frown of those famous theater masks. Dori could build her fears into actions, and her actions made possible Josh's sleepwalking optimism. A guy with such obtuse confidence needed to know someone was looking out for the bad in life. Lately he understood this. Maybe that's why so many women had that patient-but-decisive voice down pat, as if they'd learned to endure men having to catch up with their insights.

"Okay," Josh said. He'd act to head off trouble. Now he kissed his wife on the cheek, the forehead—"Mmmm"—and on the neck before rolling over to sleep.

Under the sheets, one hand reached out for a familiar, smaller hand—again.

2

It started one Thursday, when Dr. Stokes was picking up her seven-year-old son, James, from a playdate. She hated that term, "playdate"; she hated when mothers tried to add the luster of romance to their maternity, the golden seal of adulthood to their children's affairs; and she hated the smug cuteness that had become one of parenting's stations of the cross. Upper-middle-class grown-ups using the terms "playdate," sippy cup, "wee-wee," "poopie diaper"—they talked like this among themselves, using the word "poopie" even if there was no youngster in sight. And yet, the audacity with which they dressed their little girls! The sexification of kids, the toddlerizing of adults: Everyone in America would look, act, think, and covet like an eleven-year-old before long, thought Darlene, Chairperson of Pediatrics and Child Health, Intensive Care Unit, St. Joseph's Medical Center.

Remember to smile when you walk in, she told herself.

On her way to collect James, she drove alone through Sand's End. Here was the greenest part of green Washington Harbor. With sidewalk-free streets and an eager flagrancy about its wealth—green being the color of jealousy for a reason—Sand's End was pitched on a knoll, a quarter mile back from the shore. And even if this moss-grown hill rose from the waves without the boon of a beachfront—and though the local tree-line foiled all views of the sound—the knowledge of water's approach gave sandless Sand's End its *arriviste* appeal.

Darlene had her own name for it: The Land of *Yes, but Something's Missing*. Houses here had clean white foreheads and soft-lit windows that all promised, whether it was true or not, a limited span of human emotion inside. Each neat yard looked so equable it—it, they, everything—might have been on Paxil. What businesses there were had gathered together on the fringes of town: a Blockbuster; a pharmacy; Grapevines 'N' Baskets Fine Wines; an Aveda hair salon. The community newspaper, five to seven pages every week, strummed what music it could from its few strings. But here was the trouble: Whenever Darlene would shake her head at all this landscaped complacency, whenever she'd buy into the cliché that humanity's unfathomable complexity got flattened by all these big houses, she'd end up admitting that life here was without question serene, undemanding, pretty—was in fact a model of what most in the world aspired to—and finally she had no way of knowing whether places like Washington Harbor were missing much, or she herself was. It was September. And these habitual thoughts of hers got interrupted by an uneasy pang.

That baby's mystery sickness had gone unsolved for a month and a half. Zack Goldin. Had she failed this patient? Had one of her underlings, Dr. Weiss, screwed up? Why would a child have just *coded* like that? In the tests, there seemed to be nothing wrong with the baby. But it was troubling: the discordance between the emergency-room note and what Mrs. Goldin had said; the woman had utterly contradicted Darlene's subordinate doctor, claiming she'd told Dr. Weiss there had been blood in the baby's vomit during her first visit. (Darlene had to trust Dr. Weiss on that, but did she really believe him? Well, wasn't it her job to back him?) More to the point, what sort of mother doesn't want all the possible tests done? The only people who don't want more tests are those who are uninsured. Doctors become skilled at knowing after one quick look which patients are insured; *those* people were insured. And the mother didn't even wait for the result of the last test.

Standard procedure was, whenever a baby codes a report needs to be filed. There were, unfortunately, legal implications to everything these days. But she was thinking this one had the smell of trouble about it: Baby codes, mother accuses us of lying, says it's due to *our* negligence. That was something Darlene needed to clear up; that could mean possible lawsuits.

Darlene's car ride ended in the almost-there edge of Washington Harbor real-estate speculation, the third driveway on a trickle of a street called Meadow's Drive. Each house was a blunt "raised ranch"—a home in which the second floor stuck out over the first, as if the house had an overbite. When the playdate's white father answered the door, Darlene introduced herself, thanked him for hosting her son, and forgot, of course, to smile.

"No need to thank me, Dr. Stokes. We love James, really." Mr. Hechler bounced a little on his toes, in what Darlene thought a liberal's overexcitement at having a black woman doctor over to his house.

I've got one of the "good ones" here, Darlene unfairly imagined Mr. Hechler thinking. *A doctor and everything!* It struck her pride that, as her mother had wanted her to, Darlene had made it; she'd gone from Bushwick's little "Purple" to someone who might as well have been a Rothenberg or a Rubinstein.

"... they're playing Risk in the kitchen, James and Sabrina," Mr. Hechler was saying. "Come on in."

Hechler had a goatee'd, up-and-comer's face; his sharp chin and long craneish nose articulated a life moving persistently ahead.

Stepping over the family's sleeping chocolate Labrador, over its chocolate ribs, he led Darlene to the kitchen right as her seven-year-old son was losing Africa.

James, coffee-skinned and curly, grimaced up from the game board. "Hi, Mom. I'm not winning." Across from him sat Sabrina, a little girl with light hair.

"*Hellooo,* Mizz Golovin," said the girl in cartoon princess British, addressing Darlene wrongly with James's (and Darlene's ex-husband's) last name. "Charmed, charmed," said young Sabrina.

From across the kitchen, a blond woman rushed to Darlene. "Hi, I'm Sabrina's mom, Linds Hechler"—her hand offered. After a frowny internal debate, she added: "Nice to meet you, Dr. *Stokes.*" Evidently, Mrs. Hechler had argued herself out of apologizing for the daughter's last-name *faux pas.*

Mr. and Mrs. Hechler stood side by side now—firmly built, sparkling people. A doubles team; Darlene felt as if she were in a game of two-on-one. The wife, tan-armed in her summer dress, was smiling at Darlene with glasslike blue eyes. Darlene wondered: Was James feeling as she had at his age? Looking at the father, wondering what that species is like?

"James is really good at Risk," the woman said. "Considering it was his first time. Does he play games a lot at home, or . . . ?"

The woman was smiling into boring chatter with such enthusiasm—jumping so eagerly into this conversational rut—Dr. Stokes guessed, unkindly, that she was a housewife.

Now Sabrina stood. "James is better at it than I used to be when I started," the girl said. "Isn't he, Mom, better at it?"

Mrs. Hechler gave an encouraging laugh, in the attitude of *You were good, too, sweetie.* And Mr. Hechler said, "It's Sabrina's birthday in a week," ostensibly talking to Darlene but really beaming at the near-birthday girl.

"Charmed, charmed," Sabrina said.

Dr. Stokes had met her before, but seeing the kid in the context of her parents was like looking at a fossil record—picking out what of the adults' faces had endured in hers: the mother's doll eyes, and her father's strong nose. Whenever Darlene saw James's little friends alongside their forebears, she felt reminded that we're all pretty much Mr. Potato Heads, having been thrown together out of a very limited kitty of nostrils and ears and temperaments in some embryological playroom.

"Happy almost-birthday," Darlene said, grabbing Sabrina's hand and shaking it, mock-businesslike, which made the girl laugh—a bedside-manner trick Darlene had learned from more sociable doctors in Peeds.

"Sometimes I play chess with my mom, right, Mom? Which is a more difficult game," James said in his trusting way. His grin showed across his fine-boned face. "Don't we?"

He was rubbing his dimpled chin; a skinny little muscle flickered in his arm. He often rubbed his chin. He had the bright, likable look of a child model whose comb-defying hair kept costing him the big commercial. (With a Jew and a black woman for parents, frizziness was preordained.) Hadn't Phyllis Stickney written that our African ancestors had used their strong hair to lift the Pyramids to their marvelous heights? *Good, although it was the Jews who'd built the Pyramids,* Darlene thought. So James had twice as much claim to that feat.

"We'll have Coldplay CDs at the birthday party," Mrs. Hechler was saying, laying the accent on *Coldplay* like someone dropping the word "Harvard."

"Sabrina asked for it on her own," Mrs. Hechler added. A boast of a smile narrowed her eyes. "Isn't it great? She likes the same music we do. They're both our favorite."

"It's my dad's birthday coming up," James said, in his excited young voice. "He is going to be forty, but he died." And then he raised his eyebrows.

Darlene went, immediately, to stroke her son's hair. She searched the hints of James's grief, though any clue she followed was subtle enough to look like a child's happy unconcern. He angled his disarming face to her, and he blinked a few times before anyone talked. But sadness had flooded the room.

"Yes, November twenty-fourth," Darlene said, privately dying, "that's right, James." Then she looked left to conceal the unrest of her face.

Above the granite kitchen island, some never-used copper pots hung from a rack. A few newspapers had piled up on the dark stone countertop; a *Wall Street Journal* exposed to view had been underlined in pencil.

This was when it started; that is, when James began mentioning his father after months of silence on the topic.

THROUGHOUT THE RIDE home, Darlene worked that motherly trick of glancing back at her child and watching the road at once. The child-safety seat belt across James's little chest emphasized his little-ness. Now and then he rubbed his chin.

In silence, Darlene was planning out what to say. She didn't want to be overly investigative ("Are you thinking about your dad a lot these days?") or too broad ("So, how're you doing?").

Parental happiness, she realized, was a Condition of Not: *not* nervous, *not* sad, *not* disappointed. Whatever pleasure she'd had these last years had been a defensive state, in other words: defined merely in opposition to trouble. She wondered whether this were true only of other single parents who had no social lives.

"Hey, James, you know how your dad's birthday's coming up?" she said—trying to make it sound light.

"It's not really coming up," he said. "November twenty-fourth, and that isn't for a little while, I think, November twenty-fourth."

James was rocking forward to feel that pleasant push-back from the safety belt. And he smiled at her, a small one.

"Would you like to do something for it? Celebrate it? Perhaps we could look at pictures of him, at your dad, and then have dinner with Grandma Golovin?"

"Okay," James said—that was it. *Okay.* But his fine-boned face did look relaxed when he said it. Darlene wanted to stop the car and hug him, she was overcome by such affection. Yet she had no idea what her son was thinking now, what he was feeling. James's teacher, Mrs. Castiglia, had said James was "difficult to read" (but sweet), and no wonder. His mind was opaque.

James and Darlene drove through Sand's End and came out on Washington Harbor's middle-class side. The newer, fenced-in neighborhoods—the Harbor Souths, Driftwood Gardens, the Madison Park Estates—were planned developments made up of multiunit superstructures divided into linked, rhomboidal condos. Guarded checkpoints protected these condos from their neighbors. On Searingtown Road, the neighbors were attached businesses—Verizon Wireless, Kinko's, Pomodoro's Pizza—with identical gold typescript on all their shopfronts.

"*New* pictures of Dad?" James said in a delayed, hopeful voice, his lips parted slightly—a prayer as much as a question.

Darlene wanted to meet his face with a gentler try at her own mother's unsentimental consolation.

"Well," she said, "there aren't any new pictures, James."

Her brown eyes fell soft on him. "But we can look at the old ones, okay, baby?"

All along Searingtown Road, the minor businesses stood winking through their *One Week Only Sale* signs, their *X Percent Off* come-ons. Last time Darlene had driven by here with James she'd said, "Look"—as if he would have gotten the joke; as if her only steady companion were a grown-up and not seven years old—"Look: Civilization and Its Discounts."

The quiet in the car now was heartbreaking. He massaged both his eyes with his palms, a very adult gesture. This was another of his habits, like his chin tic.

She said: "James, I'm really sorry your dad isn't around."

He always rubbed his eyes hard enough to give the impression of wanting to trap what he'd just seen and stuff it back into his brain.

"That's okay," he was saying helpfully. "Like *your* dad, he—" James stopped himself.

Darlene drew back heavily in her seat. A flicker, the briefest automatic irritation. How silly! She was still sensitive about it. Her fatherless childhood. And for that split second, she'd felt not as if she were listening to her seven-year-old, but to some neighborhood tormenter. The moment went. And the ensuing guilt about it stirred up in Darlene the rawest affection—a longing, an ache of sensitivity to the fact that her son was sitting right there behind her, like a nostalgia for the present, for his frizzy hair, narrow chest, his smooth little arms poking out of his white T-shirt.

"That's true, James." She smiled, but a tiny spark in her throat signaled, unless she could restrain it, a potential cry.

"My dad wasn't around for me, either"—Darlene said in her serious, leaden way, unable or unwilling to sound light now.

Charles Stokes: On the Internet she'd found 207 men listed by that name, none of whom lived in the five boroughs, Long Island, or Westchester.

"And you don't ever have to worry about talking about my father with me, okay?" she said. "Or *your* father."

"Okay," he said, squinting at her; lately she'd decided to get him checked out for nearsightedness, but hadn't yet. He squinted a lot.

"We have each other, James, you understand."

James went serious himself, nodding, an imitation of her, probably. "Okay." He was so young, his seriousness weighed as little as he did.

THAT MIDNIGHT, READING *en route* to sleep, Darlene thought perhaps there was a stranger out there who was her half sibling. That recurring thought made her lay down her book (*On Native Grounds*, Alfred Kazin), shut off the bedside light, and bump out her lips as if she'd gotten a shred of dinner caught in her teeth—slightly bothered. How many times can the same realization bother a person? Midnight is the time when random thoughts come. What sort of family bonds could there be with strangers? Bonds made of speculation, of complete unknowing, bonds made of smoke. Siblings connected by common disconnection. She turned over and tried focusing on the warmth and smoothness of her high-thread-count sheets (Darlene hadn't fully abandoned nice things when Leo left). When she found herself in the city, Darlene would sometimes look at unknown people she'd pass and wonder, *Doesn't that one sort of clomp when she walks, like I do?* Or: *Isn't her nose sort of wide like mine?*

The dark bedroom, the midnight hour: always a tangle of such random thoughts. She couldn't think about Charles Stokes if she wanted any sleep.

She reached to her Kazin again, and clicked on the light. She liked to read for edification, but what she really loved were those moments of confirmation—the "Aha! I knew it" that came with finding an elegant proposition, something she'd more or less thought already. How wonderful to see expressed an idea she'd somehow known but hadn't managed to say.

> The age-old Jewish belief that the only possible salvation lies in thinking well, which is thinking one's way to the root of all creation, thinking one's way to the ultimate reason of things . . . ,

Kazin wrote. Where had *that* been in Leo? For James's sake, Darlene thought about Judaism often, studied up on it, told him what she found, and tried not to be weirded out by those ceremonies that seemed so foreign to her. Maybe white-bread Jewishness, bookless Jewishness, only existed in America? she wondered. But Darlene was too worked up. Down went the book and off the light.

Events of her day were taken up again as she thought, *That woman, Sabrina's mom, saying, "Our daughter likes the same music we do."*

Darlene laughed—she made herself laugh. *And then saying, "Isn't it great?" As if Coldplay were Stravinsky or something*. Darlene thought she knew Coldplay, whose singer wept out every lyric without variation or even logic.

Yes, this was good; her pet subject. Isn't rock and roll something to be outgrown? These parents—*Hey, my kids are making the same consumer choices I am! Look, our daughter follows the tenets of Big Brother ahead of schedule*—had their souls polluted by a kind of uniform smog of bad culture. —That cloying woman, Sabrina's mother, with her never-used pots and pans that hung there in that kitchen like a jumbo wind chime—the Land of *Yes, but Something's Missing*—(Darlene was getting sleepy at last). She had designs on writing an essay about our culture, calling it "Rot." When would she write it? Never, of course. Busy with administrative duties, with research, with patients like that baby Zack Goldin. For example. Something amiss there— Mrs. Goldin's affect was off when hearing the results of the test—she was too confident; no result seemed a surprise to her. Darlene bothered with her pillow, wondered if, more than other doctors, she needed always to be right. She knew plenty of people—men—who got wrapped up in their self-worth. But her own confidence was different. She *was* almost always right, humbly. She pushed through difficult questions without arrogance, until no uncertainty was possible. Her son and painstaking analysis: the two of her passions never to have cooled.

What really happened, with that baby Zack Goldin? Maybe Weiss screwed up the report? He had seemed so adamant, though. Having seen so much good mothering herself, she may have had the perfect nose for sniffing out something fishy.

Dr. Stokes opened her eyes in the dark.

3

MARTIN SEIDEL WAS A GREAT TALKER, VERY SHORT, HARD-CHARGING, cocksure in the way of a celebrity. He wasn't a celebrity; he was a sixty-six-year-old family lawyer, one of the nonequity partners at Gottlieb, Gold, & McNulty LLP, and bald. His chin was raised and he strutted, pleased in his look. He knew himself. Five foot two, expensively dressed, trim for his age, your basic class-clown type, he wanted people to see all he'd done with what little material he had. He gathered the scant hair on the sides of his head into a tiny nub ponytail.

He didn't ride the subway to Gottlieb, Gold, even though it would have borne him into Manhattan without delay. Rather, he honked and stutter-braked and *fuck you, asshole*-ed his mornings across Flatbush in his tank of an SUV.

Martin Seidel loved to sing. (In college, his tuxedoed comedy/a capella group, the Penguins, had entertained at fraternities' mixers, including his own.) These days, windows raised, he tore up his throat on expert harmony while he commuted from Ditmas Park, Brooklyn. His narrow-lawned, three-floor Victorian home was another source of pride: almost thirty-four hundred square feet, ailanthus tree in the back, private driveway, and yet it had the convenience, the *with-it*ness, of being categorically not in the suburbs.

"Remember, dinner tonight with the Spinnells," said Martin's wife, Natalie, passing him his coffee mug (one-half decaf) as he left for work.

"Mmm. I'm on it, sweet," he said. His precise voice had long been scrubbed of all its Brooklyn. He tried for a warm, urbane, cappuccino-and-croissant tone. After a swig of one-half decaf, he talked now in *parfait* Inspector Clouseau accent: "I buy zee wine."

His wife, Natalie, inured after thirty-four years to his "voices," his comedy ümlauts and high-camp tildés, took back his mug and said only: "Riesling, please."

Martin had loved other women during their marriage—in fact, he'd recently gone through a tough breakup with a Gottlieb, Gold, & McNulty associate—but he never stopped thinking of Natalie as his forever companion, his "bestest buddy," his life partner. (An equity partner, as he liked to joke.) "Give me a kiss right now, seevooplay," he said.

Gottlieb, Gold, & McNulty was a midlevel firm midway up Trump Tower, fifty-eight stories of glass-and-steel arrogance. It had a huge, brass maw façade—the goldlike standard in ostentation. Martin rushed inside, through the pink marble lobby, beyond the three-story waterfall. When he got to his twenty-seventh-floor office, he sucked at a few Altoids for his nine o'clock meeting with Josh Goldin, who was a prospective client and much more than that.

More than fifty years ago, as a boy, Martin Seidel had spent five summers in the expensive captivity of sleepaway camp with Josh's father. They'd first met when Seidel had lifted himself from a green lake onto a white dock and shivered over to young Lewis Goldin. Martin Seidel was a nerdy ten; Lewis Goldin was eleven and done swimming for the afternoon.

"You think the homesickness ever wears off?" Martin Seidel had said. Neither remembered how Lewis Goldin answered, but from that moment and for the next twenty-five years, they were very great friends until they weren't. After college they bummed around together for a year in plush, life-as-a-dream Aspen. But they hadn't seen each other since Martin introduced his best pal to his favorite mistress. (Now ex–best pal, ex-mistress, to some degree ex-existence.)

That day—was it fifteen years ago?—had been awkward for Lewis Goldin, who had been a friend to Martin's wife, too. Soon after, Lewis Goldin had bought a bed-and-breakfast and taken his own wife to Vermont. A big move like that is a starting-over and

Lewis's friendship with Martin Seidel, once the shedding of old skins was complete, went away, too. This was a defeat for Martin. Martin Seidel didn't like defeat. Here was a man who ached easily under sentimental deliriums. Intense emotion was always right up front—sadness and particularly joy—in Martin's lingering looks into your eyes, the solemnity of his flattering talk, in the way his laughing at your jokes made him fidget within his Italian suits, as if bee-stung. He was vain of how sincerely he teared up. But he was clever, too. Meeting with Josh, he would mix business with nostalgia, and reclaim his old friendship, getting to the father via the son. The son whom Martin had also liked a lot. It would be a good morning.

"Mrs. H.!" He called for his secretary. He'd had one of his periodic glimpses into the future, and as usual, he liked what he thought he saw. "Please buzz me when Josh Goldin gets here."

"Well," said Mrs. H., "I just told the security desk to let him up."

"*This* short middle-aged putz is Marty Seidel?" Josh Goldin wondered. For one thing, Mr. Seidel was twenty years balder. Whatever hair he still had—a level stripe horseshoed around the back of his head—found its *raison d'être* in that gray-black spit of a ponytail. The scalp was sleek and reflected overhead light, but the rest of Martin's face had wrinkled to a kind of dried-apple look, scored by brown marks. Bodies tell time as surely as clocks.

"I know you're here on business, Josh. But it's great—here, sit, sit—s'great that I have you back in my life after all this time. That's what it is; we're back in each other's life. I really do love you guys, you and your dad, all those Sundays, with bagels at your place, remember? I want to say that first, before business. Okay? And your mom, too. So. Now, what do you want, good-looking? Some coffee? Donut? Hold on. Mrs. H.? *Mrs. H.!* Oh, hi, sweetie, c'mon in a sec. Here she is, J., the secret weapon, the old soldier," Martin said, pausing to simper a mischievous, affection-seeking face at his secretary. "Can you get my guy J. here a coffee? Do you know how long we go back, me and this kid? But we haven't seen each other in fifteen years—more: twenty. But I'm so *glad.*"

"Come on, Marty," Josh said, "you're making even me feel old, my friend."

Behind the façade of Josh's smile, he was scrutinizing. Decades before, Martin had taught him basketball. With a grunt, nine-year-old Josh heaved shots underhand. At blacktop outdoor courts, the orange-painted hoops had chain nets that if your shot went through, jangled, like house keys—an addictive sound. Martin Seidel had sometimes swatted away Josh's desperate hurls; the outdoor ball had made a cartoon, roadrunnerish *ping!* That old, basketballing Martin Seidel—or rather, that *young* basketballing Martin Seidel, giant, athletic, amused—was more real to Josh than this short earnest version whose lips, like his hair, had thinned. "There's the warmth you get," Martin had said, on meeting Josh today with a soft-palm handshake. "You feel that with old friends. You *need* that warmth."

He was absurdly emotive, like a character in a silent movie. But was "absurd" a fair description of five-foot-two Martin Seidel?

Martin Seidel was aware that you longed to laugh at him; he encouraged and even participated in it. ("Look who's turned into a short, emotional fag—me!—but who cares?") Josh had found himself smiling when Martin followed that with, "Wow, to get you in my life again, boy. Tell me about *you*. That's what I care about. Remember when you were a kid and we all used to . . ." It wasn't a calculated effect, this absolute earnestness. Sitting in the confident posture of a ladies' man, Martin Seidel believed his words, at least he did while they fell out of him; his brown eyes slitted in soulful goodwill. He held the edges of his desk—which had a glass overlay covering its cherrywood top—as he took hold of his past. You didn't ask why, if you were so valuable to him, he hadn't ever called *you*. Josh had found his lawyer.

"If you *are* going to sue, get a plaintiff's attorney," Martin was saying. This was after the Goldins' recent history had been, in its crisis and clatter, relayed. "I can recommend a good med mal guy."

"No, no." Josh brought up his palm, showed a beatific smile. This was meant to indicate, *Thanks, but it would be easier to take the high road*. He didn't like thinking about suing because he hated remembering that hospital day. Even in describing it, he'd kept things summary, he'd shut out the details. But here it was anyway, the vacant knocking of ignored memories. He took in a breath. "We're not going to sue."

"Okay," Martin said, "so good." He nodded. All foolishness, all play, had left him. "All right. So what can I do? Why'd you come, if it all turned out okay?"

"Well." Josh sighed, beginning into greater detail of his story: the mistakes St. Joseph's had made, and that shifty, unfriendly black woman Dr. Stokes.

Martin Seidel tilted his face—as if trying to suss out a muffled noise in another room, a neighboring skyscraper, a far-off country. He gave no indication of whether he would help Josh in any way. Deliberation tightened his lips.

At last Martin said: "Nah. I don't think they'll do anything, this hospital. Okay, suppose, if they *are* worried that you'll sue them—I mean, worried that they shat the bed and want to cover their *tuchas*— they could 'come after you,' like you say. I mean, it's unlikely. It'd be stupid, it'd be aggressive, but I've seen these places do stupid before. People get stupid; people get aggressive. What good would it do for me to sugarcoat it for you? They might. It's like a woman in a divorce hearing. You know, how they sometimes accuse a husband of child molestation, a bullshit accusation, if you'll pardon my saying so, just to rock the guy back on his heels." Martin's eyes changed; his look etched into a wise melancholy.

"People always come with the hardest charge, whether it's true or not. It's, you ask for ten million when you want one million." His manner was pure lawyerly know-how. "Like in that Terri Schiavo case—the family accusing the husband of murder. Murder for that poor schmuck after his wife is sick like that. Could you believe the balls?"

"That's kind of what my wife said, that they'd come with the hardest charge. If they come."

Josh was sensing invisible patterns, hidden complexities in the world, things he would never have perceived before.

Martin Seidel noticed this rise in the temperature of Josh's worry. He said softly: "And I guess they could accuse you or your wife of being reckless when you took the baby out of the hospital." A large part of kindness is in the gentle exploration of scary possibilities. "But this, I would argue, you did only after they made it clear *they* f—ed up."

"Well, they didn't actually accuse us of—you know."

The tenderest look yet had gathered in Martin's eyes. "Don't worry, pal. So. Okay. Big deal," he said.

Yeah, sure, the hospital could possibly, and Martin was just thinking out loud here, could possibly imply that the Goldins were to blame for the baby's getting sick. But it'd be a major headache on their end—*major*. Plus, they never did figure out what happened with the baby, right? They, meaning the hospital. Which is something big-shot doctors never like to admit. They look for reasons to make their own incompetence vanish: Martin's lawyer talk was gathering speed. "Physicians can take really short-term custody of a child, I think like seventy-two hours if the child is in 'imminent danger.'"

"That's what they did!" Josh said, leaning out of his chair with that familiar client's vehemence, as if recognition and worry were trying to yank his body away from this office of bad news. "That's how, Martin, what they said when they made us come back with Zack, with the baby—"

Martin cut him off. "Wrong."

His face seemed to say: *How satisfying it feels to pass along this knowledge.* He would give Josh the words that would unite them, client and attorney, father figure and son figure.

"They may have *threatened* you with that, Josh. However, CPS—Child Protective Services —has to take these cases to court for disposition at the end of that period. In other words, they didn't go through the steps, or you would know it, right? Did you hear from CPS?" Martin lowered his head, as if slightly embarrassed for Josh. "They told you to jump, you said, 'How high,' and they never called CPS. They *imply*."

"But they had the police come and get us—"

"And you just went back. It's not your fault. You didn't have *me* then, in your corner. And now you do."

In its kindness Martin's voice sounded drugged and leaden. "And, the real good news? The legal system is unlikely to respond to doctor recommendations anyway. They've got to do an extensive review of the all the patient's records, to see if such cases rise to 'reasonable suspicion.' And even what I'm saying is worst case. A woman's right to care for her child is a strong right. Very strong. So, don't worry. Okay?"

"Okay."

"I'm serious. Say okay again."

Josh chuckled a bit: "Okay."

"Look at how he says, 'Okay,' like a worrywart. You guys are totally clear." He slid, for no apparent purpose, but with frowned engrossment, his desk's bobble-head doll of Buddy Holly a quarter inch to the right before looking up at Josh again. "And I assume you kids have nothing in your files that—hey, what's the matter? I said there's nothing to freak out about."

Josh, though smiling, still had a particle of unease left in his heart and observant Martin had found it.

"Nothing," Josh said. "It's just, I was working very hard before all this was happening, coming home late. And, also—well, I feel bad to have left Dori alone so much with the baby, so now the thought of someone accusing her of—"

"Hey!" Martin said. "Don't apologize; don't feel guilty about working for a living." He pitched himself closer, pulled a face like a man with a secret. "It's, Christ, I don't know, like we have this thing in our society against work. *Real* work. In movies, TV, you'll see it. I started noticing it, now I see it *everywhere*. I mean, wipe that bullshit out of your conscience."

"See what everywhere?"

Having set up a cliffhanger, Martin pulled at his cuffs and took a mini red-and-white tin out of his desk, dug out a chalky tablet from the Altoids case, and sucked with enthusiasm.

"Why is it," he said grandly, "that artists are congratulated when they have no lives outside their art, but businessmen are lambasted, are called assholes, when *our* work is our life? The guy splattering his paint on a canvas fifteen hours a day gets romanticized, he's a hero, movies get made. But the man who works just as hard on *useful* things, the smart fellow who gets a kick out of putting food on the table? Of having a nice car? He's selfish? You're a successful person. Don't ever ask forgiveness about that."

Josh, who had an ear for a sales pitch, merely nodded with politeness. The glass overlay on Martin's desk was translucent if you looked on it from above, but when Josh leaned back, seeing it at a different angle, its inch-high side looked green.

Martin's remarks hadn't "popped" with Josh. So, he thought, this was a meeting of two alert men. Josh's father had been—Martin imagined he was still—athletic, hilarious, likable, and occasionally glum. Lewis Goldin had been the kind of guy about whom you imagined that something was going on beneath his surface, but no one knew what that something was.

All right, Martin thought. *Time to show off the goods.*

"Tell me," he said. He nodded and made his high-significance face—a jeweler about to present his signature diamond. "What does she look like, this Dr. Stokes?"

"What's she *look* like?"

"Hey, just tell me. How's she look? Would I ask you a stupid question? Don't answer that." He went into a teasing frown meant to point up wounded friendship.

"Now, Josh," he said, "really, this woman doctor. Her voice, her attitude. What's her body type?"

"Well," Josh said. And he told Martin his few, limp recollections of Dr. Stokes.

The attorney said, "Good, good," dreamy-voiced, nodding, and then he inhaled before diving in:

"This doctor's like so many of these women department heads I've read about, I'll bet. Not to mention, the black thing; she feels she has something to prove. Dr. Kildare mixed with your junior-high lunch lady. No, wait, let me go on. I see her, no sense of humor, dorky, probably alone. Tell me if I'm off here. Was she wearing a wedding ring? No, right?"

The hasty fighting mood, the indifference to liberal sensitivities, the starkly us-versus-them stand, the gift for turning an adversary into an object lesson in some point or other—Martin Seidel really took to his work.

"I see her staying late in the Pediatrics Ward because she's got nothing else going on, I see her judging good people like you, 'Oh, this honky's just a businessman.' I know how she drives herself to work in the morning, too fucking slow, radio off, no music to sing along to. Oh, no—not *her*. I see how this woman eats ice cream watching the Hallmark Channel. Maybe they don't say 'honky' anymore, I don't know. She has no kids of her own, of course; I see how she makes frown faces in the mirror, 'Oh, poor *moi*'; how she holds up her hair and squinches her eyebrows and sucks in her cheeks. 'Does this make me look better?' No, lady, it doesn't. I see how she *hates* to catch a glimpse of her body in the glass before she gets her butt into the shower. I see this woman in high school, sitting out the slow dances because A) she worries when she lifts her armpits that people'll smell it, and, two, who's asking her, anyway? I see how she'd make a face when you first fuck her, like: *Oh, thank you, thank you*."

Martin loved seeing Josh's emergent look of disapproval—and took it as proof that he, the one-and-only Martin Seidel, was good at his job. He was fairly soaring.

"And I hear the way she'd tell you, 'Uh, no, I'd *rather* not,' when you want her to get on top," he said. "She's afraid you might see her naked body. Heaven forbid. She owns this one sexy lingerie thingy, but *just* one, and it's loose in the tits, you know why? Because she gave herself too much credit when she went to Victoria's Secret and walked the aisles blushing that one time. *That's why.*"

Josh couldn't even nod; shouldn't he be outraged?

Martin called his approach *Shock and Aww.* Let clients think (or rather pretend to themselves) that they're the good guys who have less malice than their attorney does. Let 'em believe they're eating at the Tree of Human Fellowship, all the while despising their adversaries in the privacy of their own souls; let them hate in innocence, in other words. He loved playing bad cop.

Point made; time to wrap up.

"And most of all," Martin said, "I see her *not giving you any real trouble.* Know your adversary. And your Dr. Stokes won't know how to take on the famous Marty Seidel"—upgrading his ending—"Martin Seidel."

And the famous Marty Seidel, Martin Seidel, leaned back with his hands on his belly. Josh wasn't one to be caught looking stunned and so the trusty smile had returned. But Martin had spotted that flicky look in Josh's eye. The impressed look of a client having an understanding: *Maybe my lawyer's an asshole, but he's __my__ asshole.*

"So, we're good." Martin's voice had cooled, and he was even blushing a little. "I mean, they won't fight, but if they do, bring 'em on."

FUCKING CELL PHONES. *One day,* Josh thought, *kids'll look back at these cell phones the way we look at those old cars you had to wind up with that crank thing.* Imagine if TV reception only came in sixty-five percent of the time. . . .

Traveling downward ear-poppingly fast in the Trump Tower elevator, Josh spoke again into his headset mouthpiece. "I think we're good, honey," he said, and then, at nearly maximum volume, "I said, *I think*—hello? Hello?"

The other person here with Josh—a fake blonde in a red shirt—made sure he saw her annoyed expression when he kept saying, loudly, *"Hello? Dor?"*

Either his wife's laugh or a gust of static upset his ear.

Wednesdays being one of Josh's three days a week in Manhattan (a TV airtime salesman earned the best part of his livelihood at lunches or after-work beers, and clients never came to Long Island), here Josh was, in the biggest, richest city, and, still, no cell service. *It's the network, my ass.*

Squinting, putting a finger on his other ear, he said, *"Honey? You still there?"*

And she came back with: "You are cute, Mr. Goldin. I love to hear you yelling. Were you going into your deal about those cars with the crank thingies again?" She sounded terrifically happy; also the connection wasn't choppy anymore.

"So, thank God, right?" she said. "No, the lawyer *really* thinks there's not much to worry about? And you *are* cute. Aren't you?"

When she was happy, this was a question she'd ask at random, thrusting it into unrelated conversations, like an Internet pop-up ad. Josh'd answer in a tone meant to be humble and flippant, a wry twist to his lips. His reply, always the same, came out almost ironical enough to qualify as a dissent. But not quite. "Yes," he said.

"You liked him, this lawyer?" Dori was saying pleasantly.

"Yeah, I don't know."

Josh was surprised to hear that equivocal note in his own voice. Martin Seidel had done something that had bothered Josh, right at the end there, when their meeting had passed from business into handshakes and elevators.

In having chosen a lawyer, Josh was handing control of his life to the most blunt personality he could imagine. That was fine; you wanted that in your attorney. But now, away from the dispassion of that wood-paneled office, Josh was viewing the lawyer's hot smile of complicity in a starker light. Were they similar, he and Martin Seidel? There may have been something in this. Martin Seidel went at life using the battering ram of his charm. But if Josh also wielded *his* charisma, there was at least a dissimilarity of approach; there was very little brainwork to Josh's public face. He simply gave free play to who he was. Martin's effects were different, calculated, a little unsavory. Again, that was all right. If there ever was going to be a battle, you needed a lawyer with an iron hand and not a feather touch. Josh remembered warmly the lines of conspiratorial delight around Seidel's mouth. If the guy was almost unctuous, his near unctuousness was tied into an avidity, an *oomph*, that transcended and validated it. Thus convinced that he and Martin were not the same, Josh again had combat in his eyes.

Over the unstaticked cell connection, in high spirits again, he led his wife on a sightseeing tour of their lawyer's inspiring certainty; he walked Dori through Martin's toughness, his strategy, his cunning outburst on Dr. Stokes.

"Crap, hold on a sec, Josh." Dori left the phone to go to some minor baby concern; Josh looked at his image in distorted reflection, stretched and bulged by dents in the shiny metal on the elevator door. The blond woman noticed him looking at himself.

Dori's voice dopplered back into earshot as she said, laughing, "Oh, I wish you could see Zack now."

Whenever she was in this great a mood, when she did her characteristic hop from one subject to another, Josh dreamed up her presence automatically—Dori smiling in that red Jemima bandana, dark curls twisting out of it, curls at her strong forehead, at her ears, curls behind the neck—and he could see her full red lips, all of it beautiful: He saw his wife as if she were here on the sinking elevator. Recently, the constant vividness of Dori made it just a little harder for Josh to picture other women. That's why the way Martin had ended their meeting had bummed Josh out a little. He'd ended things by being disrespectful to Dori at the elevator bank.

"Zackie's so cute today," Dori was saying. "In his high chair. Wearing his Naked Volley Ball Team shirt. Ooh, he's talking, 'Ma ma ma.' Listen. Remember that babysitter who said that thing about how he had above-average intelligence?"

Sometimes, Dori caught herself rabbiting between topics like this, and Josh smiled now—predicting she was about to come back to the subject at hand.

"No, this is great," she said. "This Martin whatever, Seidel, he was sure, he said?"

"Yeah, I think we're good." Josh, outside already, walked under the buxom shadows of midtown, going west along that curbed equator, Fifty-seventh Street.

A salesman's social face must in essence be a mirror; a client strikes you as the kind of guy likes to tell a story, let him talk, then come up with tall tales of your own. Client wants to swap jokes, you're Will Ferrell. But if the client flashes sour, the *real* salesman knows to bounce back his own brand of toned-down sourness— more placid, more acceptable, but still a reflection. The key is you can't be an obvious ass-kisser. "Honey, the guy took a few details and spun a whole case from it," he was saying. "Martin notices things, like me."

The sidewalk was a clutter of people. About a third of them were here and, additionally, elsewhere: tethered to Bluetooth headsets, iPods and iPhones, BlackBerrys.

Dori was giving the throaty laugh that meant she was up for play.

"Mr. *Goldin*," she said, in the style of a teasing high school girl, which, because men are simple, Josh enjoyed. "You think only you notice things because you're a salesman? No, so what you're establishing is you're more observant than the average whatever?"

He liked goosing his morning with just this kind of conversation, but static gunked up his cell connection again. Without warning, the call quit.

Just as well, he guessed; Josh shot ahead into his workday. He dialed a buyer for McDonald's, Denny Lembeck, whom he'd planned to meet for a noon lunch at Smith & Wollensky. The fourth ring of his call sounded a double-long pulse of escalating volume—Josh getting passed off to voice mail.

For young businessmen, there was an ethos of leaving outgoing voice messages. To come off as cool—which was pretty much the whole ball game—you had to act as if you couldn't give a shit about anything, least of all recording this message. By the time Denny Lembeck's canned "Please leave your name and . . ." ended in its deflated mumble of "Thanks," the voice had collapsed into the studied apathy, the lethargic surliness of a teenager's *back-off-Mom* mutter.

Josh left Denny Lembeck a buddying message; consistent friendliness was the charismatic architecture of his own personality. McDonald's, of course, was extra important—and extra challenging this year. The scatter market looked weak right now, with the economy up in the air because of Iraq; even buyers like McDonald's were feeling pressure to take their ad dollars online. And what could that mean but a shitty pricing-season for cable broadcasters? Like workers at the bottom of the food chain, cable stations were the first casualties in any economic pinch in TV.

Yet it was Wine Week, thank God, which was a New York salesman's home-field advantage. Once a year, on a whim of promotion, top-drawer Manhattan restaurants gave patrons ten wines for only ten dollars. Smith & Wollensky would be lousy with would-be kings of the deal, and there would be expert-level gamesmanship: each salesman trying to inebriate his client without losing his own head.

Josh's phone became, for a second, an angry hive in his pocket; it shook and buzzed. A text. Denny Lembeck, maybe? No, it was Dori: *Don't get too drunk at the restaurant, sucka!!!!*

What a lovable goofball she could be. Faithful, klutzy, maternal, hug-crazy Dori. Just this weekend they'd been walking to dinner when she'd halted midstride to say: "Let's just stop and make out for a minute."

Memories insisted on popping up at random. First time he'd

ever had sex with her, on that Hamptons trip, they'd kicked things off by taking a shower together, one of those great mutual soap-ups; she'd cut short the foreplay by saying: "Well, my boobs are clean, anyhow." Such memories happened all the time.

Josh thought again of his meeting with Seidel just this morning, and the way it had kind of clouded over at the end.

When lawyer and client had stood for the good-byes at the elevator, the older man had asked the younger if he'd wanted a drink later at Restaurant Daniel—where Martin would set Josh up with a beautiful waitress he knew there. "If she even *talks* to me, this girl," Martin had said, "she'd go crazy over a guy like you."

Martin had held the elevator open while Josh tried not to get restless inside it; Martin's face had turned naughty. "And don't give me that married guy stuff," Martin said. "I wouldn't condone dating two women at once if you were single, but I don't fault a prison convict for what he does with his cell mate."

Josh frowned. Martin was testing out the jokey tone he hoped to use with Josh's dad. (There was the sense Martin *was* talking to Josh's dad, through Josh.) A lot of Boomer guys whose mores had been created in the '50s and smashed in the '60s now behaved with this fervent, naughty-boy-scout shamelessness, their pendulum having never swung back.

"I'm kidding," Martin said, with a wink, "—unless you do want to meet her."

Josh had laughed and admitted that he viewed celibacy the way a recovered drunk looks at abstemiousness—it was scary to think of never fucking anyone else for the next fifty years, but it wasn't bad if you kept things in units of right now. If it feels right and doable today, this week, this month, then why ruin a good thing? As he was saying this—and for some reason the explanation felt like bullshit coming out of his mouth now—Josh realized that people begrudged him his relationship with Dori. Guys like Seidel could intuit that Josh had a special thing going, and their envy ran as ill will.

"The French are *laissez-faire* compared to us about extramarital affairs," Martin had said. "They are more mature as a culture because, you know, they've been around a lot longer."

At times like this, Josh's Flawless Father goal thing seemed especially intangible.

"... You see, Josh, to the French, life without adultery, *that's* what's depraved...."

About a year before that hospital thing with Zack, Josh had almost cheated, or sort of cheated. Now was the first time he allowed himself to meditate on that night without pushing the recollection away as if it were a plate of bad food. It had been nothing, but it had been something, and then the stuff with Zack happened.

Josh had taken a client (an E. J. Johnson guy) to Larry Flynt's Hustler Club. The girl, a stripper, had skin that flaunted its shrewd tan. Even in the vesper light of that place, she made you envy that pole of hers. At one point she balanced herself downside up, all thigh-and-ankle work; her hands splayed five feet above the stage. She'd painted her nails a lively color, the fingers evidently cheery about something. Off the pole, standing before him, she had small breasts, the slightest agency of gravity making a smile of their undercurves. She was probably the only dancer there with organic boobs; all the others were sporting a fleet of free-standing silicone zeppelins. But Josh liked women's bodies to be natural. This stripper had glossy shorts, which her stomach flowed into with perfect concavity; it was exactly the contour you see in a tub of ice cream after the first, pristine scoop.

She wasn't nearly as beautiful as Dori was. Her eyebrows had been tweezed within a millimeter of their lives. But he found himself crazily aroused by that stripper stare, that gaze of ready-made lust that somehow always stopped an inch short of your eyes. This pout, and the faint sparkles on her body touched him: It all communicated so powerfully the message that she was *not his commitment to his wife*.

She looked so young; it was entertaining to imagine helping her out. She had nothing to do with his life, she was a fantasy of rescue, she was a cat up in a tree with faint sparkles on her body.

She twirled the ends of her red hair, which looked seared, rusted, and thirsty. And then it happened. He simply watched it go on, like a spectator being invited down from the bleachers—her taking his hand, their walk toward the curtained side room, the loud *Yeah, dude!* from the E. J. Johnson guy (this was going to help the sale, after all), how very young the girl was; the ten lighter flames she had for fingernails; the sweaty taste of her nipples in his mouth.

The unguarded way she kissed his lips seemed an acquiescence, as did her maybe-real sigh. The slight tickle of those long nails as she reached down his pants, the lift of her hips and the surprisingly rubbery softness of her down there, after he slipped his hand under her shorts.

I didn't fuck her; I never would have fucked another woman, he'd thought, zipping up, *or even get a blow job.* He'd known that this wasn't cheating, of course it wasn't. And for a while after it had happened, he had shaken his head about it and chuckled. He'd gotten a *stripper* turned on. But he'd had a pregnant wife at home. He felt really bad about it and yet he didn't feel all that bad about it.

He didn't like even small shots of guilt. He hadn't been appalled enough, he realized now. Because then the emergency with Zack had happened, and it had—his wife especially had—taught him real morality. He wanted to get all those memories out of his heart. And replace them with what? he wondered. Well, images, for one. Like bringing the baby to his lap and then, by holding Zack's hands and balancing him, getting him to stand up, which always brought a gummy smile; the way the baby had started to go "Da da da"; making the kid laugh; his cupid face. . . .

Martin Seidel had wanted Josh to risk all that? A giant *No!* filled Josh's head as if spelled out in colossal letters, in the way a Cecil B. DeMille CinemaScope title spreads across the air over a motion picture desert. His life with a family-size hole in it? No thanks.

Besides, a different wife had emerged at the hospital; Dori had gained a startling regal look that day, as she stared palely at the doctors, and with her hair pulled back she'd shown a new intelligence. Maybe all brave women had more than one face.

. . . The phone in Josh's pocket shivered again; this time it *was* Lembeck. "Yo, yo, J-bone."

A minute later Josh was listening to that same damn buyer talk: traditional media markets versus the Internet. (Christ, all this stuff seemed kind of dirty, kind of out in the alley, when compared to thoughts of radiant Dori in that hospital.) "You see, Josh, consumers now expect all media outlets to deliver the way the Internet did: with access, speed, freedom, interactivity. Even TV. Can *Sparkplug* offer that?"

Well, Martin Seidel was right, the baby wasn't going anywhere.

"Hold up, hold up, hold up," Josh managed to say to Lembeck, climbing into salesmanship. "You really think McDonald's can risk moving a big chunk out of TV and put it online? Do *you* like pop-up ads?" (How dare someone be jealous of a guy for having a happy marriage when they don't know what terrible shit may be happening behind the scenes? Well, people have always been jealous of me about something, Josh was thinking.)

"I'm feeling pressure to move is all I'm saying." Lembeck said. "That's just how it is."

Josh met this with a lipfart. As usual, a clever remark took shape in Josh's mind and reported for duty:

"So TV's going away?"

This is what pros do. They tough it out, they smile though the minefield of distraction, no matter how serious. "Come on, now. The *Internet*? *McDonald's* forgoes all TV?"

But how vulnerable, sad, and alone the baby had looked when the doctors stuck that tube in his throat.

LATER, IN ROMANTICALLY lit, carpeted Smith & Wollensky, Lembeck repeated the old gag, that TV airtime sales is a C+ business, because what student who'd made A's or B's would have gone into it?

Then: "So, you got surprises on your prime time schedule, or what? Tell me there's no more *Matlock* reruns, Josh." Buyers have ultimate power over sellers and Lembeck had the satisfied glow of that power.

"Oh, we got good stuff, my friend," said Josh, ordering a third bottle of Sancerre but not losing the sales voodoo—the Touch, as he called it. "Oh, yes, life's full of surprises."

4

THERE IS A FAMOUS AND EXPLICIT REPRIMAND AGAINST BUSYBODIES IN the good old Hippocratic Oath—that is, a doctor's first job is not to cure but instead to avoid screwing up with overmeasures.

Yes, and maybe I'm monomaniacal about a patient's health, thought Dr. Stokes, *but so be it*. Her eagerness would not be slighted. It was nobler, at least, to try.

Darlene was having lunch in St. Joe's cafeteria. She wore her lab coat—even though a woman in her position needn't have done so. If she didn't, white people would mistake her for an orderly.

The cafeteria was an awful spot on days like today when the noon hour rattled with more hospital noise than usual—loudmouths arguing with the admittance nurses; the TVs dashing off early-afternoon headlines; and the grieving patients or families, clumped by doorways and phones, reconciling themselves to the conclusive news. What breeds hospital indifference is learning to treat all of it as the same thing: noise. But as Darlene ate, she couldn't help watching one young man accept whatever misfortune the day had given him. The thing about seeing a young man cry is that it holds off that indifference. When panicked young crying stops getting to you, you're cooked. Darlene wasn't cooked yet.

SHE SAT EATING her hard-to-unwrap apple and waiting for Dr. Weiss. Lateness usually bothered her; Darlene didn't mind the holdup now. She was fitting in the pieces, puzzling together a Zack Goldin hypothesis. It was tricky, suppositions balanced on top of suppositions. And she could knock the whole thing over by just accepting that Weiss had screwed up. Maybe the simplest answer was the best.

Weiss arrived, offered an excuse that made him just another

Leo ("I was online getting Rolling Stones tickets, so I'm sorry I'm late, but the Wi-Fi here . . ."), and made a performance of slumping his thin body down into the plastic bench opposite hers.

"I don't even know why I'm *going* to that concert." Weiss spoke quickly and patted down his curly hair.

"Interesting thing about Mick Jagger," Dr. Weiss added; he wanted to delay this. "I got him figured out. Want to hear?"

Okay, this is small talk, Darlene thought. It was a strategy a lot of the young residents relied on: set up a friendly environment, which would soften the reprimand you were afraid of.

Darlene smiled politely. And she felt her eyes pulled again to that softly crying young man at the nearby table. He was basic skinny mid-twenties, but he held his mouth so taut that his chin had gone white.

Weiss was saying: "D'you know 'Wooly Bully,' by Sam the Sham? The song?" Weiss leaned forward smiling, with a blatant casualness that wasn't quite ease.

Darlene told him she didn't know the song.

"It's from a few years before the Stones came out, I think. So they must have heard it. But listen to that tune; you'll notice all of Mick's moves in it. The cockiness, the goofing on soul music—just that *sound*, you know?" He made sure to face Darlene eye-to-eye. "Aside from the stuff we all know Mick took from the Delta blues guys, Muddy and whatnot." He'd included this last part because his boss was African-American.

Whether literally plagiarized or not, this little monologue of Weiss's—the unnatural cadence of it, the underlying wink in its mock-serious analysis of piffle—seemed to Darlene to have been lifted straight from the movies. One more effect of Hollywood on human discourse, Darlene thought. It wasn't news that films and magazines and TV caused us to mistrust our own appearance— young girls holding themselves against some airbrushed ideal they see in every doctor's waiting room. But it seemed like more and more of her underlings also took their behavioral cues from cinema.

Men, especially, were susceptible. They felt they had to banter, a big jolly table, the way characters did not just on sitcoms, but in beer ads. This made it harder to interact naturally, it occurred to Darlene. Strange to be a man nowadays. Or even to talk with one.

This wasn't the kind of insight she could easily share.

"Well, Arthur, I wanted to ask you a few questions about what can't be a favorite topic."

"Zack Goldin?" he said, lowering the white disc of his face. "Yeah—he was the baby from like a month or two ago that . . ." And then the doctors walked through the particulars of the situation.

The mother had brought her child in for an upset stomach, nothing more. Weiss had followed procedure: He'd sent them home with some Pedialyte. "You can see on the emergency-room note," he said, "I have her down as a Neem." (Neem was the nickname doctors gave the acronym NYM, or Nervous Young Mom.) "She seemed the classic example, and the kid looked fine. It was a Friday, and you know how we get Neems on Fridays, before people go to the Hamptons. Anyway, that should have been the end of it," he said. But then, it hadn't been the end. The mother had come back, crazy, her son unconscious and anemic. And she claimed to have told Weiss that her baby had vomited blood, when she had said no such a thing.

". . . So, that's when you came in," Weiss said.

His gaze, though his eyes didn't move, went off somewhere— and Darlene liked this, and saw why Arthur Weiss might eventually make a very good doctor. He had the tape going in his head, watching the playback of those events, making sure that the woman, indeed, hadn't mentioned the vomit. (He cut himself off from adding: "I'm not positive, Dr. S., but I'm almost positive.")

"Arthur, I want you to know I do believe you," she said. "But regardless, you know my policy is we need to investigate. A baby coded, and a mother claims the hospital is at fault and lied about it." She looked querulous, gently querulous. "Doesn't the lack of a conclusion bother you?"

It took a little blinking for Weiss to return to the present moment. "Yes, it bothers me, no diagnosis, of course it does," he said.

Then, as if remembering he had to kiss up to her a little, he said: "I mean, you know how it is, Dr. S. You've been here for a lot longer than I have. There are *so* many patients every week to worry about that—"

Up went her hand, to wave away such trivial excuses. "Your story contradicts her story. It's an open case, and either you or she is not telling the truth. I believe you. Was I wrong to do so?"

"I'm sure about my notes," he said. "She never, never told me that. You know me, Dr. S. You know my strengths and weaknesses, my overall competence. That's not the kind of mistake I make."

"Let's assume you're giving me accurate reports and diagnoses," Dr. Stokes said. "Did something also seem off about the mom?"

Weiss, still blushing from his recent defensiveness, had no control over his face: babyish, softly grimacing, it seemed to beg Darlene to see this case in the light of common cause. He was running his fingers on the table, over someone's scratched initials: "D.H.L."; the impersonality of a hospital cafeteria feels acute in such pauses. Darlene raised her dense eyebrows. And as if Darlene's eagerness had ended the mandatory period of musing, the younger doctor said:

"I *might* know where you're going with this, but, uh."

She told him to remember that the woman was a trained phlebotomist; she told him that there may never have *been* any vomit.

Dr. Stokes leaned forward and spoke softly: "Did you see the emesis? Did anybody see it? Maybe she left you, went out to her car, did something we don't know, and she came back in."

"What could have happened? It was five minutes later; they wouldn't have had time even to get home. It's a parking lot, Dr. Stokes."

"Maybe," Darlene said, "the woman bled her child herself."

She stopped talking only to judge what effect her words had had.

Their effect was this: While still sitting in the booth, Dr. Weiss gave the impression of backing cautiously to the door.

Though he had to toady to his boss, he also was aware that he had to toady to his own future. The last thing a resident wants to start his career with is a legal case.

"We didn't see anything like that happen, Dr. Stokes." Weiss still looked down, his face in partial view. "I mean, to accuse a," he said, and left it at that.

"You'll get this more when you've been at it awhile," she said, slipping into her motherly solicitude. "But I've never seen a parent, when there isn't a firm diagnosis, who doesn't want more tests. Never, ever. Who in that situation would not want more tests? Her son was in a life-threatening position."

"Her own son, though? Why would she want to do that, and then lie? To sue us or something?" He shifted in his chair and the fabric of his green hospital getup made a dry sound as he moved. "Respectfully, that's a big claim."

"I am aware," Dr. Stokes said, "of the severity of what I'm saying. If we're going to have to gear up for legal action, her accusations are something you'll have to answer for. Maybe her accusations were to throw you off the scent."

Darlene let the surrounding noise flow over them for a moment, exactly as a poker player would after an outrageous bet. The hospital grumbling went on around them. Neither she nor the younger doctor talked. Weiss tightened his medical-school mouth.

"Arthur, think about this as if it were a case at med. This woman would know what steps to take. And she was sure everything we said was wrong. What kind of phlebotomist would allow her child to be sent home with Pedialyte after seeing blood in his vomit? A world without consequences, attendings—what would your diagnosis be?"

"Is this devil's advocate stuff? Like an exercise?" But you could see he didn't think that. Weiss had little parentheses around his mouth now, cagey frown-marks—signs of alarm. He saw trouble making its way into his life.

"Okay, as an exercise," he said. "My first question would be:

What made the baby pass out? So—what? She bled him—and then she asphyxiated him, too? 'Cause it'd be both. Like if she used a pillow or something. Seems odd." He was warming to it, to this un-rancorous debate. "And if so, why bother making up a lie about him vomiting?"

"To trick you," Darlene said. "Misdirection is the key to keeping someone off balance."

Her light of certainty faded. The "misdirection" phrase had been unfortunate, too movie-dramatic. Her allegation was wildly serious and her guesswork provisional and she felt her mouth go dry.

"Well, let's not give it a motive yet. And the methodology *would* make her son's case more confusing," she said, rephrasing. "Maybe it's not the mother, necessarily. Maybe there's a relative or a cleaning lady?"

"It's interesting." Weiss nodded—a classroom nod, someone pretending to do a reassessment for a professor. "But the time factor. All this would make it difficult, a real pain, for us to look into."

Dr. Stokes straightened up sharply, like some bird who's de-cided to stop taking crumbs, preferring instead to fly. He'd touched on a core belief.

"Difficult or not," she said. "The issue is not one of ease or dif-ficulty." It could have been Alice Davis talking, at the end of an-other hard Rothenberg & Rubinstein day. The funny thing about having interns and residents, she'd noticed—especially since James had turned three, when he'd started holding conversations—was that being the head of a unit was like having a staff full of children, people you had to teach, in a medical sense, how to walk, talk, and eat. She spent her whole day mothering, just as Alice had: Hardship had trained her for hospital work better than she knew.

"Have you ever seen a Munchausen-by-proxy case, Dr. Weiss?"

No, he told her, he hadn't. (She didn't mention that she hadn't, either.)

Darlene had studied up on it both nights the weekend before. She'd put James to sleep, tried to distract herself with TV, a glass of wine—and then she'd found herself with the textbooks, on the Internet, looking for papers, for evidence. Munchausen syndrome by proxy is among the medical world's most controversial diagnoses: a medical condition in which a parent injures her own child. In the literature, in the ER, it's almost always the mother. A woman smothers her kids, injects feces into her baby's blood; sometimes she will asphyxiate him, sometimes feed him a measure of rat poison. Often the children die. It's a mystery. In the DSM IV, it's called a pathology, but one of the most brutal: What earthly motive could explain the pathology of harming one's own baby?

"Okay," Weiss said, "but keep in mind, Dr. Stokes, the baby coded. That's a heavy indictment you want to make. A heavy indictment."

The modern mania, attention. That's what drives these parents to it. The only fulfillment these mothers are after is the fulfillment of the spotlight.

"Maybe," Weiss was saying, "there's a reason I haven't seen a Munchausen case. Maybe the very rarity of the syndrome tells us something."

He had cause to doubt. In medical school he had studied with a professor—Dr. Josh Gottheimer, of Cornell—who regularly acted as a defense witness for parents accused of this syndrome. Gottheimer, a brilliant man, had taught that false allegations outnumbered actual cases by a critical margin; that the main fact about MSBP was that it was in fact *exceedingly* rare, a "disease *du jour*."

Now Weiss was saying, "I'm not even positive MSBP, or pediatric condition falsification, or whatever it's called now, is an actual medical condition, in itself."

Like many second-rate doctors, Weiss was a first-rate blowhard. His neutral and clever face returned. Raising a didactic finger, he said, "Merely because some mothers may injure their children and blame those injuries on phantom disease, does not mean that those activities *themselves* comprise an illness in the mother." He turned up his nose. "That's how my diagnostics professor explained it, anyway."

Dr. Stokes's annoyance weighed on her mouth—narrowed it to a trench between nose and chin. She agreed that, yes, doctors must show caution in presuming that a specific group of symptoms constitutes a valid medical condition. Point taken, Doctor.

"But *what*," she said, "does that have to do with our *actual* patient?"

She realized her voice carried rudely, especially here, where the tile floors make everything sound clattery. But she couldn't help herself—and most residents probably thought she was a stickler, anyway.

"Dr. Weiss," she said, "we don't have to be careful about what it's called, or whether by itself it constitutes a unique disease, or is merely abuse by another name—what matters is, if we think this mother may have harmed her son. Everything else is academic."

Darlene saw that Weiss, out of a politeness he barely had, strained to hold back a rebuttal he couldn't wait to make. "We*ll*," he said. He smoothed his hair down as he weighed his ego versus his need to defer. He had a cowlick that fishtailed up after every pass of his hand, and—as happened with annoying people—this quirk of his appearance seemed the soul of everything Darlene didn't like in him.

"Respectfully, Dr. Stokes," Weiss said. "What's that guy's name in England, who had all those patients—"

The answer was Dr. Raymond Pitt.

Darlene knew about Dr. Pitt. She'd been reading up on him, part of getting herself in position to light the fuse, should this come to that.

Thirty years ago Ray Pitt, a British pediatrician, had a patient whose story didn't make sense. A little girl had passed bloody urine for her whole life. Relentless treatment, long hospital stays had become the girl's second affliction. Medicines and tests of all sorts ruled out drug rashes, fungal infection, renal disease—and to no benefit. The mystery endured. Samples of the girl's urine would contain blood one hour, nothing alien the next. The pathogens would vary,

too—*E. coli* in a morning sample and then, at night, a different or-
ganism. The mother, according to Dr. Pitt's *Lancet* article, was "concerned and loving, and yet not quite as worried as the doctors were."
Pitt—with what Darlene imagined to have been an Archimedes-
like *Eureka!*—realized that all but one batch of tainted specimens
had, at one time or another, been left alone with the girl's mother.
On a hunch, Pitt took the patient's urine without telling the mother.
And then—minutes later—asked the mother to collect some specimens *herself* from her daughter. Pitt tested both the mother-gotten
sample and the hospital's. The mother-obtained urine was bloody;
the hospital sample showed no contagion. The woman had been
adding her own menstrual discharge—along with other things—to
an altogether healthy girl's urine samples.

If this mother's culpability seemed quite obvious after the fact,
Pitt had cautioned, remember that—at that time—nobody would
have thought it conceivable a parent could have such an oddly defi-
cient soul.

The girl had suffered twenty-two hospital admissions, eleven
X-ray procedures, intravenous urograms, cystograms, barium en-
emas, vaginograms, urethrograms; she'd been knocked out six times
by anesthesia, had gritted through five cystoscopes; not to mention
suffering all along through toxic drugs and antibiotics, catheteriza-
tions, vaginal pessaries, constant infections, and bacterial, fungicidal,
and estrogen creams, a merciless litany. She was six years old. This
woman had wrapped her daughter in misery, and for what? For a
dream of attention. Sixteen specialists had weighed in and they all
treated old Mum with tender, solicitous interest. For two years, she'd
been a famous heroine—while real mothers, the kind of women the
world over like Alice Davis, kept doing all that they did for their
children, for no attention at all.

Dr. Pitt—who had since become Sir Raymond Pitt—had found
a bit of gratifying attention, as well; he'd chanced onto a strange and
singular case, and through it discovered and christened a new disorder, the thing on which to pull together a reputation.

Now, at the table opposite Darlene's, the quietly crying young man straightened up in self-respect, closed his cell phone, gave a short laugh to shake off the sadness. As if without meaning to, he began humming "Hey Jude," and left.

Dr. Pitt's syndrome—as Weiss didn't have to remind Darlene— had become heavily scrutinized; a number of the knighted physician's diagnoses had, in recent years, been proved incorrect.

"I just think it's wise to be extra careful," Dr. Weiss said softly.

He understood he'd found the right approach now, reverent caution. It was the same note he used on dates who he judged too pretty for him, a cold curve of the lips.

He mentioned a recent case, Professor Gottheimer's example of overzealous diagnosis. A child's brain had swollen from oxygen deficit. Many doctors ventured many guesses, in a convention of rival diagnoses. Sir Raymond Pitt, by now very publicly a big cheese, was asked to look into the baby's death. Pitt decided, with dry poise, that the mother had likely killed her son—a solution he'd come to without having met the family or examined the child's body. He built his evaluation on news that the baby had had blood in his nostrils and cuts on his nose. Pitt saw this as evidence of smothering, a fight— *some*thing foul. Conundrums don't sit well with men who've transcended backwater hospitals to become Official Authorities of the Realm. Meanwhile nobody had told the mother that she was being investigated; she got pregnant again. Of course, there was a feeling people like her shouldn't be allowed to have kids.

"I think I read about this case," Darlene told Dr. Weiss.

As Weiss remembered it . . . When the woman gave birth to her second child—a daughter—a judge sent policemen into the delivery room to take the baby. The Manchester *Guardian* championed the woman; later, a hospital investigation determined that the case against her had been flawed. She'd likely cut her son accidentally while attempting to resuscitate him; and the hospital had prescribed him medicine found to have killed other children. *Well, even so,* said the custody courts. By then there was no way to reunite the mother with her surviving child—four years had gone; the daughter had joined a foster family. So the mother sued Dr. Pitt for recompense and won millions. The administering hospital was, like the doctors who had brought the case to Pitt, ruined by it all.

Darlene wasn't surprised. Having tracked the falling stock of Pitt's prestige, she knew there must have been at least one case like that. Two hundred fifty of his other cases had been put under official "rereview" for "serious professional misconduct." But Darlene had judged this fact an apple to her oranges; what did her suspicions of the Goldin family have in the final analysis to do with Sir Raymond Pitt?

Still, Dr. Weiss was bringing certain difficulties up to the magnifying glass, where Darlene had no choice but to eyeball them.

She admitted now that, yes, there *was* a problem with most Munchausen cases: When a parent caused illness in an obvious way, you just made out a report to Child Protective Services immediately. "But," she said, "when they exaggerate some real disease, something that their kid may already have, or when they make up a false history whole cloth, it's harder to catch them"—Darlene hesitated for a moment, wondering if she was giving a lesson or getting one—"so it's important we don't make a referral before all our ducks are in a row."

Weiss answered carefully, as you'd remind the boss that you'd out-putted him on the eighteenth hole. "I think that's right. About the ducks."

"Dr. Weiss," Darlene said with some renewed punch, "I know you're a very busy resident, as all our residents are. But Zack Goldin is your *patient*. And that means . . ."

Weiss relaxed. *Cue the speech,* he thought.

Back in Darlene's office, she planned and concocted. She would phone counterparts at Long Island Jewish and St. John's Ambulatory, and have Weiss get on the phone with Betty Van Der Meer, of Long Island CPS, who might have access to additional records. All this could be done without having to make an official referral.

She knew her hunch for what it was: merely a hunch, and maybe flimsy. No one had in fact seen the mother doing anything wrong, certainly.

"Call *today*, Dr. Weiss," she said. Her solid deep voice made the vein thudding in her forehead more noticeable.

Here was Dr. Stokes showing the deepest force of human feeling. *But why?* Dr. Weiss thought. Weiss didn't know what Darlene's personal story was. He didn't know that the idea of mothers harming their children could work up the most intimate fury in her, a great private disgust, ever since she'd learned of Munchausen in med school, when she'd invisibly begun her own pregnancy and her classmate Sue Abrams-Murray had said, with jokey mock fatigue, midway into a lecture called *MSBP—Danger Signs and Tactics for Identification*: "Can you *blame* those parents? Ugh. When I have kids, that's what I'll probably do." Sue Abrams-Murray, like Dr. Weiss, had no idea that, in Darlene's family, motherhood wasn't some life change that women joked about, like a little fat around the middle; it was a thing imposed by the world, terrible and wonderful. It was a locked tree-house door that kept women in the profoundest joys and most terrible misgivings. Darlene *did* love her son. Oh, Lord, did she: picturing his little body in his seat belt, as he'd said, "Dad's birthday is November twenty-fourth," turned her chest to cream. She subordinated her life to this small person, just as her mother had done for her; just as *she'd* been meant to. (Not that Darlene wouldn't have liked to give dating a try, but then she told herself, "Oh, yeah, a fun-loving, fortyish single mother in the suburbs who works eleven-hour days, that's what men want. . . .")

But these Munchausen women? Using their babies to meet their own juvenile, crazy, malicious, criminal ends?

No.

5

Zack had a single tooth poking up from his gums, narrow, white, and unaccompanied. It looked like a *No Sale* tab in an antique cash register. He faced happiness with his mouth hung open, which meant you saw that nub tooth a lot.

He was thirteen months now, fair, blue-eyed, and he clapped lightly with any music.

"This is hip-hop," Josh said. "You like Arrested Development, Zackie? Daddy used to get some action to this."

The baby sat unwhimperingly during car trips, calm and chubby as the Buddha. His face had the grin of incomprehension on it. He loved to say his "Da da das"—or at least, that's what he was saying today, as he and Josh drove without Dori to Central Park.

The morning was sunless and mild for October. The grayish sky was nicked here and there by white jet trails. Josh carried his son in a BabyBjörn.

After entrusting his car to an eighteen-dollar lot, and then avoiding the park's blacktop walkway—which had become a game of Frogger, him dodging bicyclists and inline skaters—he legged Zack up a brushy, off-the-path rock face, with roots and gaps and leaf litter at every turn. It was steeper and more naturish than it had appeared. Finally, he and Zack emerged to be charmed by the sleight-of-hand that was Central Park. Here, at the biggest of the smooth, bright meadows, dog yelps and Frisbees in the air, Josh forgot he was in Manhattan. Because even the archways and the mottled statues, the stone stairs with their pummeled steps—each one hammocked in the middle by the applied force of a million feet—were out of sight, out of mind in the meadow. Near the closest garbage can, a chipmunk stooped and rubbed its claws together like a miser. Josh spotted his old friends Nathan and Todd (and their BabyBjörns) across the counterfeit pastoral of the Great Lawn. And past those guys, just beyond the strip of trees that framed the park, stood the reason you couldn't ever totally forget where you were—New York's skyline, whose presence exaggerated the feeling of play and even of protected youth: The city was looking in on you, peering over your cradle.

"Fuckers," Josh said affectionately, upon greeting his friends.

A week earlier, Josh had earmarked the afternoon as a "Just Guys" hangout, one that would also give his wife a day to spend on the lam with her own friends. Among other couples this set off the equivalent of atomic fission; Josh's buddies each had wives, none of whom were close, and all of those women had separately planned spouseless get-togethers. So all of these people, released from their orbits because of Josh and Dori, had gone spinning out in divergent directions to break up more and more nuclear families.

Immediately now, Josh and his friends set up a rotating child-care scheme; each would have a turn watching, while the other two threw around a football.

Josh, the athlete among them, whose spiral most often found the soft of your hands, said, "I'll sit out first, since I was late."

"No shit," said Nathan. He loved even the limited physicality of a football catch. "That's *right* you will."

"Learn how to throw," Josh said.

Josh always had to *see* these old buddies to remember how much he enjoyed them: to recall how different solid, long-term, masculine affection was from the diluted camaraderie he fell into so cleanly. Real friendship was a space opening out where male ambition could be lifted, examined, and laughed at for the slight thing it was: All that guys really needed to do was trot around on fresh turf with a ball and some good-natured insults.

He'd known these buddies since before JV hoops, before growth spurt, dry humping, and fake IDs; Todd, who'd grown stubble but somehow lost a bit of his chin, or gained more neck; Nathan, who'd had scuzzed, Andre Agassi hair in the '80s, then the tattoo/Caesar-cut/goatee combo plate of the '90s, and who was now especially easy to rag on about his declawed fatherly existence. Nathan came from a long line of gangster-defending lawyers who made a bundle flipping real estate properties with lax eviction guidelines.

"It's not that your daddies suck at football," Josh said to the kids—two girls and Zack, all about a year old. "It's that they *really* suck at football."

"Heads up!" Todd yelled some yards away. Then, in falling volume: "Sorry, sorry, sorry . . ."

"You always were a superstar thrower."

The fun thing about lifelong friends was to wring a few more drops of embarrassment from the old humiliations. Like when Todd saw that Nathan was on his cell phone. He said: "Nathan's talking to his wife?" And he made the whip sound: "*Wha-psshh.*"

Meanwhile the kids played under the big hippopotamus clouds and Josh's gaze. They shared time with a plush giraffe doll (passing it, tugging it, dropping it). Josh picked up the doll. Zack thumped his fists to the ground, again and again, getting his playmates' attention, as if at a board meeting among cavemen. It intrigued Josh. Through yips, cries, and giggles, pointing and grabbing, through clapping and stomping—baby gestures even brought their feet into play—these one-year-olds were communing with each other: Josh saw requests, disappointment, even intrigue. Now little Zack held the giraffe. He had the plump-faced satisfaction and the numerical benefits—a girl on either side of him—of a maharajah.

The cuter of the girls, Arlen, patted Zack's foot with hers. The ignored Cassidy eyed her contemporaries coolly, without a smile. She tried to touch feet with Arlen, who withdrew hers. When Cassidy tried again, Arlen noticed her with a vague antipathy, and then turned to offer Zack another pat of possession. Even with toddlers, it was the timeless triangle, somebody in, somebody out.

Cassidy's father was Nathan, a violent and arrhythmical quarterback who kept throwing short. "Sorry." Overhead, a plane was going by, a slow comet.

"My bad," Nathan said, hands on his scalp. (His hair had gone the way of all high school triumphs.)

"You just want to make me run after the ball," said Todd, running after the ball.

Like most men, Josh pictured himself eternally at twenty-five. But his friends' faces had grown, if not necessarily fatter, then clearly wider—as though air had been let in. Like presidential reputations and the price of things, these guys seemed inflated by passage of time.

Josh noticed and noticed but never made anything of it; this was what made his aliveness a shallow aptitude. The observations seeped through a tiny hole in an otherwise closed mind. Because he sometimes had difficulty expressing them, he had the odd feeling his perceptions were smarter than he was. This didn't mean he failed to have them, or to experience the virtue of his own ideas. Just that, disturbingly, they never led anywhere: He saw children acting out adult patterns, adults patterning into old men, and it passed, flared his own experience for a moment, and then dimmed again. He had only to think something for it to be gone.

"How's my Zackie?" he asked. And he was aware, as he did so, that he was working his flirty charms, even here with children. "Making out like a bandit with these girlies?"

His son dreamily smiled. Todd, who'd overheard, chuckled. And Josh was lost in one of those moments, pure warmth, when you understand that a kid is a thing of your own making, your own DNA. Zack was so cute in his denim overalls. One gentle poke to the stomach and he'd giggle and open out his hands like the Pillsbury Doughboy. At the edge of Josh's vision, the sky kept yanking up a red kite, this way and that.

The guys stayed there for three pretty fun hours; the bustle around them continued to play out just as Josh imagined it would, and therefore seemed eminently ignorable. The pasty middle-aged in their inexcusable shorts; the overhead lather of clouds; the zitty teens, pulling sullen faces next to their parents—Josh noticed the world beyond his friends and child only when the early sunset began to lavenderize it for his pleasure.

During Todd and Nathan's final catch, the leaves around the Great Lawn hissing and falling, two women in autumn wear (thin sweaters, pencil skirts), saw Josh watching the children—a handsome man alone performing the devotional observances of fatherhood—and came to his side to praise the babies, find out his situation, squint under the weather, move their bangs around. They were a catalog photo, this pair of thirtyish scrutinizers; the flat colors of their clothes set off the drama of their linen-pale New York skin. The sky started grumbling promises of rain; neither noticed. One of them adjusted her clothes, to shift the midsize breasts in her sweater; the other had said hello in a voice that crept on intimacy. Josh sat with his ring hand deliberately hidden behind him. But a flip book of images ran in his mind, excerpts from the volume he always carried there: *Dori naked in white tube socks that first time in the Hamptons; Dori's hair falling between their mouths just as they kissed; Dori laughing, wiping her lips on his forearm*—each picture racing to the next before Josh could register it completely. But what these left him with was the essence of his wife, and he saw the other women a little less well now. Josh, with a concluding saddish smile, let them know the conversation was over.

"Bye," said the one in the sweater, smiling at him from over her shoulder as she left.

It had been a great afternoon, but these women did clip the wings of Josh's enjoyment; he felt a little bummed out. This was the faint gnawing that, with monogamy, he was somehow diminishing—if not risking—his shining self.

"Dad da da," Zack said.

"That's right."

With the first drops of rain, a thousand people around Josh looked up at once.

ZACK AND JOSH beat Dori home. When Dori called, Josh was in the process of changing a diaper, holding his breath against the humid obnoxious stench of shit. He'd grabbed the changing pad out of his backpack (he'd always thought backpacks were for nerds) when he picked up the phone.

"Hi, Mr. G.," Dori said. "Almost home."

"Good."

Josh took a baby wipe out of the little tissue-box thing. And he swabbed Zack's ass—which was dotted with brown up to the small of his back, goddamn it. Josh thought of Todd's joke about Nathan from earlier. *Am I whipped?* he thought with horror now. *No,* he thought, *I'm not whipped.*

Dori was phoning to see how Zack was doing. And also, she said, because she missed her two men. "How was your day?" she said.

But his synopsis, oddly, didn't catch the fragile, wonderful peace of the afternoon. "Zack's been crying all day," Josh lied without really knowing why.

"Oh, Mr. Goldin." She was laughing. Then she said, "I'm *sorry.*" Josh recognized the faintly babied voice that assumed worked-up, as opposed to real, empathy.

"Yeah," he said. "Well."

For Josh to complain any more would have seemed wimpy; he kept quiet long enough for Dori to say:

"I *hate* my friends; I told a joke that nobody got. We were all around the table at Serendipity, playing these stupid riddle games, and Kim says, 'The only clue is a noose and a puddle.' And so I said, 'The Michael Hutchence Story.' Pretty funny, right?"

Josh enjoyed life most when he didn't have to think about stuff. His unarticulated idea had always been that perfection in life was possible, if you ignore your way into it. That's how he'd entered adulthood. He'd met Dori, and without his having to make any effort, a number of excellent transformations had happened: The mattress on the floor had turned into a real bed, his fridge had filled with items more complicated than beer and milk; he'd been lifted, in other words, into adulthood. But how had he gotten here— removing a brown slime-smeared diaper, trying to avoid the animal smell of it—so quickly?

It was when his son had had the Incident—Josh had been forced to think about and do stuff he hadn't wanted to. Like the Flawless Father Plan. Through no volition of his own, Josh had become Nathan these last few months.

Before Josh had even met Dori, she'd had him by the ears. They'd had friends in common who had talked her up to him; the cool sound of her name—Dori Glodz—had intrigued Josh: that jolt; that electric kiss in the *dz*; the buzz it gave his mouth. He'd been dating a lot of women and so didn't think much of it at first. But the sound lingered in his ear like a piece of music too fine to appreciate on first hearing.

They were both twenty-four, an age when you move from feeling bored by the world to being a little intimidated by it.

On their first date, *Donnie Brasco* at the Ziegfeld followed by tapas and sangria that was a hair to the left of undrinkable, Dori wore open-toed shoes, even though it was a chilly night. For a few minutes she kept her scarf on indoors, wrapped three times around her neck. She avoided looking at him when he talked, which was the only habit of Turkish manners she'd picked up from her father, and which Josh misjudged, at first, for shyness. He liked her kinky black hair. He liked that there was a wispery thing about her. She was very sexy. She was an olive-skinned, blue-eyed beauty and he appreciated her looks with every fiber of his glance: her clean skin, fine nose, her lips. He sneaked a downward look at her long throat, the declination of her breasts.

He liked that, after some sangria, exhilaration was her main characteristic; she was seized entirely by whatever she was speaking about. When she meant to be funny, blood worked warmly under her cheekbones. When she recounted the sad movie they'd seen, she put a truly distressed hand to her cheek; at first, Josh thought that sensitive gesture—that rich sympathy—had been facetious. (He later saw how this would bear on their marriage: Whenever she was glad, Dori's mood wouldn't have a single speck of frost on it. But she could hardly contain her body if she was pissed off. She'd sit bouncing her knees and wriggling her feet.)

He remembered having really flirted with her that night, lifting his chin, smiling—the mystery inflection that's meant easily to be solved. Their conversation had been pithy and young.

"I'm not really even Turkish," he remembered her saying. "I mean, my dad is, but."

"So you don't speak it or anything?"

"Oh, God, no," she said, shifting up into a less grinding topic. It was clear she was embarrassed about it.

"I was raised I guess kind of Jappy," she stage-whispered, a mock-intimate confession.

Her mother was of that rarest breed, the fair and naturally blond Jew. Dori had identified herself completely with, and grown up mythologizing, her mom's cheerleading days at Dix Hills Half Hollow High West—even as she knew nothing of her dad's childhood adventures as the brave, young Jew known for racing his scooter for money along the Irmak Road, which closely followed the turns of the Bosporus like a little sister.

"Jappy's not too bad. There are worse things," Josh said helpfully. "Least you get treated like a princess, right?"

On dates, he'd always gotten the laughs he'd sought; he knew what nervous daters never figured out, that bunt-single jokes got the job done better than did swinging for the fences every time. Just get on base; eventually you'll score.

As she rose from the meal, some inscrutable emotion sparked a very pretty glow to her cheeks. Swallowing as if surprised by her own actions, she touched his chin with her pointer finger. He laughed a quick, surprised laugh. And her finger arched up, yielding flaccid in his cleft like a lobster's feeler bent against the glass of an aquarium. They stood like that an awkward second, until he touched her finger. Then his hand swallowed hers.

She took an unanticipated step into him, raised her parted lips to his. Dori's warm, pliable mouth carried the delicate, acid sweetness of tomato and wine. Soft mittens of Muzak pawed at Josh's ears. The snips of Dori's teeth hinted against his lips. They both kept their eyes open the whole time.

"How do you like them apples?" she said, and laughed—a little tipsily.

Walking from the restaurant he absentmindedly identified the streets they passed; she repeated the numbers. In front of them the skyline of Manhattan brazened up like rough teeth in an open mouth. Her neck was thin and the soft babyish hair at the nape was very subtle and warm as he put his hand to her. But unhappiness seeped into her disposition, the way a chill seeps into a house not well insulated against it. "No, I'll just take the subway," she said when he offered to pay for—and split—a cab. She geisha-stepped down the stairs of Grand Central like a cat burglar. At the bottom stair, she took a last look up at him, turning back, her face steeped to the lips in embarrassment.

The second time they met, at a weekend Hamptons barbecue, she spilled beer on herself, a Rorschach splotch from her breastline to her waist. She spent the next hour pinching her summer dress in an upside-down *okay* sign to keep the dampness from her stomach.

Somebody had a boom box on the sand; they danced to "Signed, Sealed, Delivered," to the Jackson 5's "I Want You Back," songs that couldn't help but put you in a good mood. There was a slow, thick chilly wind off the ocean. Josh was groomed with careful carelessness that was sexy and charming and he told her how pretty she was. They spent the entire night together. Dori felt they were spotlighted on the stage of their peer group. They had sex for the first time. She had kept on her white socks. The music playing had been a flat tire of a song that found popularity because its video starred a chunky preteen dancing like an idiot in a bee outfit.

They were married two years later, to the week.

Later, when he'd think back on their courtship, Josh remembered the kiss but forgot the strangeness of her behavior afterward; this flattered every husband's secret idea that his wife, a tender robot, had lived her youth pulsing only toward him.

"I CAN'T BELIEVE nobody got my Michael Hutchence joke," Dori said when she got home from her day with her girlfriends. "That guy from INXS who died from jacking off with a rope around his neck? No, let's just hang out, me, you, and Zack, from now on. I don't need anybody else, just my husband and my son."

"Listen," Josh said. He was holding the baby. "I wish *you* had taken him today."

She laid her pocketbook down on the dinner table. When she faced Josh, a new crease between her brows showed annoyance.

"Fine," she said, with muted peevishness.

"It's just that I work during the week," Josh said, trying politely to explain what he was feeling. But how? What he could just about put into words was his new sense that the trajectory of a happy marriage was delicate—that with the slightest addition of cargo, the whole thing came down in an unfamiliar, unpleasant airport?

"This was going to be like, my day with my boys, is all," he said. "And I ended up sitting for three crying babies the whole time."

He did speak calmly, with a friendly-sounding resolve, as if dealing with buyers: Josh came across as likably candid.

"I know I should have said something before today." He even gave his son a kiss by his ear before going on. "I am sorry about *that*."

Realizing she was being sales-pitched, Dori gave a sigh. On its last syllable, the sigh inflated out into a chuckle. Josh decided to say nothing and let her laugh stand alone, a victory for him. Besides, he did feel vindicated—last night during *Seinfeld* she had told him what a wonderful helper he'd been lately. So, he felt, he could ease up a bit. Zack'd had his hospital thing months ago. But now the kid was doing great, no residual effects, and *she*'d been the one to say it was just a hiccup. How long do you have to think about hiccups after they're gone?

"Hold it a second, honey," he said now, in a tone that blew out any smoldering traces of argument. "Did I really just hear you say 'jacking off'?"

He kept teasing her gently, and she laughed her high-pitched laugh, less conflicted about it this time. She said just, "Mr. Goldin"— unable, it seemed, not to admire his easygoing liveliness.

He laughed, too. Simple as that, he'd leaned into the rudder and the airplane was back on course.

6

Earlier that afternoon, on their way home from Central Park, Josh and Zack had found the Midtown Tunnel closed (Sikhs in a flower-shop van, false terror scare), and so they'd driven down Bowery, through what had become a serious rain, to the Williamsburg Bridge—past Starline Motel, which was the flophouse where Dr. Stokes's father now lived.

When Josh passed the Starline, Intelligent Muhammad wasn't in his $6.50-a-night cubicle, which had a cot, no phone, a locker, and chicken wire filling the space where the walls didn't reach to the ceiling. It might have been half a foot narrower but the flop was exactly as long as his prison cell.

Intelligent Muhammad was using the pay phone in the vestibule. As he spoke, he stared at the cashier's bulletproof partition, the wall marked with slashes and carved names. Two men he didn't know sat on the plastic chairs next to him. They didn't appear to be together.

Intelligent Muhammad was on the line with Alice Davis, the mother of his daughter.

"I don't even know why you bother," Alice said. She was addressing a conundrum: how, after all the years in which they hadn't spoken, Intelligent Muhammad now called her frequently.

"I was going to say 'like clockwork,' but it's not," she said. "Or, it's like a convict's clockwork, because it can't tell time. And now it's time to change my number."

"All right. One," Intelligent Muhammad said, "I'm a new man. A convict's in *jail,* you understand? He*llo*—in no instance am I in no jail, okay?" He nodded agreement with himself. "Two, I'm just looking to get a little information." His column of quarters waited on the phone box's metal shoulder.

"It's a convict's clockwork," she said, "and now I'm going to hang up with you."

A middle-aged guy with a limp came into the flophouse from the rain: a thin hobbling dude among bigger dudes in this bear pit for humans. Nobody knew him. An anonymous soaking figure, clearly not as imposing as most of the others, but unknown—and therefore a man to be wary of.

Intelligent Muhammad noted the guy's creeping walk, and then he went on with his phone conversation:

"You can read about it. And when you call me and go, 'I been wrong this whole time,' I'm a laugh and say like 'Hello, I told you already.' It was two men who came with this gun and I'm telling you I saved some white man from them. Me saving some white man, right?—trip."

"Yes, that's what you keep saying to me. But I haven't seen anything."

"They holding the story—that's what they told me. But for real, I'm a hero." He laughed. "Not for nothing, but this going to be in Time magazine, The New York Times, some shit, I don't know."

"Charles, that's well and good," she said. (Intelligent Muhammad had never told her he'd changed his name from Charles Stokes.) "But now I'm going to—"

"Oh-ho, listen to you, 'well and good,'" he said. "I know you, talking like that."

"You don't know me," she said firmly.

"I know you." He had wanted to be polite. But manners were a struggle the way foreign languages could be at the beginning.

"You wouldn't recognize me, okay?" she said. Her tone cooled. "I'm fat as a house."

"All right. For real, though, I just want some information." He was trying to back away from his earlier rudeness and so missed the near-flirting in her voice. "Darlene don't live in California, Alice, 'cause I checked."

"I'm telling you, she does," Alice lied. "Yes, she does. In California."

"Talking 'bout, how you going to keep a man from his own daughter?"

Intelligent Muhammad realized her answer was too long in coming—he found himself listening to the void that was hesitancy—and this brought his hopes flickering up.

"I'm—not keeping you from her," Alice said, speaking fast now. "I'm not. I told you she lives in Marin County and I haven't talked to her in years myself. Like I told you."

"*What?*" he said. " 'Cause, hold up. You said Mill Valley." He cleared his throat. "Now, this some bullshit now."

"Mill Valley," she said, "*is* in Marin County"—with not-quite-persuasive condescension. She might not have had the truth on her side, but she knew things he didn't. She'd been working that angle.

"I told you it was near Mill Valley, Charles. Try calling information again."

And then she spoke kindly. "I am not keeping you from anyone, okay? I don't talk with her myself. You're welcome to look her up and find her." Alice got caught up in the sadness of her own lie and her voice wobbled: "I wish I did talk with her."

Intelligent Muhammad had looked down at his own gibbous belly; he, too, was fat.

He thought maybe he could reason with Alice. "In that accordance," he said with a thoughtful lift of the chin, "maybe we could like work together."

But the phone made that sound like when your ears pop; time to give more money. And the receiver smelled like ramen noodles. Should he put in more quarters? No—once that recorded white lady's voice cut in, he let the connection go out. His hope went.

Fastidiously, he scooped his remaining change into his hand. The quarters rasping against the phone box made a noise like a knife being sharpened.

Information to California would be a shitload of quarters.

"That's all right for Intel, though," he said to himself—this being his frequent, stoic pep talk lately.

The man in the plastic chair nearest him said, "About time you got off." The guy was fortyish Asian, and had a very sparse chin beard that looked like iron filings stuck there by magnetism. He didn't get up to use the phone—he just stared at Muhammad in angry gunfighter concentration.

Muhammad felt sad, and thought, *My life is a circle of abuse*. But what would life have been if he'd kept in touch with his daughter, who was a doctor? As is, she probably never even gave her father any mind.

She will, he thought.

7

Josh celebrated Tuesday morning via one of the offhand wonders of marriage: some nearly inadvertent prebreakfast action.

At seven, the baby was still asleep. Josh and Dori woke up together; or more exactly, together they just about woke up—eyelids opening leisurely, face corresponding to face on the pillow, chin and nose in their jigsaw fit.

Josh finger-traced the soft uphill curving of Dori's hip and next his hand found—went to—the pang-inducing fullness behind it. Just before she moved, Josh anticipated the motion, and greeted it with a matched turn of his own body: husband and wife in momentary concurrence. And then came the kissing you get in marriage, light jokey nuzzling, the kneecaps and hipbones of affection. It happened to be perfect as long as you kept your nose from the bummer of waking breath.

After, in the white snowdrift of duvet and sheets, he asked whether what he heard was her stomach grumbling, or his. (His, probably.) Next came her customary question—*What time did we go to bed last night?* She liked to count how near she'd gotten to eight hours, her benchmark for acceptable sleep.

Dori hugged him almost painfully tight now. "Do you feel showered with love, Mr. Goldin?" And when he laughed and tried to squirm out of her arms ("C'mon, honey"), she crept jumbling up against him. "Need some space?"

It was one of Dori's pet routines—overdone affection in the morning was her deal; but when she squeezed him, it always felt better than Josh let on. She never let go first, never. When he'd reverse the game, bear-hugging her and asking, "Need space?"—she'd say, "You think I'll say yes, but I don't get tired of affection."

"Hey, did you just let out some gas?" she said now, still hugging. "Did I squeeze it out of you?"

"No, but I might invoke the Whoever Smelt It Rule." (After childbirth, you can joke about anything.)

"Would you let out gas just to get away from me right now?" she said. "No, I bet you would. Tough shit, buster."

At the breakfast table Dori gentled Zack into his chair. She then tilted her head and—in a playful articulation of her love—put her hands over her eyes like the see-nothing monkey.

"Where are you, Zack?" she said. "I can't find you."

"Oh, listen," Josh said after breakfast. "I'm not going to be home tonight."

He thought this needed no clarification; today began the Upfronts, the first weather of the $18.8 billion network season. It was the unlikely moment when the big shining world of news coverage, pyrotechnics, and celebrities landed on the head of the Ad Sales pin.

"What?" She jerked her head—the movement was sharp. A spouse's anger can be like a gopher that pops up in surprising places. *"Tonight?"*

Josh said, "Didn't I tell you?"

"No," she said, blinking. "No, you didn't tell me." Her hair was still bed-straggled, which added to the ferocity.

"I'm pretty sure I did," said Josh, who stayed downright calm. "It's the Upfronts. The occasion that puts food on our table."

Because the thing now was to avoid the pull of her gravity. Arguments can tug you away from your private trajectory; they could could suck you in.

"Sparkplug's installing us all in hotel rooms," Josh said. "Probably till Friday." He and Dori were standing near the door, fairly close. The baby was alone, down the hall, in a playpen. Dori wasn't saying anything.

"At the W hotel," Josh added, as if that might help.

"All week?" Dori said finally. Her mouth was having trouble. "Because I mean—when were you going to *tell* me?"

He walked a little to the door, and she said clearly and evenly: "Goddamn it."

"Take it easy." Josh raised his chin automatically. "It's important, A). And B), I told you."

He took a step even closer to her. "What's the big deal?" He was pretty sure he'd told her.

For a second her face showed only the gorgeous flush of anger. Josh wanted to flick aside the curl that had strayed across her brow. Sometimes one such kindhearted gesture can end the trouble—like when that comic book woman in the X-Men raises her hands and calms the winds and furious tides.

This argument kept on, though. Her storm front followed predictable weather patterns: Didn't Josh know how much harder this made everything? And he had *not* told her about this before now. Also: He knew she hated it when he asked her to "take it easy."

"You *know* how I feel about you saying that to me," she said.

"Well," he said. (Had he known she hated that? He couldn't remember if he had.)

The baby started acting up in the other room—not a cry so much as an irritated *ahem*, a sort of: *Uh, hello, where are you guys?*

"God*damn* it," said Dori.

The way she stood there in her bathrobe, fist settled on the curve of her hip, the charm of the one naked kneecap peeking out—Josh found Angry Dori cute, and for that reason hard to take seriously.

It was only these last few years that she'd even allowed him to know when she was mad at him. Watching her flop through her own feelings, flailing around but making no move toward the deep end of her anger, of her own argument, had sometimes driven him crazy. Every so often Josh had said, "Just tell me you're mad at me if you are. Just because you love someone doesn't mean you can't get angry at them." Now, of course, he was regretting that advice.

He had been slacking lately, she began telling him. Letting her handle Zack's dinner alone the last three nights, for example. And

he'd been going out all the time, meeting friends without Dori, staying late—and not always for work. Sometimes just meeting Nathan
and Todd for beers in the city. That, buster, wasn't going to cut it
anymore: She needed him to help out, the way he had been doing—
or, had for a little while, at least—after Zack's hospital thing.

"Listen, Dori, I have to go to work now," he said. "You know,
work? Like, the thing that we live off of?"—matching her anger
not in kind but in dejection, because he didn't have the minutes or
the will to explain things to her: It was weird how things went so
great when people just let stuff fall into place, but so badly when everybody got caught up in their own crap and forgot about how easy
it was just to go on being happy, Josh thought.

"Hey," he said. "Zack is—don't you hear that crying?"

"You know, I *knew* it," she said. Her chuckle was suddenly listless. "I knew you weren't going to stay changed."

Her furious face went; she puffed out her lips like a sad child. "I
wasn't happy before, Josh. Okay? For a long time I wasn't."

Her gaze skidded away from his. "But then you got better."

"Whoa, wait a second—" His understanding of what she'd
said teetered, a drunkard feeling a wind on a tightrope. "Say that
again?"

And then the full meaning and message of her words registered;
they struck him as a jokelike impossibility.

"You—not happy?" He laughed. "Come on."

"But then you helped out, Mr. Goldin, you did, you were wonderful with him," she said. "We were a team."

Yes, but that was the thing—she was even admitting it! He
had helped. He'd changed his ways. So, that was settled, and the
baby was better now, and Josh hadn't had to think about it or talk
to Martin Seidel again or anything; and he had important things to
do today, for Christ's sake.

"You're bringing this up now? On Upfront Day? Listen, we'll
discuss this later," he said. Josh didn't wear a watch but he lifted his
wrist and made a show of lowering his eyes toward it.

Not __happy__? he was thinking. *Bullshit. A hard bargaining strategy she's using.*

The baby screech was still going in the other room.

"I *did* help," he said.

"I want you home tonight." Dori's eyes seemed a lighter blue, as if a curtain in the back of her head had gotten thrown open. "Please."

The surprising force of her desperation made Josh feel weird, as if he'd walked in on her doing something embarrassing.

"Honey, c'mon. I'll be back soon."

He spoke softly, lovingly, reaching for her hand; she let him take it.

"Remember," he said, "when we were supposed to go to Vermont that time, but then . . ." He understood, as he found himself unwrapping this familiar old story, that it was just so he could be the one talking instead of her.

Once he left, once the door had closed, Dori stood motionless and spacey, as if scrutinizing the knob. Then she went to Zack.

By EIGHT-FORTY-FIVE THIS prematurely wintry New York morning, rows of trucks pulled up single file to the Javits Center, disgorging four five-hundred-foot-wide plasma monitors, three thousand Fiji water bottles, forty-five microphones, seventeen digital sound processing PA systems, one thousand seven hundred prepackaged spicy tuna rolls, eighteen confetti cannons, sixteen laser light projectors, almost a ton of dry ice, everything from the big and showy (fireworks, party buses, even paid extras) to the small but reliable (cheese and crackers, those humble conjoined twins of the American party)—whatever might help Sparkplug TV to show a little leg. The Upfront presentations, the planned seduction of advertisers, were absolute extravaganzas—featuring name celebs and production values that exceeded all but the most ornate festival concerts—and almost no one outside the industry knew about them.

Josh made his way into the Javits Center—a pinned dirigible of overarching steel lattice with a black glass ceiling, some *Star Trek* set designer's twenty-fourth century take on Gare du Nord—and he smiled again: *Dori, not happy? Bullshit.* Because who had been as happy as they were before the Incident? Next time he saw her, she'd be goofy and laughing again, guaranteed.

He couldn't concentrate on this long; what you noticed first was just how crammed it was here, in the great hall, everyone waiting merely to enter the main showroom. Confusing overload seemed the desired effect. Under the faintly air-conditioned air, a great crowd of hired dayworkers were shoving iPods in your face, which played too many varied images on which to concentrate, all of it moving super-fast; young costumed people yelled slogans at you ("Feed the Need!" "Experience digitainment!"); loud violent guitar music came from every angle, from scores of hidden speakers; human video games (guys with functioning game screens on their heads) flitted through the mob asking you to play their "joysticks"; a rushing tide of diversion and food and beverages and gift bag carriers squeezed past, with video monitors for shirts, or music emanating from their belt buckles, the owners of the future. Even the promotional videos that played on the walls—the preshow show—had sponsors: Apple, Nintendo, just ads for ads, made by ad people to sell to other ad people. The room was wide as Grand Central Terminal, it was immense, and it shook and strobe-lighted and seemed to rumble beyond the limit of human sensory capabilities.

Then the same words flashed and disappeared on every wall, only to be whispered from hidden speakers, as if into your ears: "We create, they consume, you connect."

Hard as it was to imagine, it got even more crowded, as the party buses were emptied of their passengers; these had been sent out by Sparkplug carrying booze, videos, etc., to fetch the biggest buyers. The room was swarming: a press of twenty-six- to forty-year-olds, clustered as thick as rush-hour commuters. (The auditorium that people would soon enter was now empty; bouncers had been hired to build up anticipation before letting everyone in.)

There was a multitude of voices; Josh picked a few sentences out of the general noise, as if they were fruit.

"Who wants to be on the party bus? It sounds like a fun job, but that's why they give it to assistants since it's not a fun job, keeping a hundred drunk people in line. . . . "

"*Everyone's* here. It's amazing. *Every*one . . ."

". . . and they were like, are you serious, and I was like, 'Yeah, the client is right fucking here so shut up.'"

And then that whispered effect from all the speakers, the sexiest woman's voice in the world right there inside your ears: *"We create, they consume, you connect."* And a second later: *"Feed the need."*

"*There* he is—my man," said Denny Lembeck, the first important person Josh saw here. Tall, robotic Lembeck, with his straight, aerodynamic nose and those keyhole nostrils—Josh's "in" at McDonald's—came walking right up to him.

"What up, my friend?" Josh said, fake-punching Lembeck, just enough to elicit a flinch and the business advantage of a little resultant shyness. Wrong-footing someone in a friendly way was an old sales trick.

"So," Josh said. "Been a long time."

"Been a long time since we rock-and-rolled," Lembeck said, and Josh worked not to wince at the lameness of the reference.

"Wait," Lembeck said. "Didn't something happen to your kid, I just heard?"

"Yeah," Josh said. "Was nothing, though."

"Wow. Sorry. I don't know how you get your mind around something like that. Jesus, it's hot in here. Sorry, brother. But tell me, so how'd you guys land Jon Stewart reruns?"

"It was nothing to do with me, let me tell you," Josh said. "But I'm glad we did."

"This Upfront looks cool, I have to admit it. But CBS had the the Who not only playing, but sticking around after to take pictures with buyers. That's a show of respect."

"It *is* hot in here," Josh admitted. "But let me ask you this. How many of the Who are there left alive?"

"Still, though. You have to admit," Lembeck said.

Forget Dori's bullshit, Josh was telling himself now. And so he forgot it. This was his big day, the most fun time of the year. Did Michael Jordan ever not get himself up for the play-offs? Time for the Josh Touch. Besides, forgetting was the membership fee you paid to remain in the happy marriage club.

"Anyway, what'd you expect?" he was asking Lembeck, smiling. "Why *wouldn't* we land Stewart?"

One of the huge banners overhead made Josh's case for him: a picture of Jon Stewart giving a raised-eyebrow look that mocked the unconvincing smart-yet-sexy demeanor of newscasters—and yet Stewart's look *was* sexyish and smart, which was one of the secrets to that show. The banner had a caption: "Yesterday's News: *The Daily Show* reruns, now on *Sparkplug*." Another banner had lifted itself higher than the rest—a picture of a blond man holding a lighted sword, carrying the slogan "Sparkplug Sales Force takes on Darth Murdoch and the Evil Empire." (Fox was launching a competitor to *Sparkplug*, called the Optimum Channel.)

People moved toward the auditorium, the doors of which had opened. Josh felt, in the swaying squeeze, as if he were walking through the whirling brushes of a car wash.

And back in Glenwood Landing, Long Island, Dori was just now carrying Zack upstairs to the bedroom that she and Josh shared. "Such a good baby," she was saying.

She'd calmed; she was carrying Zack at her shoulder. As a goof, she exaggerated the motion of each climbed step—bouncing the baby a little, very gently, and he laughed. Such a good baby.

"Ma ma ma," he said.

"Yes, you are," she said. "A good baby." Dori stopped and, with two hands under Zack's arms, held him out from her, so she could look in his face. "A good boy." She rabbit-twitched her nose and slanted her head for comic effect; Zack laughed again.

"Such a cute face," she said, and kept walking to the bedroom.

An hour and a half ago, right after Josh had left, she'd been carrying Zack much as she was now, one-handed, while she'd reached to get some formula out of the fridge. But she'd dropped the bottle, the top had come off, and the formula spilled all over the floor.

"Goddamn it!" she'd yelled. "What else can go wrong?" Because other things had happened, too. Three days ago the cable had gone out. And so she'd had to call, just to be put on hold for seventy-five minutes—and then she wasted all of yesterday (or twelve to six, anyway) waiting for the cable guy to show. Plus, the week before, their dishwasher had broken, soap foamed out the sides, all the dishes then needed hand-washing, and the same thing had happened—an hour on hold with a corporate "service center"—not to mention that after all that, the repairman didn't even come on the day he was supposed to. Which meant two days gone. Gone from what? What else did she have to do, anyway?

She knew these weren't major emergencies; they were day-to-day. But she did need help, at least sometimes, and Josh had stopped being a help lately—hadn't shared the load. Men never let you feel all their love, she thought. They give you a little, but not the whole thing; they can't show you their cards, she thought, not like we can.

When the dishwasher had finally been fixed, Josh—on one of his silverware clearing nights—had said, "What's the point of having one of these things if you've got to rinse the plates before you put 'em in?" He wasn't angry-sounding, not affable Josh, but he squinted, as if confused by the unfairness of it all, his one chore of the day.

"You just have to," Dori said. Men could drive you crazy. It's like they expect that, if you clean a dish once, it should remain clean forever.

Then, about two days later, apropos of nothing, he'd said, "So it saves like ten percent of the work, dishwashers." As if he'd been thinking about it that whole time, how his one chore was a burden.

"Well, you don't have to scrub the dishes by hand, Josh. Doesn't that count for something?"

"*Then* you have to unload it," he'd said.

Again, there had been no annoyance in his voice as he'd said this—but he'd spoken with the jovial, concluding tone of a man acting graciously after having been proven right. This was her life, with its chores and days.

And the funny thing was that she had long looked forward to this, to quitting her job, to being a stay-at-home. But lately it seemed even harder than working—not really *harder,* but just as hard, and without the same rewards. It hadn't been easy to hide her boredom lately. She'd been sure Josh would notice—which made her laugh now, because didn't she know her husband after all these years? What did he *ever* notice?

She took no satisfaction from housework—who does? Sometimes Josh would try to include her in his daytime life, telling her about work fun he'd had. But his office hours were full of laughs that, like shadows, disappeared whenever he shined a light on them. So that was no fun for her, either.

Not that she didn't love being with Zack. And you get adapted to the baby's routines, to the crying, as if it's part of evolution or something; it's like your eardrums eventually build a coating to guard against the wails, the occasional shrillness. It wasn't that she wanted to go back to a real job, either. She was thirty-three. She could maybe get blood-drawing work again; she was an excellent phlebotomist. But she hated hospitals, all those sickies, and doctors were no great shakes, themselves. Sometimes in her most lucid moments she thought of her life as being like some dried-up thing; she remembered seeing a desiccated riverbed out the window, the summer of her family's move from the Catskills to Long Island. It was a weird image to focus on now regarding herself. But sometimes she felt like that riverbed: Whatever rush of life had sustained her before didn't even have time to pool now, before her family arrived to drink it all up.

Plus, she'd gotten a scratch on her car last week.

The Goldins had two cars, and so she wouldn't have thought

it such a big deal—*if* she were bringing in her own salary. But she wasn't. And so she never told Josh. Such a stupid thing. She'd been going to the pharmacy to pick up some Aleve and toilet paper, the kind of stuff that Josh always forgets, and the parking lot in the back was crowded. One car was parked in a nonspot, with its ass sticking out, and maybe Dori had taken the turn too quickly—but she really didn't think that was the case. No, it was just that the other car, a little Honda Civic, had parked so badly.

Anyway, she dinged the passenger door of her own car. An Acura MDX was so much taller than the Honda, she felt the accident was like a bully beating on a skinnier kid. Not that the other car hadn't been in the wrong. And in her confusion after the first scratch—the baby was in the backseat, asleep, thank God, plus Dori got nervous driving, anyway—she pressed the gas too hard and scratched the rear wheel bay (or whatever) of the other car. It was raining and there were no witnesses. And so she drove off. She felt terrible about this, it was wrong, she knew that. Because she could have left a note, or even gone into the store—but that would have meant unstrapping the baby from his heavy car seat, which takes minutes, and in the rain. No, if she had met the other owner, she eventually would have had to tell Josh about the accident, too. And he . . . would have been fine with it! That was the funny thing. He would probably have been great. But it would have been another expense and she didn't earn a salary. They were doing well money-wise, so why—she thought—why do I care?

About a quarter mile from the pharmacy she'd pulled over to check on the baby, and he was fine. But Dori's neck kind of hurt now, already, which she knew was stupid, since it wasn't a whiplash kind of collision. Ha, ha, Dori the hypochondriac, she thought. But her neck still hurt, days later. Anyway, she didn't ever take the car out of the garage when Josh was home anymore. Such a stupid thing—a six-inch red line across the side of a car. Why not tell him right away? And now it worried her so much she had been taking Ambien in order to sleep at night.

"Here we go, Zackie." She put her son down on her own bed. The baby puffed up into a blowfish face and then blew out, "Pfffff," and laughed.

Inside the Javitz Center, an unseen announcer directed people to make their way to the auditorium; the Upfront was about to begin.

"Not exactly Don Pardo," someone said dismissively.

Alyssa from the office stood a few yards ahead of Josh in the push into the auditorium, and she was trying to catch his eye. She kept wrongly thinking that he noticed her, and with each misreading of his attention, Alyssa bobbed her head, with a hello smile, as if she were trying to gulp down a large pill without water.

When he did see Alyssa, couldn't she see that he was with a buyer? If personality is in fact a series of *un*successful gestures, at least for the non-Gatsbys among us, then there was something nauseating about Alyssa. Still, Josh winked at her.

"Stewart's show is good, Josh," Denny Lembeck was saying, flexing his brow the way people do when they want a repeated observation to seem an original thought. "But it's called a *daily* show by definition, Josh—will people care about obsolete news?"

"Well," Josh said, licking his lips before going on. He had a memorized speech about this that he chewed off piece by piece, a little at a time. "Do they tune in for the news, or do they tune in for the funny, my friend? Now, y'see . . ."

The rest of his speech contained words like "demand," "enable," and "raise prices." And then, of course, buyers like Lembeck cast doubt on the goods, and that's sales's Kabuki dance.

When they reached Alyssa, who had recently been promoted to assistant, Josh smiled at her and introduced her to Lembeck.

"Hi," she said. "Where do we sit?"

"Well," he said, "first we mingle." Aware of his unattainability, she was happy just that he continued to be friendly with her.

Inside the auditorium, some early '90s Des'ree song about having to be bad, having to be bold, having to be wiser, bubbled out of a crack PA system—music with broad if shallow appeal, and familiar in exactly the same way as a surface friendship. No one was sitting yet, everyone moved from person to person, shaking hands. Even though this was an auditorium, the preshow mingling had been planned, and had a theme: Backyard BBQ. The hall had been naturized for an inside stab at outdoor fun. The lighting was dusky by design and the ceiling salted with baby bulbs to look, in this morning hour, like a sky after sundown.

In a cleared-out area behind the rows of seats, the floor had been overspread with Astroturf. Businesspeople idled between faux barbeque grills that really were just tables offering up either Dean & DeLuca *hors d'oeuvres* (salmon ficelle sandwich bites; puff pastries dappled with sugar; pineapple slivers in a fanned-out spread), drinks in plastic cups (mimosas; wild berry smoothie shooters; plain old orange juice), or gift bags (a *Daily Show* DVD; a framed print by LeRoy Neiman; a gift certificate to Sharper Image). The gift bags themselves read:

> *Electric programming.*
> *Electric audience.*
> *Electric partnerships.*
> **SPARKPLUG**

Women were touching clients' forearms and slipping into that coy but assertive mode that only they have. Men grinned and tilted close, that undertone of aggression certain types of guys bring to every activity. The unacknowledged feeling here was the approximately sexual hubbub.

The center aisle had been gussied up with plastic flowers, a carpet of live moss, and, beside every tenth seat, a real ficus tree; this bridle path ran all the way to the stage. People in ant costumes (this *was* a make-believe BBQ) handed out programs and smiled from inside their dumb outfits, making the best of it.

Josh was glad-handing his way through the party crowd, which included: gray-templed types eating and drinking here, high-fiving

there; a waitstaff that nobody saw except when they wanted something from them; women of no-nonsense makeup and upmarket
blouses; and a surprising number of fidgeters—lame salesmen bad
at simulating calm on this play-off-intense day. But the best sounded
comfortable speaking their short, expository sentences:

". . . Now more than ever, quality is a trademark. . . . We take
pride in the fact that we wrote the book on focusing on quality, each
and every minute of the schedule. . . ."

Again and again, faces that Josh hadn't seen for a while sounded
happy notes in his memory. Here was one Ford buyer whom Josh
recognized mainly because the guy'd famously boned his assistant
in the Pastis men's room during Wine Week: "What's going on,
bro?" And another sort of familiar guy, Bill Handke, was one of
Sparkplug's lineup planners—Josh once gave him Yankees tickets
when a buyer had canceled at the last minute. "What up, brother?"
he said. And some unseen jackass kept making that particular noise
of contrived hedonism, the falsetto whoop.

The piped-in music had given way to live Dixieland. The players all sported the sort of clothing worn by bands at hokey events
and never in real life: spats, gaiters, suspenders, red armbands, bow
ties, straw fedoras. The music was sluggish and muffle-brassy and
seemed to come from underwater.

There were a lot of out-of-towners here. Even among strangers,
Josh could always spot his fellow New Yorkers: suburban or Man-
hattanite, they all shared a vibe—a clever and frank self-interest,
a tacit impatience around the mouth. "Less sophisticated" people
(from smaller places) took some getting used to, he thought. He was
surprised that he was so snooty about it. But Josh found their jokes
not really jokes, as much as references to their own mischievous-
ness or gluttony. "Our bus may not have been the first one here, but
we're closest to the bar ha ha ha"; "The waitress this morning goes,
'You don't want *another* pancake, do you?' And I said, '*Ho,* yeah!'
ha ha ha."

Resisting the party tide, Josh set himself in an unavoidable spot near the mimosa table, his hands pocketed, his smile in place, and made better and better jokes to all those whom the social currents kept delivering right up into his understated friendliness.

"You look like you had a rough morning, my friend," Josh said to a hollow-chested Merck buyer named Chaz. Josh never once peeked over anyone's shoulder to see if a bigger shot was nearby; he just kept practicing the schmoozer's jovial art.

"Breakfast pizza?" a waitress asked him. She presented a tray and wore a little steel nose ring.

"Absolutely, if you'll have one with us," said Josh, getting from the waitress a surprised, coquettish laugh, because when you're on, you're on.

At that moment, in Long Island, Dori was bending down next to her bed, trying to find something she'd hidden under it.

"Just one minute, Zackie," she was saying.

Chilly wind dribbled into the room, testing a seam between the window frame and the wall. Dori had worked up a sweat. She was carrying Zack, and—even though she was wearing her robe—the wind made her feel the perspiration on her back as a long stripe of coldness. She didn't go get a sweatshirt, however, because she didn't want to leave the baby. That was the hardest thing about babies. Not the crying—it was that you couldn't leave them alone to do other things, even for a second. You didn't feel right doing so. You couldn't even go to the bathroom without them. *Goddamn it, Josh,* she thought. (She'd told him about the chill from the window like five times. Now she was probably going to get a cold.) Dori often mentally took her own temperature, or squeezed her throat to see if she could detect swollen glands.

She didn't know why she'd made such an ass of herself with Josh this morning. *That's not the way to do things,* she thought.

She'd been surprising herself lately. One minute she'd be in a great mood, the next, bam, yelling at Josh in her head, or even sometimes out loud—and at Zack, too. She'd never been a screamer until recently. Like when the dishwasher had broken, she'd just *lost* it.

Threw a fork at the thing, and screamed, *"Fuck!"* And Zack had looked at her as if she hadn't known what was what.

"Here it is, Zack," she said now, still kneeling at the side of the bed as she took out a plank of wood that had been outfitted with canvas flaps and Velcro fasteners. This was called a papoose board.

She popped herself up, showing her face above the side of the bed, in a kind of peekaboo game with her baby. Dori's face had a relaxed love-look for this game with Zack, her lips turning up with that voluptuous pleasure you can't fake. She was ecstatic, carried away.

She laid the board down on the mattress, lifted Zack to herself, kissing his cheeks, saying, "Mmmmmm mmmmm mmmmm," and then, gingerly—with her hand behind the back of his head—she placed her son on the papoose board. Then she fastened and strapped in his head and wrists. She looked over to the clock—10:37.

At precisely 10:45, Sparkplug TV was ready to start its official presentation of the new television season. There were a lot of men choking their ties more snugly into their collars—and giving what looked like an early-Beatles head shake as they did so—while the women adjusted their skirts or patted their hair: The sexy thrill of deal making had dissipated; it was time to put personal selling on hold and watch the crazy expensive hullaballoo of *Sparkplug's* promos.

Josh reclined, legs crossed, with the ease and comfort of a man wearing slippers at home. Doug Moscow, the young sales exec, sat near to him.

"Can you believe this shit?" Moscow said, the carefulness of his face making it clear that he couldn't tell whether to make fun of *Sparkplug's* presentation, or to be respectful. "The production values on this are more than on the He-Man Awards." (The televised "He-Man Awards" were Sparkplug's year-end awards show.)

"Well," Josh said. "I can believe it, know why? Without this there'd be no He-Man Awards, no *Sparkplug* at all"—and then he winked at Moscow.

That was Josh's best trick, maneuvering people that way, tempting and winking them into place—bringing the Touch even to all these desperate graspers. Because by ignoring what was lame or nervous in people, Josh could momentarily convince them that they, too, maintained a steady hand on life's steering wheel.

The lights dimmed; the big video started. It ran on six huge-screen monitors positioned behind a massive stage. It showed a blue sky; clouds that began on one screen moved seamlessly through the gauntlet of monitors, as if a perfect spring noon were staring the audience in the face, complete with a faint-breeze sound effect. Slogans passed through this fantasy sky, and the sound of Glenn Close in full angelic mode spoke the phrases as they passed: *You say multiplatform, we say multilicious. Media mashing. Welcome to playtopia. We're multiplatstorming the scene. With megatainment. And a media hive for instant platification. When multitunities knock, we answer. Multiplatforward thinking. It's all about techspotential. Technobbing. We're televisionary at Sparkplug. Let's get down and digital. It's multibadonk badonk.*

When the video was finished, lasers spelled out "Sparkplug" on the ceiling in sizzling red lines. Kate Wilbur, who sat on Moscow's other side, sought out Josh's attention and rolled her eyes.

The voice of Michael Buffer, the famous ring announcer, could be heard saying: "And now, let's get ready to *rummmmble* with the stars of Sparkplug's new, original narrative programming: *It's a Living* and *Celebrity Dogwalker.*"

Next to cross the stage—beside some interchangeable, WASPy actresses who were cast as their TV wives—came a procession of wishful Seinfelds, dark-haired loosely Jewish funnymen mugging frantically, the footlights sinking into their pancake makeup.

"Some of these shows look good," Doug Moscow said cautiously. For an answer, Josh said, *"Huh";* he acted interested in Moscow's insights, and even would feign uncertainty in his own opinions ("Guess you're right about that, Doug")—allowing his subordinate the moments of confidence he needed.

And then, rising via platform from under the floor onto the stage, Jon Stewart himself appeared—while behind him, the Jumbotron screens flashed: *Feed the Need*. Stewart took the microphone and, in the deep voice he used for sarcasm, said:

"Now first of all, uh, I do want to say I'm here just for the money. From you."

This was followed by the sort of grateful, first-joke laughter an audience gives to anyone who's been funny in the past.

At Josh's amiable smile, Moscow relaxed, and knew it was right to laugh along, too.

"So, I misunderstood," Jon Stewart was saying. "I thought you guys were offering me the *Nightline* job. Are you not *ABC*?"

Stewart enjoyed this joke, and to show this he turned from the microphone and covered his own laugh by moving a fist over his mouth, as you'd do after a burp.

"No," he went on, "I love"—and with practiced hesitation, during which he made a performance of looking over at a hanging poster of a WWF star, Stewart delayed saying: "Basic Cable." It was clear he was going to test the limits of a comedian's immunity—the license to insult you to your face.

"Ah, the minor leagues," he said. "Soon I'll be signing up to read the listings on the TV Guide Channel. . . ."

While everyone else was laughing, Josh peered around the room—an unhurried look like a sundial's shadow. How was McDonald's enjoying the monologue? How about GM? Pfizer?

Jon Stewart was a pro, and charming. But as his schtick went on, he started reciting jokes from a script written by the head of Sparkplug's Promotional Department; the monologue became a funny guy doing a reading of a less funny guy's imitation of his act. Most of the laughs came when Stewart went off-book.

"With material like this," he said, "no wonder you have me on after *Hulk Hogan's Beach Party*. Feed the need! That's our theme. Same slogan you see on the stationery for the Cali Cartel. Seriously, TV's extinct, it's going away." This got a nervous silence from the sales half of the crowd; the buyers leaned forward. Stewart was a maverick. Josh, however, realized that the nonconformist bit, mixed in with the sales presentation all around, would give the event an air of "authenticity." By allowing Stewart to tease them like this, Sparkplug looked cool in an uncorporate way, as if proclaiming, *We're in on the joke.*

Stewart said: "They know how to force you to watch commercials, these people. Next, the cast of *Grey's Anatomy* will meet in a bag of Doritos. *The Daily Show* will be available now through a snortable line of some new comic drug. Or delivered through Jell-O shots. They know what the kids want!"

After the booming applause, Stewart was followed by the rapper Ludacris, who was here, it seemed, just to announce and give a chest bump to the CFO.

"I get down to *bizness* on Sparkplug," Ludacris said. "MTV gave up on videos, so these dudes are going to show them what's up. That's why I got onboard with producing *Ol' Skool Videos.* Because sometimes you just need to get up on the roof, and get down to business, if you know what I'm talking about—so get your checkbooks out, it's Harry Rigbert!"

Sparkplug's CFO Rigbert emerged, a tall doughy late-middle-aged guy with Groucho eyebrows, and the small voice of a born, bred, and trained nonperformer.

He said: "Stewart and Ludacris are the only warmup guys I ever use. They can warm up anybody." The joke didn't go over; his dark smudge eyebrows lifted nervously. "So welcome to the Sparkplug Upfront. Our combination fashion week, fashion show, and demolition derby. Jon Stewart was kidding, but in many ways he was not. Kids understand content combined with program. You can't escape it. Now in a host of ways, technology has finally caught up with our content."

Behind him, timed exactly to his remarks, a video began to play, which, Spike Jonze–style, parodied '80s music videos. "Colonize the short attention span. Promos that work as art, commerce, and digital wallpaper. That's what we offer."

State-of-the-art special effects appeared, buildings blown up, laser gun fights, men transforming believably enough into werewolves. "Real-life content. So for us, the proliferation of screens is the liberation we've always dreamed of. Give us a screen, we'll entertain you. That Jon Stewart skit everyone's discussing? That wrestling match between Snake Jarvich and Muscle John Van Hurtskill? It's available to your customers exactly when and how they want it. On their phones, computers, iPods, wherever."

He leaned on a see-through Plexiglas podium that many in the audience hadn't noticed until now. "Look, we're in this together. If we don't work for you, we don't work. We know your customers. They're the ones Googling, blogging, mo:Blogging, IM-ing, iTuning, gaming, podcasting, hypertasking, shoutcasting, and innovating. And, oh yeah, looking for great TV content. We *feed that need*. We are a pure-play content company with a global footprint and a multimedia playbook. And that's what we do, supported by killer consumer research. We lead by listening. Our brands are programmed by our consumers. And that's why our network lineup changes so frequently. We *feed* that need! That's why we offer spankin' new brands, like xFart and VideogameShowz."

All Rigbert's hours of preparation, all the glitter and show, had worked; this fifty-two-year-old man sounded natural using those terms.

"No matter how right we get it," he said, "we never lean back. That dude on our logo, punching out wimps? Today he's kicking butt in 171 territories, and 479 million homes. Find a place with electricity or a Wi-Fi connection, and we're there. My team has an exceptional amount of soul. Just like our viewers and you, our clients. To show our gratitude, we brought a show of soul for you right now. The most downloaded talent in the business is here. Now, let's blow the roof off this mother!" His voice cracked, a man uncomfortable saying "mother" as a modified swear word. "Ladies and gentlemen, Kanye West!"

Different JumboTron screens now appeared on either wing of the stage; a paid audience of young kids, ringers given twenty-five bucks each to cheer, were led sprinting in front of the stage through a side door. And Kanye started into his thing, rapping before almost three thousand businessmen (". . . ain't sayin' girl plays a nigger/but she still make a brother wanna pull his trigger . . .")

When Kanye was done, the ringers were led quietly off and out of the auditorium.

At the same time, miles away from here, Dori had finished putting her son's arm in a splint. She'd used her housework bandana and her purplish silk-cut velvet scarf to tie the splint carefully in place, and—padding it where wood might irritate Zack—she'd placed two washcloths between the splint and the baby's elbow bone.

"Shh," she said, because the baby had started to fuss a bit. "I know," she was saying. "I know, Zackie." God, he was being, for the most part, so good. And she was in frenzied high spirits.

This little person, her son, who had a tiny spit bubble in his mouth now, and made cooing noises, filled every part of Dori's life—every part of it, even though he hadn't even been around until sixteen months ago. This person who couldn't talk or do anything, he was the element that, in all the world, most determined her happiness or her regret—and governed the future she wanted for herself and for her family—because, really, even her relationship to Josh was shaped by this baby. How cute he was, just lying here, smiling even with the restraining strap over his forehead; she thought about how very much she loved him. At moments like this, life felt as if it had returned; the riverbed seemed filled with living water.

Dori went to the medicine cabinet to get the butterfly needle, the alcohol, the dressing, and she closed the door behind her—out of superstition, or silly anxiety that Josh would come home and walk in on her—but she hadn't latched it all the way shut; the door swung open, bit by bit, its creak making a *yaaah* sound like a bothersome baby. This was the most focused, the most engaged she'd felt with the world in months.

"This is really going over!" Moscow was saying into Josh's ear. "Don't you think?"

"Yeah," Josh said, "I mean, it's Kanye West and Jon Stewart, so." He was still peering around. Where the hell was Merck sitting?

A sixty-foot-tall image of a young mother (an actress, really, who was holding a one-year-old baby actor) was talking on the jumbo screens now, saying: "TvSchool: It's how I educate my children."

Pamela Polansky, the pretty blond CEO of Sparkplug, strode onstage, with purpose meant to trump any man's. She followed the image of the mother with:

"They consume. Go after 'em. You heard from Jon Stewart, the funniest man in America; Harry Rigbert, the most rocking CFO in America. And now, you get me. Seriously, it's so great to be here, talking about our ongoing partnerships. We'll get you David Spade up here in a minute, on video feed from L.A. I just want to say: We have partnered together on many fronts for many years. The evolving digital landscape has created even more ways to reach your target audience. Women say the size of your ROI doesn't matter? It matters," she said. "But seriously." And with that, the clouds image came back, she stood as if suspended in mid-sky, accompanied by the most soothing harp and synth string music.

"They are out there. We are helping you go get them."

Is this too calming, this music? Josh wondered. *Will it put people to sleep?*

As soon as he thought that, as if on cue, a little electric guitar—nothing too disruptive, but a tad boisterous—came to join the synth strings.

"To that point, we'd like to show you the results of our recently completed and uniquely insightful study." Superimposed on the clouds were pie charts, numbers, pictures of kids playing video games. "We first looked at engagement, which we looked at as a deep consumer connection to a network's content. Our network is proven to *feed the need*: There is a seamless integration between our on-air and online content. What you want to know is, 'How

effective is my advertising when it's in the context of this brand?'
So we've come up with an important new metric that we're calling
Conveyance. Conveyance speaks to the idea that consumers extend
the positive feelings they have for a network brand to the advertiser.
What do guys really want? They want to be entertained! They want
action! They want action-packed content conveyed through a vari-
ety of platforms. Online at SparkplugTV.com, guys get more action.
Let's take a peek."

The guitars took over now, the screen showed explosions, car
crashes, gunshots.

"We target men like Anna Nicole Smith targeted aging billion-
aires," the CEO said.

The music stopped. It was dramatic, the way her voice was now
unaccompanied, leaving the facts to speak for themselves.

"The most striking and relevant piece of this Conveyance study
in relation to today's multiplatform world is that we found Conveyance to triple and quadruple when Sparkplug-branded entities
crossed multiple screens. As one of our clients said recently, it's all
about connection marketing. And we couldn't agree more. Our audience look to us as the navigator. And our audience is leading us
to new relevant brands, which means more touchpoints for *you* to
reach your consumers."

The music came back, building slowly from silence. "We are in
the sweet spot of relevance, positioned to get your name onto every
screen there is, including mobile devices. Home-page on their television. It's like a new best friend they've known all their lives. One of
our clients joked that it was insidious. Well, we want"—and here her
voice got amplified and reverbed, as an ironic touch—"Total Global
Domination-nation-nation. . . ." There followed some laughter.

She began to speak more naturally, as anyone would, when coming to a stretch of less mumbo-jumbo. "One thing that we're very
excited about is country music, on our new Saturday-night program
I Want to Make You Smile. Love to make them smile. Here to tell you
about it is multiplatinum recording artist Randy Travis. . . ."

"She should have mentioned that cable is still undervalued," Josh whispered, sort of to himself.

THE THING WAS, Dori had bled enough people in her previous life to learn the best way to avoid leaving a mark on a patient's arm. She'd often watched nurses take old people's blood out of the same line that they'd used to feed them their IV fluids.

She took the small, flat pin of the butterfly needle by its two little wings (it actually looked more like a bow tie than anything else). She gave it a tug, to make sure it was attached securely to its flexible, see-through tube.

The butterfly needle was perfect for bleeding little children—it was small, and once you used a bit of tape, it stayed comfortably on the arm. Still, Dori had to be extra careful now: Though a butterfly needle didn't leave a mark, it was sort of blunt and could produce an agonizing jab. That was what the splint was for—to steady the baby against the cut.

Zack's arm was pale and meaty. That fold in front of the elbow— where doctors place a stethoscope to measure your blood pressure— offers the safest vein access; a phlebotomist usually takes blood from any palpable channel there (the vasilica vein, the cephalic vein, or the median cubital vein). When Dori dabbed his arm with alcohol and then inserted the needle, gently, expertly, with love, Zack blinked at her, scrunched his face, and let out a sucking-in-breath whimper—but he didn't cry. She loved him for that.

This wasn't done as a test of her husband's love. Most of the time she and Josh were together, it was all loving looks between them— both were smiling, or winking at each other. Or that *had* been the deal, until lately. Why did Josh make her so angry? Okay, she knew why—but *so* angry? Even after the Incident, even when he was good, he could never learn the basics of her, he never quite figured out how to clean or cook things exactly as she liked, the small niceties that are nothing but really everything to a woman. Of course, she needed to be better at telling him when she was pissed—she knew that. *Maybe in telling it*, she thought, *it'll be less intense the way I feel it*. But confrontation was hard for Dori. That's why standing up to the doctors had been good for her. Still, she probably should go into therapy—it couldn't hurt, she thought. But bringing it up to Josh would be so embarrassing. And how to go in secret, when he controls the money? This morning had been bad. Bad because she'd made a scene. And she knew how he hated anything that would slow his day down, or affect his glide. There were smarter, subtler ways to make her feelings known.

"Shh, that's good, Zack," Dori was saying.

One key factor—besides keeping the baby's arm steady—was that she needed to obstruct the vein proximal to the puncture location. And once blood could be seen to spill slowly back through the tubing, that would be indication that the needle had hit the bull's-eye.

Well, if doing all this wasn't a test of her husband's love—or even a sort of totaling up of debts—it would bring more of his love out into the open. Because if a woman never feels the full power of all a man's affection all at once, there are ways to increase how he rations it out. When a man goes face-to-face with what he thinks is frightening, his love will show itself—maybe only fully then. And in unadulterated form, too—because all the other parts of day-to-day life are cut out of it.

Zack still wasn't crying, the darling; his lips were slightly chapped and pouty and Dori felt full inside with affection.

It killed her that she wasn't always totally herself with Josh, that some of her always hesitated, watching how he accepted her. She thought marriage meant she was supposed to share all of herself. Because sometimes, she thought, there *was* a real sort of combination between people, like a joining, but other times you progress like a net, with a million little separations. Still, when you're going well, you say the right thing at the right time. At other moments you don't think of what to say until it's too late and you don't connect up. (This morning, for example.) All the same, how could a person share all the thoughts, all the weird impulses, all the *stuff*—some of it not even there for more than a second—inside her head? How can you open the all of who you are to someone else? Dori never asked herself why someone would want to. Or why anyone would think they were supposed to. It didn't matter, anyway; you just couldn't. It wasn't possible.

But there are some things you can do, Dori thought.

"Here we go, Zack," she said, as the inside of his bleeding tube slicked red with the run of his blood.

Dori felt hopeful and even kind of a new person. It was hard to put into words. That had been the thrill after the last time, too; a sort of rock-and-rollish feeling, a *fuck you, world!*—seeing herself as someone wilder and more rebellious than she had ever been. If she and Josh didn't have to be a hundred percent *one,* a hundred percent together, blah blah blah, then she needed to become something on her own. One problem was that she believed her husband was more a part of *her* than she was a part of *him*, if that made any sense. And that hurt; why couldn't the current run the other way, at least sometimes?

"Shh. Shhh. Good boy, Zack."

But she felt Josh haunting her suddenly, looking her over—as if he were finding her eyes and shaking his handsome head. Even now, she felt herself go under the spell of his charisma. Maybe this whole thing was stupid—

She tried to swallow down the fear that's prelude to all ratio-nalization. She didn't want to rationalize this True Thing, this Pure Act, away. But, shit, Zack *did* look a little uncomfortable now, with his head and arms strapped to the papoose board. He was frowning. Was it worth it? Dori had so much compassion for this tiny thing, her son, paler now but still cuddly. She knuckle-rubbed his cheek and warded off her doubt with intense, blinking eyes.

Because so many people that Dori knew did exactly what they wanted to do—they had affairs, say—without any consequence; she certainly wasn't going to do anything awful like *that*. Haven't you ever had to do something another might consider bad in order to do something good? she asked Josh in her head.

Here's the thing: She wasn't trying simply to rekindle the romance with Josh; they didn't need that. She was moving them to a deeper place, a more (for lack of a better word) spiritual understanding, she thought. Like *closure*, kind of, but without having to end anything. It felt as if she were being guided by some unseen hand to this. Was she proud of it? Well, yes. This was motherhood. And if she was careful and gentle and made sure nothing could go wrong (which she really *could* make sure), then it was necessary. Because wasn't it beneficial for the baby to be in a happy home?

She couldn't allow regret into the guiltless hum of her mind. Sometimes bad things are bound up in good things. Just as Zack was surrendering to her, Dori felt as if she were surrendering herself to something larger, her marriage. She was so innocent herself. She whispered her hand across her son's cheek with such great tenderness, she wanted to cry because she felt so filled with motherly love she didn't know what to do with herself.

"Sweet baby," she said. This was a good, safe thing.

I'm very safe in the way I do this.

She kissed her baby boy, over and over, as gently and compassionately as any mother ever had kissed a child. She would have to remember to hide the papoose board and the butterfly needles close by, in case she needed to do it again.

AT TWO-THIRTY THAT afternoon, just as the Upfront wound down and the crowd headed to the after party at Giles's Club and the coziest part of this whole C+ profession—steak lunches, midday partying, everyone tiptoeing to the threshold of a deal—Josh got the call from Dori. It should have been a great time for him (who'd always made better grades than C+, by the way).

An Upfront paralleled, in truncated form, the familiar rhythm of a salesperson's day: It replaced meetings with meetings-plus-

Ludacris. And afterward, as after any business meeting, there were drinks and food.

Giles's Club was a large dance space with a bar and music; a supernova chandelier impended over everything; the club had the ambiance of a cruise ship's dining hall, but with the dials turned louder. And Josh had begun to feel the sense he occasionally had of being like a pool shark about to run a table. Josh knew he was starting into the Touch. He felt it coming in the middle of the COO's closing speech. On the way out the auditorium, he'd bumped into the OfficeMax buyer, had forgotten her name—never a good move for a salesman; any deal with her slipped off his line like a wet fish—but it didn't matter. He'd felt the Touch coming and it would make big sales for him today.

Now, in front of an ice-sculpture swan at Giles's, Josh chatted with Marc Silverman, the philosophical and newly married Toyota buyer. Silverman had a perfect yarmulke of baldness at the crown of his head.

Each atom of Josh's concentration stood on guard; it was like when the hustler from Josh's favorite old movie felt himself part of the pool table and the stick and even the cue ball, and his shots came so smoothly that his arm appeared to slide along a track. He absorbed the countless expediencies of the room and knew exactly how to play each turn, exactly which balls to hit and how they would land in their pockets.

"Falling in love late in life is like dealing with Paul McCartney," Silverman was saying. "You make fun of him quite sincerely, you express disappointment with his recent work—but when you meet him you're still in awe." The man spoke merely to have something to say. And he laughed at his own jokes with his mouth open like a panting dog's. Josh almost expected the guy to have a floppy prosciutto kind of canine tongue.

So Silverman was tough; no one liked talking with him and dislike is the one thing a salesman can't let you see. But Josh knew when to shut up, when to retire into the background, when to strike.

Marc Silverman was a bloodshot drinker who showed tiny beet-root tendrils in the whites of his eyes. After his third glass of wine—*that's* when he was most vulnerable to a big buy. "How many spots do you want on Stewart, tell me," Josh said, taking from Silverman his glass of Cabernet Sauvignon—the magic third—and visualizing a ten ball rolling across green felt into the heart of the corner pocket.

Other salesmen talked around them in entertainment-sapped voices:

"Let's get out of here."

"Yeah, I've had enough."

"I hate getting old."

"What's the alternative?"

But Josh was born restless. He felt as if he lacked not just the desire but any aptitude for taking it easy.

Next, he was bullshitting someone he'd just met: State Farm's Brittney Newman, flown in from St. Louis, winking and talkative, who leaned into Josh as if she were an aunt of his, as if they shared memories and private jokes and partialities. They were deep into a conversation. "I live for massage therapy," she said. "I stay alive for my masseuse."

He saw that he would have to flirt with this much older woman, but in an innocent way, with no hint of carnality. He didn't know what her weakness—what her third taste of Cabernet—was. But feeling her out, being naughty with her in a perfectly unnaughty way ("Not foot massage, I hope. Because you know where that can lead: ankle massage"), he was backspinning balls in, playing lunatic angles ("Let me lay a crazy idea on you; rather than spread your money around—what do you do, ten million on cable alone?—to various networks, let us make an all-or-nothing proposal to win the full extent of your cable business"). He leaned over the bar, where a draft-beer pull was sneezing up glasses of Heineken. Sales is a beautiful, precise game when it's played well. Brittney ("Britt") Newman twirled the ends of her brown hair.

And then Josh got the call from Dori. He and Britt had been watching the A-Team's Mr. T, who had his arms around two sales-girls; a circle of people crowded around this spectacle, three deep, laughing and taking pictures on their cell phones.

Josh answered his call.

Dori was at the hospital with Zack; it had all started up again. "You have to come *right now*!"

If Josh had had his wits about him, he might have caught that she didn't sound scared, or tender, but annoyed with him. She had the edginess of someone already past the threshold of a horrible op-tion, standing impatiently on the other side of it, waiting for you to catch up.

And, in the way that you don't fully remember what it's like to be drunk until the next time you're tipsy, only now did Josh under-stand he'd never really lost his sense that trouble was spread wide in front of him.

As he honked and sped and worried his way back to St. Joseph's Hospital, his stomach crumpled; his life was dangerous and quick-sanded, and he'd fallen into the worst of it.

III

The sympathetic heart is broken.

—D. H. LAWRENCE

1

James Golovin, Dr. Stokes's son, four feet seven and chewing on his collar, dragged his incompatible emotions into the living room. That was where his mother and some relics of his father were to be found. It was November 24 and James felt both happy and nervous.

Darlene sat opposite the bookshelves, phone to her ear. Obviously she was talking about old music, which—as James definitely knew—Mom used to listen to with things called *records* and *record players*.

"Do they show anything, the records?" Darlene said to the phone as James walked in. "Is there something we can point to as implicative?"

Softly—because James felt afraid to bother his mom, even though she was never nasty about it—he said with a dry mouth: "Ma?"

And Darlene gave an apologetic smile; she palmed the part of the telephone you talk into, and whispered: "One minute—okay, James?"

Then, speaking into the receiver again, her voice quick and less musical than what James usually heard or liked from her: "You're making, for example, a house visit, I assume?" House visits were the best way to examine mothers face-to-face. This would be the Goldins' first visit. "All right, good," Darlene said.

James chewed his lip and looked at her. (Was being an adult mainly about acting sort of angry all the time?) He tried, by focusing really hard, to send his mom a psychic message: *Get off the phone now. It's Daddy's birthday.* And—as sometimes the school bus came just when he'd willed it to, or the traffic light would change magically, as if on command—James's mother now gave him reason to suspect he could command telepathic Jedi tricks.

"All right, Betty," she said. And she winked at James, while at the same time telling the phone, with a constricted, wrapping-things-up pace: "Uh, *okay*—yes, that's right: G-o-l-d-i-n. I'm amazed, as always, by how helpful CPS is. Oh, my pleasure, many thanks again"—and she hung up.

"Okay," Darlene said, hitting her lap heavily with both palms. And then she watched as her child tried to find something new about a dead father through the man's photo albums.

"Is this before you knew him?" James said when they got to a picture of big and robust Leo—at that time a young guy smiling in Polaroid brightness, cheeks quite rosy under wide, dark eyes. You really saw his birthmark in this one.

"I took this shot," Darlene said. "It was at Tufts: See the library in the background?"

"Was he smart, my dad?" James asked, and it was all over the kid's gentle eyes just how terribly he needed the answer to go his way.

"Oh, yes. Very."

Saying this brought Darlene an unexpected gloom. She didn't want to lie to James, but she also didn't want to let James think she and Leo had a perfect marriage; what she hoped was that he wouldn't ask too many specific questions. (Although she had always gotten by without idealizing *her* dad.)

"So, um"—James hadn't given up the hopeful tension at his eyebrows—"what did Dad study again?"

Darlene ran her hand down the side of her son's face and around under the chin: a caress in the shape of a backward *J*.

"Your father majored in history," she said. "He really wanted to know about what happened in olden times." And quieter: "You ask me that every time, sweetface."

James's skin felt so smooth—this tiny man, more hairless and in a way more feminine-faced than even she was.

But Darlene was thinking of something else, too.

Once a reasonable medical suspicion comes up, New York State obliges a doctor to report any child who might be a victim of abuse or neglect. Even before the Goldins brought in their son a week ago for a second, dodgy emergency visit, Darlene and Dr. Weiss had placed opening-salvo calls to Betty Van Der Meer at Child Protective Services. They'd reported—over Weiss's mute objections—that they likely had found something underhanded. That was all well and good, but maybe Darlene should have reported her suspicions earlier? She always had a great, crusading anger; if she'd acted on it sooner, she might have saved that poor baby from what was happening to him now, she thought. She couldn't stop wondering about her delays, how they might have harmed the child.

"My favorite thing in Mrs. Castiglia's class," her son was saying now, "is social studies. And that's the same as history, Mom."

Everything—the thought of parents injuring innocents, the sadness of James's half-orphanhood, the defenselessness that Darlene's own history had predisposed her to find in all children—made her feel immensely protective of her tan-skinned son. He was doing his eye-rubbing thing and, watching him, Darlene pictured a sheep on a cultivator feedlot, blinking, a cream puff without defenses from the axe.

"Well, that's true, James. However, you are good at science and English, too." And as if she worried that her son was seriously taking on a career decision at seven and a half, she said: "You can focus on doing whatever you want, you know."

"D'you think I could be as good at history as Dad?" he'd said a thousand times, and now one time more. "Prob'ly, right?" A sense of pride—which is not something men are born with—was budding in him.

"Your dad was a very smart man, but I think you may be even smarter."

Predictably, after the rocky part of the Goldin family's second emergency had gone by, the mother had refused Darlene access to her son's records—which is a mother's right—or any information about his sources of past care. This complicated the analysis. And there had been the awful scene the mother had made—yelling, crying, *deny*ing, etc. But what kind of kid codes twice, is anemic twice, and then each time returns quickly to normal health? What could that be but Munchausen's?

James—having paged back through the photo book—pointed to a different picture now: his father at eight or nine.

"Did you know him here, Mom?" he said.

"James, you're being silly," she said, then hoped that hadn't sounded accusatory. "You know I didn't know him when he was little."

"Oh."

They studied the photo together (Leo extra skinny, his chin dimpled), Darlene and her son sharing a tacit awareness that James looked a good deal like his father. (Except for James's woolly hair.) Darlene's gloomy feeling widened out into something worse, something big and despondent, and she closed her eyes as if that might wipe her mind clean.

PCF was a tough diagnosis—Darlene always knew that. The harm doesn't have to be direct; a mother may—rather than purposefully making her kid ill—simply make up some false history, hiding from the doctor the key to the problem. In these cases, recognition is more difficult, and the legal system is unlikely to respond to a physician's recommendation to remove the child. Especially if the doctor hasn't seen any of the patient's old records. (Luckily, CPS can force the parents to give over all that stuff.) But Betty Van Der Meer had found nothing in Zack Goldin's file. That's why it was time for CPS to pop up at the Goldins' house for an inspection.

The next photo Darlene and her son looked at came from the early '90s—James was dipping backward and forward through the album, with haphazard pleasure—and the picture showed Leo and Darlene hand-in-hand, at dusk, slightly blurred, on a Manhattan street. Who could have taken *that*? Ah; now Darlene remembered—

her mom had. This was a record of the first time that Alice had visited the Madison Avenue apartment, that place with those silly chocolate leather couches and the projection-screen TV; afterward they'd gone out to dinner together, and Alice had snapped a spur-of-the-moment photo. In it, Leo's face was turned in handsome profile; he'd been running ahead of Darlene, who'd tried in her lumbering way to keep up. That the young husband's turning to look back at his young wife had untucked his shirt a little moved her heart now; the twist of his body had emphasized the muscles of his chest.

Maybe she needed to date.

"Do you still want to look at these, James?" Darlene was tamping down the inclination to take the book from him.

Turning from the picture to her son, she felt softened and overwhelmed by his eyes. Those calm impassive *big* child eyes—dominating his face—were now, as they so often were, just staring at her. Those eyes were not quite like hers yet, but as he grew into his features, they were getting more so. Sometimes she'd glimpse, as in photographs under developing chemicals, the arrival of her own selfhood in her son's lion-colored, maturing features. But then he looked like Leo, too.

Who the hell would hurt their own child?

"Maybe we can call Grandma Golovin now, huh?" said Darlene, closing the book of photographs.

2

WHEN DORI WAS A KID, HER FATHER OFTEN WONDERED IF SOMETHING was up with her.

Nothing serious. He just imagined that, as with his wife, what made his only child hard for him to understand was that she was an American.

He was first confused when Dori had tried to skip out on elementary school: telling her father that she'd fallen so in love with her teacher, Mr. Kaufman, and that it would be best for all involved if she could just steer clear of Mr. K. for a while. That had been first grade, when they'd lived in the Catskills—a tough place, with its fretful mix of hasids and hayseeds, for a Turkish reform Jew to make a living selling paper goods. Then he bought a stationery store in Queens and his daughter quit talking about being in love with anyone. Next they moved to Woodmere, Long Island, one of the so-called "Five Towns" (these being Inwood, Lawrence, Cedarhurst, Woodmere, and Hewlett—South Shore communities linked since the 1930s for no reason anyone remembers, and *in toto* so principally Jewish that Five Towns Radio still advertises "The Best in Jewish Music, 24/6").

Woodmere was a torpid village that needed a park, a movie theater, a rec center, *some*thing, but didn't get anything. And none of Dori's friends had a swimming pool. But certain things flourish in boring towns, among them ingenuity and legend. Legend had it that a local golf course's greenskeeper fired a salt-pellet rifle at trespassers. Dori's ingenuity was to make this into an after-school game. When you're eleven, commonplace things acquire the bump of mystery, and if (like Dori) you rarely saw any plot of land bigger than a quarter-acre yard, the breadth of an empty golf course—its mild steep-ups and baby-size beaches—make an excellent fantasy world. Her sneakers got scuffed, like a boy's, from sneaking around the front nine, where she and a few school guys hoped to annoy a stranger into firing his low-impact rifle at them. Her father worried that Dori's hands looked large, kind of boyish. And weren't there any *girls* to play with?

At twelve, Dori fractured her shinbone riding a neighbor's 100cc Yamaha. For a while, she stayed indoors. This was when computers and she were young; Dori played violent video games—dragons, tanks, pixilated arrows and blood—and her dad started again to wonder if something was up with her. Dad sat for a talk with Mr. Eustis, the junior-high guidance counselor (Dori's father left his assistant, Nelson, in charge of the store, which he didn't like doing). Mr. Eustis directed him to Judy Blume. Ten weeks in a row, on the 7:57 to Jamaica Station, Dori's father analyzed *Superfudge, Tales of a Fourth Grade Nothing,* and *Blubber,* getting sideways looks from the sports-page readers. Then he'd linger through the last chapters, sitting in what he liked to call the *entrepôt* of his stationery store, while Nelson handled the long customerless desert of two to three-fifteen P.M. If Judy Blume was right, parents cause problems when they make life-altering decisions without consulting their kids. (This was a strange country where he'd landed his family.) Hadn't he moved his daughter when she was very small? It seemed weird to think about how he could have consulted a six-year-old, but he felt guilty, anyway. He wanted to be fully American, and was certain that the pull of tradition could be offset by gestures, by silly poses that had only to be maintained. (Assimilationists suffered jealousies as did fundamentalists; the difference was in their angle of approach.) So he became solicitous of his daughter's opinion after the fact. And he made sure he talked up the wholesome pleasures of girly things. He was the only parent on Wallace Lane who wanted his daughter to start dating really young. And so, when Dori found herself in Cindy Xenakis's closet with Alex Pucciariellio playing seven-minutes-in-heaven, she giggled as Alex placed his hesitant hands on her. Dori closed her eyes, sighed, and knew that something was definitely up with her: Boys were up with her.

She loved their touch, the big *actually* boyish hands of them. She had hazy ideas about becoming an actress, because boys liked actresses. But with no stage or footlights at her disposal, she had to practice by becoming a convincing liar. No boy could stay mad at her; Dori's excuses were exquisite. Alex Pucciariellio was a guy whose skies were so bright and warm you couldn't help but like him, but Dori lost her virginity, in the tenth grade, to a different boy. She had sex with a guy who wasn't even her boyfriend, a soccer player named Charles. (He had bright red hair, and a face often moved to a similar color by emotions he couldn't justify.)

She'd done it, in part, because the boy had looked so sad and hopeful and nervous whenever they talked; she'd felt bad for him. Afterward, word got around. She realized, to her surprise, that her classmates weren't ready to accept her in the way she had accepted herself: as pretty and popular enough to be above reproach. To compensate, she started studying the queen bees, the girls whom boys really liked best, imitating the lazy sideways dip of their heads, the braid twist, their lingering eye contact, their laughing along when guys made cruel and dirty jokes, the light physical contact of their touch on some boy's arm while talking about the day's earth science exam.

In eleventh grade, Dori had been courted heavily—as had many girls her age and echelon of popularity—by anorexia. Its charms were legion, the ease, the expediency, the opportunities it offered for drama. But she was never one who let anorexia go all the way with her—not like the zombies walking the halls with their ringed eyes, the gulag kids, all thinning hair and dry, yellow skin—the girls who had abstained themselves right into the hospital. Dori skimped on a breakfast here, a lunch there, but that was it.

This having been the late '80s, a lot of Dori's teachers were ex-hippies, and so the bulimia/anorexia cases earned tons of caring attention; the thing that seemed nicest about it to Dori was that the administration worked to ensure that no one made fun of them; at least, nobody dared make the kind of Turkey-is-a-food-not-a-country jokes that they had to Dori.

One such *ano* girl—Naomi, whose give-away was her over-size head on a toothpick neck—sat behind Dori in Spanish. Dori befriended Naomi; Dori's Sweetheart Court friends couldn't understand it, but she liked talking to the girl, black nail polish notwithstanding. She liked offering her a little help. Part of it was that she enjoyed wheedling bulimia stories out of Naomi, the whys of the problem; and it wasn't just an eating disorder. Naomi cut her skin with bottle tops—mostly the calves and forearms. This all caused such exciting commotion at school: Everyone was instructed to feel so *bad* for her. But Naomi still seemed incurably glum, and that was the other part of it for Dori—the second reason she hung around her sad new friend. Her companionship seemed actually to help the girl. Naomi stopped cutting herself, and had even started engaging with her lunch. That's how Dori had first decided to become a nurse. She would always wonder what happened to Naomi, whenever anyone asked Dori why she'd made the first steps into her profession—but they'd lost touch, irretrievably, after junior year.

3

THE GOLDINS HAD TO GET UP EARLY TODAY. THE VACANT SUBURBAN SKY was a little pink at a quarter to seven. It seemed mortified to have been caught at whatever it had done while the world slept.

By 8:40, it was time to appraise the severity of their hospital problem. They'd entered that lawyer world where anguish might be renegotiated, paid off, or tossed on a technicality.

"Pure horseshit," said their lawyer, Martin Seidel. "And that's all it is."

Not that Josh wasn't anxious. Horrible questions tousled him with their grubby hands. Hadn't CPS or whatever asked for their files? What kind of files? Who had *files*? Wasn't the head of the Pediatrics Department just out to get them?

Zack seemed okay again now, though. That had to count for something.

"You didn't do anything wrong," Seidel said, expansive as the occasion required. He sat with calculated informality on the edge of his glass-topped desk. And again, very slowly: "I'm going to say this again, for the benefit of the cheap seats: *You didn't do anything wrong*. Don't let them get you questioning yourselves. These big corporations—yes, we're talking about a hospital, but a *corporate* hospital—these big corporations, I've seen it. I've seen it; I've seen it."

He shook his head in genuine, do-gooder loathing. "I can tell you when CPS—I can tell you that CPS has been known in the past to go hard. They go after people. But now the media has been tough on them in recent years, they've lost a lot of fights. They can't beat a family like you guys, because A) it was *they* who screwed up, not you, not to mention that you are the parents. That is the salient point here. See how happy Zack looks now. I mean, on the way in, did you hear Mrs. H.? Mrs. H. said, she said: 'What a cute-looking baby.' "

"That's right," Dori said. Her nose was always red now, a sensitive red. Josh understood why, the horrible insult: Not just her motherhood had been called into question, but also her sanity. But what a trooper she was! Josh was so proud of her, for how well she was bearing up under this. She was so admirable, that was what killed him about it: She'd guessed exactly what the hospital would do. She'd tried to warn him against a legal action. She understood the system so well. But it hadn't saved them; here they were anyway.

"He really is a cute baby," she was saying.

She fitted her chin into her collarbone to peer down at Zack, who was sleeping on her legs. His brow as he slept was flat above the smooth eyelids that stole her heart every time; his cheeks looked delicate.

Dori kissed the top of his head, quietly, as she thought about all that had happened to her.

Maybe it was only because Josh had been sort of a cock about helping with parenty stuff, but when Zack was born, her thrill for her son got into her skin and stayed that way. It was, that first half-year, something she could *feel*, a poison-oak affection. But that intensity, the skin prickle, is impossible to keep forever. Which is only natural. Motherhood has to come down to earth sometime.

"No, he is *such* a good baby," Dori was saying, soft enough not to wake him up. "Forget *me*—why would the hospital want to put him through this?"

"Fear." Seidel shook his head. "They're scared of you."

"Well," Dori said. This came out angry-sounding, but in truth, sitting with this lawyer (whom she'd never met before), stealing peeks at her husband's worried face, Dori suffered the unavoidable dwindling of morale, the slump in energy, the shields weakening a bit in the light of this morning. She had to make an effort here; no one would believe a hospital would be *totally* wrong.

Josh reached over to touch his son, and Dori felt terrified of what could have been in his mind.

"How long?" Josh asked, still leaning to his son but eyeing Seidel from under his brows. "We've got to work it so this goes away, buddy."

He spoke with vehemence and certainty. This irritated Dori—that typical Josh *smoothness*, even here!

Josh sat back and now held his fingers intertwined; Dori didn't notice that he squeezed his hands in a nervous strain. His fingernails looked like mini sno-cones; red followed by a white that was bloodless.

"How long, Martin?" Josh asked.

The lawyer could offer them only the hung jury of his hesitation before he finally said: "I can't promise anything." He trailed off on that, his least favorite phrase in the language.

Of course, he didn't tell the Goldins about the prospect of a *felony child endangering* charge, which could bring eight years in prison. Nobody at CPS or the hospital was talking about that yet, and Seidel hated giving clients scary information. He was just never in the mood for it.

"But beyond their looking around, we don't even know if anything's going to happen," Seidel said. Then his eyes relaxed beautifully. "The legal system, thank God, is unlikely to respond to doctor referrals to remove."

"But either way," Josh said, "we'll be hearing from them soon, you're saying."

"Remove?" Dori said, a sob halfway up her throat. Like that, her underarms had gotten sweaty. "Referrals to *remove?*"

Seidel shook his head. "They won't take Zack away," Seidel said. "I promise you, Dori." It was a fairly believable hard-guy face.

When dealing with a couple, Seidel generally addressed the nitty-gritties for the husband, then offered the more broad-spectrum banalities to the wife.

"The truth is that they don't have Zack now; you do," he said.

"Sounds obvious, right? But I can't tell you what an advantage that is, even after both times you brought him in."

Josh looked around in an uncomprehending way. *Both* times? His memory had syncretized the two visits to St. Joe's; they seemed to him like a single afternoon of fear and sitting around—that impossible medical compound, anxious boredom. Would he be asked in court to differentiate them? Would he have to provide details?

Well, the second trip involved more yelling, a clearer degree of antagonism from Dr. Stokes. That was almost as bad as the worry: having to watch his wife take the woman's rudeness. Dori's chest had shivered, puffed up, stayed like that; when the tears had finally come they did so in a violent fit. Josh had wanted to kill Dr. Stokes for that. The strange accusation in the woman's face was outrageous and offensive; it was too *retarded* to consider, he thought.

"You did say 'remove,' " Dori said.

Seidel told her again, gently: He would not let that happen.

Watching Dori, Josh got a vivid bolt from his memory: curling himself behind Dori, when she'd been pregnant, one hand on her taut, warm stomach, the other on her forehead, everything lucky.

"So, Martin," he said, "tell us what *is* going to happen."

"Well, you see, Child Protective Services has to try to prove a lot before they can even begin to . . ."

Josh—as one skilled professional watching another—recognized Seidel's fluency, his calm guarantees, for what they were. Essential to the grit and sparkle of the guy's competence was a vocational pleasure; Martin Seidel had found a terrific project to work his way into: Josh's life.

Josh was already developing the survivor's proud, stubborn insularity. *Nobody, not even a guy whose job it is to sympathize about this stuff, can really understand what it's like to go through this,* he thought, *unless they've been through it themselves.*

"Temporary custody," Dori was saying. (Even now, Zack looked so peaceful there on her lap, as legal phrases packed his bags around him.) "That means they take him away." She shook her head at the madness of it. "From his mother."

At this, Seidel faltered. For a while the only sound was the note of Zack's surprisingly dainty and musical breathing. And Josh was holding himself so stiff it looked like he felt nothing at all.

Over the last few days, Josh had hoped, at work at least, to put across the impression that he was still thriving. But after some break-room whisperings overheard or imagined, the distress in Josh's own smile let the truth slip. His false front was thin and uncomfortable.

"Okay," Seidel said, with a tone of: *Stay with me here, people.* "That's the bad news. You ready for the good?"

"Yes, definitely."

"Good. Dori?" Martin said. "How 'bout you?"

"Sure," she said, and blinked herself back to attentiveness. "Of course."

She'd been spacing out on the hairiness of the lawyer's hand, the little dark slinky-curls that arched from his cuffs. She wanted desperately for the guy just to shut up already; she was scared shit, and didn't want the conversation veering toward her. If this guy could just stop talking, maybe he'd bring the boat back to shore now, so that it wouldn't drift by chance out onto her depleted little island.

Men just loved making their deep-voiced noise, though. But words seemed the shabbiest phonies when there's nothing to say.

And trying to listen to them talk about how horrible the accusation was, she felt more and more of who she was (mother, wife) melt away, inch by inch.

She imagined telling Josh—just coming right out with it.

"I'm very safe," she would say.

He would probably just look at her.

"There was no way Zack was going to really get hurt, Josh. I knew what I was doing," she would say. But then she would say: "I didn't know he would code that time." And she'd add: "I admit that."

Her worry had sprouted a furious vein in the middle of her forehead, but neither Seidel nor Josh noticed.

"You were a bad father. You wouldn't *help*, Josh," she'd say. "And my plan worked. It worked. For a while, it worked perfectly." But then she imagined her husband and son being taken from her—taken like faith, or sanity.

Her trance was interrupted because she saw something. For some unknown reason, out the window, a flock of newspapers glided past in a floaty *whoosh*—not just one, but page after page swimming up the air, bright in the sun, tangling, turning over, glowy little ghosts rising twenty-five floors up or whatever, how weird—but the sight was gone before she could explain it.

". . . the good news is I've already contacted the New York Center for Family Rights," Seidel was saying. The NYCFR had been set up to defend parents against overzealous Child Protective Services actions. Out the window, one last newspaper pirouetted and almost bowed as it passed.

Lately there had, Seidel explained, been a lot of "aggressive CPS attacks." In Idaho, the state had placed a thirteen-year-old cancer patient in foster care wrongly—after the girl's parents decided against radiation therapy. Well, guess what? The radiation was deemed unnecessary and potentially harmful. "The state didn't only lose custody," Seidel said, "but a not-insubstantial financial settlement."

He continued in his closing-statement tone, slow and quiet:

"The point is this: We can work with these NYCFR people; we can get folks out of the woodwork, vouching that you've shown super interest in the well-being of your son. This is going to end up an—"

Dori made an attention-getting sound in her throat. "I have something to tell you," she said.

Raising her chin, she tried to look casual: *Hey, look, I don't give a shit about CPS. I have something important here.* And she lifted Zack—with motherly magic, she moved her son without waking him—and finagled him into the stroller next to her chair. The thing was, they were going to get to her depleted little island eventually; if they investigated everything, they'd wash ashore sooner or later. So her idea now was to lead them there herself.

"What is it, honey?"

Josh looked incompetent to her now, childish. He didn't *understand*. Some evils are necessary in this life, Dori told herself. *No regrets*.

She said, "I have to confess something," and looked at the floor shyly. Now she shattered the whole framework of the conversation. "Something bad did happen. But—" And she went suddenly quiet, offering them the surprise explosive of her silence. The longer they waited, the larger the detonation would be.

"What, honey?"

"It's something I didn't admit."

Josh, at a loss before the prospect of the most terrible, astounding news, turned his confused face to her. *Could she have*—he wouldn't think it. Even Martin Seidel was rubbing his cheek with apprehension. How bad was it?

Josh thought she looked so helpless and sad now. He loved her so much; was she going to say something that shattered everything he knew about his life? It couldn't be.

"I was scared to say this before," she said. "I didn't tell you everything about what happened the first time Zack got sick." She spoke quickly as if nervously; this was a story whose delivery she had practiced.

"You know how I was with him the whole time, I said? Well, the truth is I left him alone in the car." She sat with her hands cupped, as if self-control were a match flame she was keeping lit between her palms. "Just for a second, Josh."

She looked up, and faced her husband's eyes.

"I was at the pharmacy, to get something, there was a really long line—and I didn't even buy anything, because I knew it was taking forever, but when I came back to the car, he was throwing up." She said it in her most feminine and modest tone. "No, I don't know, maybe it *is* my fault. I left him alone in the car—I don't know." She lowered her face to her palms, as if crying. "It was just for a few minutes."

Josh and Seidel exchanged a glance of condescension that said, *Oh, just look at her—this poor lovely naïve woman feeling guilty over nothing.* And Josh put his hand to the back of Dori's neck, the mildest touch, almost in the way that her baby sometimes stroked her: a touch that was no more than a breath on the skin. He felt protective and even sadder after her confession. So *that* explained her recent anxieties!

Seidel talked first, and softly: "So you left Zack alone for a minute or two. Who cares? That doesn't mean they didn't fail to do the right test for his"—he turned around to look at something on top of his desk—"his coagulation factors and blood count. Isn't that what you said?"

Dori nodded into her hands without showing her face. At the price of a little untruth, she had Josh's trust, and the lawyer's, sewn up. It made her feel humiliated and, worse, sort of vulgar, to have done it. She shouldn't have *needed* to have done it.

"Oh, honey," Josh said.

"Listen, sweetie," Seidel said. "We're in the real world. People make mistakes down here, in the muck and mire, all right? But does that mean you are responsible for your kid who got sick? No. Does that mean the hospital didn't *not* do the right test? Of course not. Or that it's right to maybe try and take your only child from you?"

Dori wore a face of great, dry-cheeked fortitude now. The face seemed almost to have been composed in a mirror.

"No." She sniffled.

"Okay, then."

Martin Seidel was back in smiles; this had been a bonding moment—all trust now—between lawyer and clients. Josh caught the smiling bug, too: He was always susceptible to it. He felt so deeply indebted to his wife, who had—in ways he now realized were kind of mysterious to him—worked so much harder than he had at raising their son. (For one example, *he* wouldn't have thought twice about leaving Zack in the car for a second or two.) All the sorrow of the last few weeks, over this small thing. And still, somehow, she was under unfair attack.

"Now I want to tell *you* something," Seidel said.

He pushed off from the lip of his desk and stood with enough winning gusto that it seemed they'd already prevailed.

"I got some tricks up my sleeve," he said, walking around to his chair—another signal that he was concluding things. "I got some famous Martin Seidel secret weapons."

His voice was so inspiring that Dori even found herself smiling. And he was keeping up his smirk while he talked, an acquired skill. "You'll see."

Before long the phone rang, one of Seidel's clients in some jittery trifle of an emergency. "*Shh*, I'm giving you a hundred-seventy-five-thousand-dollar discount," the attorney said into the mouthpiece. "You'll never get that in the history of the legal profession." He gave the Goldins a slack, contrite face but didn't end the call, which only seemed rude to them after they'd left, the spell by then having passed.

STRANGE THINGS CAME to Dori's brain. Heading down Fifty-sixth Street and into the parking garage, she imagined herself a celebrity under some public embarrassment, masked by sunglasses, with a thousand cameras and her push of bodyguards swaying nearby, outsize men with no mind for their own safety.

More than anything in life Dori wanted to be happy. *And maybe that's the difference between me and the absolute best mothers of the world*, she was thinking.

Now she had to dig through her bag for the parking stub and slide it through the cut arch in the garage's Plexiglas window.

And—because she knew this would get Josh to look at her—she gave her husband's hand a quick squeeze. She hoped to guess Josh's thoughts by the attitude of his face. But he just smiled at her: kind of sad and fully unreadable.

Soon Josh walked away to tip the the car fetcher—tipping being an obligation that falls to the husband—leaving Dori to take the crisp little Swiss-cheese paring of a receipt, which, as she held it, seemed to pass on an important ethical lesson. She had this disturbing sense that the world was trying to narrow the difference between Right and Wrong into something flimsy, like this fragile slip of paper.

She felt *off* in her heart. But some actions were right even if they seemed wrong.

The baby in his stroller scrunched his chin, looking impossibly adult and thoughtful. Dori got him to smile by imitating this face but she still ached for some ethical decree, a court order from God, whose verdict would be more unassailable than the assurances of some lawyer, a baby's smile, or a cold slice of paper. For some reason, she thought of those stray newspapers, twisting and ascending on their invisible current of air.

Dori had been told that, a hundred and some years ago in Russia, her mother's family with its occasional rabbi or cantor had delved deep into religious thought. Five generations of American comfort had, in Dori, worried and reduced that reverence of God to a light, all-purpose spiritual confidence; she, like almost everybody she knew, believed only this: *Everything happens for a reason.* She'd made the right choices for her husband, and so that had been the right choice for her baby, too. Josh, for example, was being helpful again. Maybe a trial would bring them all even closer. Everything happens for a reason.

When Dori looked up she saw that her car, big, new, and expensive, was ready to sway her out of the city and back to her home.

4

DEREK HAYES WASN'T EXACTLY SCRAWNY, BUT DARLENE HAD THE CLEAR feeling she could bench-press more than he could. And she had never been any sort of gym rat. In fact, she wasn't sure that she could even identify a bench press machine—another example of how terms one didn't know filtered their way into the personal databank.

She'd guessed right away that the stranger heading into the restaurant with a face as clutched and skinny as a talon had to be Derek. He'd been trying to spot someone whose looks he didn't know. And he was black.

Jane had set them up—serious, forty-six-year-old Dr. Jane Shepherd, chair of St. Joseph's Department of Obstetrics and Gynecology and the one colleague to whom Darlene felt comfortable revealing more than a speck of her personal life. Jane was a work friend—that is, a second-string friend. These women, like people who use each other's companionship to brighten their time on a stopped elevator, never talked outside of the confines of the thing they had in common—St. Joe's itself. And yet, Darlene found herself here, waiting for a Jane setup: a blind date, of all things. She wondered if Jane had paired her with Derek because they were the only black people she knew.

After one hesitant phone call ("I'm, uh, Jane Shepherd's friend who I think she said I might call you . . ."), Derek had selected the place—a restaurant in Huntington where the walls on the fireplaces were lined with leather-bound books, giving it the feel of Sherlock Holmes's private library.

Darlene had arrived fifteen minutes early. She'd sat waiting for Derek at the bar, alternately watching the TV (even Sherlock Holmes liked a good sitcom now and again) and casting her discerning glance on the people who passed, ladies with good backs and French manicures, men wearing collarless dress shirts. She'd been cruelly, silently dismissing each one as they circled by. *In the room the women come and go, talking about Da Vinci Codes.* She felt off her game in a way that made her nervous, alert, and happy. This was her first social night out—not counting dinners with Alice Davis or the occasional retirement party at St. Joe's—in nearly three years.

The TV was tuned to one of those cable harangue shows (two starched and insincere white men mixing it up); the question appeared to be Iraq-based (confident stuff about whether it would end up an ash heap or rise to modest success). But it was like everything else: no solid information, no real data, no accountability, no *news.*

Then Derek walked up and bashfully introduced himself. He and Darlene were led by a sway-bottomed Asian woman to their table by the hearth; taking their cues from the TV, they discussed the war. (No one called it "Iraq War II"; Darlene pointed out that this was America's first war that seemed not to have a proper name. People just referred to it as "Iraq.")

Because there were certain conditions they shared—they were educated, they were middle-class New Yorkers, they were black—there was between them the implicit understanding that neither could ever have supported Bush.

"How can anyone be happy when the world's so screwed up?" Derek said. "So, are you a red or a white person? I like a Pinot Grigio, but we can get individual glasses, too. Or a bottle."

His voice was high and young-sounding. He taught tenth-grade health, looked very skinny in a cardigan and jeans, and there was something in the studiously impartial way he laid out the beverage options that put Darlene in mind of the classroom. He was a divorcé who said, "Tell me about yourself," with such Pavlovian detachment, Darlene felt she should raise her hand to be called upon. And the way he listened—cataloging details he could recall to her later—made it clear he'd been schooled in being a good first date. Still, he listened without expression.

But being given the chance to talk about the achievements of her life—about how she'd always set some particular goal for herself, and devoted herself fully to it until it was accomplished—had a surprising and depressing effect on Darlene. She'd always been a striver and she'd succeeded. And the second part was: She'd never been happy. What could be more disappointing to an aspirant than realizing your aspiration but finding that it has left your life unimproved? She really wanted to add that last big question, to see whether it would make his hair spin around, whether it would make him revolve in his chair. Give him a real, full blast from the fire hose of another's personality.

She did finish her monologue with a smile, at least. In fact, she sat up straighter, kept up that put-on smile, and even remembered to hold her jaw away from her neck to avoid any hint of a double chin.

Then Derek surprised her, slipping out of the box to which she'd consigned him. "Hey," he said comically, "do you think we're the only black people Jane knows?"

Darlene laughed, relief slackening her posture. This shared, humorous insight would certainly lessen the friction between them, she thought.

"I'll bet we are," she said. "Do you think she wants us to found an organization? African-American Friends of Jane?" Now it was his turn to laugh. This made her give him a second look: He was jaunty, with leather-brown eyes, thick hair graying a little on the margins: handsome in his straightforward thin casual way.

"I wonder if we *are* the only black people she knows," Darlene said again; Derek gave a much smaller laugh. Then that was finished.

The food came. He told her he had no children; she told him about James. Then, as Derek sat there munching his plate of salt cod, occasionally dipping a fork into its chilly cream, Dr. Stokes found her tires locking into the pothole, the burst radiator, the stalled highway of a first date. She could think of nothing to say.

All the accomplishments of her adult life, med school, motherhood, Peeds, real estate, none of it gave her a leg to stand on against her old pre-Leo anxieties. How do you ensure another person's liking you? She was someone who always had graceful essays running in her head—so why was she able only to get one clumsy sentence out of her mouth at a time?

She thought, *I'm not going to let you ruin this; please not tonight*—beseeching not herself, but the ex-husband who was gone. *Don't do this to me, Leo. Don't.*

She patted her hair, which—while taken down from its usual tight bun—had a sheen and a smooth, unchangeable helmetish look that, as with Condoleezza Rice's head, gave it the air of being pulled back anyway.

Earlier this evening, she'd gotten herself ready in her white-tiled bathroom—wrapping her head and sitting under her mother's old hood dryer for about forty-five minutes. Then her son had walked in. His own head was bowed as if he thought something adult and formal were taking place.

She'd been startled by James's entrance and had been about to scold him. But she couldn't; even when he was in his best moods, there was something poignant about her son. He was so innocent and yet determined.

Window blinds quieted the sun on the bathroom mirror; it was the afternoon's last live hour.

"Why is that thing on your head?" the boy said shyly, taking a step back on seeing his mother.

"Well," Darlene said, also shyly, in a clipped mild voice, "because I'm going out." And then, unable to resist: "What did I tell you about knocking?"

"A rendezvous?" James's eyes popped open, nervous and sad. "With a man?"

Again, by what osmosis do words seep into our awareness? How did little James know "rendezvous"?

"I'm just going out for dinner, James. A rendezvous is pushing it."

He nodded. "Is Grandmama coming over?"

"No," she said, "tonight it's Lily."

"Oh."

Darlene rose from under the hood dryer, applied some light oil, used a wide-toothed comb to loosen the wrap, and flat-ironed her hair. She combed in some Straight Fast Hair Elixir before wrapping her head again. James watched all this, blinking.

She put down the salon care implements and knelt before him; they were eye-to-eye. "Nothing will ever change the way I feel about your dad." She had planned on saying, "how much I loved your dad"—but she ran up against herself; that Darlene stiffness. She wasn't going to lie, even for a good cause.

James's face puckered. "That stuff smells stinky."

Her knees made a cracking noise as she stood. "And I suppose it *is* kind of a rendezvous, or at least a date, to be honest." She moved her head from side to side, to catch the different angles in her mirror. Yes, she had Condi Rice's 'do. "But I'm just going out to meet someone my own age. How stinky do you mean?"

"Like burning."

The funny thing was, she had planned to tell James about the date, and was even going to make a list of age-appropriate facts to share with him. Well, kids are intuitive little creatures.

She said: "Sometimes, a person wants to have people one's own age to hang out with. It's important to your state of mind. Take you, for example. Would *you* want to see only adults all the time?"

"Okay," he said. His round face blushed copper.

"I still love spending time with you," she said, her voice so hot that, after she spoke, she thought she might have alarmed her son by the out-of-place intensity. Still, she couldn't stop herself from going on: "More than anything in the world."

"More than work?"

He had surprised her again, not least with the apparent calmness of this question. His eyes had gone dry. She didn't know that James had not planned to ask such a question, that he had surprised himself even by showing the courage to ask it, that for years he'd remember this moment as a signpost in his own growth.

"Of course," she said. "I mean, I work to support us, and I love my work. But I love you more." A heavy look of defeat passed over her face. She wanted to cancel the date; she wanted to stay home playing chess with James.

But now here she was anyway, at an awkward restaurant table with Derek Hayes, to no apparent purpose.

Derek had let her hang, like a student who hadn't completed the required reading. But eventually he opened up more. Their plates came and went, kitchen staff brought different-size forks and sharper knives and refilled glasses. Darlene was halfway through an evening out, and not even handling it—to her standards—horribly. Derek was saying that he thought music—not that he was a connoisseur, or one of those guys with strong opinons about vinyl—had "gone downhill recently."

And here was a topic Darlene could warm to. "It's not just music," she said, laying down her fork.

"I'm far from the first person to point out that we live in a culture that is unserious in a self-congratulatory way," she said. "But for me the surprise is that we've quit seeing our guilty pleasures guiltily."

He told her he wasn't sure what she meant.

"Guilty pleasures have become proud pleasures," she said. She was very nearly reciting now; "Rot," the essay that she'd written at length but never on paper, was always ready to pour forth.

"There are," she said, "scores of writers and academics who have taken to calling popular art the only acceptable form of art."

She spoke breathlessly. For the first time tonight she was a vital physical presence at the table, and this was because she had stopped thinking about how her looks were being judged. She was saying:

"There was recently an emblematic 'thought' piece I read in *The Village Voice* by the critic Joshua Clover called 'Better Decide Which Side You're On.' It argued that, as unappealing as it might be to do so, real music fans must choose to prefer Britney Spears over, say,

Norah Jones or Alicia Keys if they wanted to stay hip. This was because those other two artists play the piano, while Britney plays nothing. The critic said that 'history will judge you harshly' if you don't choose the nonmusician over the musician."

Derek was about to stick in a "Well, that's silly," but the current of Darlene's thought hurried quickly by.

"The author put forward the credible, if hardly fresh, argument that it's nonsense for critics to disregard any work of art simply because its practitioners might not be technically accomplished. Point taken. But the next line of reasoning, Derek, is as foolish and as dogmatic as the reactionary position he's just trashed. He asks us to discount music because it's made by people who *can play their instruments well*. Well, I think that is a remarkable argument. We are asked to align ourselves with Ms. Spears's music, because at least she isn't unfashionable enough actually to be a pianist."

Darlene had grown prettier on the rising currents of her eloquence, brilliance, and her authority. The flues of her nose broadened and her face warmed into its sumptuous color. If only she had stopped talking now.

"Dogmatists ask us to shrivel our world into binary arrangements," she said, "good and evil, with us or against us, musicianship versus nonmusicianship. But, hey!—at least Britney's unable to play the piano! Really, is the narrow-minded doctrine of 'technique is always a bad thing' really anything other than 'technique is absolutely necessary' stood on its head?"

She was so excited to be finally getting these ideas out, to be doing what she conceived of as "socializing," that she took Derek's frequent uh-huhs as a good sign. But the flame of his interest, his sympathy and affection for the subject, had fizzled under the wind of her chatter. He'd stopped listening two minutes ago.

"Look, nobody has to like symphonic music," she was saying. "But if your life's work is the professional evaluation and appreciation of music, and you then dismiss such legitimate geniuses as Mozart and Bach out of hand, isn't that just . . ."

As she kept on, Derek nodded as if impressed; this was the least a person could do. "You really know a lot about this stuff, Darlene."

It wasn't that he was unused to people spouting off; living in what has become a nation of blowhards, of bogus expertise, half his tenth graders had political blogs, and some of them, Derek had it on perfect authority, couldn't find Pakistan on a map. Mostly, Derek knew, people didn't need to be agreed with. They simply wanted their hobby, their breadth of interest, acknowledged.

"There's this critic in England," Darlene was saying, "who wrote that Eminem has all the 'depth and texture of the greatest examples of English verse' and that his song 'Stan' is 'more sophisticated than the work of Robert Browning.' "

"Hey. Everyone's got to have an opinion."

Darlene came up for air, broke the surface of her absorption.

"I know about this because I'm thinking of writing an article. As a story, per se, the song 'Stan' is all right—simply all right. I've been following this, buying the records as research. In 'Stan,' Eminem portrays himself as implausibly compassionate for a superstar, and the story's power derives not from . . ."

There were twelve minutes more of this. Derek, as politely as he could—because when you're making a move on the garnish, it's all belly, and civilization is out the window—tore the sourdough bread and dabbed the pieces in what cream sauce he had left; Darlene still had half her meal and plenty of argument to go.

"The reason Eminem is called a genius is multifaceted, but also simple. You get the sense reading his advocates that everybody's so proud of having spotted literary gambits. They forget that gambits aren't inherently interesting *in themselves*; Eminem's formal and technical innovations, such as they are—"

"So, uh, what kind of an article is it you're doing? Who's going to publish it? I didn't know you were a writer," Derek said, trying desperately to muscle this conversation through any number of more interesting doorways.

"I haven't decided where to try to publish it yet. But the point is, we live in a time in which audiences and even many critics prefer not to be challenged; prefer instead to be congratulated on their taste—nobody wants to feel guilty about a guilty pleasure. It's actually not even written down yet, this essay. I just don't have the time to— Here's one thing, one point I want to get across. Norman Mailer, in 1958, wrote that a psychopathic adolescence would become 'the central expression of human nature before the twentieth century is over.' And then you have Eminem, who . . ."

She was speaking quickly enough now—or maybe it was just that Derek was trying less hard to pay attention—that he had to blink over and over just to keep his eyes open.

Darlene took a sip of water before continuing. "Well, the final reason he's called a genius is, of course, race. The sad fact is that white America has always aggrandized its own performers of African-American music. Today Jay-Z is called talented; Eminem is 'more sophisticated than Robert Browning.' "

The amazing thing was, Darlene actually thought of herself as holding back. She thought she was keeping her bloviating in check. For one thing, she didn't mention that the self-proclaimed Dean of American Rock Critics, Robert Christgau, wrote that it was *specifically because* Eminem can be such a jerk that he can also be such a genius—is genius really that easy?—and that he proclaimed the rapper a brilliant artist for "having the talent to rhyme oranges," when all Eminem did was put together a nonsense lyric: *Set to blow college dorm room doors off the hinges/oranges, peach, pears, plums, oranges . . .* (A long section of "Rot" was going to be devoted to Christgau. She first thought his title had been pinned on him by others—the Provost of Latvian Hip-Hop Correspondents, perhaps?—but the Dean of American Rock Critics actually referred to *himself* that way, and often. Like some little fella swaggering into a bar wearing a sequined World Junior Flyweight Champion belt, Christgau had emblazoned that absurd title across every page of his Web site.)

Derek shifted his weight from one buttock to the other, as if sitting on a fat wallet; he was really anxious to leave.

Every essay needs a masterstroke. Darlene planned to end hers with a startling admission: that she actually enjoyed some of Eminem's music; on the other hand, if she felt the need to bask in the work of a "literary genius," she was more than likely to read a book, quite a few of which were even more "complex" than Eminem's *Encore*, which, in the words of that guy Christgau, is a "mature work" that "showcases a phenomenally gifted lyricist doing all the things he does best," and features the immortal lines: *I never touched a booty so hot/she shake it shake it/so my ding-a-ling bounces/boing, boing, boing.* We have (and this is how the essay would go out) the genius we deserve.

"Well," Derek said finally, in a voice parched from lack of use, "I just meant I liked the old-school beats." He exemplified uninterest. He sat, leaning back slobbishly, with his hands on his stomach. "You know, the Gap Band, Rick James, like that."

She'd been talking for twenty minutes, at least. Even Darlene could see that she'd bored him; more, that in having spoken "Rot" to him, she now knew she would never write it. His boredom killed it, had rendered it stillborn.

The date went on for another quarter hour, some *flan* for him, and a minor-key smile for her, but his response to her monologue had been the evening's true end.

The restaurant having been near to Huntington Station, Darlene had taken the train here. On the ride home, looking out the window, she experienced the melancholic effect of being locked outside even a repetitive world, with her face ghosting over Long Island's limited topography.

She paid the babysitter and, the date having ended so early, put James to bed herself. Here was a world where she felt comfortable, confined, and—since James was growing so quickly—where the vistas felt unlimited. He wore his pale blue footie pajamas, and the glops of toothpaste he had on his lips and chin made him look like a rabid animal. She wiped James's goo off and sat by his bedside.

He perked up on seeing Darlene.

"Was he nice? Did you have fun?"

"No. Well, he was nice enough, but." Darlene believed she owed the diligence of parenthood the thoughtfulness of some unspoken assurance. Then, after the courtesy of a pretty long silence, she said: "I would have rather played chess with you."

He wiped a last speck of toothpaste on his sleeve and the look on his face vacillated. It seemed at first to say, *You're just saying that*, but then, as if realizing he wasn't ready for such mature faithlessness, James smiled warmly.

"*I* had a really good time without you," he said. "Lily and I played chess, and I almost won the second time."

She leaned in and gave him a hug. He had been going through a "no-hug" phase, but the anxiety about her date that had blown through him had left a grain of nostalgia in its passing. His head lay against her ribs. Even from there, James could still perceive the slightly burned smell of her hair stuff.

5

THE ADMINISTRATOR TIPPED BACK FROM HIS DESK, A DOUGHY MAN IN AN ergonomic chair, his cheeks pink as a sauna attendant's.

"It's commendable," he said, "is what it is."

Peregrine Berg, an Englishman, always had this *sangfroid* to him, as if he were patting the back of his own gross bulk.

"Commendable," he said, those pink cheeks acting as blockades for his little smile—really keeping it wedged in there.

"Well," Darlene said. "I consider this simply part of the job."

They were on St. Joe's top floor, where the administrative offices were. Out the window, the sprinkle of hospital outbuildings—parking garage, A-frame doctors' offices, a "convalescence pavilion"—gave way to greater Long Island, rippling and extending out in all directions, Sunglass Huts and TCBYs hitched up against a few chastened bits of green.

"CPS doesn't think so, yeah?" Peregrine Berg said. "CPS is under the impression that you have a commendable eye. Dr. Weiss didn't spot the business with the Goldins, and he was the admitting, assuming I've read the situation properly."

Darlene knew she should have been nicer, more of an agreer. But the trouble with administrators was that they never talked with you—they only somehow talked *alongside* you. "Nothing's happened yet," she said. "We'll know I did a good job if the New York Child Abuse Consult Network decides on a hearing."

"It's not a step any hospital takes lightly"—Peregrine Berg's voice was spraying into self-satisfaction—"you know that. But . . ."

Jewish faces are in constant motion, Darlene thought, watching Berg speak. Eyebrows cresting up and down, lips pressing italics onto words. Berg was trying to turn some of the small first measures in the Goldin case into a greatest hits compilation: two hospital visits, both serious but both oddly indeterminate; and Weiss being a doctor who was inexperienced but whose paperwork was always tight as a drum.

Even English Jews, like Peregrine Berg—and Darlene assumed that to be Hebrew in England was, in its way, the equivalent of being from Bushwick at Tufts—ended up being more Jew than Brit. Funny that Darlene should have ended up always in the company of these strange, comical, and animated people.

"The key is, it's a big step, and it's an aggressive posture for the hospital to take, Doctor. So we all have to make sure we're on the same page, approach-wise, yeah?"

"I understand, Mr. Berg. And, beyond the concerns I'd naturally have for any patient who's part of our pediatrics ICU"—and this was the sort of legalese Darlene never learned to speak well—"is my understanding of what I see as the hospital's exposure. I feel confident in my diagnosis: and if this child is harmed, and it's clear we had our suspicions, *and* we have paperwork on it. I think we'd be even more susceptible to legal action if we did nothing. We don't want to end up like Long Island General Presbyterian."

Peregrine gave that chuckle—and shook his head. "No, we do not. You're protecting this instituion, and we're all aware of that." His voice turned from dull to playful. "I do *love* American English: a term of art for every sort of action. 'Our exposure.' Yes, we would be swinging in the breeze. I am grateful that you are looking out for the hospital's interests. Public relations, and all that regrettable nonsense."

"And I appreciate the administration's support," Darlene said, borrowing once again the leeched language of paperwork as she made her way from Berg's office.

The walk to Peeds took Darlene through cancer hallways, true grief territory, what she called the front line of sadness.

Truth was, she thought administration support incidental and the meeting a formality. As she understood it, by the time a doctor alerted

Child Protective Services, the headwaters had been opened; the inquiry was already a current that had swept the principals up and left the hospital behind. CPS, in consultion with the doctor, would run the whole deal itself—it would both trouble and credit the hospital bureaucracy (and a man like Peregrine) as little as possible. In fact, Peregrine was now really a sort of bystander at the table, overlooking and blessing a stack of chips another organization would play.

So who was he to mention PR when there's a kid's life involved? Darlene always felt like taking a shower after meeting administrators. But you had to bullshit, keeping them at bay, all the while knowing what the real point of the thing was.

Getting investigations to start was also thorny. Everyone remembered the overzealous 1980s, when any kid stuck in an imperfect family had been snatched willy-nilly and dropped into the howling foster care system. But everyone had also learned—after brushing the stove a few times, coming away with a number of high-profile burns—that waiting for a preponderance of "reasonable suspicions" also carried risks. As it turned out, there hadn't been any jackpot medical documents in the Goldin case. But there was always the potential that, while a mother like Dori Goldin coolly denies the evidence, she might just be ramping up efforts to show that her child is truly ill—and thus exposing the patient to greater thresholds of risk. All the same, it was no easy task getting a CPS caseworker to visit the family and make a forceful report (an undertaking of worm-like dispatch, what with Long Island caseworkers handling up to twenty investigations at once). And in the meantime, St. Joe's and now CPS would have their own reputations, and their own legal fates, mingled with the Goldins'. Medicine hadn't kept pace, entirely, with advances in the law and insurance; the spaces where one could encounter legal trouble had become much more sophisticated than were the avenues for the cures themselves.

LATER, SHE GOT a call that dunked her into a surprise like freezing water—as if her office chair had trapdoored into the polar sea.

Two rings; she picked up, said hello, and the past came to intrude on her.

A man's voice on the line said: "Uh, this Darlene Stokes?"

"Yes, this is she."

Darlene steeled herself in her chair. Somehow, through some agency of intuition, she knew.

It can't be, she thought.

"Hey, Darlene," said the man on the phone. "This your father speaking."

Her heart bent, tightened into some fist-size thing.

"Oh," was all she managed. "Oh."

Darlene, in her scientific and careful style, had toughed her way through life by knowing what was knowable. Neutrons, electrons, and protons seethed all over the place, the matrices of the living cell, all holding their posts. Understanding life's components was to have some handle on life as a whole; this had guided Darlene through her entire education and beyond. All things alive are built from cells and all cells come from preexisting cells; there are no exceptions.

"I go by a couple a names," the man was saying. "Charles Stokes, Intelligent Muhammad, that's me." His voice ran surprisingly flat. "Your daddy, you know."

Darlene forced the dryness in her mouth to the shape the word *hello*.

All things alive are built from cells, but even the most basic living systems aren't just the tally of their neutrons, electrons, and protons. This is what always troubled Darlene. Systems theory says it's the arrangement that matters—the mess of joined, circular, sometimes time-delayed relationships between these particles. And so, you may know loads about neutrons or protons and almost nothing about the systems they make up. The details of the physical world sometimes seemed like a welcoming person who'd change its mind and take off when you got close.

"This wasn't easy, you know. You a hard person to find, Doctor."

She said, "My telephone number is listed in the phone book."

Also: Neutrons and electrons were constrained; but a human could bounce, shift, turn up anywhere.

"Manhasset wasn't the part of the map I hit first, you understand? You got to understand where a person lives before you could look."

"Yes," she said, "I suppose that's so"—her voice quite throaty. Thinking of what to say felt like smoothing out a crumpled paper scrap: as if she'd written an old note, keeping it hidden in a pocket, for precisely this situation. But time had turned the paper blank. It had faded away by the time she'd pulled it out.

"Why," she said, "—why are you calling me now?" One word flashed in her mind: "Money."

For the ten thousandth time Darlene tried picturing him. For a hopeful second, she called up an old stately savant at a cherry desk, puff-haired like Frederick Douglass, his mouth gripped by thought.

"You know, Alice—your moms—she wouldn't tell me no address. She was talking 'bout California, Mill Valley, Marin County, all these places."

"But why *now*," Darlene said, "after—" A boulder in her throat kept her from going on.

(Her mental picture of him *had* been Frederick Douglass, basically; she'd forgotten it, but a grade-school photo of that leonine reformer had whipped up young Darlene's great unspoken hope: *Maybe he's like <u>this</u>*.)

"Doctor." He was laughing. "I made it this far, I can't stop now."

Darlene squared her jaw, a little nod of annoyance that won her no points in a telephone call. *If love is a light, then I live in darkness,* she often used to think, long ago—with all the melodrama and truth of the teenage temperament.

Intelligent Muhammad answered her silence by cushioning his voice. "Just calling to see, if possible, we could, I don't know"—all swagger gone. "I only got one daughter," he said. "You, I'm talking about, Doctor."

No one felt more proud of her profession than Darlene did. But that word "doctor," so curt and clacky all of a sudden, brought a warm feeling to her embarrassed cheeks.

"That's the *real*," said Muhammad.

She said: "Charles, listen . . ." Had he told her his name was *Intelligent*? She decided not to try it—

—and he said with more unforeseen softness: "I don't want nothing from you, you understand me?"

". . . I'm quite busy," she finished saying. She recognized to her great surprise that, after waiting nearly forty years, her strongest wish—it was almost a spasm in her arm—was to hang up on him.

"I called a lot of hospitals, looking," Muhammad said. The quarters he now added to his pay phone bubbled into the connection; it sounded like small rocks plopping into a stream.

"I've thought"—Darlene regretted her honesty even as she said it—"to look for you, too, actually."

As if he hadn't heard, Muhammad said: "In that accordance, I'm like most people. Out here, just trying. You got to play this game they call life."

Darlene felt, for the first time ever, something not unlike a teenager's burning embarrassment over a parent's shortcomings.

"Talking about, I'm not a scheisty person, Doctor. Believe that. But give a man like me a chance *some*times, I don't know."

She took the phone from her ear. At the last moment she kept herself from hanging up. She listened again. But her agitated mind, a double-tugged wishbone, could have broken either way. After a lifetime of hoping, she had nothing whatsoever to talk about.

"I had some bad luck," Muhammad was saying. He couldn't *stop* finding things to say. "*Bad* luck."

She closed her eyes and pressed massaging circles on the lids. Even after having been told her whole life that Charles Stokes had been a loser, Darlene had still entertained the most childish, middle-class hopes about him. One distasteful thing about this call was having to face her own banal prejudices, like some white person. Frederick *Douglass?*—it was like a joke.

"But we *family.*" Muhammad's voice scraped a little in exasperation now. You could almost feel him steeling himself to ask why his daughter was so damn *mean.*

"You understand—family?" he said. "I know people on the outside they have to, you know, get by the best they can, bust they ass, but you know what I'm saying? I just want to meet, is all."

If she were going to talk with him it should have been on her conditions; she'd have prepared. What did she want from this man now—from this call she'd ached so badly for as a child? He wasn't helping; he wasn't clearing a space for her to say what she really had wanted: a father when she'd needed one, in the long-ago past. He couldn't offer that.

"I just want to meet you," he said.

But she'd already decided: *I'm going to hang up.* She began to move the phone off her ear again. *Right now.*

Yes, sometimes the world does seem like a welcoming person who takes off when you get close. But other times it seems more belligerent, even argumentative. It hisses at you.

Darlene's expected gut responses—enthusiasm or trepidation or even a thud of anger—never turned up; instead she just listened to herself say into the receiver:

"How will I recognize you?"

6

THE AIR WAS FREEZING AND UNSTEADY AND NOW THERE WAS SNOW.

Snow fell on the four gas stations at what residents called "the four corners." It fell on Glen Cove Road's Blockbuster Video and on the adjoining McDonald's. It had been shoveled clear out of Pizza Hut's crescent-shaped parking lot and on the truncated, four-car slot of its eternal antagonist, Domino's. Beeping yellow municipal plows had built their white peaks on either side of the road. But the snow had already started to reclaim the territories it had lost. McDonald's blacktop looked again as if a doily had been laid over it. White semicircles had formed in the bottom halves of the fence links that separated the franchises from one another. Glen Cove Road, though it was filled with these small, enterprising buildings, remained entirely free of architecture—the stores were just cubes of industry. Yet the snow made it all nearly a fairyland.

Two blocks down from the main intersection, bearing a sharp right under a traffic indicator that blinked a cautious, slow-down yellow through reflecting snowflakes, Dori Goldin stood at the window, looking at the weather. And then she turned to stare at her sleeping son. She thought: *I can't even remember my life without him.* This was sort of true.

She left the window, took a step to Zack. She was alone in the room with him.

What Dori really had difficulty remembering was herself. Herself—as she'd lived before giving birth. She would often stare at her own face in pictures from, say, high school, looking at that girl as if at some little sister—a person who was not anyone's wife, not anyone's mother.

Dori didn't snap on the bedroom light now; she leaned over the baby's crib in the half-dark. He looked happy, sweet-dreaming at seven-thirty P.M.

He can tell I'm looking at him, Dori thought. *He always knows things in his sleep.*

Zack twisted a little from her touch. His skin still surprised her: its softness, his cheeks as she ran her hand over them, his neck, the meat of his arms.

She loved these quiet moments, her and the baby. She considered looking for the clicker, firing up some cable news, just to get a weather update. But she decided against it. She wanted to be alone with Zack now, in the quiet.

Sometimes, when she'd turn a few pages in those old photo albums, she'd get nervous and and find herself asking, *Where's Zack?*—as if he'd been somehow lost in the past. As if even there, he was her responsibility.

Even after thinking, *How silly*, she'd miss him a little—her son who was disappointingly absent from pictures shot before his birth. Wasn't that a mother's love?

But how could she have explained this concept to the stranger from this morning, with his muddy and suspicious assumptions, who had stepped into her house to track her fitness as a parent?

"Hello," the thirtyish stranger had said, "I'm Jim Plates, Child Protective Services."

Jim Plates was astonishingly handsome; it must have been a distraction to his job. His clothes were standard, of the kind Dori recognized from junior salesmen in her husband's office: the wardrobe of men who couldn't worry—as a man like Josh could—about the fatness of weave, the sumptuousness of dye, the subtlety of pattern. But above the collar—and even past the cuffs, in the power of his improbably tanned hands—Mr. Plates was beautiful. Wide-jawed, spike-banged, hard-browed: It was as if you'd squeezed some kind of surf god into a Secret Service man's suit. The dissociation kept throwing off Dori.

Plates had stood at their entrance, and offered Dori his hand.

It felt calloused and sunny and firm, like a summer's walk across a beach parking lot.

"Mrs. Goldin, is this time convenient for our little visit?"

His look of concern and etiquette was so strange and outsize, like a lion asking the proper way to eat a walnut. And she had to invite him across her threshold.

"You understood I'd be coming?" he said.

"Not coming *today*, but yes, that you were sometime." She talked vigorously, as if to sound like more than the almost five feet six she was. "Please, come in." Her biggest smile.

He put his sizable head into the room before he stepped in—hesitating, rubbernecking a bit, taking in the house. She understood that everything (the furnishings, the cleanliness, the warmth) was up for inspection, would be receiving a grade. He held a small cardboard pad. How could that little sister of hers, the Dori at seventeen years old, have known one day that the achievements of her life would receive an assessment by New York State?

Mr. Plates stood looking for something special—but what? Dori couldn't stop staring at his jaw and hair, where snow had left damp marks. Mr. Plates didn't seem surprised to find her gazing; whatever it meant to him, he was used to it, a hesitation in the way people processed the information of big Jim Plates. "And where is"—Mr. Plates checked his pad—"little Zack? He's going to be joining us, too?"

Mr. Plates had a low voice that flounced up at the end of sentences, a demure turn of apology even as he had somebody else on the ropes.

"Zackie's in the kitchen, which is right this way," Dori said. The words were coming at a nervous gallop. "No, he's in the high chair. I'm sorry, strapped *into* the high chair. This is making me nervous. He's not alone—or maybe my husband has gone upstairs." They heard footsteps cross above. "He is upstairs, my husband. He's just getting ready for work." Her hands were shaky.

Mr. Plates gave a kind smile. "Ma'am, Mrs. Goldin, don't worry,

I understand you had to leave your son alone to answer the door. I'm not here to judge you. I'm just here to make, oh, an assessment. But it's not an antagonistic process."

"I'm sorry, I can't help feeling like I'm being judged."

"We're just forming an opinion on a claim—the claimant is being judged, too, in a sense. Hey, I should meet Mr. Goldin, too, huh?"

"I'm sorry. Josh! Come down, please! It's Child Services is here!" She turned to Mr. Plates again. "You understand"—and now it was coming out more smoothly; the guy's being handsome was making it easier, not harder. It didn't feel like the grubby hand of the city, the mud and sadness of falling into the clutch of bureaucracy, that she had feared.

"Believe me, I know exactly how you'd feel," Mr. Plates said. He aimed his eyes on Dori and his forbearance breathed something like warmth into his voice: "I'm just here to make a preliminary report."

"Oh."

Dori took this big man to her kitchen, poured him a cup of her coffee. The thumps from Josh's feet upstairs accelerated.

Little Zack sat belted, indeed, in his high chair. He looked healthy and blond and showed that silly, four-toothed smile. A nice thing: He reached out to Dori the second she came in. Easy and unself-consciously—his mother was an object he coveted. And he made a happy sound like *"tut,"* showing four teeth that leaned into each other as if jostling for a view of the world outside his mouth.

"My sweet boy," Dori said with all her might.

Upstairs, Josh stood at the corner of their bed, squirming his feet into shoes, jackhammering his shirtfront down into his pants. The key was to walk in extra cool and relaxed. Like a newscaster heading light and springy to the anchor's desk—and thus to seem *un*startled by the sight of this CPS fucker. Lips still smeared with toothpaste, buttons to be buttoned—he was hurrying. Dori wouldn't do a bad job alone. Dori had never failed to impress anybody, which was one of the things that was so mystifying about St. Joe's picking this fight with her. But Josh was desperate to bring their combined forces to this battle. It was the two of them, fighting to remain a three.

In the kitchen, Mr. Plates sipped his coffee as if he had all day to shoot the breeze—as if he were a prized guest, favoring one of the Goldins' small, wooden chairs with his full, packed body. He was eyeing little Zack very closely.

"You have a great kitchen," Mr. Plates said.

It was really, really strange having this guy in her kitchen; when she looked away from him, panic gurgled in her stomach like the last slop of foam in a sink.

"Thank you," she said. She tried to be nonchalant about the slight mess: the stuffed bunny doll that lay flaccid in front of Zack's chair; the two dirty dishes on the counter. But when she looked back at the strange man in their home, she felt calm, as if hosting a friend she'd forgotten she had. She felt like she might say any stupid thing. The state had devised, she thought, a brilliant tactic—if bureaucracies had recourse to tactics—employing someone as graceful as Mr. Plates.

"It's usually spotless in here, Mr. Plates." She fed Zack from a jar of "Stage 2" apricots. She changed his bottle. She felt like the guest star of a Martha Stewart show about baby care.

She smiled at the man, took an awkward step, and tripped, in her own kitchen.

"I know it is a very artificial procedure, Mrs. Goldin," Mr. Plates said. It must have been that every normal person buckled a little under the artificiality of these visits—which reassured Dori that she was processing things in the normal way. Nothing of what she'd done—the creative action she'd taken to improve her family—was showing.

"And we're aware this course of action puts folks out of ease. I've been in a lot of homes. I know things get *prickly*."

Something about the word "prickly" made Dori start—

Josh burst his way in, leading with a spruce step to the unfamiliar man; and Dori could tell that Josh hadn't found what he expected. On seeing Mr. Plates, Josh's eyes, for a moment, squinted as if sizing up a sexual rival. Then she felt him gauging *her* level of attraction to this man—but finally he stepped forward, Professional Josh again, offering the meaty shake of his own big hand.

"Glad you're here—Mr. Plates, is it?" Josh said, smiling, sitting. He was playing the guy, she saw, as one more pal in the locker room, man-to-man.

"Just another step on the road to putting this whole idiotic thing behind us. Did you know the hospital screwed up? My wife predicted this. I mean, we're just normal people. We just want to go on raising our son, doing all we can to make certain he doesn't get sick again"—not overconfident but not insecure, either. The fine line, walked skillfully.

"I'm sure you do," Mr. Plates said. He put his coffee back firmly in its saucer.

"Glad to hear you say that," Josh told him. Everything they said, it was like they were shaking hands again.

"I was telling your wife this sort of visit is not antagonistic. But so many families get *snippy* when a representative arrives."

And Dori understood, in a way her husband did not: Mr. Plates was gay. CPS had sent a homosexual to assess her fitness as a parent. The visit felt even more absurd to her than it had ten minutes ago, and she was angry at what she now recognized as having been her attraction, which had been like trying to have a conversation with a recorded voice on an answering machine: He could hear her, but he wouldn't respond. She thought: How could *this* man know about the stresses that made up a straight family?

And so the Goldins found themselves spending the next hour with gray-eyed Jim Plates, Child Protective Services, a strange man taking notes at their breakfast table.

Dori's fury roared back. She didn't like being judged by him; it sharpened her senses. CPS was *inviting* her to get a bad report. Because didn't homosexual men often "dislike women"? She thought she'd read that somewhere. But that freed Dori of her tripping anxiety. With her anger to focus on, she became, oddly, the most relaxed person in the room. Josh kept trying to sell every answer, and Mr. Plates seemed afraid of somehow knocking a mobile with his giant head (he hunched even when he sat), even though there were no mobiles in sight. And Dori was serenely wondering: How could those people have set her up in this way, sending a man who couldn't tell anything about the kind of person or mother Dori was?

And it was funny to her that Josh couldn't see it—Josh, who felt he noticed everything.

"Okay," said Mr. Plates. "Just have to run through these questions, which are standard."

"We are aware it's serious," Josh said again. "We just *know,* however, once you spend a minute with Zackie, you'll see we're really, really good parents. Not to pat ourselves on the back. But I almost think the best thing would be just for us to clear the room and let you spend some time alone with him."

It was as if he were offering Mr. Plates the chance to take their son on a test drive. He was right, though: the baby was being so good. Not making any fuss or crying at all.

"No one could love their child more than we love Zack," Dori said. Her voice came out quite loud and emotional and anybody would have understood she was telling the truth. "No one," she added.

That's it, honey, Josh thought, with a senior partner's pride.

Mr. Plates activated his pen by thumping its bottom against his pad: *click*.

"Okay, this is the prepared-questions part of the program." His condescension played as a lengthening of his smile.

Mr. Plates's questions were easy; the answers fell absolutely in the Goldins' favor. How many hours a day is one of you with him? (*The whole day*.) How many times has he been seriously sick, besides *the* times? (*None.*) Even Plates's hair seemed fussy to Dori—its part made a precise scalp trail, pale and straight as string. Um, has Zack been sick since the last hospital visit? (*No, he hasn't.*) How do *you* two get along? (*Great!*) Have the police ever come here to break up an argument or for any reason? (*Of course not—no. No.*)

The questions weren't just repetitive. They showed that the families whom CPS usually confronted must have been quite different from the Goldins—and also why Plates himself seemed so relaxed here. "...So, have either of you been arrested or charged with drug use, or any criminal act?"; "Do you have any dependents from earlier relationships?"; "Are you, or have you ever been, in family counseling?" (*No, we never had any reason to be in counseling.*) Between questions, the only sound was the salt-shakerish *cha-cha-cha* of Plates writing.

"All right," he said, lifting his gaze from the pad. "On to the next bit. Listen, I have to tell you that I'll check all your answers with the authorities."

"Sure, sure," said Josh, trying hard to keep up that smile.

Everything Mr. Plates did—his own over-smile; the tight grip on his pen; the eyes that kept trying to catch Zack unawares, as if he were the candids photographer for a yearbook—seemed meaningful and cunning to Dori. A trap in her own home.

Who knew if any straight couple would seem odd to this gay man? All the ways in which she and Josh didn't get along, the failures of understanding, the disjunctures of ambition, of mood: It must be a wonder to this man why any heterosexual couple didn't fight, abuse, torture. Really, she was being goaded by the hospital, she knew it. And so she was extra careful not to make a mistake.

She forced herself to stare into those lulling gray eyes; she managed not to look away. Behind his liveliness there was something else—steady, wise, above all judging. A part of him that seemed really to know Dori. Everything hers was being made cold by his being here, by the reprimand of his presence.

On the wall, they'd hung a framed poster of pale spaghetti emerging from a grinder in patriotic red, white, and blue. But the picture was off, Dori noticed now—half of it was angled faintly higher than the other, damn it, like someone with shoulders at a slant.

As Dori kept telling herself, *Don't look at it,* Mr. Plates asked if she'd please pick up Zack from his chair.

"Really?"

"Yes, I'm afraid this is the talent portion of the program," Mr. Plates said amiably. "Well, I'd just like to see"—he told not Dori, but Josh—"how the child interacts with his mother."

Josh heard the request as an outrage, a humiliation—but Dori took it as a *time-out*-like relief, the opportunity to hold her son.

And Zack was a dream. He made a laughy noise, opening mouth and eyes wide, in anticipation of his mother's touch, clapping his little starfish hands.

"Upsy baby," she said with a tenderness no one could fake.

The Goldins were so close that what Josh felt watching his wife was the gratification, the warmth, you have for yourself if you manage some little victory—a behind-the-back catch, a fifty-point Scrabble word—with surprising poise.

Now Mr. Plates rose and walked over to Dori and something happened to Josh; the reality of the threat landed on him.

As this stranger drew near his child and his unquestionably innocent wife, Josh grated his teeth with anger—fight as opposed to flight. He burned to attack this trespasser. To jump the table and beat the living shit out of him. The ridiculousness, the privacy violated: It was as if the state were following his wife and only child into the bathroom.

"Could you turn him to me, please?" Mr. Plates was saying, leaning closer. "I know it's difficult."

"All right."

It must have been easy to feel generous, to flaunt such an unblinking pushy manner, when you visited so many terrified rooms and faces.

Mr. Plates got out a penlight and fired it at Zack's eyes. The baby cringed and turned his head to stare up at his mother.

Dori held and *shhh*-ed Zack. Above the baby's head, she smiled at her husband in the brave, hopeless way of the sun just as it's swamped by clouds: a brightness about to be overcome in all that storm-rack and shadow.

Dori's smile made Josh rally. He stood. "Is this necessary?"

It was; "Can you just point Zack a little more toward me?" Mr. Plates was saying with his humorless twinkle. He acknowledged nothing but his own agenda, his own schedule.

Mr. Plates put away his penlight, set down his pad, and stood, too. He asked if he could have Zack just a second and set his catcher's mitt hands to receive the child. It's rarely graceful when a man takes hold of somebody else's baby, but Mr. Plates was practiced—and Dori had to stop herself from speculating about what else he'd held in those giant hands, and the fact that they were now on her baby. Zack, good kid, didn't struggle against this unknown shoulder. Mr. Plates bounce-stepped back to his seat with the baby as if on a slow-motion trampoline, the way he'd been taught to carry children. But there was too much up-and-down in his gait; the baby started to whimper.

This made Josh terrified: Did this mean their baby looked scared, abused, that he would cry too readily? He feared Plates reaching down, making a note on his pad: *Ready crier*. And in fact, he did write something down, holding Zack with one hand while he worked the pen. Without turning the angle of his head, Josh tried to read from the cardboard pad. Plates had jotted what looked like a picture of a cloud, whatever that meant. A code of some kind, or just a bored squiggle?

Mr. Plates cooed what seemed authentic fondness at the baby—"Hey, hey, there, handsome boy." The guy's own affection for Zack seemed one of the great insults of the morning. The wretchedness Josh felt was a faint cousin of what you must suffer relinquishing your child to a foster parent.

Another striking thing was Mr. Plates's total absorption as he made silly voices. He shook his face, lowering it toward Zack. It was always bizarre to see a strikingly handsome man talk to a baby. Zack raised a hand to Mr. Plates's nose slowly, reverently—like the vague lost astronaut in *2001,* plucking at the world in awe.

The baby made a happy noise. Josh waited: Write *that* down. Write the happy noise down, you fucker.

Dori got angry, too, and unexpectedly hurried from the table. Mr. Plates seemed not to see this. Josh understood what the guy was measuring, as he sat the boy down on the table and played with him. It was ingenious. He moved at the boy from different sides, put his big adult face—his neck pleating with chins—near one ear and then another. He was seeing if Zack saw all motions as threats. It was so clever it made Josh despise the man all over again.

And Dori had walked to the open kitchen door but stopped; she gazed out at the living room intently, as if a movie were being projected there. Her face clenched its concern—misery creasing the bridge of her nose, even the great pink lips getting pretty small.

Josh tried to will her to turn to him, so he could shoot her a frown that said, *Come back.* She took a step into the next room.

"Where did your wife head off to, Mr. Goldin?" Plates said, not looking away from the baby.

Josh couldn't say his wife was having a tantrum—though surely she was. He decided to lie, to risk that Plates wouldn't turn and see Dori right there. "Bathroom, I think," he said.

"Fair enough. It's on this floor, right? I saw one as I passed."

Josh understood—figuring a man like this for house-to-house work. It was a long-standing debate in sales: How attractive did you want your sales force to be? Unsightly, and you made all your sales calls, unconsciously, a negative: Who wanted to spend time with that fugly Sparkplug crew again? But too nice-looking, and the buyer felt self-conscious, overmanned, outgunned. Who wanted to feel like a toad? A man this handsome would make most families worry about how they appeared as a social unit—and then they'd forget that he was here to notice everything but that.

Sending someone like Plates had been CPS's way of making the visit social, and feel true when it wasn't, Josh thought. It wasn't true. It was a lie.

"We like to have both parents in the room, just for the report. You get that, don't you, Mr. Goldin?" It was Mr. Plates's chastening indifference that made you feel you were giving your child away.

Josh said, calm as he could manage, "Honey?" He'd also spoken overloud so she'd understand: It was meant to sound as if he were calling to a far room.

Dori didn't want to spend more time with this assessor who had no basis to assess from. She stood her ground.

"Mrs. Goldin," Plates said sensibly—not as if she were in another room at all. "Please come back to the table. I know this visit is difficult."

Dori returned: Her reflection was vivid, gray, and wavery in the face of her oven, which was set in the wall a few feet from Mr. Plates's profile.

"Look, people freak sometimes," said Mr. Plates. He lifted his manful shoulders. "You couldn't do this job for five days without accepting that. I don't hold it against anybody. This is in no way the weirdest thing I've seen. Three weeks ago, a woman slapped me. That's how whacked out. And now I'd like to remove Zack's clothes."

She'd already gotten back to the table as the guy lifted Zack's shirt off. She hadn't anticipated this. She had thought it would be a visit to test their emotional condition. Shouldn't only a doctor be allowed to examine their baby's skin? Because she was pretty sure the butterfly needle hadn't left traces; but maybe the tiniest marks were there, if one knew what to look for? And Dori couldn't imagine— because she knew all the ways in which she was ordinary—that, in the whole history of the state of New York, she could be the first mother to have ever bled her child.

Mr. Plates was scanning the baby's chest: zero bruises. He moved his fingers like a garmento examining cloth for imperfections, searching the places where discoloration, where damage, was likely to be found; above the ribs, in the hollow of the armpit—and Dori flinched leaning closer to the man. His eyes moved toward the shoulders; soon they would be traveling down the arms.

Please, she thought, *don't look at his arms.*

And Josh, heart in his mouth in spite of himself, was thinking of all the children this man must have examined who really *did* have bruises—and he imagined what it might have been like to see four knuckle marks on Zack's rib cage, or a welt on his leg; he thought how much he himself would have hurt anyone who'd put such things there.

"There's a good boy, Zack," Mr. Plates was saying, "letting the funny man come in from the snow and give you a little examination."

He hooked his hands under the baby's fingers, and Zack smiled, squeezing Plates's thumbs. Zack looked to Dori just like he had on the papoose board, his arms spread; Zack seemed almost to be expecting this move. The sight forced the blood to Dori's neck and shoulders and cheeks. She felt faint. Plates was looking at Zack's wrists (many parents must squeeze dangerously hard there), and now, especially, at the biceps (another universal handhold). But his eyes—Dori felt her own heart banging—had passed right over the delicate pale forearms, with their thatch of blue veins. He held Zack's arms out for another moment, and then he let go. The baby was slow about lowering his arms, as if he were on the papoose board, after all. Dori lost all her breath again.

Mr. Plates looked at her. "I'd like you to turn him over, please, Mrs. Goldin. And thanks for your help, this is just a formality, really." And the big man checked the child's back, the undersides of Zack's legs, all the places where his eyes had, in other homes, found evidence and sadness, indiscipline and anger.

"You want me to change him, Mr. Plates?" said Josh.

"Sorry if my hands are cold, Zack," Mr. Plates said. Without looking at Josh, he added: "I've got him, Mr. Goldin, thanks."

The rest of the kitchen part of the interview was easy. He tapped

Zack's knee with one of those pint-size medical tomahawks, check-ing for baby reflexes. With every chop his tiny foot spurted out.

Zack, with his open-mouthed, face-scrunching smile, looked like Josh's grandfather had when *he'd* laughed—the thrilled cheeks, the gleaming, pinched eyes; he was successfully imitating awareness. But he had no idea what was happening.

"Almost done, Zack," Mr. Plates said.

And yet, another half hour trembled and passed. Mr. Plates made no effort to leave. "You can get him dressed again, Mrs. Goldin," he said. By now, a lot of Josh's anger had burned off. He just felt nervous and exhausted—it was becoming hard to remember what their house felt like without this big man in it. Plates stood, and Josh raised his eyebrows at his wife, as he had at the end of hundreds of dinner parties, when the last guest had yet to slump toward the door. Dori, who had been—not counting her two-minute freakout—so helpful during the examination, having made sure the man hadn't missed how healthy the baby looked, now seemed as worn-out and relieved as Josh did that it was ending.

"Oh, one more thing," Mr. Plates said. "I'd just like a little house tour."

"Really? Okay, that's fine."

And so Plates intruded everywhere: the baby-proofed family room, where all risky edges had, as in a pinball machine, been pad-ded with bumper cushions; Zack's room, with its foldaway changing board and a mobile that dangled blue triangles from the ceiling—and where, finally, tall Mr. Plates *did* snag his head on something. He was taking his notes through all of it, a walking condemnation that wouldn't quit.

Mr. Plates scribbled about everything, the food-preparation area, the guest-entertaining zone, about the entry and exit halls. And, if not every *last* inch here was kid-safe, Plates must have seen that clearly, this was a house of *parents*—cautious parents who had taken pains to look after their child as best as was humanly possible. Still, as he circumnavigated the home, for some reason Dori believed that he'd be staying out of *their* room; they would, she assumed, be allowed this one molecule of privacy. But when Mr. Plates came out fom the little garden room at the back of the first floor, he pointed upstairs and said, "Which door's the master bedroom? I think we missed that one"—and Dori exploded in panic.

The papoose board was under her bed. It was simply tucked beneath the box spring's skirt. And it would be as impossible to hide as the sun in a movie theater: It would shine out everywhere. It was the burning center of the house.

The intruder stuck his head into the bedroom—Dori's blood jumping in her own forearms. But Mr. Plates dithered before entering, a three-year-old shy to wake his parents on Christmas morning, bashful at the threshold.

"Nice," he said, finally stepping in: red toile coverlet and curtain, a wall-framed wedding portrait, Dori in her white and Josh in his yarmulke, just another Jewish wedding on another big wall in Long Island.

Dori cursed herself. Was she crazy—well, not *crazy* crazy, but at least at fault here? The acknowledgment finally reached her. Dori felt the way you might when, after driving your car calmly down the street, you understand with a jolt that you're going the wrong way, and that danger is barreling toward you. That you're headed for a crash of your own devising.

Josh, sensitive to changes in his wife's emotional weather, rested a hand on her back—his are-you-okay touch. She was too freaked to respond.

Mr. Plates walked toward the unmade bed. And all he would have to do, Dori understood, was drop down on one knee. If he looked under there, everything would be finished. One look, and no more CPS, no more dragged-out worry, no more protection by Seidel, no more Zack, no more Josh. No more anything. It seemed he was on the verge of kneeling every second. If he dropped a pen, for instance. If he caught a glimpse of anything suspicious. Dori didn't know many gay people, but she'd thought someone once told her that they noticed more, that their senses were as alert as dog's ears. This man could end her life.

It was then she saw a snippet of the papoose board, its corner just barely poking out from above the box spring's skirt. She was holding Zack now, and each shift of her son's bulk pulled her collar to different shapes.

Mr. Plates gestured at the unmade bed, faced the Goldins, and smiled.

"Yeah," he said, "until my girlfriend gets around to it, my bed stays unmade all day, too." He elbowed Josh playfully in the ribs. "I know how it is, buddy."

AFTER THEY SHOWED Mr. Plates out, she told herself that she'd done something few mothers would have been ballsy enough to do.

It had been brave and important, she thought, giddy with relief. It had been *necessary*. Because you've got to keep the family together. You have got to keep the family together.

She'd avoided the car crash.

At the front door, Mr. Plates had thanked his hosts. He'd said that "they would be in further touch" with the Goldins. Dori wondered who "they" were. "More people like me," Mr. Plates said. The smile almost seemed genuine—slack-mouthed and built on what he'd have liked you to believe was kindness. He dropped his pen by accident.

And Dori had gotten cocky, lowering the baby before Mr. Plates one last time and saying: "D'you want to show the man how you can walk, Zackie?"

Zack took five steps across the carpet, his arms straight out. Lately, his legs had been finding their use slowly. With elbows and knees in the unplumping stage that marks an end of earliest life, and his cute nonsense tries at sentence making—facets of an individual self falling into place—Zack was plodding out of babyhood. He lurched, as if the floor were treacherous, then fell back into Josh's waiting hands.

Dori bent to retrieve the pen that Mr. Plates dropped. "If you have a busy schedule," she said, "do you say you have a full plate?" And she handed him the pen.

Mr. Plates had risen into solemnity and said: "No, Mrs. Goldin, I do not."

Josh had let out a soft, amazed chuckle: what a woman, joking even then!

But later, and into the next day, Dori feared talking casually, as if CPS had bugged her house or something. As Mr. Plates had driven off, she'd taken Zack to the family room, stood the child in front of her, and knelt with the hallowed, stubborn dignity of mothers.

"Show Mommy and Daddy how you walk, one more time," she said. And Josh had looked upon this, his family, and drawn comfort from his good fortune.

IV

Love covers all sins.

—Proverbs 10:12

1

Under the attentions of CPS, Goldin family life ran on an alternating current. It went on like this for six months: Some days, the threat would hiss and crackle; others, the baby would galvanize his family with some proud signal of progress. He referred to himself by name for the first time on a Tuesday morning. One week later Dori learned she would face a judge for a "Parent Suitability" hearing. Martin Seidel (Dori had begun to freeze when the firm's name came up on the caller ID: GOTTLIEB, GOLD, & McNULTY) phoned to alert the family to a slew of future visits from Mr. James Plates; on the same day, Zack mastered the indispensable, masculine art of kicking a ball—which in Josh's eyes made the prospect of additional hours with Plates doubly, triply, quadruply ridiculous. The only abnormal element in his son's upbringing, Josh tingled to say, was Child Protective Services itself. It raged and burned within him, this knowledge—some days he felt like a kind of Big Mac, his feet the lower bun, his head the upper, and in between layers and layers of squashed resentment; he felt toasted and precariously balanced, above all these shelves of anger, pride, optimism, and more anger.

Josh and Dori fought. He'd leave for work in the morning without having remembered to do A), she'd been at Pathmark but hadn't picked up B), and the affronted one yelled. That was just the stress, making its predictable mischief. What surprised both Dori and Josh was the discovery that their sputtering little blowups actually bound the family even tighter. It gave Dori the sense of getting a look at all sides of a person—in the same way that, once she'd accustomed herself to it as a newlywed, she'd felt closer to Josh each time she entered the bathroom after he'd spent time in there beyond the standard thirty seconds of noisy man-urination. The solid knotty smell he'd left was evidence of another thing her husband did; one more avenue by which his personhood was expressed. And *now,* she was being reminded that Josh was a clean arguer: He fought about the issue at hand, and never pried under it, never gouged at her personality. So during this half year, Dori had the steady sense of her marriage getting even better. They'd fallen into the needy, poignant togetherness of soldiers hemmed in by occupying armies.

Dori realized that, forgetting even the risk, this had made further bleeding of Zack unnecessary—at least for now. She had achieved the desired effect.

All this, of course, was offset by the threat. The fear that, when they read certain addresses on certain windowed envelopes, dark forces were looking to take away Zack: to dissolve the family. The envelopes dropped Josh into dark funks; they made Dori's stomach flip. Sometimes she simply turned the envelopes upside down, as if in some deep part of her, her soul were neatly burying its head in the sand.

As much as Josh hated finding the thumbprint of state bureaucracy on his table, he hated even more that his office had taken on the vibe of a sickroom. Everybody showed Josh their concerned face. He hadn't told anyone, but the news traveled (his having been forced to hurry from first the break room and then the Upfronts) because of a sick kid. Friends and clients left overwarm voice mails, where the bounciness was offered as unspoken support. ("Listen, Josh, you're a good dude—and Dori is a great mom.") How'd they even know? How do secrets breed into gossip?

Colleagues materialized at his door, poking their heads in, just to give that underlippy smile you reserve for those you have to console. The vice president of programming wrote from L.A., saying he didn't know a more attractive young wife than Dori, and that he would be happy to forward those impressions in an *amicus curiae* letter to the court. (The VP's sister was in her second year of law school.)

All these folks were people who, on an hourly, daily, and annual basis, Josh felt he outshone—in every way that mattered. And now they felt sorry for him. Even the newly married ex-intern Alyssa sat down to exchange sympathy faces with him for thirty minutes one Friday afternoon. And all Josh could wonder, as he strained through that half hour, was who could have *married* such a person?

When he returned home to Dori's healthy face, and her optimism in the teeth of offical scrutiny, he reflected how lucky his own marital choice had been. At least he had that. It was one thing to love your spouse when you were stretching your legs in some calm heaven. But who could have endured all this better than Dori? What a lift it was to look over and find her beside him in the foxhole.

He needed to shoot his rage at specific targets. The incomprehensible *they* became Mr. James Plates—who retained his glib golden color throughout the winter and spring months, on the four occasions he visited their home. And Josh especially hated the black lady doctor whose name ran riot through the stationery of accusation, Dr. Darlene Stokes. He didn't suppose he'd ever hated a fellow human being as much as he hated Darlene Stokes.

Removing a child from his family was—and this made Dr. Stokes loathe Child Services with fervor nearly equal to Josh's—beyond her power. It exceeded the authority of any physician. So Dr. Stokes had been working intently with CPS—and with CPS's Betty Van Der Meer—helping to write reports of detective-story heat. And some of that language would make its way to Marty Seidel, and then via fax to Josh. Next Josh and the lawyer could go over the sentences by phone together, the accusations that Zack was in terrible, terrible danger: from *Dori*, of all people!

"You know what I think it is?" Seidel asked. "I swear, I think this is it. Some people, a certain kind of person, can never, ever, find it within their heart to trust a pretty brunette. I swear that's what I think maybe it could be."

One detail that Darlene had nearly overlooked, from the Goldins' second emergency-room trip, was now finding its way onto the CPS forms. Zack's skin had presented a slight irritation in the tender bend of his right arm. A raspberry and poison-ivy stipple, just above the standard baby coloring of cream and rose. Did this indicate he'd been bled? Was that why the tests had indicated anemia? The Goldin mother had had medical training. Drawing blood from your own child: In the casebooks of MSBP, it would rank among the kindest of methods. But it seemed almost too cautious. That kind of care (Darlene considered this at night, as she tutored James in his own self-maintenance: fingernail clipping, molar brushing, ear scouring, a body's lifetime housework skills) didn't seem likely to occur alongside the wild, secluded passions of MSBP.

Before long Dr. Stokes had her wish granted, however. Facing down the creeping doldrums of state bureaucracy, she and CPS got the Child Abuse Consult Network finally to agree to set up a hearing. The CPS agent Jim Plates had found something damning. The parents and their lawyer didn't know it yet, but finally a judge would decide if Zack should be removed from his home and into protective custody. (This being a hearing, the state wasn't required to share any evidence with the defense.)

It's a tough stand to take, Dr. Stokes told herself. *Removal.* The warmth of her desk lamp often made her neck hot; she'd been working so much on this lately that sometimes, on sunny weekends in the park with James, she'd feel a burst of office anxiety—when all that had really hit her was a splash of sun. *But it's the right stand, and the only one.*

The process moved by measured steps, like a humble petitioner's walk across a palace, or a climbing team's assault up a mountain. Or for that matter, Darlene's own medical education: You advanced on territory, held it, assembled tools, took preventive measures—and then on a crisp morning you made the next ascent. Were the judge to rule in favor of removal, Zack would be taken immediately, with a second hearing to be convened thirty days later. The next question would then be "continued out-of-home guardianship." And *that* would be revisited, every ninety days, for a year and a half. What could be a fairer, safer, more transparent process than that? After that time, CPS would make a bid for "permanency"—and the very phrasing made Darlene imagine Peregrine Berg's chuckle. And Berg was right, she thought: We Americans dressed the largest and most terrifying of our transformations in the most innocent of bland locutions.

Of course, if after all these steps, a parent was diagnosed definitively as "DSM-4—factitious disorder by proxy," the state would seize the child for adoption. There wouldn't be a shadow of hope for the parents. And this is what Darlene wanted to happen to the Goldins.

Darlene handled all this in what no longer really qualified as her off-hours: the hours when she wasn't busy as division chief, or seeing new patients, or recruiting new doctors, or setting the curriculum for the pediatrics residents, or organizing "ground rounds" (lectures on cutting-edge developments, delivered by physicians whose stars had risen high enough even to be observed from St. Joe's); or conducting her own clinical research—comparing ventilator modes for treatment of respiratory failure; testing blood-pressure-elevating medicines, called "pressors," for kids in shock. Meanwhile, her actual, away-from-St.-Joe life had gone topsy-turvy. Darlene's father had managed to introduce his criminal record and inelegance to her world.

The first thing Intelligent Muhammad had said on meeting Darlene had been, "Yeah, you my daughter, all right." He had looked her up and down: elbows, knees, ears, big jaw. They met at the Manhasset train station, by the information desk.

Darlene didn't think he looked that much like her, with his baggy pants and baggy neck. But Darlene saw that he did *stand* like her—a mistrustful inclining to one side, which Darlene had always chalked up to her time at Tufts (not quite white enough; not quite street enough), but instead proved to be choreography from her genes.

Intelligent Muhammad was thicker and rounder than Darlene—

in a way, his ample body had spread to become more feminine than her own. And he had her slender nose with its wide nostrils. Most of all, when he trudged across the parking lot to shout at a car that had honked at them, the galumph of her father's step was so much hers it gouged Darlene's heart. It was like watching her own destiny locked in the body of an old man.

All she needed was to read one Internet story about the Starline Motel where he lived: the $6.50 rooms, the chicken-wire walls, the knife fights in the stairwells. ("Hey, it's all right for Intel, you know?" Muhammad said. "Talking 'bout, they know me there.") She temporarily installed her father that afternoon in a proper bedspread-and-curtains room at the Clarion Lodge by LaGuardia airport.

She asked Peregrine Berg if he might find custodial work for someone named Intelligent Muhammad. She told him only that the guy was a "relative"—while, of course, asking that he remain discreet about her connection to this ex-criminal. And then Darlene said to her son, "We're going to have a visitor for a while."

"Who?" James said. "Is it Grandma Alice?"

"No, not Grandma Alice." She said this calmly, because a child should never see his mother lack control. "It's someone Grandma knows. Well, it's your grandfather. My father."

She thought he might smile. You could never tell with James. He winced, as he had when she'd said there was no Santa Claus— the sullen face of a brainy kid resentful that, while he's been making a *bona fide* effort to understand the world, the adult he'd trusted had gamed the system, had kept him tied in ignorance.

"You told me you didn't talk to him ever," James said. A meteorologist might have described his mood as "cloudy"; his mother was dismantling their neither-of-us-will-ever-see-our-fathers-again club.

"That used to be true," she said.

"Oh," was all he said.

Darlene hadn't told her mother about Muhammad. Forty years old, and still hiding her bad decisions—her mother would think it a "terrible idea," a "fool's mistake"; but she also wondered if keeping the truth from her mother was her way of telling herself it *was* an awful decision.

When she left for work, she wondered, *Will he steal from me?* When she got him his locker and his uniform, she thought, *Will he steal from the hospital?* And then she tut-tutted herself on the car ride to St. Joe's: Her sojourn among suburban whites, among Leo's people, had turned her into a damn bigot.

Yet Darlene resolved never to allow James to spend time alone in the house with that man. *That man*—her father. (And once he did move in, she regretted her charitable decision every time she noticed one of his hairs, the single helices, the dark squiggles he left on her white porcelain shower tub.)

But if Muhammad harbored late middle age's need for creature comforts, he accepted Darlene's hospitality in the way he'd taken the free Clarion Lodge room: as someone James's age might have done—with seeming apathy, the sort of mental sidestep that dodges tenderness. Darlene read this as arrogant *riffraff oblige*—it seemed Muhammad accepted charity as a *favor to her*—and not a grown man's chafed pride. She often didn't know what he was talking about, anyway, and listened to him in a more or less intentional fog. As if any comprehension of him would dig up some feeling best left buried.

Still, there he sat in Darlene's suburban TV room, this felon who'd pushed crack on Bronx school kids ("Never junior high school, though. For real—but when you fifteen, sixteen, you old enough to make your own decisions"), sipping Coke and watching *SpongeBob SquarePants* with his grandson and a Caribbean nanny, while Darlene was out working to break up the Goldin family.

"Don't you get tired of this show ever?" Muhammad said. "This cartoon dude running around like he retarded?"

The nanny raised her eyebrow at Muhammad.

"I do like *Rugrats* better," James agreed solemnly.

"Bet." Muhammad scratched his chin. "The cartoon rats and

all them?" (Neither he nor James realized they shared a chin-scratching tic.)

"Bet," little James said, though he was sure there were no rats in *Rugrats*. He didn't exactly feel at ease with his grandfather. But he thrilled to the man's speech, the tough-guy voice with its dramatic bassy sediment sounds, as if Muhammad swallowed loose, dark sand. Also, the old guy cursed a lot.

When *Rugrats* came on, his grandfather changed from Coke to beer and didn't say anything more.

AFTER HALF A week in his daughter's house, Intelligent Muhammad felt like somebody who, after being rescued from drowning, realizes that the boat is in many ways as unappealing as the choppy water—realizes that he's still damp, cold, seasick, and far from his own, solid land. He couldn't relax with these tight-ass people, especially that Trinidadian lady whose job seemed to be to spy on him. She wasn't stingy with tales about criminals that she had known—lawbreakers from the far-flung precincts of her own family. "My uncle tried to reform him. Get him the job, find him the wife—but no way, you can't give a rodent feathers and tell him, 'Fly.' "

He knew, too, that his daughter wanted something from him, and that it was the same thing he wanted from her: the night when they'd both crack open beers at the table (teenaged Alice had liked her beers; he guessed Darlene would, too) and make sense of their lives to each other. Whenever it got quiet in the house, Darlene looked at Charles with an anxious, expectant face. And Charles felt the meaningful words collect in his throat: "So, yeah, you my daughter: What you want to talk about?" But he never spoke them.

When they did talk, he'd say such things as: "Like my man Rakim say, times was hard on the boulevard."

And she'd give her shaky, embarrassment smile, which guttered like the fidgety light of a candle.

Worse, the magazine story about him, the tale of his heroism that would have made such an introduction unnecessary, never happened. "It can take months, really months," Ralph Dunn explained on the phone. "There's fact checking, copyediting, then you have to twiddle your thumbs waiting for the right news peg." He'd answered this call from Muhammad late at night, sounding exhausted and surprised. "Then if they have to cut pages because of ads—but you probably don't want to know all this production stuff. So, who in editorial gave you my phone number? We're in the same position; just have to stay, you know, cool."

But for all this, when Darlene and James were asleep and Muhammad sat alone in the pearly, late-TV screen-shine, or took a half-hour soak with Darlene's bath beads and milk creams—these calm, expensive pleasures reminded him that he was a lucky man.

The hospital, however, reminded Muhammad of jail. A hierarchy of colors made clear, with near street-gang firmness (green shirt plus stethoscope stood for this, white lab coat and name tag for that), the societal order, the caste game. Waiting out his nightly rounds, cleaning up after the nightly sick, Muhammad thought about his daughter. All that high school, college, extra college, sticking her hands in dead bodies, ass kissing, just so she could wind up locked up in these corridors, under uglying lights. This place even gave you that familiar high-octane lemon taste of cleaning product on your tongue. His daughter the doctor, stuck in a world that had the same mood as those supervised daily laps around the prison yard. What would be wrong with a nice office, her own practice? Not to mention, people here—not the visitors, but people stuck here, the long-term unwells and the workers—had numbed themselves to the shit around them. You learned to become your own anesthesiologist. Like in jail.

He'd meander the hospital halls during work hours, shirt half-tucked, hands in pockets, trusting that people wouldn't notice him enough to say, "Excuse me, can you help with something?" He was a sharp guy, familiar with the necessary means. Head down, using the prison-learned lie of put-on shyness, Muhammad didn't talk to anybody. That way he wouldn't have to say he was Darlene's father.

He guessed his daughter the doctor didn't want people to know they were related.

He guessed right. One afternoon, curious Muhammad asked his supervisor, "How you think I got this job?" The man just said he'd received the blue carbon and the clipboard and that was all he knew.

That afternoon, Muhammad, before mopping corridors, headed up to Darlene.

"I just want to say, you know, thank you," Muhammad said. "Doctor."

It was late in the day—if early in Muhammad's shift—and he stood at the door to his daughter's office. He seemed self-conscious to enter. She didn't invite him in.

"Oh? You're welcome." She smiled. "That's all right. No need." But what word should she follow this with—the problem she'd felt fourteen mornings and fourteen nights running now—what should she *call* him? Intelligent? *Dad*?

Whenever she hung out with her father, Darlene felt as if she'd lost one of her basic senses: not touch or taste but sight of who she was. Her soul bent to the distortions of a funhouse mirror; Darlene felt like she was squinting to recognize herself. *Oh, yeah—that's me.*

"Bet," he said. He gave the typical compacted nod of pretend casualness.

She'd been looking over some official forms and she covered them with her hand, the way a person would the mouthpiece of an interrupted phone call. She also had some Reese's peanut butter cups sitting out; as happened pretty often, she hadn't eaten yet today. She stripped one of its brown paper petticoat. She looked at nothing but this snack. Then she bit into it, down into the gunky *snugness* of the peanut butter inside the chocolate. Her father didn't take the hint, though. He didn't excuse himself and walk away.

When she realized he was still standing there, she looked at him blankly, expectantly: the way James sometimes did. And it was the first moment he felt the burden of fatherhood. He was sure his daughter was looking to him for something, for answers maybe, and he owed her something in return, something responsible. This one moment of dependence called for reciprocity, for kindness. This was the bargain, the biological deal, he'd avoided for four decades.

Severe inarticulacy weighed on him, tamed him like a punishment there was no parole for.

Out in the hall, footsteps clomped toward them. Next, there came the *shh*-and-*crack* of a soda can opening; "Hey! You're getting it on me!" Orderlies, two of them passing. They slowed, quit talking as as they walked by, and peeked in at the doctor talking to the janitor.

Muhammad had stood this whole awkward time scratching his jaw; Darlene realized that her son and her father shared this chump mannerism, and it annoyed her. What a cockamamie thing heredity was, that this trait had gotten picked, by senseless nature, to leave its stamp on her family. What other qualities had this this ex-con imparted?

"All right, then," he said, not going anywhere.

With his janitor's mop plunked in its wheeled pail, here stood her father chewing his lip. His eyes still had that shifty back-and-forth that had cost him so much business in his time before Iceberg.

She felt him taking in everything: degrees on the wall, the stylish brushed steel lamp, books and books, the confidential Child Services forms on her desk, the small photo of Darlene's mother standing in her backyard, arm around her daughter, all the accouterments of familiarity that (for Darlene alone in the world) filled this office's bland hospitalness with some little homelike warmth. Muhammad's eye rested on the photo of Darlene and Alice—Darlene regretted she hadn't thought to turn it facedown, so her father wouldn't have to confront the daily matter of preference and rejection that life without him had become.

"I know, Doctor, you see me as, like, a hard case or something. But I can be grateful." When he spoke, his voice had lost its staccato mix of grievance and cunning; it was no longer a tone meant to impress you with its hardships, its strategies. "And I'm a worker, so, as regards that, it isn't nothing to worry about."

I know I'm not the father a classy person like you deserves, his embarrassed little smile seemed to add. Wretchedness can be mistaken for decency, sometimes.

She smiled, too, and said, gently, after a short wait: "Well, you know, I'm glad to hear that—"

What she'd almost added, or at least imagined having added despite herself, was the word "Dad." Foolish, so cheesy, and yet she pictured her father's face turning affectionate if she'd used that word—his face turning thankful. Who could say how he'd really have reacted? Maybe he was only kissing her ass because he was afraid she'd have him fired? But maybe not.

With a tight nod, he left.

Maybe from here on out, by a buildup of these small kindnesses, the two of them could press some father-daughter connection into shape. Maybe this was what family was, Darlene realized: worked-at forgiveness. This, the reality of family life, was what Darlene wished she could plug into the CPS forms, with their steady requests for indifferent data that would always overesteem a family like the Goldins.

A ping from her computer bumped her from these thoughts: incoming e-mail, AOL's slow dawning *whoosh*. She looked up: a name she didn't recognize, with the return address of gannet.org, which she thought might be a newspaper. The subject line read: *Goldin Case*.

She opened it, thinking that the e-mail would credit all her good work, and maybe even—who knows?—offer some confirmation of what Darlene now knew about families.

It turned out the reporter knew many things about her: but not that. She read words she hadn't seen in two decades, the names of places she hadn't lived in since college, and old causes and beliefs that made her smile a little. Then a warning went off inside her, a sense that the journalistic digging hadn't been neutral but avid and perhaps antagonistic; she read the words "Leo Golovin."

2

MARTIN SEIDEL'S INSPIRATIONS FOLLOWED A TROPICAL PATTERN OF drought and flash flood.

No matter what—no matter how long and dry the case stretched ahead of him—he remained a true believer. Whatever the merits, he *believed*: in the winnableness of a position, in the cosmic integrity of a cause. A loss never meant the system, the case, the client was imperfect; it just meant he hadn't thought hard enough. Sometimes it took him awhile. But Seidel, all spontaneous dazzle, understood himself to be slave to the big idea. Seidel did not represent so much a carefully engineered and regulated electrical system as he did a lone lightning rod on a flat plain.

The Goldin-case *eureka* came when Seidel had been sipping a coffee that, in its blue, Hellenic-motif paper cup, had the smell of a burned gym towel. He'd just been jogging; he lifted his exercise-warm face and thought: *Holy shit, I got it.*

He left it as a message for himself on his own voice mail; his fingers were so excited he nearly couldn't dial: "You know what it is about that black lady who's a doctor?" Angry at his own shins, his aching upset knees, he was finding relief in the painkiller of a hunch. "She's like one of those Japanese soldiers, fifty years after Nagasaki, who wander out of the jungle not realizing the war's been over forever."

Three hours later he was telling someone else: "It's some civil rights bug with this woman, I bet." He was on his kitchen phone, talking to a newspaper columnist named Gregory Hollister. "We solved all these problems in the '60s, thank you, you did your part, you educated us, we honor your service and sacrifice and commitment, why are you still resentful? Why target?"

"I get it," Hollister said. "But how would you know she's on some crusade?"

Seidel had never worked with this guy Hollister before. "I don't know," he said, "you're the reporter. I'm the attorney."

Hollister sounded like a kid, and not necessarily a hungry kid. He had that laid-back voice they talk in nowadays; you were expected to do all the homework and big-picture stuff and even take out your handkerchief to wipe their noses for them. But Gottlieb, Gold, & Mc-Nulty had built a relationship with the *Long Island News-Independent*, an upstart paper, the new "family alternative" to *Newsday*. The editors had transferred Seidel to Hollister—and this lawyer always worked his spiel hard, however unpromising the jury box.

"I'm an educated guy who isn't meaning to come at you in a non-PC way; we're all sophisticated people." Seidel cradled the phone on his shoulder to take off his jogging shoes; judging from Hollister's voice, Seidel was pretty sure the guy was white. "Take you, for instance," he said. "You're not, uh—"

"My family's origins are Scots-Irish."

"Exactly what I was trying to say. See what this is, it's a family story, a family that's like hundreds of thousands of your readers. Okay, they're Jewish, so what? This story is about, we're all afraid of the assault on the family." He grunted, pulling the last shoe from his heel. "Crazy rules, some woman decides you aren't raising your kids the hundred percent top-notch way, and some agency can take your kid? If it wasn't a great story, would I be calling on a Sunday?"

"Right, right." The sound of Hollister's typing was soft but audible. "The assault on the home by insidious outside, institutional forces," the reporter said.

Seidel congratulated him, saying that the kid really seemed to get it. But there may have been even more to the story—

Selling without overselling; that's the key to things like this. Things that involved race. (Hell, maybe that's the key to everything, thought Martin Seidel.) A man's talking points are his fate, says today's Heraclitus.

"I don't know who this woman is," Seidel was saying. "I'm pretty sure the only thing she knows about families is she wishes she had one."

He outlined the Goldins' plight with elusive, feinting strokes: repeating the word "family" until there emerged from it an under-story of homespun values; lingering an extra quarter-syllable every time he hit the very black-sounding name "Stokes"; talking, of course, with modern regard for the difficulties—the likely almost *maddening* difficulties—that "minorities must face in the medical profession"; finally chewing over, with excellent politesse, the crazy zeal of some of these doctors—black *and* white.

"It is transgressive," said the young journalist. "It runs counter to all our assumptions of who exactly represents 'the other.' I mean here, the unmarried black woman represents the top of the hierarchy—she's the doctor, the institution."

"Exactly. Like the turn in *The Sixth Sense*, in terms of the hierarchy thing," Seidel said, massaging his ankle.

Seidel, without saying much outright, kept filling in his picture: an angry black woman (one with no wedding ring) who was trying her damnedest to break up a happy white home. This is a *very* compelling story for your—for any—paper, you have to admit. Just think of it: a family, a good family, powerless against these accusations. Christ, the doctor might end up winning—the kid could be stolen! And the accusations are flimsy, really flimsy. . . .

"Ask the woman herself," Seidel said. "*You* be the judge. But why this doctor may be going after them—and why the hospital is backing her—*that* is what makes for an interesting side point, too."

Seidel felt good enough to push it a little. Not that anyone's bigoted here. Obviously. But let's not be over-PC about this, either. You have to understand: We know about Jews and blacks. Or rather, about blacks, and the problem they have—some of them have—with Jews.

"So, okay, so where would you suggest that I begin with this?" Hollister said.

Seidel didn't want to laugh—but he couldn't help a *tuth!* sound. "You go, you look into her background, and I'll bet you here's what you're going to find: There's going to be some unfair patriarchal court system that screwed over her family, some white guy who broke her heart, some school she didn't get into."

You had to be careful with these kids: You couldn't present something as too tedious, too much hard work. "Guarantee you'll find it in a day."

This wasn't a story of just racial issues, though. As their lawyer told it, the Goldins brought together many threads and fears of present-day life: loss of privacy, institutional mercilessness, formless threats to the American home, but race was the final element, making the decisive push in convincing Gregory Hollister about the story's newsiness. Of course there was race, the *coup de grâce*.

Hollister could already imagine going to town on the Goldins, making a seventy-inch splash of them. The whole page. Though he worked in the jittery industry of deduced facts, a young columnist needed to be sure. Hollister hadn't moved past the nods and fusses of his first editor, the *you better quadruple check it*s that would body forth a career's training in tabloid discretion.

"Let's say I'm wrong," Seidel said. (He'd felt Hollister beginning to balk, to beg off a little. That's why he was going through this part of the routine.) "—If my client *is* doing what this woman Dr. Stokes says, that's a great story for you, too. Either way, you win: a family's threats from within *or* without."

Hollister, who was twenty-six, wrote a twice-weekly column. He was a fair guy. Fairly smart, too, Dartmouth grad—although the good offices of his profession did little for the liveliness of his mind. Hollister had Tucker Carlsonish ambitions; he walked under the banner headlines of his life wearing a bow tie, seeing himself as commander in chief to a subscriber army, to the riding-mower battalions of Nassau and Suffolk Counties. He already had at various times hoisted the *News-Independent* battle flag against Saddam, Iran, welfare, North Korea, and pale liberals who talked

French to their manicurists and insulted our troops the whole time; he came at these targets honestly. They were surely endangering the Republic, these people. Plus, you can't get your readers into a lather—or yourself, incidentally—by worrying the subtleties. Lately, though, Hollister had been surprised to find himself getting really invested. He'd even been moved to tears rereading his own prose, especially when it carried the imprimatur of a professional byline. His articles on the families of lost soldiers and children in grim straits (tears of compassion); his reportage of unlikely U.S. Olympic victories (tears of joy); his reviews of bios of Founding Fathers (tears of love). He was a nostalgia dealer who'd gotten heavily into his own supply.

"Tell me about Mrs. Goldin, the mother," Hollister said now.

DORI WAS SITTING at the long arc of her mommy group when Josh phoned. He'd just ended an excited twenty phone minutes with his lawyer. Rescue was to arrive in the form of a newspaper reporter.

"That's great, Mr. Goldin," his wife said. "That's wonderful news—oh, no. Stop that—Zackie, that's *really hot*." Dori came back on the line. "Zack almost got somebody's cappuccino."

Dori kept her end of the conversation vague (none of the members of mommy group could know anything about CPS) while Josh laid out what was expected: a columnist, probably a photographer, some afternoon this week, maybe a few snapshots of Zack.

"Great," she said.

She flipped closed her phone, pulled Zack into her lap. "You guys—" She pulled a mopey face: "*Sorry*. I know I violated cellular silence." This was group code: no intrusions from the nonmaternal regions of life.

But now, all Dori could think about was the newspaper reporter. Finally, some hopeful, exciting news. She could feel a flush spreading along her neck and collarbone. "What topic were we on? What'd I miss?"

The mommy group had a distinct past-meets-present feel:

Imagine an Amazonian communal child-rearing circle spliced with a coffee klatch.

It met Sunday mornings at The End Coffee House, one of those desperately "uncorporate" corporate latte chains that plagiarized the book of suburban home furnishing. Interiors here ran to neutral colors, bleached maple tables, and soft, backless sofas—your aunt's living room raised to a higher power. The cups were stamped "kewl koffee" and "peace-out tea"; everything here had The End Coffee House logo in squiggled *f*s and tongue-out emoticon *O*s. Corporate humor often surfaced like this, with all the elements of real humor (levity, ostensible sass, wackiness), except for the wit, the actual joke; except for the *humor*.

"I'll tell the story again, Dor," said one of the women—Francie, the chubby-faced mother of little chubby-faced Mila. Francie was a former recruiter of legal personnel and a pretty good friend of Dori's.

"I just told everybody: Mila was just tearing around the house, going, 'Soovee, Soovee,' and I'm just like, 'What is this kid *talking* about?'"

The other women scrunched with delight, remembering.

Francie went on: "Then I saw out the window, her daddy pulling up; Mila was saying 'SUV.'"

The ensuing laughter, since the women already knew the joke, was a flare-up of communal affinity, an approval outburst. Dori could never have explained to Josh how soothing this was. These eight women passed their lives around the way they would photos, for group inspection and giggles. One who had a tightfisted husband shared stories of her illicit eBay abuse. Another, eyes small and baggy, always stayed up late watching TV for hours after her husband nodded off, and then needed a nightly Lunesta to fall asleep; another who was overweight swore that she and her husband had tantric sex every Friday in their backyard hammock; many watched the Food Network and believed that Mario Batali's show was condescending. Whatever their differences, they saw one another in the flattering light of shared circumstance. Anything you did, it felt as if someone else in the circle had done it, too. Except for Dori.

She gathered Zack deeper against her chest, feeling the warmth there, as from a big tabby cat. For the last two days he'd been sick with one of those baby colds: sniffling, tiredness, no lust for the bottle. Lucky for him he had a former medical professional for a mommy. *Wow—the newspaper,* Dori couldn't stop thinking.

"Mila can be such a terror," Francie was saying pridefully, "running around every morning, just yelling: 'Daddy's gone, Daddy's gone.' "

"Really?" said another mom, Liz. "Mila can be a terror?"

Liz was picking at the crumb heap that had been her blueberry muffin. She was the oldest here; Liz must have been pressed right up against forty-five. Her son had screamed and colicked through his first year. Her tired drab eyes showed the light of life only when other women were trash-talking their own children.

On all sides, toddlers strode back and forth with their drunkard steps, or squirmed in their strollers. But Zack stayed quiet in his mother's lap. He was staring and blinking at Dori with the neediness of a faintly sick kid. She actually sort of liked—should she say this?—when he had a cold. There's a fringe benefit to kids being a little sick; they're more affectionate and needy. Even as he was sitting there, she felt nostalgic for his presence, for that body warmth, that gratifying human weight on the leg—almost as one would appreciate some soldier boyfriend the night before he went off to war. She rubbed Zack's hair. It's weird that a person can love anything this much, that your heart can twist just because a baby coughs.

And now that Zack was becoming a fully operational, talking and interacting creature, the feeling would probably become even more intense. Assuming nothing happened with CPS.

Don't think about it, she thought.

Dori sipped her café americano. The paper cup featured '60s shibboleths in a serif-laden script. The back read, "In the *end*, we'll remember not the words of our enemies, but the silences of our friends"—*Martin Luther King*. The front read, "And in the *end*, the love you take is equal to the love you make"— *Paul McCartney*. Both felt true to Dori.

She took her americano with no cream and no sugar, for her husband's sake. Her husband, of course, shoveled every kind of crap into his own mouth without a care. This particular inequality was a continuing favorite among the group.

"Come here, baby," that Francie woman was saying. Having stopped her daughter's running, she bent to the girl for a peck on the forehead.

Each woman in the group would occasionally slip out of the conversation to give her own child a kiss or a bright stare, a spotlight of her mother love. In these moments, it seemed that good parenthood came easily. Good parenthood could be acquired and consumed, it seemed, like a blueberry muffin.

Now one of the women began a questionable story about somebody who breast-fed her son until he was seven, but Dori didn't laugh as heartily as she once would have; she had a secret she so *badly* wanted to share.

Dori was like a poison ivy sufferer, craving the reckless comfort of the scratch. Nobody knew the trouble she'd braved for her family, and she couldn't ever tell about it.

Imagine telling!

How brave she'd been—having managed the deed, having pulled it off. Like any terrible secret, hers carried its thrill, its soft whisper of pride. You sort of love anything that you risk your life for.

Did they already know? Not exactly what, but that there was *some* secret? Dori wondered if she'd been like a tinted window: obscuring all the details of her mystery, but not hiding all hints of its existence, not its silhouette. Not hiding that *something* lived behind the glass. Well, she had the urge now to make a shattering admission: *Can I tell you guys something really nuts?*

Sure, they'd say.

But what after that? The telling would sound crazy. And Dori knew she wasn't crazy. She just knew that certain husbands needed pushes. One push may get them to help out with stuff, another and maybe they'll notice their wives. There are ways to push that make you look naggy, and then—there are other ways.

"Is Zack sick?" Liz was asking Dori, as the mommy group wound down.

"Oh, Zack's fine." Dori smiled. But right away her smile just ran out of gas.

Dori felt like two people. The dark, shocking, fascinating one had to get buried. But that one was what, lately, made her seem most interesting to herself.

"Are you okay?" Francie asked her.

Think of how considerate of her husband she'd been, compared to these other women; rather than just doing what *they* did—becoming complaining wives, or harpies, or having affairs—she'd found a way to get her husband's attention while remaining likable; complaining would have just driven a guy like Josh away. Besides, who wanted to whine all the time? She'd made him a better husband *and* remained attractive to him.

Even with this awareness, her mood dropped all at once out into fear—fear about that newspaper story, about what it would mean for her. It's odd how quickly panic can turn up. Dori now looked at her friends guardedly. She was really upset. She understood she'd been stupid even to want to tell these women everything; maybe that urge had been a kind of shock?

The idea of all Long Island reading the hospital's accusation gave her a terrible queasiness now, like a tuning fork twanged way down in the stomach. In a word, she felt exposed, and actually brought a hand to cover her throat. Francie's daughter Mila was running around the table, and Dori weakly turned from the sight of her. Suddenly she didn't think herself able to look at children; this guilt came on like a thickening of her inner self, something that might be increasingly hard to carry around. And so, to help herself with the carrying, with quiet resolve, unexpectedly, and by spelling out a bunch of phrases to make absolutely sure that the kids nearby wouldn't understand (h-o-s-p-i-t-a-l), Dori began to tell the mommy group her story—not as it had really happened, of course, but as that newspaper would report it—starring an innocent terrified mother, a child in danger, a self-important angry black doctor, and a gloss of mystery. The women got too absorbed to notice Dori's face of eagerness and guile.

By the time she reached the good part, the CPS part, her friends were crying and she was, too, all of them (including Dori) really quite moved—distraught, offended, *ruined*—by a first-draft version of a story that, already, was no longer particularly even Dori's own, but a sort of communal peace-offering against the odds of fluke heartbreak. Dori's virtuous anger had silenced her fear. CPS had nothing; *they* had Seidel; Seidel had this reporter; and she had the justification of having been in the right.

Before long, the public account of her story would allow many people to feel the catharsis of another family's tragedy, would allow everyone to push pause—if only from time to time—on their own problems, their own problematic lives.

THE TELLING AT mommy group had gone so well. And yet when she got home she realized it still hadn't fulfilled her somehow; she had half a mind either to do it to Zack again, or to admit everything. What if she told Josh, just came right out with the truth?

She could imagine how the exchange would go: "I don't understand why," he would say. "We were *fine*." "Fine was never enough for me," would be her stalwart response. It would feel satisfying and movieish to say it. But then what? No, she would have to bear this secret in herself, forever, which made her sad, and the sadness turned into melodramatic pride.

Dori was on her knees in the upstairs bathroom, scrubbing their shower that just wouldn't clean—one of the chores for which Josh *still* never thanked her, or even seemed to notice.

Every evening, just before Josh got home, Dori put on lipstick to greet his arrival. Tonight would be no different. He was out playing golf with a Ford buyer—his idea of a working Sunday.

She knew husbands. She even knew about the provoking male ego that would strike them at odd hours, demanding not just that they be good at their job, but *better* than the other guy. She knew they'd always wonder if they could score that younger woman, that sexy young secretary by the copy machine. Finally, she understood, she really did, that family nights at home must have tasted pretty bland after the thick meat and scotch of Manhattan business dinners. And so that's why Dori always worked to be charming for him.

Josh came home at four-thirty: it was very bright out. Maybe they'd grill, eat in the backyard? she wondered.

"The Yanks are going to get Tejada, I heard," she said, right as Josh walked in, reciting a last-minute article she'd read on the 'net.

"Ah, I don't know," he said sullenly, pulling back from the kiss, lifting their son in a rote way, "they always say shit like that."

"Daa-ee."

"Hey, little man," Josh said mechanically. An equivocal shine, almost the shine you get from tears, was lighting his eyes. And he passed Zack—out of habit—to Dori, though the boy had stood on his own for months.

He went alone to sit on the couch. Something was weird about his manner. He sat watching the cloudless sky glaring its blue intensity over their salt-and-pepper driveway, over the gravel that looked like TV static.

Then, in reaction to nothing, he just cracked. It was so odd. Sitting there, looking out the window so his wife wouldn't see his face, he'd just started crying—for the first time since the last hospital visit. He hid his face in his hands.

"What is it?" she said, coming to sit, to rub his back, to be his protector. "I thought Seidel told us things were going well. CPS has no case, right?"

He turned to her with his mouth opened; a saliva bubble wobbled on his lower lip. "I know. I know it's probably almost over." He wiped his mouth. "It's so hard, though. Maybe I've been keeping it bottled up, I don't know. I don't know."

She watched as he was reduced to jerking sobs, no talking; he cried as if the dam hadn't been just cracked but lifted, taken away. Men were weird, the way they held everything in as they did.

"Isn't it *so* hard, though?" he asked her pleadingly.

Josh looked at his feet. Cruel misfortune is said to bring wisdom. But disaster had brought no real lesson. Worry remained worry, and sadness, sadness. That was all. What was supposed to have been illuminating in fact gave no light.

"Don't you think it's *hard*?" he said again.

"Yes, I know we did nothing wrong," she said calmly. "So I can't believe they would take him. And I know he'll be fine, healthwise. Dr. Keller even said so. It won't happen to him again, I'm sure of it."

The struggle in her brain made her face look stiff-boned, open, and eager. Her desire to tell him everything downshifted into a minor nod, a gesture of self-sufficient dignity. "And if it does, we'll deal with it."

He blazed in his stupor. She was startled by the intensity of his eyes. "How can you be *so* strong?" he said.

She was gently scratching his hair, consoling him, saying, "Shh," and thinking, for the first time, and with regret, that he might have been a weak man. At least, weak compared to her.

V

The sympathetic heart is sometimes broken,

sometimes not.

—Saul Bellow

1

THE QUESTION FOR JOSH HAD ALWAYS BEEN: HOW MUCH BLINDNESS does a happy life require? Josh had grown up watching the *Mr. Magoo* show, in which a wealthy man took on the challenge of failed eyesight by sallying into the world as if everything were fine: He walked off the edge of a girder (the hard hats pointing, yelling, panicking); but just as he stepped off into space, some crane swung an I-beam up under his shoes. Or he would saunter into an animal pen, mistaking it for a doctor's office, and caress a tiger in the belief that he was petting a kitten—and the jungle beast would purr and nuzzle. If Josh could mosey through his days like Magoo through a room, narrowly avoiding the furniture of human faults, wasn't there a chance the world might be flattered, and agree with him, and transform itself into a series of blessings? But if that worked, it led to another question he hadn't thought about before: What sort of life did that become?

However.

A greater sin than emotional blindness is to play at love without purpose, to be caught just visiting the high points of your own existence. Josh loved Dori honestly, faithfully, and blindly. And that was the reason he failed to avoid this strange shipwreck of his family life.

JOSH CONSIDERED MAY 27th the most truly horrific day he'd known.

Afterward, certain noises would act like fuses, setting off exquisitely painful fireworks of memory. And Josh couldn't *stop* remembering: the sound of a police cruiser crunching and spitting over driveway gravel; the doorbell—its three notes, down-up-down, which led him to a sight he couldn't place: cops in uniform, wearing somberly rigid expressions; his own stupidly merry: "Who is it?" Car doors now made him anxious, as did his own last name, pronounced by an unfamiliar voice. And the most evocative, most horrific: the swishing sound of that squad car pulling away, as it left his driveway and life empty. This police car, these strangers, had taken his son.

Mr. Plates had found, on his third visit, a butterfly needle in Mrs. Goldin's possession.

The police had arrived at seven-thirty A.M. on a Monday. Josh'd had his dress shirt open, a tie flapping, unknotted, like a scarf. (Coffee made Josh sweat through his shirt.) The doorbell rang; Zack started clapping and laughing. Josh said, "Shh—hey, cool it, buddy," which in hindsight felt like the most excruciatingly mean thing he'd ever say to anyone.

In the doorway stood a policeman, a policewoman, and a different, terse woman from CPS. Somehow Josh would remember that string puller Dr. Stokes as having been there, too, as if she were part of the group that shouldered into his house and asked, "Mr. Goldin, where's your son?" (Josh still conflated "that bitch" and faceless CPS. He had, without realizing it, found religion—a bitter and imprecise personal religion of anger and fear. Like all religions, Josh's condensed individuals to symbols and types, to devils and martyrs and angels, and offered the possibility of redemption.)

What can you do when some female cop gets in your face with her arrogant nose? What can you do when the police have legal authority to kidnap your son?

I could've done more, Josh thought again and again. *I could have.*

Dori—walking from the kitchen—had a more immediate grasp of the situation. Her eyes narrowed and she sucked in a breath; and then, as the CPS woman handed Josh a legal document, Dori ran full-speed into the kitchen.

Breathing hamster-quick, blinking like mad, Josh was trying to make sense of the blue sheet of paper (it said "Retrieval"; it said "suspicious evidence . . .") when he looked up toward a banging sound. The policewoman was already inside, knocking at the bathroom door. "Mrs. Goldin? Mrs. Goldin? This isn't going to help anything, Mrs. Goldin."

The male cop approached. "Mr. Goldin, do you have a key for this door?"

The policeman was tall, with a midcareer softness at his middle; his features were a collection of pale and carefully shaved ridges. The face of this cop—the noticing half of Josh's brain recorded— was managing a tricky job. Determined, sympathetic, superciliously without remorse: *This is an unpleasant duty, I understand*, he seemed to say. *But let's be frank, it's a situation that couldn't happen to me*; it was the expression of an undertaker who would never die.

And then Josh had found himself at the door—he'd had no idea where its key was; the house was Dori's world, it functioned invisibly for him; he remembered his affronted hand knocking on it. He didn't like to (and couldn't) remember what he said; he was mortified to think of his own sturdily affable voice asking his wife to come out and hand over their baby.

Josh did remember something else, too; looking over his shoulder—helpless, powerless in his own house—while the male cop nodded and mouthed: "Thanks." Somehow that was one of the worst things to remember, the policeman's embarrassed *thanks*. Dori opened the door looking furious and dignified, her face pinked by crying. She evened her hostile blue stare on Josh, a little slow resentment, before she turned to the police.

This made him feel like ice; it was the strangest sensation. Really, he felt built of ice: cold but also brittle, all fractured inside—as if shatterable, as if see-through.

The Goldins nodded their heads in disbelief, they asked what right these people had to take Zack, they offered up outrageous threats, they asked for specifics about what CPS had actually claimed, all in the space of a minute; but in the end the parents were left just to blink and blink, numbly. No one had needed to tell them why.

The policewoman, her hair up, carried their son to the police car. Zack's thin friendly face rested on the woman's blue shoulder.

Josh gnashed his teeth watching this. As a father he was so unfit for this moment it disturbed his balance like vertigo, like light-headedness. The serenity of the baby's uncomprehending, impassive face looked as it had that first night in the hospital, with the merciless tubes connected to his body—*So these are the things that I can expect will happen to me, as your son.* That calm felt more horrifying than tears would have been. In the coming weeks, Josh kept seeing this, kept picturing Zack as he bounced along with the policewoman's stride, his noodle arm around her collar and shoulder. The back of her neck had a patrol tan and showed its perpendicular cords; Zack's arm looked very pale in comparison.

Dori stood next to Josh and a little behind him in the doorway. Up on frenzied tiptoes, she tried grinning at her receding son, waving as if at a cruise ship's good-bye rail.

"Bye, honey!" In a sickening, sham-cheery voice. "We'll see you soon, okay? Bye! Bye! Bye. . . ."

The male cop appeared at Josh's side. "Thank you for not making this, you know, any worse than it needed to."

Josh thought of what to say. "Fuck you," he managed, without force.

The other man nodded, as if truly sorry.

"You seem like good people. Do what you can to get him back. That's the only advice I can give you is do what you can."

The policewoman handed Zack to the CPS representative, who carried him into the intricate rigging of the big police car. And then Josh couldn't see his son anymore. The sky was beginning to whiten on this bright sunless morning. The police car's engine started; the gray mini rocks under the tires popped and ticked. Josh found himself running after the car, sidewalk and lawns and a streetlight bouncing in his vision as if he were watching someone's frenzied video footage: He hardly even realized that he was huffing down the street alone, on exhausted knees, waving bye to his son. This was another sound that, later, he couldn't stand: the tapping, shushing sound of dress shoes on pavement.

2

AT NINE-THIRTY A.M. MONDAY THE SKY GLOWED WHITE LIKE THE FACE of a medium-watt bulb. Darlene didn't notice that ache at the top of her vision—the cool paleness of this warm morning—and neither did Intelligent Muhammad. They were both too happy.

Darlene wore a gentle smile of faint superiority. She didn't even know her father was a few hundred yards behind her, she was so pumped up.

We've won, she thought. *It's gone from subjective to objective.*

They had proof now: no question anymore. CPS's man, Plates was his name, had found, on his fourth visit, a butterfly needle and papoose board in Mrs. Goldin's possession. *It's impossible that we won't win.* And now she could get back to the real work of being a doctor. Mr. Plates hadn't had the power to confiscate the damning items, so it was important they move quickly. Before the mother could use them again.

St. Joe's electric door sighed open and inhaled her.

Intelligent Muhammad was rushing, too, squeezing his rolled-up copy of the *New York Press*, and sucking on a green lollipop—he preferred its bullying crisp tang, its tongue-spark, to real apple flavor. (People where he came from ate many more fruit imitations than they did fruit.)

Half an hour early for work and yet he hurried. Past the various *ologies* of grief (nephrology, cardiology, the terrible bummer oncology) and through their smelly messes, the stink that months here hadn't taught him to overlook; past the Big Bird statue; along the paw-tracked wall and past the saddest place in this sad building, the Peeds ICU; coming, finally, to the end of Pediatrics's blithe pastel hallway. He'd reached his daughter's office.

———

BEFORE MUHAMMAD KNOCKED, Darlene was planning Grand Rounds ("CPC: An Infant with Decreasing Movement After Birth," presented by Joseph DiPietro, M.D., FAAN, the Phoebe Lichty Distinguished Chair in Pediatric Neurology; Professor of Neurology and Pediatrics, Columbia-Presbyterian). Her vision blurred over this busywork.

Some nurse had left a slightly disquieting fax on her desk. The *Long Island News-Independent*—whose article, at this point, was still days away—had sent tough questions at her, mostly *no-comment*ish questions about her time at Tufts, her marriage, her age, about whether she "has ever been wrong in a diagnosis." Where had they learned about her and Leo? Who hadn't ever been wrong? She'd called her mother-in-law and her sister-in-law; both had said that they'd never spoken about Leo and her with any reporter. ("Regardless of the way you two ended up, I've never held any ill will toward you," said Leo's sister Alyson, with the convivial indifference usually shown to busboys in frou-frou restaurants.) She also had a tense voice mail from Peregrine Berg, who had been cc'd on the faxes ("Well, Doctor, there's good publicity, but, ah, there's the other kind also"). Still, Berg likely didn't know that good news was on its way, that CPS had found its clincher.

And now Intelligent Muhammad knocked, then simply opened the door to her office.

"Hey, Doc." Her father used a lively, social voice; his grin worked to expand his nose. "I got something to show you about."

He, this uneducated janitor, not at all exceptional, standing with his lollipop miles beneath her in any reasonable topography of status, of achievement, a guy crinkling his newspaper and wearing a floppy work getup, filled a weird place in her life now. They were friendly. But not yet personal enough for her to tell him she was busy and send him away.

" 'Bout to take your mind on a journey," he said.

———

THE NEW YORK TIMES MAGAZINE, its editors having wavered at first, decided some months ago to turn down freelancer Ralph Dunn's account of mysterious post-Riker's heroism. By the time the magazine begged off, Dunn's story lacked a "news peg"—words like a funeral ring for any freelance story. Still, after having pocketed the kill fee, Dunn sold the article to the last place most professional Manhattan writers deigned to try: the *New York Press*, a shambling, copycat *Village Voice*. Before publication, a *Press* editor threw cold water on Dunn's prose; the printed story had the pith of a TV spot:

HERO EX-CON RISKED TAKING BULLET, TURNED LIFE AROUND
By Ralph Dunn

Charles Stokely looked up from his breakfast last November, and saw a sight that changed the most hopeful morning of his life in an instant. Not 10 yards from where he sat, two thugs pulled out a gun to rob the greasy spoon where he was eating. "That's when I realized I had to act," says Stokely, who had been released from prison just that fateful morning. . . .

"I don't know what came over me," says Stokely, about the next moment. "I really don't think I ever considered myself a hero." But what he did was the stuff of a man possessed by heroism. . . . "While it was happening, I remember thinking, if I die, I hope my daughter learns I was doing the right thing." Instead, his daughter found out nothing about it. Because she didn't know him. . . .

For another three paragraphs, the article hurried like a very pragmatic subway, making its few express stops of past detail and present-day surprise.

The way Ralph Dunn had wanted to write it, this story of baffling kindness would have made a point very unlike that of the

"Dori Goldin" article that the *Long Island News-Independent*'s Gregory Hollister was cooking up. Dunn had wanted to make a point: Goodness—isn't it a shock when you find great goodness in people, almost like when you find great evil? Saints and perverts venture too far out on those dangerous waters, not you, not your neighbors. That tone, that unambitious take on our nature, colored Ralph Dunn's article, even after the *Press*'s acid-bath edit. Dunn's Muhammad was a fearsome, outlandish black question mark.

The real-life Intelligent Muhammad had asked the *Press* not to use his Muslim name. And in what Muhammad considered another sacrifice of Mother Teresan gallantry, he decided not to share his *real* non-Muslim name. (At any public mention of their relationship, Darlene might actually freak on him, he'd thought, wrongly. Life on the outside was hard. Maturity was hard.) "Stokes," after enough back-and-forth to annoy Dunn, became "Stokely." Still, Muhammad shed the chafing habit of sainthood and made sure the article bragged a little: his daughter the doctor; his new "turned-my-life-around" job; his great courage, etc.

And at least he would get to show Alice, and, more important, was showing Darlene. This counted, didn't it?

But the article unsettled her. Darlene read it glumly. The particulars (crime, bravery) seemed to match the story Muhammad had been telling, his heroic-self tale, and yet the reporter condescended to him—vaguely but certainly. The guy might as well have referred to Muhammad as a "black thug." It made her uncomfortable. She felt protective of him; he was after all family.

"That's my big power move right there," Muhammad said, pointing at the paper. His left eyebrow was arched like a worm touching its toes. It was the expression Darlene would remember about this meeting—the face of a proud and restlessly anticipating simpleton.

"It's the story you'd mentioned," she said. "It came out."

"Yeah." His eagerness seemed to squeeze the back of his neck; his chin made its way up a few more stairs of expectation. "Yeah, that's right."

Darlene tried piecing together something to say, some flattery. But the flattery broke apart on reaching her throat—the words, like uranium and plutonium, fizzing into nothing tangible as they came in contact with each other. Why did she have to be so honest all the time?

"Well, it's not *The New York Times Magazine*," she said—and immediately regretted it. "But still—" Her smile was a lame offering, a shaky fingertip's hold on the ledge of politeness.

That was the best she could do.

"All right," he said. Absently he rolled up the paper and then held it behind him. "Wanted to show I was, I don't know—"

But he did know. He'd wanted just to throw his hat into the ring of respectable citizenship—however grubby, however inelegant the hat may have seemed; however unwearable a second time.

And of course he'd wanted Darlene to say something encouraging, but now he just hoped she'd say nothing at all. He hoped, especially, to get out of the office soon.

She looked at this nervously smiling, benign-eyed father in his professional loser jumpsuit, a man conditioned into transparency—and she managed not to hurt his feelings; managed not to ask why he didn't see that the reporter had condescended to him. She'd manage to say: "You must be proud."

"Well, it's not *Time* magazine, but," he said, and smiled.

She wanted also to ask the article's unasked question: *Why?* Why would a onetime criminal, nobody's idea of a hero, this screwup who'd abandoned his daughter, risk his life to save a stranger? But why did anyone do what they did? She thought about the father of the Goldin case, that man named Josh Goldin. She wondered, with a small shrug, if he knew what his wife had done.

In fact, Darlene—driven by clear notions of right and wrong—had no conception of the anguish that her actions were causing that man named Josh Goldin.

3

EMOTIONS WERE VARIABLE AND WEIRD IN THOSE DOWN, RAVING FIRST days. Josh was bewildered. After he'd run after Zack in the police car, Josh simply walked back into his house, without having remembered to close the door, not knowing where he was headed. He knew something terrible had happened. But he couldn't yet find a context in which it was real.

People don't have the circuitry to handle so many incoming emotion messages, so much incoming pain. Our central nervous system, that vintage switchboard, is unequipped; we go numb in the overload. And so, like Zack, Dori and Josh didn't cry that morning.

After they'd called Martin Seidel, and then phoned their parents; after they'd answered questions for that reporter; after they'd hugged each other, and talked, and reassured for hours—and after Dori went off to call her mother again—Josh sat by himself on the couch in Zack's room, lowered his good-looking head to his hands, and slumped gently into a light sleep. And yet it was only one in the afternoon. He hadn't even been tired.

He awoke minutes later—very calmly—leisurely twisting his robust upper body in that half-conscious stretching that people do first thing in the morning. All at once he stopped twisting and his stomach tumbled; he made a huffed breathing sound. Guilt swept over him, along with the expected fear. How could he have forgotten? Perhaps when your family is accused in this way—perhaps when your child gets taken—even memory has to avert its eyes.

No one had told them or their lawyer why this was happening. No one had told them, specifically, that Mr. Plates had found something in their house.

———

SITTING IN THIS child's room that had been decorated in light blue by Dori (cloud-on-sky painted walls, gingham-print miniarmchairs) Josh faced his likeness in a mirror. He felt agonized with tenderness for himself. The youthful jawline, glassy look, the unbumped charisma of his nose went right to his heart. Josh felt like a kid himself. A kid whose parents had gone without him on a long trip.

Josh took three personal days from work. He wanted to be with Dori and to have phone meetings—at home—with Martin Seidel.

"You can visit him this Saturday. That, the state's got to allow," Seidel said, in answer to their first, desperate question. "You can bring him packaged toys during visitation, but not home-baked treats, due to they always think there's a risk of poisoning. There's nothing we can do till then. But I promise—"

Dori tried to tell the lawyer: "Don't promise, just *do* it"—but to her amazement the basic elements of speech failed; her thin body listed forward and her voice was a ripped howl.

"We're not going to let this happen," Seidel said, as if it hadn't happened already.

Dori and Josh had stood together, listening on speaker phone, and the fuzziness of the voice technology had felt like an outrage that was allied, somehow, to the larger outrage.

Josh still couldn't cry. He was a parrot in Yankees T-shirt and socks who said, "I can't believe this," over and again, an unthinking voice. Zack's Batman action figure, splay-legged indecently on the kitchen table; a "sippy cup" in the cabinet next to Josh's own drinking glass; the bumper cushions with which Josh had babyproofed the nasty corners of the house—these were all sinkholes of grief. But he couldn't cry.

He just zombied around, dribbling away the hours, screaming curses, but only inside his head. He was disoriented, it seemed, by their Zackless home. It felt cold in here, as if the third person's—the littlest person's—body heat were actually missed.

They learned that Zack had been put in a temporary foster home. That's the way bureaucratic "retrieval," bureaucratic abduction, works: the state scampers over to a licensed provisional family, carrying a retrieved child in its teeth. The process is disheartening and slack: Any husband-and-wife high school graduates can become short-term parents (after being judged physically fit and taking a TB test). Some do it for altruistic reasons; but there also exist people who will enter a brief dream of parenthood for the $150 a month plus expenses, only to hand the kid back after no more than a few weeks.

"How'd CPS take him, Martin? Huh? I thought the visits went well," Josh said. He'd felt permanently confused. "On what basis have things changed?"

"For these preliminary removals they don't have to tell us anything. That's the shitty rule this state has. American justice, huh? And unfortunately, right now their standard of proof is basically 'more probable than not.' More hearsay is allowed in these removal deals. I can't know. But that's just until Saturday."

Dori's parents came over: ineffective attempts at solace, the barren vocabulary of consolation, and many awkward silence-filling hugs.

"Hey, Dad," Josh said. "It'll be all right." He found himself in the ridiculous position of comforting his father-in-law when he himself needed comforting.

Dori's father, Sergius, couldn't look Josh in the eyes now. It was very odd. Josh would say something, and his father-in-law's face seemed alert only to frightening inner questions; his gaze lifting no higher than Josh's collar, or his stomach. He couldn't face his son-in-law.

Later, Dori stood in Zack's room, so immersed in her spell that she didn't hear Josh when he called to her. "Dori?" He could never have imagined what was in her mind, but he may even have shaken his head a little at how she just stood there, unable to hear him. "Dori?" (In some sense, he'd be shaking his head the rest of his life.)

Where was that strength of hers, that hospital gumption? He

would have to be the man, the strong one, now. He worried he'd never be able to comfort her enough. But he would try. He felt as depressed as he ever had, he'd entered a subhuman state, he was a fiasco in both mind and body. And yet: no tears.

For some reason Josh remembered something: the joy with which Dori on a snowing afternoon had run to the streaked top of a giant, plow-made embankment and waved, goofily, for him to chase her. Her cheek lifted in silhouette to the falling snow, the meticulous beauty of her smile—then his memory switched. He pictured his son's nonsensically small sneaker, how Zack's foot had swung just above the woman cop's scornful black police belt. It just wasn't possible that Dori had done what they said, right? Right?

Josh went into their son's room now and led his wife to the kitchen.

BETWEEN STRATEGY SESSIONS and bouts of Dori's crying, and amid the doses of grief that came in stages or abruptly, the Goldins slouched through the long spells of waking hours. They even performed their familiar domestic rituals, if more quietly, and with far less than their usual attention—ordering in sushi and eating outside on the deck, even watching TV (*Sex and the City*) on the couch, the two of them clinging, sticking, to each other. He had a flash of something like anger at Dori, didn't even feel like touching her—why? Had she maybe—was there any way—could it be that she'd? As soon as he thought this question he cursed himself. Walking the take-out containers to the garbage on horrified legs, Josh realized that the thought alone had made him nauseous. How could he doubt her?

Josh and Dori didn't take their eyes off the screen for most of the TV shows they watched; nor did they really watch. It seemed a betrayal to order sushi, to eat it, to breathe, without Zack.

At breakfast a few days after Zack's abduction, Dori sat in red underwear and the T-shirt she'd worn to bed—still cleanish but unironed, blue. Her hair was messy with the sweat of a long panic.

"Don't pour me any cereal, please," she said; she sat tilted forward, gazing at the legs of her kitchen table, at their baroque candlestick shape. "I'm not hungry."

Should she tell Josh what she'd done? No, she couldn't. She admitted something to herself: Because of the person she was—the impulsive worrywart actress she could sometimes be—she was doomed to go too far now and again. Even when she meant well. This thing *had* been a stupid gamble. Really stupid. How could she have been so careless? During that third CPS visit, Josh hadn't been home, and (for ten seconds, as she'd put Zack down) she'd let that guy Mr. Plates into her bedroom alone—for *at least* ten seconds. How stupid could she have been? Well, she hadn't wanted to act all shady and follow him around like a guilt-ridden dork. Had he found her butterfly needle and/or papoose board? Is that why this had happened?

If she ever got custody back, she'd never do it again.

"Okay," Josh said, "no cereal."

He turned and he smiled at her—a pretend one; he was trying to prop her up. He believed his face held something from their happy life of two days ago. And smiles can be little contentment generators. When you pretend to be a few clicks better off than you really are, sometimes you actually begin to feel some small upturn in your mood. That's what Josh hoped, anyway.

"Josh," Dori said. She left her mouth open as if to tell him something; she looked on the verge of saying something heartfelt and important.

She closed her mouth.

And he said what he'd been saying, again and again, for forty-eight hours: "It'll be all right." What if they didn't get their son back—as awful, as impossible, as it was to contemplate—they would have to move on together, right? He considered it his duty to prepare his wife for this possibility. He licked his lips and planned to start telling her this tough truth. Taking a fortifying breath he simply said: "It'll be all right."

He mistook the strange vehemence of her eyes for anger at him.

He squared his shoulders. "I'm sorry I haven't cried. I know I may not look it, but I'm really upset, too."

Despite what Josh thought, to Dori he looked extremely, wrenchingly sad. It was all there, how awful he felt, how baffled, how bodily wrecked, how ambushed by his own thoughts.

"I understand that I haven't, you know," Josh said, "but—"

With a gesture, Dori cut him off.

She'd felt something like pride about his having not wept—pride about what in fact was his continued, boyish state of shock—because she took it as proof of Josh's strength. Strength she had doubted was there.

"We're a good environment for Zack, aren't we, Mr. G.?" She blockaded her leaky nose with her hand. "Whatever our failings as parents? He always seemed okay to you, right? Aren't we a fun household for him? Aren't we happy, I mean, as a family?"

He got up from the table and walked around to Dori. He bent to hug her. "You're the best mom, you never did anything to hurt Zack," he said, though she hadn't asked for reassurance on *that* question.

Sweat had clammed her skin. She smelled faintly sharp, as if she'd just pedaled on her workout bike, or carried her son from where his captors held him and taken him all the way back into her life.

The fact that he'd had even a moment of doubting his wife made Josh hate that awful Dr. Stokes woman even more.

4

Three days after CPS took Zack, the *Long Island News-Independent*'s Gregory Hollister lifted the Goldin family into a news version of the display window—where big scandals go until their expiration date arrives.

VAGUE ALLEGATIONS PUT LONG ISLAND FAMILY IN JEOPARDY
By Gregory Hollister

It's the horror that mothers have always had to face in tyrannical countries all throughout history. An armed thug arriving at your door. Taking your child away, leaving you helpless and powerless. It happened to a young American woman this past Saturday, and not in Nazi Germany or Mahmoud Ahmadinejad's Iran. This nightmare befell Dori Goldin, of Glenwood Landing. And it befell her in her Long Island home.

Dori Goldin and her husband Josh were feeding their not yet two-year-old son his favorite meal of Cheerios and milk when the police came pounding on the door. Outside, a squad car was parked crosswise at the end of their driveway. The car had its flashing lights on, breaking the serenity of this tree-lined Eden and calling the neighbors' attention to the unsuspecting Goldin family.

When Dori opened the door she stood face-to-face with a large policeman holding a warrant out with one hand. The policeman's other hand rested on top of his gun.

Dori, a pretty, upbeat thirty-three-year-old former

nurse's assistant, is being accused of the unlikely charge of trying to harm her own son, without any evidence of wrongdoing on her part.

Child Protective Services has been trying for almost a year to build a case against Dori Goldin. But what had been a whispering campaign had suddenly gotten very loud, a roller coaster ride of allegations into the controversial realm of Munchausen syndrome by proxy. And tonight the Goldins' young child sleeps miles from his home.

The Goldins blame their downward spiral on a Long Island pediatrician named Darlene Stokes, a single mother who has never diagnosed a Munchausen case before.

Unlike Dr. Stokes, many specialists believe Munchausen by proxy is not really a specific syndrome but just another word for physical mistreatment of children. While the condition frequently called Munchausen by proxy can endanger children, experts say its misdiagnosis can destroy families forever.

Zack Goldin, who had been sick but appears well now, has shown, and continues to show, no signs of abuse, according to the Goldins' attorney. The hospital has no comment.

Dr. Stokes, 39, is St. Joseph Hospital's shortest-serving and youngest division chief. Given that she holds a position of authority at the hospital, the New York Child Protective Services agency has to take her accusations seriously. But whether she has any proof or not, Dr. Stokes has the power to order the confiscation of infants from their homes, at least temporarily. That's the authority of doctors under the law.

It's this authority that is now coming under scrutiny. Martin Seidel, the Goldins' lawyer, maintains that

Dr. Stokes was "rash and irresponsible to the point of negligence in her misdiagnosis of my client." Mr. Seidel claims that Zack Goldin suffered two bouts of severe anemia that puzzled the doctors, who were "immediately hostile to the Goldin family, at the time when they should have been helpful." In addition, Seidel says that CPS examiners came up with nothing to substantiate the doctor's claims. Indeed, no criminal charges have been filed.

When asked about the whether there is any factual basis for having made the Munchausen claim against Dori Goldin, or for having removed Zack from his home, Dr. Stokes and CPS officials again offered only a "no comment."

Experts say Munchausen by proxy is extremely rare, but the disorder has been diagnosed with much more frequency since the 1990s. It often results in notoriety for the accusing physician. Dr. Nate Dennis, a Great Neck psychiatrist who has testified in defense of parents in a number of Munchausen lawsuits, is suspicious of the upswing in recent cases reported. "This is an incredibly uncommon thing. We call it a needle-in-the-haystack disorder. And yet doctors seem to keep finding it. Is there some immense outbreak of Munchausen all of a sudden? Or are doctors getting carried away, mistaking needles for regular old hay?"

Defending babies or defaming parents?

A number of recent cases appear to back up Dr. Dennis's point.

• In 1998, Shana Lasdun was actually convicted of murdering her daughter, Anne. The New Jersey mom was said to have poisoned her baby because doctors thought they identified what seemed to be radiator coolant in the little girl's blood. And the Lasdun family had a half-finished bottle of antifreeze in the basement.

While serving her life sentence, Mrs. Lasdun gave birth to a second baby. Soon afterward, that second baby also showed extremely high levels of ethylene glycol in the blood. Doctors determined that both children had a rare genetic disorder, methylmalonic acidemia, which causes deadly hemoglobin anomalies. Lasdun was cleared of the baby's death.

• Four and a half years ago, doctors at Mississippi State University Medical Center warned state officials that Deena Jacobson might be responsible for her severely ill child's medical condition. The state took custody of six-month-old Beau Jacobson, but two weeks later, the baby died in state custody. Soon after, Starkville Medical Examiner, Dr. David Elkin, decided that there was no evidence of Munchausen by proxy. Mrs. Jacobson, who was never charged with any crime involving her son's illness, was exonerated too late.

• Five months ago, Boston officials awarded $2 million in damages to a woman whose daughter died during an epileptic fit suffered while in foster care. The mother, who was accused of having Munchausen by proxy, had warned social workers of the dangerousness of the child's seizures, but she was ignored.

Ronny Meadows, spokeswoman for MAMA, Moms Against Munchausen Allegations, said: "Often the accusers have ulterior motives. My association works to fight the attack on blameless mothers."

Pernicious presumptions
According to MAMA, as well as experts like Dr. Nate Dennis, all cases worldwide in which the Munchausen label has been used should be reexamined.

No scientific test exists to catch Munchausen by proxy. Instead, doctors examine parents—usually mothers—on the fly, in search of danger signs that she might be inventing indicators of illness.

Cases like the Lasduns' demonstrate the risks involved in trying to evaluate mothers for vague "danger signs," according to specialists. If you have a very sick child and you are anxious about it, that "corresponds" to one danger sign. If you are thought to be to be an overly involved advocate for your child, or are "obsessed" with your child's illness, or request multiple opinions, or have worked in the medical field, you are judged a Munchausen risk. Another danger sign is if your children have various symptoms that don't fit with known diseases.

Some experts reveal that many who have been accused of Munchausen are eventually cleared when their children are correctly diagnosed with rare and unexpected maladies. According to MAMA, two danger signs are appearing "too calm" when faced with a sick child, or acting particularly upset and bold with doctors. And, right out of a witch trial, the final indication that you have Munchausen is if you strongly deny that you have it.

Guilty until proven otherwise

Besides profiling the mother, doctors evaluate a baby's medical records. Zack Goldin's medical history showed no abnormalities.

The case against Dori Goldin, in the words of Seidel, "hinges on innuendo, hearsay and guesswork."

"It seemed that Dr. Stokes was upset that my wife knew about medicine," Mr. Goldin said. "No one there knew what to do, until my wife told them what they were doing wrong. They didn't like that." (Dori Goldin was a medical professional. One more "danger sign," according to Munchausen advocates.)

"In America, you're innocent until proven guilty. Except in these cases, they can take the kid away before anything is proven."

Again, Dr. Stokes refused to comment.

Even if Dr. Stokes is shown to be wrong about her diagnosis, she will avoid legal punishment or any consequence at all, not even a fine.

Dr. Nate Dennis, who often works with MAMA, said, "These cases entail the security and well-being of children on one hand, and the rights, stability, and welfare of families on the other. In this case, in which the Goldin child has no verifiable injuries, and no one has seen the mother doing anything, it seems to me like there might be a rush to judgment." Often Munchausen cases rely on videotaped evidence, showing a parent harming a child.

Dr. Dennis said he's seen some doctors misrepresent evidence, wrongly incriminating parents, because these cases bring doctors a lot of attention. He declined to say whether he thought this was true of Dr. Stokes.

Once a mother is marked as a suspect of Munchausen by proxy, she often is shunned by her own neighbors—even if she's later found not to have done wrong. Often, if their children are ill again, they fear they will be arrested just for taking their kids to the doctor. And if a child is taken from the home and then later returned, experts say the separation can be quite damaging.

Every parent who is caring for a critically ill child is in danger of being falsely charged with engaging in Munchausen's by proxy.

Have any parents accused of Munchausen ever been

found to have harmed their own children? The answer is yes. A few mothers have been rightfully diagnosed with trying to do serious damage to their own kids. Often, though, those mothers have been caught on video. And luckily, there are laws in place that safeguard children from real perpetrators. But sometimes, however, as in the case in which at Mississippi State University Medical Center Beau Jacobson died in foster care, the officials err on the side of the doctor at the expense of an innocent mother and her baby.

Because there's no single location where medically acknowledged Munchausen cases are registered, no one knows for sure how common the condition is. Estimates by some experts put it as low as one in well over a million, according to MAMA. Numerous cases have been reported in Long Island this year alone.

Josh and Dori Goldin will go before a judge in a month for a 30-day hearing. That's when they see if they get their child back. Wish them well.

Every few months, the *News-Independent* would break a sweat in this way, throwing exhaustive "special reports" together. But their Munchausen package was the grandstand play of the year. Editors padded and kitsched up its thirty-four hundred words, in full tearjerk mode, with "candid" pictures of the Goldin family. The most affecting shot—mother and son on a swing set, cakey Rockwell colors—broke off what had been one fleeting playground moment and exalted it. Dori's wistful smile, like her son's sweet naïve laugh, got repackaged into a sacrament of such enduring and magical schmaltz you felt a pull at your heart. And there was more.

The article, large and central as it was, had gathered around itself a few tepid moons: a six-hundred-word sidebar called "Syndrome Diagnosed More Frequently Since '90s"; a pair of clinical quarter-pagers ("Syndrome Involves a Wide Range of Factors; Spotting Munchausen"); and a curt summary profile of the Goldins, its every detail a soft hint: These people, this woman with her wide, earnest forehead, very pretty if in no way unusual, could be *you*.

5

Very early Thursday, the bedside clock glowing *3:17* a.m., Josh's first tears soaked his eyes, warm and persistent.

For the past two nights Josh had dreamed about Zack's abduction over and again, but each time he'd added a happy ending, with the cops having admitted, "We made a mistake": Josh's brain—as any bodily organ would—trying to heal the bruise.

But not now.

He woke with a start, feeling the departure of his shock as a tangible phenomenon, a protective crust being ripped from who he was.

A terrified frown twisted his mouth, all his numbness gone. The images came again: Zack's expression as he'd been stolen, staring at his father with eloquent, weeping eyes. Josh's recollection had changed to give Zack tears, and that policewoman a scowl. Rage, that devoted propagandist, airbrushes memory whenever it can.

He wondered with self-pity if all this weren't harder for him than it would have been for other people. Good fortune had tucked him in so securely until now. What a jerk he'd been, acting cocky (not on purpose) about others who'd suffered difficult times. How often had he thought, even if he hadn't put these exact words to it: *I'd never get in that position, that's for sure*. And now he was in a *worse* position—worse than anybody he knew. He was very publicly unlucky now. That idea, on top of everything, was so unpleasant he just couldn't think about it. He tried to pray, in Hebrew. *Baruch atah adonai, eloheinu melech ha-olam*, but what came next? What did those words mean? He didn't know their English definitions. He thought he'd be awake through this endless night.

But the hours did pass. By morning Josh had managed to scoop up a few atoms and rites of his diminished life. He'd rolled over to put his hand on Dori's soft hip and slept.

"Oh, my God," Damita Melendez cried in the coffee lounge. "It's Josh!"

She brought a hand over her mouth just to look at him, as if her boss were a car accident, or a deformity picture in a medical text. She went to hug him; the other person here, Mark Santella, followed her, and—when the woman's hug was done—he squeezed Josh's shoulder manfully. "How you doing, J.?" All this behavior learned from movies-of-the-week.

Josh said, "Good; all right; you know."

Then, one second into this chat, they had nothing further to say. Boilerplate consolations only get people so far. Every individual tragedy is uncharted.

These were his first moments back at *Sparkplug*. Jennifer in HR had told him he could (or should) take more time. But, not a guy to ask, "Am I ready?," Josh wanted to prove he was managing. He thought it might get his mind off things, a return to the sales fraternity, to that kick of competition and juvenile fun. He could picture the handshake, the laughter, the clowning that was its own pleasure.

Besides, he'd already had a seven-thirty A.M. phone meeting with Seidel today (a nothing appointment, though: rapid-fire strategizing, conference calls to the journalist, a helpless clammy feeling the whole time, and two hundred more unmentioned dollars to be paid later). So he was doing all he could, wasn't he? Didn't he still have to live, and to earn a living?

Therefore he'd gotten to work very early—the office seemed vacant—and of course he'd come straight here, to the coffee lounge.

And now tweezered Damita, the owner of the shapeliest eyebrows in the world, was saying: "It's crazy. For them to—"

It took a second, but then was clear that she wouldn't finish her sentence. (And those brows of hers really were impressive, angling up like peaks on graph paper.) So Josh nodded. "Yeah, thanks." And next, just to occupy himself during the silence, Josh furrowed as if he were trying to remember something.

Damita finally completed her thought: "You know, for them to take someone's kid like that"—and right away regretted having said it.

Santella fired a glare at Damita: a bid to tell her to go on tiptoes around a griever like Josh. Josh noticed this; grievers very quickly become look connoisseurs.

Santella said, "It is, she's right." He was working a sudden crick in his neck; he weather-vaned his head left and right, like an owl. "It's fucking crazy."

The coffee machine gave its throaty noise. What was Josh feeling—annoyance, surprise, embarrassment, sadness? Yes. But he smiled.

"Um," Damita said. Her mouth turned pale under its lip gloss.

She and Santella nodded, in agreement of nothing, their eyebrows lifted, their expressions strained—a pair of beat cops waiting at a crime scene for some detective to come explain the mystery to them.

"Yeah, *any*way," Josh said. He felt at the start of someone else's life, someone jinxed, someone pathetic. He had the old unthinking impulse, before he stopped himself, to ask: *So, how are you guys?*

Instead, he just blurted out, "I, uh," and then had to take a step toward the counter, had to lean against it. Santella and Damita exchanged a hasty discreet look: *Yikes.* Because with that one uncertainty, Josh had drawn back his veneer of everything's okay. And the other two had shared their second glance, their message, of the sort Josh would intercept a lot in the coming weeks.

This was what he'd feared. Josh had promised himself, upon coming in this morning, that he wouldn't creep anyone out. And he'd actually hesitated before first entering the break room. To his surprise, he hadn't felt comfortable enough just to stride in. It was hard for a guy stupefied by the hypnotist's watch of grief to come around to small talk.

That was all it had taken for Josh: Damita Melendez's horror-struck face. He realized yet another sad fact, one more thing that that bitch of a doctor had taken from him: He'd lost another family, his family of the break room.

As THE MORNING got going, he felt strange discussing his problems with colleagues—discussing Zack; he felt unmanly. Everyone approached him in the same way, with chin and voice descending. "I heard, uh, I mean, how are you doing? You know, with ... everything?"

Don't talk to me, he'd think. *Just shut up.*

The more compassion these people offered, the more his old life seemed untenable. His grief had gone public. Sympathy is poison to salespeople. Salespeople needed to be Teflon.

In the days leading up to when they'd taken Zack, Josh had taught the baby amusingly to sigh after each gulp from his bottle —a Pepsi commercial–like "Aaah": very funny. But where was Zack now?

Could my friends maybe think Dori really did it? Josh thought. *Holy shit, what if they think I'm the one who's accused—me and not Dori?*

Josh shook off this idea, managed some reflex gratitude, a few mechanical responses to his colleagues—but he couldn't bear their expectant eyes. They had suspense in their faces, like people wondering if you remember their names.

By ten-thirty, he was sure his predicament had already struck its blow to his own face. He imagined himself as having gaunt cheekbones and protruded eyes, the almost-squirrel face that belongs to insomniac grief.

Eleven A.M.: His college roommate called to see how he was holding up. "We're fighting through it, Dori and me, thanks," Josh said. "Good," the roommate said, but then he, too, had nothing to say. (The cracks in old friendships are measured in awkward pauses.) Josh struggled to lift that dark boulder, his mood. He needed to put his failure, or not failure, he meant to have thought his *problem*, out of his mind. And so Josh, being Josh, delivered a smoother account each time he told his story. By lunchtime, he realized he was wrong about his appearance: His face had the handsome beam of suffering on it, as in some mural of St. Sebastian. And by recounting the article in that more Josh-like way—better polished after each telling—he guaranteed that the story had fewer rough and hurtful edges as it came out of him. What was wrong with that?

He looked forward to his lunch meeting at two-fifteen with David Wohl from Novadyne, makers of Cytocal; a chance for more banality to help him forget.

"You got units that sell for what, like twenty-five thousand dollars?" Wohl said. "That's more than I'm looking to spend."

Josh tried to ease into the friends-from-way-back timbre of professional selling. "Hey, Jon Stewart's kicking old-people tail, too—*your* demo, I'm talking about."

(Coincidentally, he and Wohl had gone to college together, where they'd bantered through a colorless near-friendship.)

"Nuh-uh, Josh. Not at the twenty-five thousand range."

David Wohl was born in Binghamton. And though he'd lived in the metropolitan area for a while, he boosted the upstate manner in his speech rhythms and dress. He wore Haggar pants, short-sleeve button shirts; he began sentences with little challenges, with a *Look here*, a *You got*. Hundred was *hunn-erd*. Once, Josh had taken him to watch the live feed of NFL draft day at ESPN Zone's skybox, and Wohl went crazy about the mini-TVs over every urinal in the bathroom.

"Nuh-uh. Can't do that price," David Wohl was saying now.

"Yeah, it's a lot, and costs per thousands are in like the high single digits, compared to last season," Josh said. "But Dee Dubbs—the show is performing like you wouldn't believe."

Under the table his feet roamed agitatedly. Josh, given to effortlessness, had found his smiling self capable of having forgotten—for thirty seconds, a minute. Yet it came back, it always did come back. Already it was unignorable, like a toothache, or a noisy mouse between wall and wainscoting: *Zack, Zack, Zack.*

As David Wohl kept talking, Josh's mind went in a strange direction.

Jesus, does this guy not know what happened to me? he thought, relieved that he might not have to talk about it again, but also sort of offended. (The story had been very prominent in the paper. Furthermore the problem was his; it had become who he *was*.)

Near the end of the lunch, David Wohl, after a pause, did say: "Hey, sorry to hear about . . ." And Josh felt a certain sneaky relief, gross-hearted and shitty.

Wohl barely recognized that Josh ended their lunch as quickly as a guy wrapping up a mediocre blind date: check, handshake, bye.

By the time he'd gotten back to the office, Josh felt totally wrong again, in having talked so much today about Zack; the squawk of a phone ringing in some nearby cubicle seemed not merely climate noise, but a judgment, an electric *tsk tsk*. Josh's punishment for having disclosed his sadness, for his having grooved, just a little, on these people's pity.

On his way to the men's room he passed the lounge without, of course, stepping foot inside it. But, looking in, he saw Alyssa standing alone by the microwave, no one paying her any mind. And to Josh the world seemed very sad.

Doug Moscow was in there, telling how he used to skim cash from the registers at some bar he'd worked as a ski bum in late-'90s Telluride. Moscow talked up his larceny without shame. "It was awesome." Everyone thinks his own degree of involvement with something bad marks the far edge of acceptable.

"It was totally easy, kind of like working here," Moscow said, and even Alyssa laughed.

And so, as it turned out, Josh's difficulty was to be a paper tiger—at least to everyone else at *Sparkplug*. They'd feared and pictured the uncomfortable initial second, a rising of the curtain onto who knew what. Once people realized that Josh wouldn't break to smithereens if they looked at him—that, by lunchtime, he ended up seeming "cool about it"—they were able to relax. They could even take pleasure in the release of their own pent-up worries, by comparing them to someone else's misfortune. They went about their jobs without getting in his way. "What dedication, coming in here," they'd say, in relieved voices. "That guy's a fucking trooper." It was cathartic.

Then came the news that the young sales exec Paul Damphouse got promoted, and everyone talked about that.

6

At St. Joseph's Hospital, administrators had the impression that Darlene Stokes, like so many brainy doctors, had no mind for the world—not as it happened outside the lab or the ICU, anyway.

Many things in that Goldins newpaper article irritated her; the columnist had written that a doctor had authority to confiscate infants, which was untrue. What's more, it was as if she'd been penalized for not commenting, when the law, the dictates of her profession, her very morality—none of these *allowed* her to comment. (The reporter must have heard about patient-doctor privilege, right?) Still, while Darlene did recognize that the Goldin publicity was regrettable, she saw the difficulty as you might a pathogen, something diligence and time would flush out—out of the hospital system, out of her life.

She was thinking these very thoughts when she ran into Peregrine Berg; he was standing behind her in the lunch line at St. Joe's cafeteria, that brightly lit, dully painted dining hall. All around, patients cautiously moved and bent in their complete anthology of stoops and slouches.

"Oh, *I'll* get that for you," said heavyset Berg, stepping nimbly ahead of, and paying for, Darlene.

"The hospital's taking care of my soup?"

"A courtesy, and a pleasure," said Berg, handing a twenty to the cashier, his smile missing the stamp of delight.

"Very kind of you, but—" Darlene said. "It is a surprise, that's all."

Then Darlene's peripheral vision ID'd the man who stood behind Peregrine Berg: Eric Stone, the fifty-year-old VP of Hospital Affairs, Marketing, and Medical Staff Relations. That's when she realized this was no coincidental meeting; these men wanted to talk to her about the story.

At the lunch table, salt-and-pepper-headed Eric Stone turned his eyes, his smooth restrained face, on Darlene:

"Can you believe this weather? Seventy-six today, forty-eight yesterday. And they say there's no climate change, right?"

The man's voice was pulled taut by repressed feeling. "All right," he said abruptly, "St. Joseph's supports you, that's paramount to us, Dr. Stokes." He'd groomed his hair back from the peak of his forehead using a gel that had preserved the rows left by his comb.

This Mr. Stone had a very energetic posture. "No local newspaper reporter is going to change our commitment to our patients." He was keyed up. "Or our defense of our physicians."

Darlene warily said thank-you to her bosses.

A red apple sat on Mr. Stone's tray. An ancient patient walked by: Tolstoy beard, Kafka body—there was infinite hope, just not for him.

Laying down her plastic spoon, she was still in the thick of politeness. "Pardon me if what I'm about to say comes off as an ingratitude." She gave a sternly expectant nod. "I would've thought that administrative support didn't need an announcement."

Mr. Stone turned to Mr. Berg, as if he couldn't trust himself to stay calm in answering.

"Of course, of course," Mr. Berg said quickly. "But this story has brought other reporters out from under their rocks, yeah? And that means a lot of unwanted—you know, a lot of *stuff*. But it doesn't matter. That's why we came to meet you, you see."

Darlene sat there, quieted, while Berg kept on with that shifty something in his face. "We wanted just to show you that we don't *care*. Who is going to support a mum with bloodletting expertise whose baby shows signs of bloodletting?"

"It's a point of pride," said Mr. Stone, a bit head-in-air about it. "We back you. A hundred percent." He moved his big body in the chair. He was speaking excitedly. "They used all they had. They got their picture in the paper. It's done by the end of the week. Mark my words. We're a hundred percent supportive of you here."

They wanted to be thanked? The hot feeling in Darlene's face became a twitch in her legs.

"All I did was make my recommendation to CPS," she said. "If the child is taken, that's CPS's call."

Berg had kept his smile at Darlene. This was hospital politics, and Darlene knew she had to appear grateful to men who had merely allowed a doctor to report a suspicious mother to authorities.

"And any race stuff, well." Mr. Stone waved off the subject of bigotry, not even bothering to tread carefully.

Darlene now let a pause in. She didn't really know Mr. Stone, but she'd seen a wide sampling of his administrative type, his species of managerial man—covetous extramarital eyes, trendy cell phone that they'd pull out during lunches, your classic "postthinking" American—to whom God, in that mysterious way of his, had ceded the future of the world. Darlene had once planned to smack this unthinking type across their handsome go-getting faces in her essay "Rot." (In fact, although not especially introspective, Mr. Stone himself was a devoted reader of Civil War histories, an unsentimentally charitable man, a good father/husband.)

"We know," Stone was saying, "that there's no truth to the charge that race played any part in targeting this mother."

Had there been the slightest vocal lift at the end there—the questioning lift? *Targeting?*

"Anyhow," Berg said, "and all that."

"All we ask is that you have Dr. Weiss or yourself provide us with a weekly progress report on this."

"It's CPS's call, mostly," she said, almost to herself. She was tough-minded and terrible at being unlike who she was.

"We know. We just want to keep involved. There's a case to be made that we were overly generous in giving the family so long before we acted."

"All right," she said. "A report a week. Straight to you. I'll write it myself."

Back in her office, she'd psyched herself into a headache just by recalling the conversation, its pride-bruising tone. Why'd she get so mad? Hadn't the administrators said they'd support her?

Behavior is merely one's ideals infected by circumstance, and by past gripes, Darlene realized. She remembered, as she often did, the many patients and administrators who (going back to her resident days) had stared too long at her ID card. Their squints asked: *Can this black woman be a doctor?*

Annoyed as she was, she still felt confident in the case.

But the reporter Gregory Hollister was cooking up something else for Saturday, the morning of the Goldins' appointment to see Zack. He would change the story, taking it out of its lumbering stride and into a manic gallop.

7

MUNCHAUSEN DOC HAS RADICAL PAST
By Gregory Hollister

Dr. Darlene Stokes, the St. Joseph's Hospital pediatrician at the very heart of the Glenwood Landing Munchausen trial featured exclusively in the *News-Independent* for the last week, has a past history of Black Power radicalism and "antiwhite protest," according to sources close to the doctor.

When in college, Stokes, now a single mother, belonged to an antiwhite activist group called the "Melanin Society." No whites were allowed in the group, or in their campus housing. A "Manifesto" written while she was a member called for a dramatic reordering of the world's political power, "by any means necessary." The manifesto claims that, since "us black people are dying more than any other people on Earth," the HIV virus was "probably made by some [white] scientist."

"I'm not saying this case is racially motivated, per se," the Goldins' lawyer said. "But I am saying it is possible that such impulses or biases may, subconsciously, have played a part. I have tried to come up with a reason why this doctor is hounding this family, and unfortunately I can't find any other logical reason."

As St. Joseph's Hospital's shortest-serving and youngest division chief, Dr. Stokes considers herself an authority on Munchausen syndrome by proxy (MSBP), which St. Joseph's spokeperson Andrea Truncali calls "a mental illness"—although many experts believe it not only to be extremely rare, but perhaps nonexistent.

"It really is a diagnosis of the month," says Dr. Nate Dennis, a Great Neck psychiatrist who has testified in defense of parents in a number of Munchausen lawsuits.

And now word has emerged that Dr. Stokes's radical past may have played a part in her decision making, at least according to one person who knows her well. In an exclusive interview, one of the doctor's former in-laws tells this reporter: "[Dr. Stokes] didn't know what a family should be like, because she didn't come from one."

Dr. Stokes, a single parent, was raised in a fatherless family unit, according to this former in-law. Dr. Stokes had been unhappily married to the late Leo Golovin, a white Jewish real estate broker, who filed for divorce from her in the 1990s.

According to the former in-law—who requested anonymity because she "didn't want to get too involved with a legal case"—Dr. Stokes was "incredibly angry" and "possibly anti-Semitic" after the breakup, which occurred some four years prior to Mr. Golovin's death. The parents of Zack Goldin are Jewish. The Melanin Society no longer exists, according to a Tufts spokesperson.

"I didn't want to come forward against someone who used to be in my family," Dr. Stokes's former in-law said. "But I thought it was important to say that [Dr. Stokes's] feelings about [her ex-husband] may be affecting this case."

Following the recommendation of hospital attorneys, the doctor would not comment, not even to say if she's ever been wrong about such cases before, other than to say, "I certainly am not a racist."

Still, other experts who have reviewed this case at the request of the *News-Independent* have concerns about

Stokes's diagnosis. "Without talking about this case particularly, it strikes me that doctors are quick to cry MSBP,"
Dr. Lewis Krauskopf, a Philadelphia psychiatrist who
has testified against doctors in numerous lawsuits, said.
"I have known of cases where bias plays a role."

In fact, this case troubled Krauskopf enough that
he said he filed an objection with CPS, citing the "frequent inaccuracy in making this diagnosis, the extreme
hardship it places on this family, and mitigating circumstances." Mr. Krauskopf would not specify what mitigating factors he was referring to. . . .

The story got picked up by the wires.

8

DARLENE HAD TO READ IT TWICE, THAT'S HOW SHOCKED SHE WAS. SHE actually laughed, seeing the Melanin Society get mentioned; it felt like an amplified version of catching a very old shot of yourself in someone else's scrapbook—that tricky sensation of how weird it is to see the ways in which other people view you. Words, Darlene thought, are amazing little implements. Because of words something can be awful and untrue, while still being factual.

Weirdly enough, the one person who also grasped how that dichotomy shaped this article was the Goldins' lawyer, Martin Seidel.

Seidel folded his newspaper with librarian fussiness, then placed it on the seat just next to his. He was traveling by train to meet his clients; the Goldins were to have their first supervised visit with their son today. He wanted the article in savable condition.

This was Seidel's third time going over Hollister's piece. Earlier, at home, when his wife had asked what he was reading ("I *know* that look, Marty"), he'd answered: "Nussink," in *Hogan's Heroes* mock-German. "I see nussink, I hear nussink. . . ." Like a lot of needy charmers, Martin kept even those closest to him at a distance, in his case using jokes and wacky voices and shallow declarations of affection; these barriers also held Martin at a remove from himself, where he wouldn't have to encounter that stranger, the real Martin Seidel, too often.

Now he was thinking, almost ruefully: *Well, we did it*. It probably wasn't true, about the doctor being a racist—or, at least, the crap about how Dr. Stokes let her supposed racism blind her. But lawyers needed to do what they had to. In fact, didn't he *owe* it to his clients to perform the best he could? Suddenly the train was in a tunnel:

that quick windy *whomp* like a smash of the eardrum, then everything quiet but the stutter of metal wheels over train tracks. Seriously, what were the chances a nice Jewish family like the Goldins actually *did* this thing to their son? Seidel, a fairly religious guy, even thought of praying for the Goldins now. But he had the strange feeling that it wouldn't work here—that prayer, like cell phone reception, was disrupted by being in a tunnel.

I mean, if you look at a case like that, he was thinking, *isn't it one of the most ethical things I could do, in fact, to spread these rumors?* So in this way, this quickly, a liberal guy combed over his guilt.

He thought about what he'd read in the court filings about Zack Goldin's temporary foster family and felt even more secure in his belief that he'd done the right thing.

Danielle Kirk, who liked to be called "Yelly," had such baby-fattish looks that people put her at early twenties, not her actual thirty-four. She was bouncy-awkward enough to make people feel personally invaded: When you talked to Yelly, you could never be sure she wasn't going to lose her balance and fall on you. It wasn't so much that she wanted to lean into people as to move somewhere past them. She hoped one day to "go off the grid" entirely—a cabin somewhere with a good vegetable garden, a desert pueblo with a drinking well but no TV, a Hudson River houseboat tricked out in solar panels, no address for tax returns—*any*thing to get clear of prepackaged culture.

Until that future day, however, Yelly was renting one and a half carpeted bedrooms five blocks north of Long Island's Roosevelt Field Mall. She shared this small home with Tyler, her genial, eternally (and disappointedly) bicurious "husband"—in fact, mere housemate and sometime lover. It was Tyler who'd hatched the idea they get married to become temporary foster parents, for cash.

This had been a slow week, foster-parent-wise; Tyler and Yelly were boarding two children, providing the benefit of their interim supervision. One was a colicky black newborn, Lucas, who seemed to like his crib near the slightly open window. The other, nineteen months old, white and sad-seeming, was Zack.

Sometimes, Yelly would tell Tyler, it's just a bad mix; whatever you do, now and then personalities are like two positive heads of a battery—the fit wasn't right. That's how it was, she knew, between her and Zack. Something about the way the boy moped—no matter how happy and smiling Yelly would be—scraped at her insides. So she came into the living room now (where the two boys slept) braced for more rejection. She raised Zack by his armpits, hefting him toward the changing table that he was already a little big for. "*There* we go, Z-man," she said, lowering him to the hard surface. " 'Bout an hour, you're going to see Mommy and Daddy, those naughty, naughty people."

She un-Velcroed his Huggies. Already, Zack was making Yelly's morning a little difficult. He wasn't resisting her, just not actively helping. "The kid's got some Gandhi in him—he's a conscientious objector," Yelly would tell Tyler. Tyler never fully listened and actually assumed Yelly was complaining about Lucas, the black kid. At night, when Tyler gave Lucas a bottle, he'd whisper in the boy's ear, "Go a little easy on my lady, huh? Guy-to-guy, here: You're making my life rougher than I need it to be right now."

Yelly would tell her friends: "You have to love kids to get into this gig." Temp fostering earned $150 a month, per kid, plus expenses, and if you had the extra space it wasn't a bad deal. An added roommate who didn't get a TV vote. Yelly had an evangelical response to her own life; what she did felt so *right* to her, so essentially smart, that it seemed ungenerous not to pass the tip on to others. "Also, it's good training for when, you know, Tyler gets around to making me round."

What made the job hard, though, was that if you liked the kids, you knew they were leaving in four weeks. So it was better, all in all, not to like them. Yelly had come to understand what it was like to run a B and B; you were professionally, indiscriminately hospitable—but felt, in some deep sense, taken for granted. Because the kids tended to come in fresh from a bad story, and they never treated Yelly with great appreciation. "Of course, they don't care if I've got a story, too," she told her friends. "Hey, that's cool. They're kids. You shouldn't expect too much from a kid. It's really helped me understand my own mom."

This morning, Yelly wasn't just running a hotel; she'd have to be a chauffeur, too. She had to ferry Zack to his therapeutic day-care session—but it wasn't too much of a downer (just another car seat, buckle in, buckle out) except that she had to drag along the other kid. Yelly's husband, Tyler, would, under normal circumstances, have baby-sat Lucas. But Tyler was an artist—collage and multimedia— and this morning he was schlepping his installation piece to a Great Neck gallery. For twenty-eight months, he'd taken Polaroids of five hundred and forty-four strangers. He'd seated each one of them, separately, in the same desk chair, asked for an affectless posture, and given them each the same red clown nose to wear. The culmination of his labors, *The Nose Project*, occupied an entire wall.

"*Lucas,*" Yelly called to the other baby. Next to Zack on the changing table, he had started to fuss. "Zip it."

Yelly caught sight of her own torso reflected in the chance mirror of her turned-off TV screen; an odd, upward angle, her heavy arms occupied. Her black T-shirt (Nirvana, *Nevermind*) hung down over her thighs, and she could just about see the bottom of her underpants; it was seven-thirty, and she hadn't gotten dressed yet. Her T-shirt's famous image, that naked swimming baby reaching for the green dollar bill, made for an eerie third child in the room. The image always brought her up short: When hadn't *she* been that baby, trying to get some extra money, under oozy, difficult, even heroic conditions?

"So, okay," she said, "I'm taking breakfast orders. On the menu—formula." Yelly, who forgave herself for naturally favoring the white baby (genes), always worked to make up for it by feeding black children first. It offset, she felt, the innumerable times in their lives that whites would find softer treatment.

In his resistant way, Zack was captivated by Yelly: She was not ill-suited to foster-parenthood. Attributes that functioned as red flags to her fellow adults made her mesmerizing to children. Her openness, her wide variety of smells (different ones in different zones of her body), her individualist's approach to makeup, her self-chopped punk hairstyle. At home, Zack liked to throw himself onto couches, rustle his head under pillows, and make up word sounds that made him laugh. Here, he was reserved and watchful: Yelly did all that other, silly work for him. And on a preconscious level, Zack didn't want to commit his at-home personality to this new house, out of some inchoate sense that it might somehow render his accommodations permanent. But he did raise a hand to Yelly's face now. She was pink and moist.

"Aww," Yelly said. She kissed him on the palm. "Baby taste." She turned to Lucas. "Now, you."

Her husband hadn't left yet; Tyler took long showers. They both did. For that reason, this room always felt moist to Zack; someone always seemed to have just left the bathroom, or to have spilled water into the rug, or to be steaming some vegetable. If anyone left, say, a tissue on the glass, it stuck. (A mediocre napper even at home, Zack had slept especially fitfully in this humid place.) Little Zack, unattended for a moment, gazed at the room. Two pink bassinets flanked the TV, which was now showing *Sesame Street* on mute; the white walls had tan scars marking the removal of taped-up prints; next to the changing table, bright-spined paperbacks made a pile. Zack liked to arrange these books into Lego-like stacks (*Jewelry Making & Beading for Dummies; Search Engine Optimization for Dummies; Living with Hepatitis C for Dummies; Parenting for Dummies*). He'd push them over, then begin the pile all over again. If she would just get him off this table, he could start a new stack.

Yelly sensed he wanted something. "Yeah, Zack, but we gotta hurry." The two kids, together, paid half of Tyler and Yelly's rent— more, if they cheated a little on the expense reports. "You're gonna see your mommy today."

Zack had extremely few words ("Ma," "Da," "Zack," "ba") but he did have thoughts, or pools of meaning he understood somehow. He looked around for another adult in the room. *This is not Mom* was pretty close to describing what he was thinking. He expressed it by crying.

"Hey, not now," she said. To end his sudden tears, she bent and touched his face. But they weren't a real family; this empty act could no more be mistaken for a mother's touch than the wind that fills out some dress on a clothesline might be confused with an actual body.

She saw in the dark-gray TV a reflection of Tyler: thin legs, ballooned by the screen's curvature, stretching up to the shaggy groin region and his dangling, still damp penis, and even the soft belly, the wet stringy chest hair. He had his red nose on, for a goof (there were no self-portraits in *The Nose Project*). He touched her, and having misjudged how near he was, she jumped.

"God*damn it*, Tyler!" Her heart was galloping. "I asked you not to sneak up on me! I have to take both these kids to see Zack's parents—*alone,* remember?"

9

Josh listened to the husky breathing of the Lexus motor. Neither he nor Dori spoke.

Josh had become prey to a kind of ballplayerish superstition. If either of them were to say the wrong thing (or really anything at all) it would jinx today. Also, playing the radio would have felt disrespectful. So Josh and Dori glided down Old Country Road in what was the street's quietest vehicle.

This is the route they would drive to the Hamptons or the North Fork beaches. (This whole thing was so unjust; were such vacation days gone forever?)

Old Country Road was Long Island's open-air sales experiment—a six-lane constellation of franchises. A state name, a food product, a logo, a daily slogan, a region; they lined the road like corporate embassies. California Pizza Kitchen, Nobody Beats the Wiz!, Boston Market, Western Apparel, Olive Garden, Ruby Tuesday, Nathan's Famous Hot Dogs, Pizza Hut, McDonald's, Taco Bell, Chili's, Romano's Macaroni Grill, Cozymel's, Burger King, Wendy's, The Cheesecake Factory, P.F. Chang's, Brooklyn Diner, Cold Stone Creamery, Fuddruckers, OfficeMax, Circuit City, RadioShack, Best Buy, Urban Outfitters, CompUSA, Office Depot, Home Depot, BJ's Wholesale Club, three Loews movie theaters, a Costco warehouse, each a consulate of a discrete retail philosophy, a discrete browsing experience, and a discrete set of shopping memories. Of course, Josh and Dori had many associations with each one (fond, bad, desirous), and looking at the shops sparked as many thoughts and feelings as songs on the radio would have. But there was no way to turn them off, and Josh didn't hold it against himself.

Dori's face transformed in expressive ways, even in the silence;

anxiety pinched her mouth and let go; her brow wrinkled, unwrinkled; Josh was afraid she was reading his silence as directed *against her*. When in fact it was a sacrifice offered to both their futures, a good-luck hedge. He patted her hand.

"Honey," Josh said. "We'll get him home."

But what Dori had been thinking about was Martin, Josh's lawyer; she didn't see him as *her* lawyer, too. She wondered if attorney-client privilege would cover confidences she shared with him—but kept from Josh. It was a problem that she returned to whenever she felt guilty. Having a lawyer she wasn't sure she could really call her own made her feel put-upon, unappreciated, and anxiously greedy.

It was time, she thought, for her to start forgiving herself.

"I'd like to kill them," Josh said, startling her. Them —doctors, CPS, the world beyond the family, the mysterious incalculable menace gathered *out there*.

"Me, too, Mr. Goldin. I think I'd really kill them." Dori closed her eyes and leaned her head back, dramatically. "If I knew we could get away with it," she said. "And get Zack." The harmony of features, her plump mouth, that long neck—all of it was boosted by her sensitive pose, her shut-eyed grandeur.

"Hey," Josh said when they reached a stoplight, "we'll do this."

He talked because he knew it would soothe her, at least a little. And he needed to keep talking for himself, too; he thought it might be reassuring to have someone depend on him; it could make him feel secure and comfortable.

But here he was, Mr. Professional Small Talk, and that itself was what seemed so odd to him now: Words themselves felt *lame*; they couldn't get near the powerfulness of this emotion. The talk itself was a barrier, an icy layer covering a deep lake of the unsayable.

His face squeezed by feeling, Josh turned to his wife and managed this in one shot:

"I love you more than anything, and I really think we will get him back, but whatever happens I want you to know that I'll always love you."

This also ended up, disappointingly, just words. Not as eloquent as he had hoped. Josh had wanted this to have the weight of a prayer or something—a magical command to make it all, *abracadabra*, better.

Still, Dori's cheeks went red under the heat of Josh's affection. His devotion, his friendship, his cuteness—his *Josh*ness—yanked like a magnet at the cold, iron-gray secret inside her heart. But to let it out, to tell him, would be suicidal!

The thing to focus on was that she cared for Zack *so* much. How to explain to those CPS people that her love of family had been why she made sure Zack would never really get hurt?

"I love you, too," Dori said. She opened those eyes, exactly Zack's blue, at her husband. For a moment the atmosphere in the car felt a bit less brittle. Dori set her hand on Josh's lap—her usual place. "I really do," she said. But because nothing had changed, the spell petered out in the ensuing silence, the ensuing awkwardness. And the traffic light turned green.

"That article will really help," Josh said, facing ahead again, driving, falling back on his bright actiony voice. The voice of small talk.

His mind snagged on a memory, an image. From a minute ago, two at the most: Dori closing her eyes, leaning her head back in the seat. Why did this pose catch in his mind? Drop it. But he couldn't. Dori had seemed aware of the beauty advantages in raising her profile just a little against the sunlit window, her eyes shut in melodramatic, wifely vehemence. It seemed she'd been just playing a part, hamming it up. Josh, the trained noticer, never off duty.

But he cursed himself for noticing.

United front, he thought, smiling at her again.

WHAT DORI BEGAN doing was counting the seconds of quiet, measuring how big Josh's smile was, how long it remained on his face. It was freaking her out. Usually, a smile was good news—unless it operated like a cynical smile, a silent lie. *He's smiling a fake smile because he knows*, she thought. *What if now he believes the hospital and not me?*

Dori looked out her window, to the franchises that kept sprouting there, prefab one-stories that cozied right up on one another. She knew Josh was still smiling at her without even having to look. And she felt as if in a dream where every signal took its opposite meaning and the basic facts kept getting all fucked up.

She even had a speech ready—she'd been coming up with one for weeks, a full explanation of herself to Josh. But she kept changing it, except for the opening line: *I'm very safe about it.*

She let her hand slip off Josh's lap—her hold on self-control, on everything, had gotten shaky.

That line—*I'm very safe about it*—had been her constant internal soundtrack these last weeks. She thought the words almost without registering their meaning: when showering, fixing coffee, making her bed, failing to sleep at night. Her internal patter ran not unlike Josh's external patter: constantly.

Would he forgive her if he really did know? The way she always forgave him his faults? (And this whole thing was his fault, partially, wasn't it?)

She was slow to realize Josh had begun talking to her again. He was going on about something. She smiled at him, a bluff of comprehension.

Don't people have to forgive, in order to love someone else? she thought. Yes. Yes, they did. Forgiveness isn't a virtue. It's a necessity, she told herself.

LITTLE ZACK WORE his tie-dyed shirt (sunset colors, orange and blue) and his cinch-waist jeans. The Goldins were surprised almost to tears that whoever'd dressed him had picked an outfit that Zack often wore.

"Oh, my God," Dori said, and her hand flew to her throat. Josh had a palm on her other arm, and so could feel the bolt of pleasure—her whole body tensing—when his wife caught sight of their child approaching through a glass door.

These sixty official minutes of Goldin family reunion were taking place in the softly lit auspice of "Meeting Space" at Family Foundation, Inc. ("Family F is just so much less impersonal than our old contract for therapeutic day care," the bureaucrats of Long Island agreed among themselves, at breakfasts and staff conferences. "They've got an indoor slide.") The Meeting Space walls were decorated with corporate murals (smiles, houses, eight-petaled daisies), and posters in multicolored fonts: "Spend the DAY; You can PLAY—but don't get CARRIED AWAY." Below, in a smaller and tighter black font, ran the legend: "All conferences are supervised by Family Foundation professionals to ensure that parental contact does not put any children at risk." Cameras had been discreetly positioned not at the corners of the walls but in the wide, grin-faced clocks; this rendered moot the question of free will.

The Goldins had waited at the blue conference table. Seidel was there (hundreds more unmentioned dollars), along with the reporter Hollister—who, upon learning that Josh graduated from NYU, tried to strike up a conversation about, of all things, semiotics and comp lit. Josh had wanted to focus all his attention on Dori, to try to surround her with some of his calm. A chubby, black-haired man with a trim goatee and wearing blue orderly's scrubs had entered with Zack—the guy led their son by a gentle hand.

"Oh, my God!" Dori said again. "My baby!" She hurried to him, shaking a bit, as if she were the only object in the room touched by some little earthquake that had just rumbled through. (She'd known the reporter would be here, and had imagined this moment, how it would play; and it felt as special as she'd hoped.)

Zack heard his mother, saw her, smelled her. "Ma!" he said. Zack opened and closed his hands in her direction. The simplest request: *Bring me this.* The words came rapidly and excited as barks. "Ma! Ma! Ma!"

"Yes, yes, little Zackie. Mommy's here, Mommy's here."

Josh was aware of Martin giving the reporter a deep, significant nod, as if to say: *See, what'd I tell you? A family.* Josh noted how young and skinny Hollister was, how the guy's small digital recorder was going (the red operating light held steady) and that he was also writing in a small pad whose cover actually read: "Reporter's Notes." It seemed as if he approached this whole thing as a role-playing game.

What struck Dori as strange—a kind of sooty, foreign object—as her son swayed and ruckled into her arms, was that Zack was holding a bottle the Goldins had never given him, a generic brand of bottle she didn't recognize.

"Hey, bud," Josh was saying, kissing the boy's head and tawny hair. Even missing his son, he'd forgotten everything about Zack's physicality: the powdery innocent smell, the after-bath warmth, the surprising strength in those meaty arms. Zackie kept saying, "Ma! Ma!" and rubbing his face into Dori's. (Had Zack forgotten "Dada" so soon?)

Dori hugged—and then Josh saw that she, heartbreakingly, took in the clock, to gauge how much time was left. The chubby black-haired guy nodded. "Don't worry, I'm not here to rush anybody."

He wore a name tag, "George N.," a grinning blue bear to one side of the letters and a sprig of four delicate flowers on the other: Josh hadn't realized he'd be passing the minutes under some stranger's eye; but this was the sort of thing he had to accept now. George stepped around the table, where he, Martin, and the reporter all introduced themselves, like team captains at the fifty-yard line—everyone, with the considerate formality of their manner, apologizing to the others for their presence here.

But Josh noted that when Dori walked Zack to the slide, when she brought her nose to his, and especially when she lifted him into the air, George grew extra alert, watching for foul play. (His movements had that Babe Ruthian daintiness of the lively overweight.)

Josh begged, "Let me hold him," and he thrilled to the grabbiness of his son's fingers around his shoulders, the little face riding in front of his, the soft breath falling on his cheek. Josh took a deep, noisy inhalation of Zack, as if he were smelling fresh bread. Who knew, until children were taken away, that the smell of them was so *nourishing*?

And then, when Zack was on the slide, Josh saw his boy looking for someone else: The child's eyes passed over the three men and his mother, but then moved to the door from which he'd recently entered. Josh couldn't figure it out, but after a second he understood: Zack was searching for the parents he now lived with. He was sure these foster parents were perfect, and this notion made him angry again, so he lost the value of ten precious minutes with his son.

Finally, Zack toddled over to Hollister, whom he had never met before.

"Why, hello, young fella," Hollister said.

With every infant's alert but self-absorbed eyes, Zack half considered, half wrote off this strange man.

"Look at *me*, baby," Dori said to the child's back, softly. Zack's having walked over to Hollister hurt like a kick in the heart; her son wasn't pouring out the love or attention she'd craved and expected. The first tears brightened the edges of her stare.

But Zack did turn around to her, blinking.

Dori almost lost her composure now; she gave a burst, a laugh/cry hybrid. She waved at him, a silent hello. Zack's chubby face went plump as his eyes switched to joy. He'd already begun to forget that other woman who'd been his mommy this week.

"Ma."

Zack's white Keds were so tiny, Dori felt a wave of affection that she'd have called "wanting to eat him up." She shot over to lift Zack in another embrace, greedy for his weight.

Near the end, Dori reached into her big leather bag and came out with a yellow box that held a Murray Wiggles doll—which Josh thought looked kind of gay, especially with its red shirt and high-waisted jeans. But Dori had picked it out with both the supervisors and the reporter in mind.

Zack, once the box had been opened for him, fired off rounds of gibberish. Then he laughed at his private joke. (This was how he said thanks.) The gift rule here was nonsharp toys, but no food, nothing that could be poisoned.

"It's time to wrap up, folks," George said; he threw his watch a look that carried a touch of the pantomime in it. "Sorry to be the one to have to say." His body clock was calibrated to know precisely when an hour was up.

(Yelly was sitting—not to say hiding—in Family Foundation's upstairs offices, watching TV while she waited out the bio parents.)

Dori dropped to a knee, squeezed Zack's hand. Josh put his palm to Zack's head; he hoped the boy didn't have a clear idea of what was happening. He prayed Zack wouldn't cry now. If he did, these last minutes could make the whole hour seem a lot worse in memory.

Dori said: "Are you sad to see Mommy go?"

But any thoughts Zack may have had played very indistinctly under his calm appearance. He swiveled toward the door.

Seidel asked George—for the benefit of his clients and his journalist: "Your legal mandate is strong to try to reunite the legal family, correct?"

"That is the state's policy, yeah," said George. He carefully—neither quickly nor slowly—removed Dori's hand from her son's and replaced it with his own. "But it's not our mandate. All that's CPS's deal." In his non-Zack hand, he picked up the Murray Wiggles doll. "We're just a private corporation. We contract with New York State."

Seidel kept trying to play his clients' natural advantage. But Josh was thinking, *Come on*—irritated almost to offense by his lawyer. *Not now, Martin, huh?* He wanted his wife to be able to say good-bye in peace.

Dori's thoughts were elsewhere: She demanded to see the foster mom. "I have to know he's in good hands. I have to know."

"I'm sorry, Mrs. Goldin, but—"

"I have to know."

And then George lifted Zack onto his own shoulder and kind of turned himself backward, so the boy could face each of his parents.

This was something attendants had been taught how to do. "Say good-bye to your folks, now." Dori nuzzled him and kept herself from crying. "I have to know," she said weakly.

Josh lowered his face toward his son's. "Okay, kiddo," he said. He felt Zack's familiar little nose hovering very close to his; Josh let his forehead drop gently against his son's. Zack's nose kinked up in a lazy smile, a lot like Dori's on a good day. He had his mother's plump lips, too. All this crumpled the core of who Josh was. He began to mouth a strange question, a question he didn't know that he'd been dying to ask:

Did Mommy hurt you?

Josh just about said it out loud.

He hated himself even for thinking it. He inhaled carefully through his nose, to calm himself, and told himself to shut up with any doubts, she couldn't have, all right?

Then, once again, he began to ask: *Did Mommy hurt you?* He felt the throb in his throat, the pressure from keeping this volatile question corked there. But what would he do if he found out she had? Go to the police? No, shut up, she didn't, you idiot.

Josh watched Zack's small, happily oblivious face move across the room for the door, past the murals and clocks and signs.

"Bye!" Dori sounded so desperate. "Bye, Zackie!"

Childless at least for now, Josh led his wife out into the bright day, and across the undistinguished strip of grass that led to the macadam parking lot. Dori had her edgy manner going; to Josh's amazement she seemed fairly, and suddenly, self-sufficient now. She didn't need, in other words, to lean on him as they walked to the car; nor did she cry. Nor did he. But neither did they say anything.

Family Foundation, Inc., sat at the Old Country Road boundary of the Plainview Business Complex—not far at all from a tidy, shadowless soccer field. And as the Goldins made their silent way across the sunny parking lot, they could hear referees' whistles, the earth percussion of kids running, and shrill crashes of laughter.

10

A CULTURAL PHENOMENON, LIKE ANY WHIRLWIND, IS HARD TO PRE-
DICT. Some news articles, like local cloud systems, just drift over the
country. You can't forecast which stories might gather force and
momentum, which airstream will go squally and funnelform until
it tornadoes out into national attention.

Hollister's Munchausen series had already grabbed some decent local notice. The columnist had been interested to experiment
with materials from the classic tabloid story: mixing up the emblematic signifiers. Threatened family, the power of bureaucracy,
the mysteries of medicine, and a radical past, black in charge,
white in weakened position. It was a good, challenging experience.
(Hollister had read the old Tufts screed about the aims of Melanin
House with both great sympathy and the eyes of a copy editor.
From a subjective point of view, he appreciated many of the Melanin House arguments.)

The day after the latest article had come out, a producer at
Fox—five A.M. coffee in her hand like a little ingot of daylight—
had flattened four morning papers across her desk. The *Long Island News-Independent* was the second she read—on another day,
she might not have picked up that local rag at all—and she knew
instantly what would be her story for the noon hour.

She could book it into the lunchtime show—a midday chat, segment two, during which anchors were encouraged to go passionate
and free-form. She called the executive producer. "I think what we
have here is a single black woman doctor out of control. Come take
a look."

And seven hours later, some good-looking someone with no
medical training, who'd never met Darlene, said almost that very

thing in the confines of a million TV screens: "What I think we have here is a doctor out of control."

He was a second cohost, new to the broadcast, and—excepting an ankle injury he once had gotten set in Barbados—he'd never stepped foot through the doors of a hospital.

Later that day, Sanjay Gupta included it in his CNN medical minute: Munchausen, rare in practice, difficult to diagnose. At 5:35, MSNBC had it on Tucker Carlson; the scent the anchor nosed was social engineering, a doctor attempting to legislate ideas upon a family, ideas that couldn't be won at the ballot box. And then it was everywhere.

Television vans, their satellite dishes rigged up for maximum impressiveness, gathered at the hospital. St. Joe's was reporter-haunted—print and broadcast people wandered the grounds, though they were forbidden to enter the premises. TV guys with their hearty skin tones, clear eyes, and strong teeth really stood out. Something in their out-of-place expressions, their air of playing hooky from rude health to spend time amid all this disease, put everyone on edge. That was the third day.

In the early going, Headline News, Fox, and CNN found space for rational voices—experts who were cautious and sensible, offering caveats and specifics—on sets that were as complicated, bristling, and bright as any sci-fi battleship. But their points got crowded off to the side, as this story narrowed to what everyone agreed were its base elements: race, medicine, the embattled family, politics.

Some guests condemned Darlene and St. Joseph's for refusing to leave the shadows and be interviewed, although these commentators were themselves familiar with (and often appreciative of) doctor-patient confidentiality. Then there were the guests—often young people, with alert eyes and fresh jackets—who had the most fun with Darlene's two-decades-ago involvement in campus politics, with the residence that had been her only cheap option for housing.

And you're saying, Tucker, that the doctor lived in a house that had been officially designated as African-American only?

It was a strange sensation for Darlene. She'd always especially disliked the television shows in which hosts acted as fight promoters, putting two arguments together in a ring. And now she'd been reduced to one of the arguments.

Coming up: Tough talk—two congressmen say the hunt for abusers may be out of control. Cathy Fadiman of Mothers for Family Legal Reform, and Dr. Frank Crenesse of Cleveland General. After the break.

One odd consequence: After ten days, the word "coags" had become a nationally recognized term of art. It became something that—whatever its actual meaning—you needed to ask your baby's pediatrician to check.

When did Dr. Stokes know the public case had tipped against her? It was in the small pause before anchors said her name, the little lift of the eyebrows. Of course, the pro-Goldin people argued their case with marathon hostility—and there really was no other side, no Darlene side; a doctor could only say that MSBP was difficult to diagnose, patience was required, nothing was really known yet. It was ideal programming (since no development could spoil the story until the hearing) for a cable news hour's second segment, the eight-minute B-block.

"If there is evidence of parental wrongdoing—and that's the big if right now, Greta—we certainly haven't seen it."

Many times that sad, solitary June, Darlene thought this: *I am symbolism reified.* A woman who'd often been made to feel not black enough at Tufts had become the face of blacks endangering white families. And Josh, watching the same reports from his own home, had a bitter laugh at his own expense. He had—politely and generously—feared coming off as racist when he'd met this doctor. How could he have known that, all along, the racism lay on *Dr. Stokes's* side?

Of course, Darlene kept a list in her head of the press's mistakes: No one had told any reporters, nor legally could have, about the butterfly needle CPS had discovered, the redness on baby Zack's arm, or Mrs. Goldin's strange behavior in the hospital. Or that the baby had been fine until Mrs. Goldin had removed him from the attention of St. Joe's staff—at which point he'd coded, and Mrs. Goldin changed her story. Of course none of this—no evidence of any kind—could come out, except at the hearing.

HMOs, tests, doctors, city bureaucracies—Chuck, I think most of us get a sinking feeling when we hear those words. We need to raise the veil of secrecy off the workings of this kind of stuff.

Print coverage continued, too; the *Long Island News-Independent* had a proprietary interest in the story. Through congressional votes, foreign redeployments, administration scandals, it led the paper seven times in a thirteen-day span; most popular was its headline "The Child Snatchers." A split-screen photo: one side, Darlene Stokes, the other, Betty Van Der Meer, of Long Island Child Protective Services.

Darlene learned not to answer the phone before checking the numbers on the little screen above the keypad. When James answered one of the nasty calls (he didn't tell Darlene what he'd heard; he just widened his eyes), she changed and unlisted her number. When protestors appeared at the corner of the St. Joe parking lot (with picket signs: "Protect Long Island Families from Medical OVERREACH" and "BAD Medicine"), Berg actually sent Darlene home, counseling that she take the next few days off.

Ms. Grace, there's something I want to remind your audience: The mother is a medical professional herself who had the simple audacity to question a doctor's verdict. Have you ever tried telling a physician you think they're wrong? Or asked them about something you read on WebMD? Well, just imagine your doctor didn't check your baby's coags, and you try to call them on it. How do you think they'd react?

The only time Darlene went out was to pick up the Chinese food. At Uncle Dyai's, two men seemed to whisper about her as she stood bumping her knees against the counter, waiting for her check and the warm brown bag with the greasy bottom. At home she kept the curtains and blinds drawn, in case someone heaved a brick, the way people with Southern accents did in civil-rights movies. Students at James's school sent him home with judgments, questions, and insults.

James's face took on a kind of *smeared* look, his eyes terribly sad-making in their wide-open gentleness, when Darlene invited him to speak about it.

"Mom, am I in trouble now or something?"

Why would he ask that? Maybe she'd been so busy lately that any extra attention he got seemed suspicious?

"Sweetie, we're just talking. I want to make sure we're all right. We haven't done anything wrong."

"Certainly you haven't, James," said Darlene's mother.

From her spot next to James on the couch, Alice laid her plump hand on her grandson's back and patted him. (Alice often sneaked the boy some junk food against Darlene's wishes; there must have been a Dunkin' Donuts box stashed among the pill bottles, romance novels, and juice packs in the huge, ridiculous wicker bag she carried everywhere.)

"Your mother is saying she's worried about you, James."

The boy nodded, and over his head Alice gave her daughter a look Darlene could not decipher. Ever since Alice's own health problems began, she had begun offering, with Buddha-like calm, the advice and examples from her life. But in the last weeks, she seemed to have barked up against a wall—a limit beyond which she couldn't travel. This was the first time Darlene could remember not being able to make sense of a look from her mother. It seemed that Alice wanted to say more, to add a few words that discretion wouldn't allow. (Also, she pointedly made sure only to visit when Muhammad was working.)

"Everything okay, Mother?" Darlene said.

Alice didn't answer. She just held that same look at her daughter.

Are we looking at a classic liberal overreach, Maury? Is this a case of the nanny state gone too far? My mommy sent me to bed without dinner, do we need to hire an attorney, am I headed for foster care?

When Darlene watched, she understood why life had steered her from the humanities, and down the long, smooth corridor of the sciences. There was a hardness to medicine that cheered her, that was different from the softness everywhere else. People only wanted to hear *yes* and *no* when there was no other possible choice. When there wasn't, they preferred the *maybes*, the *it could have been*s, the *it's a matter of opinion*s that let life progress in a variety of directions. *Yes* and *no* only allowed two-way traffic; what life required, what everyone needed, what science didn't allow, was more space to fudge.

I think there's a whole group of people out there, with charts and graphs, just waiting to social-engineer our families. . . . Now I want our audience to keep in mind this is a document from twenty years ago, but I think it's indicative of an attitude, a cast of mind if you will. "White people introduced HIV into the black community, on purpose." Are these the people who we want setting social policy?

Even if she'd had the legal right to respond—and she probably would have been allowed to answer some of the more bullshitty racial stuff—Darlene would have thought it beneath her. After all, what were her motives? They could hint and allude, but she was working out of the clearest altruism: a baby in jeopardy, a doctor stepping in to save him.

Without asking permission, she began going back to St. Joe's, sneaking in side entrances, working ever later, not wanting to come home. She still believed hard work would trump everything— people may not like those of us who work harder, but the truth will out. In America, because of the quality of your mind and effort, you can go from being an Alice Davis to a Rubinstein or a Rothenberg in one generation.

Getting home very late one night, after James had gone to bed, Darlene switched on the tube; after hesitating, she took a cautious sip of some TV news. Not too much, she thought—just a minute or two. Was she hoping to find something on herself?

Feeling especially irritated by the denuded shuck-'n'-jive routine of the local black weatherman, Darlene went out to stand on her front porch. *If I liked cigarettes*, she thought, *I'd do my depressed smoking right here*. At least there were no reporters camped out now (four of them had rung the bell during those horrible first days).

Darlene, who'd been looking at pictures of lungs since she was twenty-one, had never smoked a cigarette in her life.

The scarce Bryant Avenue traffic on this nine-thirty weekday night occasionally made its sound—its sad old-mannish sighing—just beyond the end of her long driveway. For a while she listened to the passing cars, watched their lights surge and vanish like days into the boring darkness. She had the strange thought that many of them had heard about her, but had no idea they were passing her right now, the woman standing here for a smoke with her no-cigarette. Many of them probably had said in the last few weeks that they hoped she would go to hell.

"We're having a meeting in my office, right now, Dr. Stokes," Eric Stone, VP of Hospital Affairs, Marketing, and Medical Staff Relations, told Darlene's voice mail. "If you're engaged with patients, hand them off to a resident and come. *Now*, please. Any resident."

"We are a business," Stone said. "That's not boorish, though it may sound it." His facial expression of mocked-up gentleness hadn't roused the dead spot in his eyes. "We are in the business of helping people. It's a business of which I am very proud to be a part."

The implication, the admonition Mr. Stone didn't need to spell out, was that this Goldin story had put a dent in business.

Even before getting Stone's call, Darlene had known there would be a meeting today. She had tried to dress what she thought of as business: long skirt, tan blouse, but too dowdy.

Eric Stone's wood-paneled office, in St. Joe's bright new wing, had a lot of comfortable, padded chairs in it, as if the man always hosted as many visitors as he was hosting now. Darlene recognized Stone and Berg, of course, and Ellen Fitzhugh, the VP of Professional Services, Planning, and Development—St. Joe's top fund-raiser. But there were two unfamiliar faces here, a woman and a man, who also sat around Stone's desk in cozy-cushioned seats. The woman was the hospital's deputy chief counsel. The man, an outside entrepreneur, happened to be on St. Joe's board of trustees; he was the CEO of the Baldwack Group, which operated many Baskin-Robbins franchises across Nassau County.

She resolved to appear unemotional. Doctors were never included in these meetings.

Things really got going when Ellen Fitzhugh, declining to turn her shadow-ringed eyes at Darlene, reminded everyone of the "macro situation." In full-on doom voice: Three Long Island hospitals were in bankruptcy proceedings, and seven had submitted applications with the state's Health Care Commission, volunteering to merge or consolidate to avoid closing. (Had Fitzhugh's eyes always looked so fatigued, or had genuine job worries painted those shadows there?)

"And now, people are beginning to stay away from us," Fitzhugh said. "Going to Long Island Jewish for non-life-and-death ailments, even if it's a farther trip. Making a point of it. Actually driving the extra three miles with passengers who have broken arms or whatever." She couldn't have been more than thirty-five, in her pinstriped blue outfit, her shrugs of understated breakdown. "We're at twelve percent less capacity over the last month; from sixty-four to fifty-two filled."

"Empty beds," Berg said, to the lawyer.

"Three hundred fifty-eight of them," Ms. Fitzhugh said. Because she talked in numbers she appeared to have authority over the future. "Forty-eight percent empty. And we're no longer in a position to do advertising. Not for the time being, anyway."

Earlier in the meeting, Darlene thought these people had been watching her too closely; now they seemed not to pay her mind at all. Why the hell was she here?

Clearing her throat, Darlene said: "All the publicity is unfortunate"—giving Ms. Fitzhugh her straight-on stare. "But, I think, extraneous. It is extraneous." (Although the fuck-you-nigger calls she got at all hours didn't seem extraneous, nor was it extraneous when her son's school had contacted her, saying James had been teased about his reverse-racist mother. Why didn't James ever tell her this stuff himself?)

"Let me ask you," Darlene said, "how should we have acted any differently? What's a hospital to do? Do you want doctors to have this fear in mind when we diagnose and prescribe? The evidence at the hearing will show—" And she went on about the butterfly needle, the redness of Zack Goldin's arm, the mother's phlebotomy background, the inconsistencies in the woman's story, the CPS reports of suspicious behavior, etc., etc.

"I'm glad you said that," the lawyer told her, having looked at her Cross pen a beat too long after Darlene had finished her spiel. "We *are* in the right, and we need to make sure the world knows that." The lawyer was an overenunciator, lips outlined in red pencil, big Long Island hair, with unfortunately dark fuzz that crept down her jaw line, next to her ears. "That's why we're going to request that Perry"—the woman gestured to Peregrine Berg now— "do most of the speaking for us at the hearing."

And here the board of trustees businessman jumped in. "We're going to send out the Bat-Signal with this one," the guy said. "We'll just have him say what you would have said."

"Will I be able to speak?"

"Yes, of course, but Perry will do most of the speaking for us."

Because Berg's not politically radioactive, Darlene thought. *Because he's white.*

And now, of course, everyone here became intensely solicitous of her, and said in chorus: "We know we're in the right"; "We have your back"; "The truth will prevail, as it always does"; "We're all in this together"; "It's only a technicality." Blah blah blah. We all wrap ourselves up in protective cliché at stressful times. One bluntly honest comment might have set the whole place ablaze like kindling.

"It's not my decision," Peregrine Berg was saying. He smoothed his shirtfront, lifted his chin as if putting on a tie. "But I think it's not the worst call, Darlene." Then he scratched behind his ear and swallowed. He'd morphed into a thousand and one ticcy anxieties. Nervousness was the only thing that set him apart from these other automatons of surrender.

Darlene, meanwhile, kept her face calm, even disinterested-looking. But this was an outrage. The *Bat-Signal*? "I agree only under protest, which you can put on record." She had to lick her mouth, as if wetting her lips might keep the eyes dry. "I want to write up everything that Mr. Berg will say, prior to his appearance, and I want an assurance that he will read it." Her voice betrayed her; it shook and it cracked.

"It will all come out in court, Dr. Stokes, no matter who says it."

"You're promising me that—"

"Yes."

"And I want to be there, able to give my testimony at least once."

Mr. Stone and the woman lawyer smiled at her, and he said gently: "Of course. We'll make sure you get your say, even if it's in a prepared statement format. But you and Dr. Weiss will both be present."

11

Darlene, still fuming, took her anger out on unkind thoughts about Mrs. Dori Goldin. *She is one of those women,* Darlene thought. *But that has nothing to do with it.* That perfect, pretty white-girl type, she meant. The sort of woman who, back in college, had gotten Darlene shaking her head at the reflected face in her mirror. Not because of the *white* part, because of the way those people had flaunted the *pretty* part. But she hadn't ever believed herself ugly, especially not once she'd started dating Leo. So what was she talking about?

It was insidious, how they made you question the truth. "They" meaning whom? she wondered. They, those who rooted against you, she thought as she made her way down to her office. "They" meaning the world.

In a windowless, octagonal alcove off the Pediatrics hallway, two vending machines faced each other—one filled with bottled water and Snapple, the other with Pop Secret popcorn, Nutri-Grain bars, Ruffles Wow! potato chips, and Baked! Lay's potato chips. Darlene came upon her father standing between these machines. He was having a conversation with an orderly—some thin, twenty-something Afro'd worker who wore a shiny blossom of keys on his hip.

Muhammad was saying:

"Bush talking about, everything going to be fine." He leaned against the drink machine. "But the thing with Iraq is like, I don't see an end to it, for real."

"Yeah," the other man said, *"yeah"*—the forceful assent of an ignorant person, hoping his nods would change the subject. He wanted to get back to discussing how bastards at vending machine companies estimated a certain percentage of wedged-in, ungettable snacks *into their profits.*

"If you don't know, you better *ask* somebody," Muhammad said. But now he noticed his daughter standing there, just watching him as he talked to this young orderly, Kurt.

She look like shit, Muhammad thought; and he was right. Darlene's tight bun of hair had a frizz corona. And insomnia had uglied her skin a washed-out, more ashen color.

"Bet." Muhammad pointed his chin indiscreetly toward her and then said to Kurt: "I'm a see you later."

Kurt, squinting at Dr. Stokes and again at Muhammad, at last gave a confused little gold-packed smile and, before leaving, said: "Oh, uh, right. Yeah, yeah, all right."

"You okay, now, Darlene?" said Muhammad. "I been waiting here for a half hour to talk to you."

Muhammad's voice had the bait and the hook of real kindness. Or maybe Darlene just wanted very much to be caught.

She hadn't even thought of how this might be affecting him. TV vans, with the whispering everywhere? This was Long Island's Tawana Brawley, its Elizabeth Smart, its Duke lacrosse scandal. But what could she say? She tried to smile. "This is, you know, *inopportune*, certainly. But it's just sort of a *brouhaha*, an inconvenience."

She realized she was using words Muhammad may not have known, or at least wouldn't have been comfortable with, words that she herself rarely even used. "Inopportune." "Brouhaha." Had she gone extra formal on purpose, to make him feel bad or something?

"It's not a big deal," she said.

Muhammad laughed but then knew to nod thoughtfully.

"I mean," she said, "it's not about *me*, is all I'm saying. It's about the patient, of course." She straightened her posture. "The truth is that these things happen from time to time, and they never have any bearing on the outcome."

Muhammad angled his head, pushed out his lips a little, actually raised an eyebrow at her—a face of skepticism, even of disapproval.

"Listen, Doctor," he said. "I know you a doctor and everything, but."

He looked down and nodded, gathering confidence to go on. "I just want to say one thing, and then I'll quit. These white people, they not going to let you do this." He allowed his eyebrows to lower, and spoke in a whisper. "Especially not in a place like this, you know what I'm saying?"

For the first time since this whole ordeal, Darlene had started openly to cry.

"I'm okay, thanks," she said, wiping her eyes, when he had finally made his halfhearted move to comfort her.

"Talking 'bout, you think your sister-in-love did this to you?" he said finally. Her tears had made him uncomfortable. But Darlene didn't understand his question.

"I hear your sister-in-love the one who been telling the paper that stuff, radical groups and all this," he said. "Calling you a reverse racist."

Darlene actually took a little step backward. There was so much to sort out: the expression *sister-in-love*; the fact that Muhammad had heard things about her story—her life—that she hadn't; that she and her father would always be so very different; that Leo's sister Alyson would screw her over like this.

She pictured, in snatches of memory, Alyson's enormous Old Brookville house, the wide pink span of its marble entranceway, the open rooms you had to step up into, the floor-to-ceiling, two-pane back window that showed its vivid green movie of foliage, all spring and summer long. Alyson's husband made his money trading derivatives, the complex numbers on which American prosperity somehow floated. He was beyond rich. His millions made further millions for him, offhandedly. Why would Alyson—loaded, uninvolved Alyson—jump into the fray like this, trashing Darlene, selling her out to newspapers? Why did anyone do what they did?

"I don't know," was all she said.

"All right."

"My husband and I were married when we had James." Darlene sounded unintentionally snotty, her jaw tense with self-respect. "Alyson is my in-*law*, not my in-*love*. Was my in-law."

"Bet." Muhammad turned to the Snapple machine and fed it a dollar bill and a quarter. He hadn't been thirsty; this was Muhammad's barely conscious way of showing his daughter he had some money in his pocket, the $1.25 for this drink purchase.

Unlike a lot of the men in his place, Intelligent Muhammad had no craving to pull more successful family members down to where he was: the muddy slop of failure. He'd merely been interested, even anxious for her. But he'd wrongly taken her tone as a *fuck-you*.

"I'm just saying," he said.

Darlene watched Muhammad's wide back as he crouched to get his Snapple.

I'm not like this man; I've worked my whole life, she thought. *I'm a doctor*. But how could she explain it to him without insulting the person he was?

"Thank you," she said, "for your concern."

He said, "I guess we both had news stories about us, huh?"— and walked past Darlene, back to work.

12

THREE DAYS BEFORE THE HEARING, JOSH GOT OFF THE TRAIN AT WASH-
ington Harber's LIRR stop—it was farther from home than Glen
Head or Roslyn were, but was free of transfers. In Manhasset, Josh
went to get the product Dori had asked for. ("On top of everything
else," she'd said with her signature loud laugh, her one attempt at a
little levity, "I have my period.")

Josh faintly remembered the Washington Harbor family drug-
store. But it had been pushed into insolvency by a gleaming new Rite
Aid, huge and crannied: row after long row, each selling varieties of
just one thing—twenty yards of candy here, pet food there, headache relief and constipation remedies everywhere; a whole aisle for
toothpaste, another for diet pills, for holiday cards, inflatable neck
rests, straw hats, plastic toe separators, another sold little carpeted
stairways for retired dogs—it was all like some buyable dream of
wellness, any health item you could possibly want or believed that
you needed, plus a Photomat, an ATM, and, in a separate wing,
the prescription station with immodest, eye-level condom shelves,
Vagisil ledges, K-Y jelly racks. It was all a reminder of how much
Americans needed. It was ten minutes before Josh found tampons
(aisle six). Then he had to get in line at the counter, where Rite Aid
hawked yet more candy and also the DVD of Chris Farley's *American Ninja*.

From somewhere behind him, some kid whined in a minor tantrum. The mother talked fairly sternly to her son. But the boy kept
it up. "Quiet, James. This is not like you. I don't care what Grandma
gives you."

And loneliness took Josh gently, like a drowsiness. All those
months ago, he had first thought of Zack as a scream machine in a

crib, but then the baby had become a real person, and next they had stolen him. How lucky even to be able to fight with your kid.

Josh, heading to the exit, stopped to watch the argument, the mother and son upsetting the medicinal purity of this place.

Strange to say, he couldn't place the mother at first, although their lives had become so intertwined. Then his drowsiness went.

Josh recognized Darlene's pulled-back hair—as much from news photos as from his memory—and knew it was her, despite that she was wearing a distinctly nonmedical getup: unstylishly pale bluejeans, a lumpy gray sweatshirt.

Josh didn't want to cause trouble here; he needed to think about what to do. He hurried outside to wait for her.

He stood against the nearest pylon that separated the mammoth lot into sections. Dr. Stokes, not suspecting a thing, came tromping along with her heavy step. Josh didn't even notice the little boy at her side. He sprinted over. It was as unthinking as the impulse to take care of an itch, or to yank out a throbbing tooth.

Darlene worried that a strange man was running toward her, but at the very same second she realized it was Mr. Goldin, the man from the case. Anxiously she brought one hand to her collar. With the other hand she pulled James to her hip.

AT THE SAME time, Dori was walking around their home, easily spooked. She was like a mare. She'd waited to make sure Josh wasn't coming back from Rite Aid anytime soon. Then Dori swallowed to buttress herself, and she phoned Martin Seidel. "I have something to tell you," she said. "But I don't want Josh to know. Okay?"

Martin didn't say anything for a second. "I love Josh, you know that," he said, and sighed. "But, yeah, sure. What's up, gorgeous?"

JOSH SPOKE WITH outrageous volume. "You!" he said, making Darlene flinch as he reached her.

He felt really tall suddenly; he got an uncomfortable awareness of himself, here in front of this woman, as a big frightening animal.

Darlene was gazing blinkingly up at him, standing stiffly—afraid he might actually hit her.

"Yes?" she said.

He was breathing heavily. What do you say to the stranger with whom you'd stumbled into the freakish universality of scandal? "You know who I am," was what he came up with.

"All right."

And Josh felt weirdly calmed by the difference between the real Dr. Stokes and his angry idea of her; he looked at the few dark ac-neish dots on the edge of her jawline. He realized his hands were fists. It was a mistake to have stomped over here.

Darlene took a step toward her car, still holding her son's hand. But Josh skimmed in front of her, blocking her way. She searched his face for a second and then looked around, as if to find someone who might help her.

"Excuse me, Mr. Goldin," she said. She was able to talk in an even, if tentative, voice. "I'm going to my vehicle."

"It's a terrible thing you're doing," Josh said, no longer as loudly.

Darlene got a little braver, remembering who else was in her corner. "We, the state, Child Protective Services, and I, are trying to help your son. I know it may not seem like that."

A touchy silence followed. Westward, behind Josh's shoulder, the sun was lowering, and Darlene had to squint to see Josh's chang-ing expression.

"so, TELL ME already," Martin Seidel said, fearing bad news. Belated client info was the worst, the absolute worst.

"They, uh," Dori said; she exhaled and then swallowed. "They found something when they came here. CPS."

"*What?* Why'd you not tell me? What do you mean, found?"

Dori said: "I didn't do it, okay?" She turned to the window to make sure Josh wasn't back from work—though he wasn't due for a while yet. She saw her car in the driveway, the sun glinting off the secret little scratch on its side door. Sometimes she didn't think of her lies as lies. Instead, they seemed a consolidation of the truth, or truths. The real story of things always took so much effort to lay out in full detail, is all. "I didn't do anything to my son," she said.

"Hey, all right. I know that, sweetie. Of course not. But you have to tell me—"

"They found a needle, I think," she said, "I'm pretty sure CPS found a butterfly needle in my house."

She remembered now thinking there had been something up with Plates, when he'd left the last time: the considerate, complicated, determined look on his face as she'd watched him come down the stairs.

How could she have left that fucker alone, even for a second?

DR. STOKES MOVED a hand up and down her son's little shoulder. The boy clung to her. Each gathered courage from the other.

"My son," Darlene said, when she saw Josh notice James.

The kid gazed silently up at the strange man. James was skinny, with frizzed hair and whitish skin; he squinted at Josh as if he were nearsighted.

And so Josh had to fight against his own natural amiability. Just because this doctor acted touchingly scared, and was a real person with a cute kid, right in front of him—why should that matter? He turned away, collecting his anger again. He did hate this person, the depressing fact that she existed. It was windy and humid, even at sundown. The clouds looked like bloody footprints across the sky.

"You have a son yourself," he said. The connotation being: *So how could you do this?*

She was reassured now. It seemed impossible that he would hit her. There was a sort of *pardon me* aspect now to his intrusion. He even reminded her of her ex-husband a little, with his big eyes, his Long Island manner. But handsomer, and more confident. She imagined a whole personality for this man, to match Leo's. They— these Jews—seemed like the most American men she had ever met.

They'd out-Americaned other Americans, by assimilation. Odd. It struck her, too, that this Mr. Goldin was probably a better father than Leo was. She told herself that was stupid—how could she know anything about him? But she empathized still; her heart went out to him.

"You have to look at your wife," was what Darlene said.

DORI WALKED AND talked while Seidel planned. She got a different view of the car from each window, seeing how the shadows made the secret scratch look different in every angle.

Dori's excuse would go over, Seidel was saying. She *had* been a phlebotomist, and one of the tools of the trade was . . .

But the truth he kept to himself was: He wasn't sure. Man, it would have been nice to know this before. That was the problem with these hearings: They were less formal than jury trials, and so the state didn't have to show the defense all the evidence it had beforehand. Maybe it wouldn't matter. Maybe—presumably— momentum was so heavily on their side that this detail wouldn't mean jack shit. She *was* a phlebotomist, right? But why would she have been hiding a butterfly needle? It was much harder to try a case in the media when there was no jury for newspapers to sway. Still, what were these judges—goddamn automatons? No, they were not automatons. They read the papers like everyone else. They watched TV.

"Dori, *Dori,*" Seidel cut her off. "It's okay. There are ways, you know? I'll handle it. But there's no chance we can keep it from Josh."

JOSH FELT AWFUL now, walking back to his car, alone, with the tampon box. *That bitch doctor,* he thought. But it was forced; his heart wasn't in it. "You're wrong," he'd told Darlene, shaking his head. "She's a good mother." Even though he'd believed what he'd said— even though it *had* to be true—it came out sounding like a lie, an elegant, horrifying lie.

13

ACCORDING TO DOCUMENTS FROM THE NASSAU COUNTY COURTHOUSE, officials had removed Zack Goldin from his family in order to "facilitate an *immediate need for protection*." The hearing represented the state's best attempt to "establish the child's permanency." To Josh, the documents represented something else: a resistance map, offering routes, timetables, strategies.

The phrases ("protection," "permanency") were bland and insulting, but they provided Josh the only information he'd needed since the terrible morning when his son had disappeared—and really since the horrible afternoon when his son had gotten his first botched care from Saint Joseph's. That information was: Here was the end point. This was the time and location where his son would be, presenting the surest moment, the best opportunity, for his father to retrieve him. That last fully happy afternoon in the coffee lounge had communicated something strange: that the skills of his life had been wrongheaded. His talent for ignoring all but the essential—the lesson he'd learned as a salesman: that people admired you for your ability to overlook hardship, to make the thousand-mile journey feel nearly completed the moment you took the first step—was inadequate. Josh should have been more engaged, maybe then he'd have noticed his baby was sick; if he had, none of them would be here today.

Still, these last nine months had felt like a countereducation, and somehow that made Josh sure he'd earned the right to have his son and his old life restored. And this morning was a gift. If Zack had been snatched in the jungle, the court date told him that, at nine-thirty A.M. on Wednesday, June 12, he'd be passing through a clearing up ahead—which was Josh's chance to fight for and retrieve him.

What he found odd, though, on this sunless drizzle of a morning, was the informality of it all. The cataclysm that would decide his life didn't get a big courtroom, a jury, or even a jury box. There would be a judge, however—and if everything went well, they would be returning home that night with Zack.

Josh had frowned so rarely in his life that a look of determination made his features look dire. He had the air of a beach umbrella painted entirely black. It made Seidel give his client a heartening smile and a shoulder squeeze. "Here we go," the lawyer kept saying, softly, as they made their way toward the reporters.

Josh couldn't believe that anything could be so much like a movie: actual reporters—radio journalists poking their microphones connected to digital units; print reporters with photographers who aimed their cameras on long pikes; TV units hustling in three-person teams, weaving and bobbing—all collected on the damp courthouse steps. A newswoman's fancy shoes (although who would see them?) ticking and scraping alongside the Goldins as they passed the fat Greek columns. The words "No comment" dropping naturally from his own mouth, like the only phrase you needed while touring a crowded foreign country.

They came into the marble lobby (lights and footsteps spanking off the marble floor) stunned and blinking, as if they'd stepped out of a noisy TV set. It wasn't until the elevator doors shut that Josh felt control over his features and motions return. Seidel looked pleased about something. And then they were walking into a kind of basement—the Special Hearings Room—and Josh had to recalibrate himself again. He was no longer an accidental focal point for cameras and microphones, or a man recovering from temporary celebrity. He was Zack's rescuer, on the most important business, the only business.

He had imagined it would happen in a judge's cozy chambers, with a polished wooden desk and green lamp (the kind you see on *Law & Order*). Rather, Seidel led Josh and Dori into a chalky, too-bright cellar; a long plastic table commandeered most of the room.

CPS's tough hockey defenseman of an attorney was seated already, next to St. Joe's woman lawyer, Betty Van Der Meer from CPS, and a relaxed guy from hospital administration—excellently tailored. Josh recognized Drs. Darlene Stokes and Arthur Weiss. Josh had stored so much concentrated anger in Dr. Stokes's small frame that he'd almost forgotten Weiss existed.

Dr. Stokes caught Josh's eye—with her mouth open a touch, as if she'd spotted a friend with whom she was on shaky terms—and she was bashful with her gaze until it failed her; she turned away, looking at her notes, and then at Van Der Meer, as if she'd been caught doing something improper.

Josh's eyes dropped, too, but not before he became aware that he'd stared too long. His gaze went to Dori, to see if she'd noticed—that's what happened when you did something uneasy; you checked if the people you might offend had noticed. Josh hadn't told his wife about speaking with Dr. Stokes at the pharmacy. He didn't know why. He'd driven home with a guilty husband's forlorn stomach, as he had after that thing with the stripper. By entertaining Dr. Stokes's doubts, he had cheated on his wife morally. It felt much worse, especially in this room—it felt to Josh like the worst luck.

Dori settled herself into her chair with an apprehensive smile. In her tasteful pale dress she looked so touching, so out of place and vulnerable. It wouldn't have been a surprise if the antagonistic people at the table—or the stack of manila files there, the books on the shelves, the legal system itself—had apologized to her on the spot, fixed her an iced tea, and called her a taxi home.

Seidel had deliberately allowed Josh and Dori to sit first, across from their opponents, at the crux of their future. An old air conditioner above the door had broadcast, as Dori walked in front of it, the scent of his wife to Josh. The familiar body smells he wouldn't have been able to name: Acqua di Parma *lotion pour le corps*, Sephora perfume, Fekkai conditioner, the shadow of all these Dori scents suddenly falling across him. Today would be the day to determine if Dori ever got to be a mother again. At its worst, it could be the start of a grinding legal mechanism, the iron levers and pincers, that would take Dori to jail.

The judge, a woman in her middle sixties, sauntered into the room, heavyset and relaxed under the robes and prestige of the state. She had the soft, crannied face of an aging and kindly bulldog.

"Good morning, everyone," she said. "I'm Judge Tilda Wildensteen." She sat higher than the room's other occupants, behind an elevated podium with the state seal, in which a robed woman held the scales of justice in one hand and raised her other one, as if on the verge of an important point. It seemed like Judge Wildensteen was piloting a kind of oak boat with official markings.

Josh ran the stress factors, the billiard odds, through his mind. It could be good that the judge was a woman (pro-motherhood), or bad (siding with the female doctor). And her name sounded Jewish, which of course could be helpful. On the other hand, Bruce Springsteen wasn't Jewish. And this woman maybe spelled her name like his, ending in -steen, not -stein.

"Mr. Seidel," the judge said. "I think we can all agree you've done your job. With all the reporters, it's a madhouse out there. But that does not mean it will become a madhouse *in here*."

At the sound of the hearing's first notes—"State of New York, County of Nassau . . ."—Dori's cheeks flashed pink. Then the fear left her features, and she dipped her head like a soldier who'd waited months, weeks, days, knowing a battle was ahead, wondering how she might face it—and then understanding that, when you feel the grip of an event, the momentum simply carries you.

She took in the room's corners and angles for the first time, the walls, lights, ceiling: The room's functional plainness felt like a crypt for the death of families.

A bailiff was swearing in the guy from St. Joseph's Hospital, the administrator. Dori, in the mess of emotion and introduction, had missed that bailiff's entrance. But the swearing-in seemed so familiar—the recognizable liturgy of due process, the judiciary sacrament. Without ever having been in court, Dori knew this stuff as everyone in America did: from TV. Which is to say *in her bones.*

Josh mistook her calmness; he saw the look of someone freaking out, and put a palm on her knee, startling her. Her blood warmed the spot where his hand lay. Dori focused on Dr. Stokes, who sat immediately across from her. *Look at me!* Dori thought. *You don't know what I did, or why I did it, or how safe I was, or how many people I was trying to keep happy.* She tried to give Dr. Stokes her death stare. But Darlene simply stared back, a physician verifying a chart's unpromising diagnosis. Her eyes flicked away. In Darlene's world, what Dori was accused of made her nonhuman.

They had all come to play such a gigantic part in each other's lives, and this was only the third time they had been in the same room.

Darlene turned slightly so that her shoulders were aimed at the judge. She'd always felt comfortable in a classroom, and that's how this felt to her. The authority at the head of the room would say which answers were correct, and which were gappy and wrong. And it would have been easy to tell just what Darlene thought of Martin Seidel—whose puckering grin seemed to be a sort of Rand McNally Road Atlas to every spot that was coarse and unappealing in his character. *Clearly a Jew*, Darlene thought, and then pushed that vulgarity from her brain, and resented Martin for having been the occasion for it.

To Seidel, who automatically broke down the world into categories of helpers or impeders, Darlene looked primed to shout, "Objection," before the statements had even begun.

"So, Mr. Seidel, if you would start us off," Judge Wildensteen said. And with that, under the burnished presence of this judge, the event began.

"I very much appreciate it, Your Honor," Martin said. "I would like to say we are immensely grateful for the opportunity to put all the rumors and innuendo to rest." This, Darlene noted vindictively, was Seidel's weak spot: Courtesy from him always seemed truculent, the gratitude of someone who obviously didn't feel that the world had ever done him any favors. It put your back up. But this proved to be Seidel's one bad moment of the morning.

And Dori lifted her head past the hearing and took a short leap into the future. If they won, it would be her, Josh, and Zack forever. A real family that was safe—and she wouldn't have to do anything bad ever again. She'd learned a lesson. Maybe what she'd done hadn't been wrong on its face. Not really. But anything that could interrupt their lives this way, that could draw them into this court, couldn't be counted in the final measure as anything but a negative. You had to be straight with yourself. On the other hand, nothing she'd done really deserved *this*. And it was this clear look of having been wronged that Dori showed on her face—that she instructed her features to preserve. She wanted the room to see the dignity of her fighting down her tears. If she won today, there'd be trips to the park and sushi dinners and videos with Zack once he grew up enough to understand them (they'd get to find out what kind of movies and songs and TV shows and subjects and girls he liked) and they'd be a totally normal family. Compare that to the way that Donna from mommy group had wheedled her husband into staying with her for the kids—with guilt and detective-gotten credit-card receipts. What kind of a solution was *that*? Who was happy *there*?

But if Dori lost today—she'd have to find some way of keeping Josh from being mad or blaming her. Also, could the court revoke her right to have additional children? This was a question, she realized, she needed to ask Martin.

She stared in near wonder at the court reporter who typed it all; every nasty accusation—every shameful truth revealed here—would be written down, officially documented, saved in triplicate. Seidel had promised she wouldn't have to testify, but she was still terrified it might happen.

"I'd like to begin with that first afternoon at St. Joe's," Seidel said. "Could you walk me through it? This is the day that Mrs. Goldin brought her son, Zack, to your facility, in a panic about his condition. St. Joe's has an excellent reputation." He smiled. "And she was counting on you to maintain that level of care and support."

For a reason Dori couldn't understand, it wasn't Dr. Stokes who answered. It was a tall, sandy-haired man in a college dean's jacket and tie: Peregrine Berg. And he was making a show of not speaking from memory—as if to make clear that the facts weren't hot and fresh in his mind—but from a folder of notes.

"I'll take you through it," Berg said, in an English accent. And he began: the hospital, the nervous mother, the sick child, the miscommunication.

He seemed to relish any official wording. "According to HIPAA sanction, there are certain elements, certain details, we aren't at liberty to divulge. Even here, in this context. Patient-doctor privilege being what it is, the operative element in this matter—"

Seidel interrupted to ask: "Would you agree that it would have been important to check a baby's coagulation factors and blood count, in this particular matter?" Seidel turned helpfully to the judge. Then he recited the definition his associate had pulled that morning off Wikipedia. "Coagulation is the process by, uh, by which blood clots. It is an important part of healing. Platelets form immediately, to arrest hemorrhage at the site of injury. This is called *primary hemostasis. Secondary* hemostasis also occurs—proteins in the blood plasma. These are, uh, known as *coagulation factors*, a response to strengthen the platelets."

It continued to amaze Dori, the power of what she'd done. She had communicated something—through her boy, actually through his body—that she'd intended only Josh to hear: *We, your son and your wife, don't matter enough to you.* To get it heard, it'd had to be said in a hospital, and now all these other people around the country had heard it, too. And because of that, each person here had a job to do, a particular role to play.

Returning to Berg, Seidel asked: "Would you agree that it would be important to check a baby's coagulation factors, in this particular situation? And isn't that a routine, first-line-of-defense kind of test?"

"Well, you do understand I'm not a physician. My training is restricted to the administrative side of the house."

"Yes, I am aware. But isn't it routine to?"

"Well, I have complete faith in our medical staff," Berg said. "And these trained physicians observed that, if the baby had been in some *danger*, they would have begun routine tests. But—"

And Darlene, five feet away, shook her head briskly. She recognized the trap Berg had just stepped into.

"But those coags and blood count did not get checked," Seidel said, in his wrecking ball of a professional voice. "Which means the baby was not in danger. And if the baby *wasn't* in danger, then what are any of us doing here?"

There was half an hour more of this. Next Dr. Weiss was called. Darlene told herself not to worry; this was the Goldins' turn at bat, which would to be followed by Darlene and the hospital's.

It didn't matter that Seidel didn't bark or even speak particularly loudly. The voice came out low and unhurried, a demolishing force that would push down any walls you might have set up. His lethargic momentum chiseled against the foundations of your argument; things in the way of that voice broke down under the steady, chipping attrition.

Weiss was a young man, and Dori found it interesting to watch as he unfolded a chameleon's worth of colors and poses. She understood; she'd thought about becoming an actress, and she knew the way you could send your attention out into an audience, probe their tastes, and then work their preferences back into your performance. And she was maybe the first to understand something else: that Weiss was on her side. All his statements were tilted away from the definitive, and toward the marshy, the uncertain, to the "we don't really know." Dori's Josh-in-the-mornings future, Zack at his high chair, was coming nearer. Everyone in the chamber, to her, seemed to want the same thing; the sole obstacle, the only discordant will here, was the head of pediatrics, Darlene Stokes. And it felt to Dori as if the force of Seidel's chisels and hammers—with even Weiss helping in a way—worked against this one other person. Because for Dori to be right, Darlene had to be very, very wrong.

For Dori to be happy, it had required some inconvenience, a tiny donation of blood, from her son. It now seemed to require the same from Darlene Stokes. Dori understood this. If she had been offered it in the flattest terms, she would have accepted the deal; maybe that's what happiness always required—and the people who had happy lives were those who were most comfortable with that arrangement. You had to be willing to take a little blood from people to make yourself happy, and that was that.

Meanwhile, Dr. Weiss had hit a snag in his testimony. He scratched through his Brillo hair whenever he made a special attempt at remembering. But through every posture (annoyed, merely interested), his eyes never changed—obedient, careful, and above all: unaggressive.

"Did you or anyone else ever determine, and I mean *definitively determine*," Seidel was saying, "exactly what was wrong with the child?"

"Exactly and definitively?" repeated Weiss. "No. We couldn't. On the other hand, it was a question mark, it did raise some flags, because the presentation was a little unusual, and—"

"So that's a 'no' to my question."

The judge lifted her hand, even before she noticed St. Joe's lawyer fidgeting in her seat. "Mr. Seidel, please. Let the doctor finish."

"Actually, that's all I'd really intended to say. It was an outlier, so we ran more tests."

Meanwhile Darlene's face was too active. She winced, she frowned, she was killing herself throughout arguments and rebuttals. First of all, they had a guy who wasn't a doctor testifying, and now Weiss—whom she hadn't even remembered would be here—was just doing an awful job on the stand. Nearly every answer, she would have handled differently. And she hated the young-person style, talking around a problem, seeing all its sides, while waiting to be told, essentially, which door to open. Darlene would have answered yes, no; right, wrong. And she yearned to be asked, to be given the chance to discuss and defend, to protect herself and her patient.

Martin cleared his throat. He lifted a folder for everyone at the table to see. "According to this report from the New York Center for Family Rights, in most cases where guardianship is taken from the parents, the child is poisoned. In here are incidents, horrible occasions, terrible parents and families, stuff we'd all agree is possibly the worst we can imagine. Kids poisoned with ipecac, chloride, even with human waste injected right into the baby's bloodstream. Now, Dr. Weiss, was there feces in Zack's bloodstream, or ipecac, or any foreign substance?"

It isn't all cases—Darlene thought—and the question wasn't what substances Zack Goldin had *not* been poisoned with. The issue was what had he'd suffered and what he might suffer again; the issue was what she had noted and, in her capacity as a doctor, acted on.

Silences feel drawn-out in any courtroom, when a rhetorical question is asked for all to hear, and people have nothing to do but to lean forward and listen. Weiss himself looked as if he were waiting for someone else to answer.

Seidel spoke once more: "Was there any poison—were any irregularities at all—found in this baby's blood?"

"No."

"I appreciate your forthrightness, young man. I'm now going to take you through a few more of the classic signs: Was there any significant bruising on Mrs. Goldin's son? Or—"

"Not in my report."

"—any welts, contusions, black eyes, anything at all?"

Weiss glanced at Mr. Berg. This was clearly a request for guidance. The administrator took a hearty breath and raised his eyebrows. And Weiss returned his attention and youthfulness to Seidel.

"If we'd spotted any of those things, that's a big red flag, you'd see it in the file."

"So that's a 'no,' Dr. Weiss?"

Weiss, his jumping bean of an Adam's apple going, agreed that it was, indeed, a no.

The lawyer smoothed his scalp. For Seidel, it was the challenges that always woke him up. He loved a courtroom. He loved even a basement courtroom—the deepest, undersea stuff, the secret places, where complex matters got sorted and decided. But he was finding this so easy that the aggressive parts of his brain were switching off. Rejoinders he'd polished and stored weren't proving necessary at all. He'd expected to hear about the redness on Zack's arm (and he had *volumes* to offer about redness). And he was waiting to hear, above all, about the butterfly needle. But they seemed to be saving it for later; or maybe, Martin began to speculate (and to speculate about the reasons why), they were saving it for never.

And then Darlene became the third person in the room to understand that Weiss was coloring his answers toward Martin. She tried, and failed, to get Betty Van Der Meer's attention.

PACING THE HALLWAY during the first recess, Darlene went about the business of calming herself; her internal conversation became a broad concert hall of reassurance. The hospital's strategy was to lull the Goldins. Once her side presented their case—its reports, its evidence and accuracy—the hearing would begin to feel very different.

For all that she'd been through, the landscape of the past weeks had not, to Darlene's eye, contained any overly alarming or unfamiliar features. Reading newspaper accounts of the woman she'd sort of been in college (a person both more confident and more frivolous in print than she'd been in life, a person resembling her old roommate Tiphanie) had felt inconsequential. It had seemed to Darlene like summer break, like August for a college kid. The trial, she continued to believe, would be when school came back to session. Classes would resume, a fair and discerning authority would take charge of the discussion. Correct answers would be starred, drivel would get circled in red. She had ignored the media the way she'd ignored the kids outside PS 274 Elementary School, razzing her for being

brainy, for doing her homework, for being *right*. And since she always shone in any official setting, she'd remained certain of prevail-
ing today.

Yet when she saw the hospital lawyer closing her cell phone
and shaking her head, Darlene's soothing internal music faltered a
bit, and her first response was confusion. Darlene had forgotten the
woman's name—Joanne Grella—but anyway she'd stood the lawyer
by the wall, made the case for herself: "You need to get me up there,"
Darlene said, "I'm the only person who can present this case."

Joanne Grella had penciled her lips red, but the rest of her
mouth—the meaty blossom—remained pale. The way Joanne Grella
saw it, a lawyer's mouth had to be as clean as a doctor's hands.

"Dr. Stokes, I want to say I understand where you're coming
from. And I need to add from a personal standpoint how much I
admire and respect your passion. But this did happen at St. Joseph's
Hospital, and we all agreed that Perry Berg would speak for us."

"I am not hearing anything about a needle. And I'm not hearing
anything about a baby's arms."

"And we certainly intend to bring out everything we can.
Have faith in the process. I will speak with Eric about your testifying," Joanne Grella said. (Eric was Mr. Stone, the hospital's VP of
whatever.)

Joanne threw Darlene a condescending smile. "Let it take its
course. I understand how difficult and confusing a lot of this must
have been for you, the stuff in the press. But we're used to it, it's our
job, and we are going to protect you, our position, and this hospital
by not allowing you to remain the issue."

"That little boy is the issue. I'm comfortable with who I am."

"Yes," Joanne Grella said. "I think that's certainly true."

EVERYBODY FOUND THEIR seats, the hearing resumed, and Josh
couldn't lift his eyes from Darlene Stokes. She no longer loomed
for him as a figure of demonic punishments. Some of her shine had
abandoned her; she looked like a single, professional, middle-aged

black woman in midcareer. It seemed strange that this person could have been the cause of so much pain, along with the deeper discomfort of mistrusting his wife. Josh, in his own internal conversation, had begun to accept it as the most natural thing in the world that a trained phlebotomist would keep a butterfly needle in her house. Because the court was accepting it, too—"Look at your wife," she'd said? Well, lady, look at *yourself.*

Betty Van Der Meer, Child Protective Services, let Joanne Grella lead her through testimony. "And what was the reaction of Mr. and Mrs. Goldin to CPS's legal inspection of their home?"

Mrs. Van Der Meer kept the file open in front of her. "According to our caseworker, Jim Plates, Mrs. Goldin's behavior was a bit, it says here, confrontational."

"Objection." Seidel sighed. " 'A *bit* confrontational'? This is a mother meeting a man who intends to take her kid. Did he come expecting a soufflé?"

"Okay, Mr. Seidel," Judge Wildensteen said. "Sustained."

Betty Van Der Meer blinked at the lawyer. In the last few weeks, *Newsday* had strutted out stories of infractions by Betty Van Der Meer's Child Protective Services of Nassau County. The paper hated to swim in the *News-Independent*'s wake, but there'd been lots of juicy, satisfying stuff. Civil suits, cases reopened, that great prim phrase "overzealous personnel." The truth, as Mrs. Van Der Meer well knew, was that any bureaucracy was like a restaurant kitchen. Certain routines and practices just didn't seem hygienic when exposed to a very bright light.

"Okay," Joanne Grella said. "We can move away from this topic. Unless you have any specific observations you'd like to offer, Mrs. Van Der Meer?"

"Well, I wasn't present at those visits, remember," Mrs. Van Der Meer said. "CPS always works in concert with a presiding medical authority. And we rely on our professional partners to be fair, honest, and conscientious."

"And in your opinion, has St. Joe's always met that standard?"

"Yes."

"I'm passing a copy of our emergency-room report. Could you read that to the court, please?"

Darlene began frisking her pocketbook for notebook and pen. She scribbled down six words, tilted the page up from the table where Joanne could easily read. *Redness on Baby's Arm.* She underlined the last word: *Butterfly Needle*.

Mrs. Van Der Meer, meanwhile, was reading Arthur Weiss's emergency-room notes.

"Was there any material in this report, the first visit the Goldins made to St. Joseph's, that you would characterize as anything but conscientious and fair?"

"No."

In cross-examination, Darlene had expected Seidel to address many questions to Mrs. Van Der Meer. He had only two.

"My firm has checked over four hundred reports made by Dr. Weiss. And we have not discovered evidence of a single error. Now, do you see anything on this form, Mrs. Van Der Meer, about a report of blood in Zack Goldin's vomit?"

"No."

"Fine. You characterize Dori Goldin"—and he nodded at Dori, who dipped her head, made shy by the passions of motherhood—"as 'confrontational.' Did Mrs. Goldin, in fact, make any attempt to restrict or obstruct four inspections of any part of her home?"

"No."

"That's all I have."

And Darlene began to fear that the butterfly needle was no longer going to be an issue; it had just fallen off the edge of the trial. Joanne Grella cleared her throat.

"Judge Wildensteen," Grella said, "we'd like to return to the matter of what St. Joseph's did discover. So I want to address my next questions to Dr. Arthur Weiss."

"Excuse me," Darlene interrupted. And she stood, having followed the counsel of her conscience and her ego.

Judge Wildensteen, with the first real surprise that her voice had sounded in this courtroom in quite some time, said: "Doctor?"

"I'm not a lawyer, I don't really know this format," Darlene said. Then the proper terms came to Darlene's mouth; you couldn't be a TV-watching adult—even, like Darlene, a not especially diligent TV-watcher—and *not* know them. "I need to speak with counsel," she said.

"But, Dr. Stokes, you are not the witness."

Darlene gave a short, quick nod. "Not yet," she said. "That's what we need to confer about."

Martin said: "You know, Your Honor, I don't know that I've ever seen plantiffs object to their own questions."

"I'm sorry, Your Honor," Joanne said. "We're fine. We'll just need to ask for a few minutes."

Before Darlene could say anything in the hallway—could offer the measured, intelligent case she had built for her participation—Joanne Grella whirled on her. "Is it true?"

Her face would have made it clear, had Darlene had any talent for noticing this kind of stuff: They were antagonists, she and her lawyer.

"Is what true?" Darlene said. "No, none of this seems true."

Joanne quietly seethed, shaking her head. This encouraged Darlene to follow down the course she'd prepared. "In my professional opinion, it all seems correct without being true."

The lawyer's face went stiff with resentment, with unfriendliness, with dismissive sarcasm. "This is perfect. You don't have any idea what I'm talking about, do you?"

Darlene stood there, eyes squinting into the mystery of Joanne Grella's expression.

"Eric sent this at the end of the last break." Grella bent to open her briefcase, then pushed a faxed copy of a newspaper into Darlene's hand. The headline blurred under Darlene's fingers: She saw today's date, her name, the hospital's, and a strict, formal police portrait of her father when he was twenty pounds lighter.

"Your father," Joanne said, "is a drug dealer?"

"Well, I've never entirely thought or considered him as my, I mean we don't really—"

"This man lives with your son, alone in the house with him?"

"How does this—?"

"There was a story about him in one of those free papers in the city. You don't think to tell us about that now? You found a job for your drug dealer father *at the hospital?*" Arms at her side, her mouth pressed tight, Joanne Grella looked as if she were making a great effort not to break into little sections. "I've got to hand it to you both, I mean, he really went the whole hog, he hit all the bases. He even got a prison name, it's *Muhammad? Intelligent Muhammad?* And he organized other African-American prisoners in demonstrations while he was in jail?"

This impressed Darlene. "I didn't know he did that. Is it true?"

"Of course it's true—it's in the media, so it's true now. It's true about St. Joseph's, is what's important." Joanne snapped the article back. "We're both women who've done well in tough fields." She spoke more softly but not less angrily. "I'm going to let you answer. Tell me it's not true. Tell me I'm not fighting to break up that family while you leave your own son in the custody of a convicted felon, and we'll go in there together and you can answer any question you want. Is it true?" She took a step toward Darlene: "Is it true?"

Darlene chewed her lips, patted the fuzz at the top of her head; the question remained unrequited between them, impossible to flick away. "Yes," she said. "It's true. As you said, it's there in black-and-white."

"Do you know the expression 'The press will have a field day with this'?"

Darlene didn't want to answer, or even know if she'd been expected to answer.

"Well," Grella said, "I never really got that phrase, never really understood it. 'Cause we used to have 'Field Day' in elementary school, something nobody liked, being taken outside and waste your time running in circles. And so, the real analogy, the press is going to have a Fourth of July fireworks bonanza with this, a Christmas party with Macy's floats, etc."

Joanne Grella closed this discussion by laughing: "This doesn't end, this case." The sharps of her teeth had shown. "The bad news here doesn't fucking *end*. All those meetings you had with Peregrine and Eric, three separate meetings, didn't you hear them asking you for anything in your background, anything they should know about? Didn't you understand that was what they were asking? This is about the future of the hospital now, okay? You think you're the only one with a responsibility? You're also—we're all—responsible for the jobs of everyone who works in that hospital, the patients who are in there now who need us to be able to provide quality care. Do you ever think about any of that? Of course not." And Joanne stalked back into the chambers.

It took only twenty minutes for Dr. Weiss to float through the second half of his testimony. His speech had the confident, easy swing of a person who believes he's matching the sound of an imagined, ideal self. He offered a list of procedures to which they'd subjected Zack that first night: lavage, guaiac, liver function, endoscopy. The story he was relating followed the theme of St. Joseph's as a high-performance medical luxury vehicle: no possibility untested, no corner cut.

"Did anything strike you," Joanne asked, "as at all out of the ordinary?"

"Well, no—other than that Mrs. Goldin was clearly upset. But even that isn't really atypical—there's a word we have. Mrs. Goldin was what we call a NYM." He ran the letters together as a word: "Neem." "A Nervous Young Mother. You can always expect to see more of them on Fridays—something about the weekend, families being alone with the baby. As you can see, that's what I wrote on the admitting form."

"So was there anything about her conduct that seemed to you, in any way, suspicious?"

"I would say that Mrs. Goldin overreacted. At least she did from our perspective, even given the great strain she must have been under. That was a big reaction, hostile. But she did continue to make herself available, allowing us to provide her with information on Zack's condition throughout the evening."

"So what was the source of the hospital's suspicion?"

"Well," Dr. Weiss said, "that would be Dr. Stokes."

When Seidel got his chance again, he said:

"I see the letters NYM. I notice the words 'Munchausen by proxy' do not appear on your admitting form. When did you first hear them, in relation to Mrs. Goldin?"

"From Dr. Stokes."

AT THE LUNCH recess, Martin led the Goldins through the muddle of reporters on the steps, slipped them into his SUV, and drove to a diner by the courthouse. (Through his car window Martin addressed the microphones and notebooks. "We'll have a comment just as soon as this thing's over. But the legal system is fair, it's sympathetic, and sometimes the best strategy is just to trust in the courts.") The diner was a mile up Mineola's surprisingly bare Main Street, that grove of telephone poles.

"I'm incredibly encouraged," Martin said. He sat facing his clients, at a booth of bulbous maroon cushions in the sparkling 1960s mode. As if LBJ had just become president, the hottest thing was omelettes, and America had yet to commit any kind of grave blunder. The heyday of diners: You could settle into a tall egg cream, flip the Dave Clark Five on your car radio, peel out from the lot. That had been the moment in which Seidel could have lived, pleasantly, forever. "I'm very happy."

Martin grandly filled his role as advocate and legal interpreter: smiling over questions when that was appropriate, or frowning his brow when *that* was; telling unkind jokes about the competition; taking not a single bite from his hamburger until he'd explained, cleared up, until he'd given the relevant details; nodding as he held his drink almost to his lips, the popping microclimate above his Diet Coke tickling his nose.

"You really are confident? You're not just saying that?" Dori asked, her voice light and shy as a snowflake. "You really think they're just going to let the whole thing go?"

This phrasing seemed strange to Josh, so he changed the conversation's direction. "Well," he said, "it does seem like it's gone well so far, doesn't it?"

All morning Dori had had difficulty eyeing Josh straight on. Her look would creep up to his, then slide away.

"It's going terrible for them," Martin said.

"I was only afraid it was like Muhammad Ali," Josh said. "And they're playing a rope-a-dope."

"They could have been," Martin said, and finally sipped his Diet Coke. "Only, it's like round twenty-nine now, the crowd's left the Garden, and janitors are about to shut off the lights. That's how bad an ass-kicking."

Martin had not intended to discuss the press—it would have been more pleasant to discuss winning a case on its merits—except there was no other way to explain why the opposition had lain down. "Not to mention, and I'm going to go kind of off-road here, take us extrajudicial for a second: That last bit of news was very, very good."

Martin's office had texted the story about Intelligent Muhammad. Dr. Stokes, noted advocate of child safety, had an ex-convict father sharing their house with her young son. "The hospital, CPS, that whole crowd. I think they're looking down the barrel of a lot of community animosity, and a whole crop of lawsuits they don't want and can't necessarily afford."

Josh adjusted the conversation a second time; again, without being aware he was doing so. "So they're finally coming to their senses, you'd say?" he said, his seat cushion squeaking as he leaned forward a little.

Seidel looked away, down at his plate, then took a quick bite of his burger. "Yeah," he said. "Yes, that's right."

"I just," Dori said, "don't want to jinx it. If we're getting so lucky."

The diner was emptying out. They could hear the robot sounds from the kitchen: jangling silverware, a dishwasher rack smashing into position; plates, glasses.

"I can understand that, Dori," Martin said. "I believe in Karma myself—maybe I'm stupid, maybe I'm gullible, but I do."

"I knew it would go this way," Dori said. "Do you remember, Mr. Goldin? I said their main concern would be to cover their own asses?"

"You did," Josh said. "No doubt."

Josh had to stop himself from shaking his head, seeing his wife so much smaller than her old self. Her affection had been such an encouraging influence, so accommodating. But these last few weeks had changed her. One of his secret worries was that he'd never receive that full attention from her, that total gut devotion, ever again. Everything about her was coming off as overstrident now—the nods, the quick treble voice, the boasting—and, strangest of all, in the manner of a legal defendant, *sly*. He just wanted to get his old wife back.

It was amazing to Josh that Dr. Stokes could have both turned Dori this way, and also gotten him to start questioning her innocence—"Look at your wife"; well, go fuck yourself. When he got married, he'd thought he could sculpt his future, like Schwarzenegger did his past in *Total Recall*. Stupid to think of that now. But it had to be admitted: He'd found himself pissed at everything, maybe even at Dori for being on trial here. Could that be? They were winning! His emotions were all cocked up, as if he didn't know whom to be angry at. He was getting so mad that his face lost its color.

The waitress, in the pink one-piece diner uniform, politely slid the check in front of Seidel—who, she understood, would be the one to pay because he was, by far, the oldest at the table.

Seidel didn't look at the check. He noticed something was up with Josh. Usually when you represented a married couple, only one of them oscillated on your wavelength; the other could go into la-la land, but it was crucial not to lose that important one.

So, Seidel began speaking about Dr. Stokes, what a positive development her "nontestimony" had been. And Josh's relief at hearing Stokes being mocked nicely burned away his other thoughts. It had been easy for the doctor to be plainspoken outdoors. But she hadn't had the courage to make the same claims at the hearing. Josh realized he'd looked forward to her testimony; he'd wanted frantically to see her proven wrong, as you'd want your favorite sports team to beat the current champions on the way to their own title. But apparently Dr. Stokes was afraid to speak. In the final measure, it seemed even she hadn't believed her own charges.

Martin said, "Ooh, hold on a sec, we've got a call." He twisted to reach for his vibrating pocket. Then his face brightened, and he held out the phone for the couple to read. "Ho—look who this is from."

DR. STOKES MADE her way, alone, across the court's lobby. She was walking oddly close to the wall. At the start of the recess, Darlene had been careful to allow the Goldins to clear the hallway—she hadn't wanted to risk words, or even hard eyes—and next she'd pretended to go to the ladies' room. This was to get away from the vivid cluster of Perry Berg, Dr. Weiss, and Joanne Grella. She'd locked herself in a stall and stared at the porcelain oval of water.

Now, as she walked the corridor, she imagined Berg and Joanne tracking her progress from the corners of their eyes. They had reason to worry: Darlene was heading to the judge's chambers.

Her certainty made Darlene feel stalking and large. In her mind, she saw herself tapping across the marble floor in giant, graceful steps. But the call she made was the act of a smaller person—she dialed her mother, for warmth, for support.

"Momma?" she said. She was grateful to hear Alice's voice.

But Alice sounded less sentimental than Darlene did. Alice

sounded, in fact, the very opposite of sentimental. "You watching the news right now, baby?"

"Momma, you know where I am, right?"

Alice answered after a long, chary silence. "Oh, yes I do: that place where you dared them to send you."

Maybe you only reach adulthood when your parents turn over the keys to their maturity; when they say, after the lessons, advice, the road tests, "Take it out of the garage, it's yours now, I can't drive it anymore." Then, once you return, they frown over the scratches in the paint, the dings in the panels, the passage of time and accident.

That's how it felt to Darlene, as Alice started to unload: While it seemed to Darlene that she had found insight, her mother had slid into adolescent self-centeredness—into unreliability.

"Baby, I've held my tongue." Tears had thickened Alice's voice. "I held it when you let that *man* come back into your life, bringing all his mess with him."

"Mother—"

"—You'd been looking for a father so long, who was I to stand in your way? I held my tongue when people started making phone calls to *me*, at all hours, every day. I held it when Greta Van Susteren sent a reporter to my front lawn to ask questions about my beautiful daughter. Baby, everybody is okay with a sacrifice. But make it for the people who *matter*. Like your son."

Darlene was passing another inquiry room, its doors slightly open. Some other Gordian knot, at the center of some other person's life, either being untangled or given another twist.

Darlene couldn't believe Alice shared Muhammad's opinion, that she also thought life was about staying back from an invisible fence that kept certain people from trespassing on green lawns of power. Muhammad having said it was one thing, but why had Alice sent Darlene to college, then?

"You worked hard to get where you are," Alice was saying. "But I worked even harder to get you where you are. And all *I* got to do was watch. And that was all right by me. That was my choice."

As the cell reception took to static, Alice's words arrived as waves, crackling, spreading, separating. Darlene didn't bother to tell her about this; it was a small blessing. But even if the words got lost, the meaning came through—as clear as though Alice were walking alongside her, tall and healthy, a hand on her forearm: *I didn't throw away my life, all those years with those Jewish lawyers, so you could throw yours away for this.*

What do you say to that? She stopped walking abruptly and put her hand over her ear. "Mother?" Two men in suits bustled past, firing road-rage looks at her, taking her in with a glance: just another black woman receiving bad news in a courtroom hallway.

The burden, the *mountain*, of her mother's sacrifice had landed on her. Again, more fully than ever. She managed only an "I'm sorry" into the phone, in case Alice could still hear her. This was all she hadn't let herself feel in years. It was much heavier now, a more concentrated from of guilt—although that didn't seem the right word for it; "weight" did seem apt, in a way that guilt did not. It was a palpable drag on Darlene; her shoulders and head felt it, her back and her legs. How could she avoid letting her mother down without letting herself down, without abandoning all she was?

"Mother? *Mother?*"

Darlene had been granted the reprieve of a definite, complete breach in cell service. That settled things.

She went to a security guard for directions. He was surprisingly lighthearted for such a formal place, where so many stories compacted and ended. He called her "sister"—this idiom, with its assumption of shared aims and experiences, usually annoyed Darlene, but it didn't this afternoon. Two turns, then she found herself before a small oak door. The brass nameplate read, "Judge Tilda Wildensteen." Seeing the name steadied her. Because certainly a woman who had risen to a judgeship—a single woman, or the head of a good family that supported her—would understand all about professional excellence. She wouldn't need any coaxing about the importance of things turning out right. Darlene would tell her: This hearing is covering up evidence, it is concealing and preventing a just verdict. I am willing to step outside it, and take any consequences. This woman would love justice in the same manner and proportion that Darlene had always loved science.

No answer came to her knock. Leaning an ear, Darlene made out the clumps and risings of voices on the door's opposite side. She took an extra breath for courage, and knocked a second time. Darlene pictured every door she had knocked on in her career, the hallway of doors she would be knocking on in her future: conscientious and optimistic, the woman doctor from Bushwick with the prim, black woman's name.

She heard one component of the murmuring break away from the general sound, becoming louder and more distinct, a man's voice, getting closer. She was surprised to realize she felt nervous. Her cheeks got warm. She patted her tight bun of hair, smoothing its force field of recalcitrant frizz.

The knob shook, and the door opened. It was Martin Seidel. His face was turned back toward the room he was exiting. "Thank you, Your Honor, counselors." His voice was relaxed and natural. "I'll bring this to my clients." Then he pivoted, and was surprised to find Darlene.

Seidel's smile, as he looked Darlene from head to foot, turned up in his eye first, a flicky show of triumph. This was a winner's smile. But as the smile reached his mouth it changed into something less than a grin: the gentle manners that the conquering may show the conquered. "Dr. Stokes," he said, a respectful and solemn note in his voice. It sounded almost as if he felt sorry for her.

In the office, Peregrine Berg was stretching his arms in a chair, making a little *Ooo* expression of release, as if about to rise from a movie seat. There can be a message in someone's refusal to look at another person, and Peregrine Berg refused to look at Darlene.

Judge Wildensteen didn't even seem to recognize Darlene at first; in her mind, she'd moved on to other business, to the next case. The warmth Darlene felt seemed to come only from Seidel, who still stood next to her, savoring the moment. "Sorry to be the bearer of bad news, Dr. Stokes," he said in a way that didn't seem sarcastic. But then he left, going up through the marble and columns and into the bright summer afternoon; he was hurrying to tell the Goldins that—if they would agree not to bring civil suits or talk with the press again—CPS and St. Joe's would drop it. Drop the whole thing, even give them a little hush money, to boot. He was going to tell the Goldins that, in fact, they'd won. The good guys had won.

VI

Countries go insane like people go insane.... Some had been insane all their lives and then gotten better again and then gone insane again. America: America had had her neuroses before, like when she tried giving up drink, like when she started finding enemies within, like when she thought she could rule the world; but she had always gotten better again. But now she was going insane, and that was the necessary condition.

—Martin Amis, *London Fields*

1

Normality strolled back into the Goldins' home, then hung around as if it'd never left.

Dori was happy; her strength returned. Here lay her baby at night, asleep in his own bed, which had white mesh around it like a ceilingless mosquito net; and there was Zack the next day walking around, pointing at everything, asking, "Dat? Dat?"

Zack at just over two years could walk on his own, but his parents often carried him anyhow, for fun, as if to make up in triplicate for the weeks they'd missed.

Dori and Josh followed Zack's every step, laughing, spellbound by—dutiful slaves to— his gummy smile. Zack's being here was a fragile present they were again entrusted with. The house, for the first time in weeks, looked especially clean. Josh and Dori kept the air conditioner on full blast—they couldn't risk Zack being too warm. They gave him a knit cap to sleep in. And Dori kept picking him up, nosing his belly, kissing him, kissing him all over; she was a natural mom. It all came so easily to her. The sun was high outside but they didn't go outside. It felt safer to keep indoors; they had Zack to themselves here. One look from the kid and Dori's throat would shut. She couldn't take full breaths—this was a mother's desire, the fullness of her greedy love. "Look at Zack, he's—isn't he just, you know, really . . ." She'd gotten incoherent with gladness.

"Yep," Josh answered, always with a smile. But there was something in the back of his mind.

(Had Zack somehow changed in the days they hadn't been with him? Wasn't his hair a little darker? Wasn't he a little taller? What did he know about being taken? What did he know?)

When Zack slipped, fell, and thumped his knee on the kitchen floor, Josh and Dori went into panic mode, the way brand-new parents would have—as if they'd gone back to their first days home from the delivery ward. But they ran the *Finding Nemo* DVD on the living room flat-screen; Zack stopped crying, and everything seemed all right. Still, Josh worried he'd need to relearn parenthood. Or, he thought that was the thing he was worried about.

When Zack was happy, or found himself under the usual baby difficulties (that bumped knee, a scary picture on the television), he'd run to his parents. And though Zack was perhaps more of a scaredy-cat than before, Josh accepted even this with fatherish satisfaction, that feeling that's like being nurtured while you nurture someone else. But there may have been something in the back of his mind.

Eventually Josh and Dori took him to Christopher Morley Park. They let him walk under his own steam, their tiny coconspirator. Zack said hello to strangers—his voice a surprise, a silly Carol Channing squeak. He liked to run ahead of his hand-holding guardians; he'd gotten better at doing so: as if on three beers now instead of six.

"Time to go home now, Zack," said Josh, picking him up with a grunt. The boy had really seemed to gain weight in that lost, abducted week and a half. He kissed Zack's hair, which smelled powdery as clean children always smell, and he worried about the sun on Zack's skin. But then he remembered Dori having put sunscreen on him earlier, taking care of their child, being the responsible parent he never could be on his own.

Smiling Dori gave Josh one of her sweet, unexpectedly nervous looks.

"I love you, Mr. Goldin," Dori said, or rather she silently mouthed it. "I do love you. You *are* cute, aren't you?"

"Yeah."

Later that night, eight P.M., Dori had Zack asleep against her chest. The baby wore his OshKosh B'Gosh overalls; his snoozing face was an assortment of comic bulges: chin, lips, cheeks all puffed. And Dori gave Josh her naughty look—it was just a flash in her eye, but he caught it.

Getting the baby to laugh by blowing onto his stomach; watching some dumb DVD together in bed; making familiar, husband-and-wife, jokey references that called up pleasant memories if not always real laughs; and the weekend coming tomorrow, or right now, or at least soon; etc.—in other words, the easeful monotony, the day-after-day accretion of slender contentments that felt like the pinnacle and the goal of regular married life, had returned.

After putting Zack to bed, she plopped down alongside Josh, or rather, halfway onto him, then cozied her mouth into the forgotten real estate of his neck and shoulder. This was no surprise. She lightly, playfully, tongued the skin there. *That* was. She shifted her tan legs and knelt astride him. She laughed in her silly loud way. He laughed, too. He had been waiting for this; it felt nice. The lifeless balloon filled with its miraculous, solidifying air. He pressed his body against hers, gratefully stripping off her T-shirt and bra and—easing her onto her back—he got her shorts off (with some unavoidable sofa clumsiness). It had been a while. Off went her functional tan underwear. Cushions got thrown to the carpet. And as Dori rolled onto her side, her naked breasts veered that way, too. The lamp overlooking the sofa was a pervert, gawking brightly over Josh's shoulder. Dori's face looked pale in the glow. Josh always dug it, how her eyes widened the moment it started, the moment of entrance. Plus that audible gulp of breath. They rolled over together. A practiced move of some difficulty. Already the deep-down flicker began. Josh tried with all his will to ignore it. But Dori's breathing went into that animal conspicuousness that made him feel huge and masterly. Yet the flicker still seemed a long way off. He knew how to ignore it. He was chugging along. Her skin felt warm. He was a piston. He slowed; he sped up. She pitched her head back into the sofa; the angle showed her throat's structural design, its underground cables, the buried treasure chest of voice box. Josh kept chugging along. His knees slipped into a gap between the cushions; Dori's heels, in rhythm, thudded the backs of his legs. He kept chugging along. He was ignoring it and ignoring it and now he couldn't ignore it. Time started going amazingly slowly. She lifted her face toward his. He watched her features sharpen, as if she were rising out of water. The amazing warmth of her. Now he kissed her ear, her forehead, her hair—

The moment it was over, time hurried ahead. It whooshed past, a train speeding off without him. He felt it go.

Easing himself backward, out of breath and naked, his boxers still at his feet, his pants God knew where, Josh immediately saw Dori once again without lust's undue focus.

"Good stuff," he said, and petted his wife's leg.

He now spoke, with the dispassion proper for the mother of his son.

"No, that was pretty fun, Mr. Goldin," she said. "And by pretty fun I mean *a lot* of fun. I almost forgot." She stood and then winked at him. "Almost, but not quite."

He ran a finger up her thigh absently, keeping eye contact. "We have a big day coming up," he said. She loved their anniversary; Dori's parents made a big deal out of her daughter's marriage day, sending presents as if the event were a holiday for all of them.

"Let's do something fun," he said, "to celebrate everything."

But she turned quickly away. "Okay." She ruffled her hair, adding to the messy postsex look. "So—you . . . want a little water, Mr. G.? I'm going to the kitchen." She was holding her head at a guilty angle, still watching herself too keenly in the mirror across the room.

Why was she making a point of not looking at him? Also she was wiping at her cheek, which seemed kind of peculiar, because there was nothing on it that needed wiping off.

Abruptly she faced him. "You don't think we woke Zack up, do you?"

"Sweetie." He pulled her back down to the couch. That A/C was so strong you felt its chill as a dank blue coating on your skin. "C'mere," he said.

And then he looked in her eyes and held her, gently if dramatically, by the shoulders. "I'm so glad," he said. Glad should cover everything, he thought: Glad that they were doing it again. Glad that Zack was home. Glad that Dori's reputation was cleared. *Glad I don't have to think about it anymore.*

Now she began smirking at her own ridiculousness. "No, we'd have heard if we disturbed him."

She gestured at a walkie-talkie monitor on the table, which would go off if Zack were crying in the other room. This parental gizmo was kitsch-colored and blocky, as if made to be used by, and not for, children.

Now Dori's composure vanished. Her lovable mouth turned vicious. This, lately, was a recurrent face of hers. A way of saying: *Well, we showed those fuckers.* Josh kept quiet, to move her off the subject that seemed to run like background noise through her thoughts.

It worked; the mood subsided, the dark clouds parted. She rested her cheek on Josh's shoulder.

"Mmm," she sighed eventually.

He patted her head. Except for these occasional flare-ups, everything seemed almost as it had been. But wasn't there something in the back of his mind? "So," he said, "did you already make anniversary plans, or something?"

Dori tipped over him to grab her clothes.

"*No,*" she said. "I told you." She went back to wiping at her cheek, at the clean skin of it.

"Hey." He put his hands on the sofa, palm down. "What's up?"

She couldn't stop a smile from uplifting her mouth. "Nothing," she said.

Before all this mess with Zack, Josh had played cards every couple weeks with friends. The secret to winning poker was noticing your opponents' "tells," the fakely numb faces, the blathered monologues and quick eyes that gave it away when someone tried to bluff.

(Dori planned to celebrate her anniversary by doing something she'd always wanted to do: go on a cruise. She'd set up the whole deal—bought the tickets online, checked Josh's datebook—in secret, to surprise her husband. She used the money that St. Joseph's had awarded them to pay for it all. He didn't appear to suspect anything.)

Dori was tilting backward to pull her underwear on, lifting her arms and legs in slapstick angles. "Whatever we do is fine," she said.

But she continued to look away from him, and when she was finished dressing, she wiped her cheek again. "Just let me know before you make any plans, okay?"

He turned—the cheek wiping made Josh turn—from the prospect of his wife, and to the window. It was getting dark out. There was one star showing, a tack that kept the blue-felt evening in place.

So what if she had planned some secret for their anniversary; if she was lying, was that so bad a lie? Should it really make him so queasy? What was *wrong* with him lately?

The back of his mind had been intruding on the front of his mind; the back of his mind kept taking up more and more space.

"So," he said in a premeditated chuckle, "what about that glass of water that lady was talking about?"

There was a pinch in his good humor; lines of doubt framed his smile. (But it was normal that a phlebotomist would have a butterfly needle at home.)

Josh's own face showed childlike in the mirror. He'd convinced himself that a woman could be targeted unfairly by a big hospital. He'd convinced himself, with his tenacious bright-sideism.

From the other room came the *smooch* sound of a freezer opening, and Dori's voice: "You want ice in it, *Señor* Goldin?"

He had convinced himself. That childhood is a mysterious time, a kind of postnatal incubation period, when babies can just get sick in weird, shocking ways. And that because Zack no longer presented signs of illness, the kid was—if they kept an eye on him—likely going to be okay from here on out.

"No ice, thanks, hon," he called to her.

He'd convinced himself that doctors and hospitals don't always know. And the truth was that his wife was a great mother. Spend five minutes with them together, anyone could see that Dori and Zack had a special bond.

Each of these statements, taken on its own, sounded plausible.

"Here you are, sir," she said, coming back in and giving a mock bow. "I believe this is what you ordered." Josh smiled his thanks, Dori sat by him, and he clicked the TV on.

Hadn't the good news reaffirmed that familiar Josh outlook, that substitute for maturity, his *life*? Well, there's a reason the word "pathogen" comes from the Greek for "birth of pain"; the unfamiliar germ—pain—had crept in. And even after the cure had come, Josh stayed anxious and watchful about his frail-seeming life; he kept the stethoscope to its chest.

"I'm going upstairs," he said, standing, "to look at Zack."

2

It was a shadowing day for Darlene.

St. Joseph's had a program for local med students: Twice a month, a doc-in-training would follow Dr. Stokes on her rounds. Today Darlene, still the Director of Pediatric Intensive Care, had to guide one such shadow all over the Peeds ICU.

Darlene frowned at Hofstra's young Anne Maxson—at the girl's petite nose, smiley mouth, at her blond eagerness. *But maybe having her here could make everything go back to a somewhat normal atmosphere*, Darlene thought.

Ever since the court hearing, Darlene had been feeling outrageous tension in the air at St. Joe's—enemy territory. But there were no reports of gunfire. The enemy wouldn't show his face. *Maybe*, she thought, *this little ritual can be the start of moving on?*

Rounds in the Peeds ICU was always an organized, nomadic movement. The "team" (Darlene, three interns, three residents, and, today, the girl Anne Maxson) walked from bed to bed, healing as they went. At least, that was the objective. Under the rotating schedule, each resident took a turn managing the entire ICU—and so became the custodian of all this youthful trauma—every third morning.

Meanwhile, the interns were responsible only for individual patients, the occasional fractured skull, the odd cancerous child.

The team always began its lap at the sickest patient. This hierarchy of need was determined by the resident-in-charge—today, that was the high-strung Bob Kraselnik, locally famous for his melodramatic nose and his disquieting pauses.

"Okay," Kraselnik said to Adam Sachs, an intern in two-tone scrubs, green top, blue bottoms, total nerdsville. Everyone was gathered around Sachs's patient, a one-year-old boy in one of the elevated beds of child illness.

"Adam, can you tell us about"— Kraselnik was saying, while eyeing the patient's chart—"Christopher Shepherd?"

"Wait," said Anne Maxson, looking up from her clipboard. "We're *starting* now?" The Peeds ICU was a forbidding place, spotless and bright.

"So, right, here we have a little DKA is what we're looking at," said Adam Sachs. (DKA meant diabetic ketoacidosis, in which the patient—already saddled with diabetes—becomes hyperglycemic, dehydrated, and insulin-deficient.)

This guy Adam Sachs's green eyes looked proud of their sleeplessness. It wouldn't be a shocker, Darlene thought, to hear that he'd renounced all food and water. Residents had it tough, but not as tough as they'd used to. He looked pissed off about having avoided the trials of finickier times. His round face, without the hindrance of a neck, rested on his scrubs.

Darlene said: "Therapy began with volume resuscitation?"

"Of *course*." Sachs had looked at his feet as he said this, but he'd said it—a crisp impudence. No resident (no *intern*, certainly) had ever spoken boldly to Darlene before the court hearing. She was aware, with a single-mindedness she might not have had six months ago, of being the only black person here.

"Flowers need tending to survive," Darlene said now to the med student, in full-on instruction mode. "Too much tending, however, and they're in trouble. One is tempted to say the same about people. Overdoctoring can be a problem."

This was received in silence.

Another resident here, a woman whose ambition made her a nightmare of vivacity, said, "Question, Adam: Any hyperkalemia?" This woman's name was Julie Roth; she gazed brightly at Darlene, no matter whom she was talking to.

Darlene felt a buzz on her hip: Her pager was going off. The LED screen showed it was Peregrine Berg calling.

"Despite what may be acute body potassium depletion, um," Bob Kraselnik was saying to young Anne Maxson in his heavy-tongued way, "there's occasionally serum hyperkalemia in, in DKA patients. Before volume resuscitation, I mean."

"Oh," Anne Maxson said.

Darlene wondered if the girl knew the definition of "hyperkalemia." Darlene wondered if the girl knew about the court hearing, about the African-American doctor who had tried to take the white baby away; Darlene wondered if the girl knew any damn thing at all.

The exhausting glow in this ICU, consistent in every inch of it, stifled all notes of organic life, any connection to shared humanity. Otherwise it might let emotion in; otherwise it might admit human sadness. There were now more unused beds here than at any time Darlene could remember. Could it be that some parents with sick children were avoiding St. Joe's—that even *those* desperate souls were keeping away?

Darlene resolved to keep ignoring her pager's buzz.

"DKA's symptoms are hard to diagnose in toddlers," Julie Roth said. Julie, addressing the med student, looked at Darlene with a grade-grubbing face. "There's abdominal pain, but babies obviously can't *say* that, you know? Because they can't talk. So, look for like polydipsia, poly*uria*—"

"Patient showed polydipsia, polyuria, *and* increased capillary refill time," Adam Sachs said, interrupting. (No one liked Julie Roth.)

Meanwhile, the med student Anne Maxson scribbled and scribbled.

And Darlene found herself teaching. "Besides poor perfusion, besides lethargy and weakness, which are hard things to diagnose in a baby, besides *fever*, a telltale DKA symptom is an acetone odor on the breath. Which is a sign of what? Metabolic acidosis," she said, not having given anyone time to answer.

Maybe some of the residents who had to work under her difficult gaze—and most fully certified doctors at St. Joe's, too—noticed Darlene trudging through the hospital halls five days a week, sometimes six, hard-faced even before the court hearing, free of makeup and chitchat, dark-skinned, arrogant in her opinions, her hair yanked into that style-free style, and maybe they'd think, as that hospital lawyer had thought the first time she'd caught sight of her, *I wish she'd just quit*. Not that Dr. Stokes had been in the wrong. A hasty diagnosis could happen to anybody. No one bats a thousand. But she made it hard for everyone, for the whole hospital. The morale here was for shit now. Dr. Stokes did have her supporters, she must have had *some*, like Jane Shepherd in Obstetrics.

When she worked on real medical stuff—not the administrative bullshit, the director of Peeds ICU crap, not the setting up of lectures, arranging these "shadow" days, not the *dealing with unsick people*—Darlene felt all right. Diagnosing curveball illnesses, walking the floor in clogs for fourteen hours straight, bringing her magic to a hemorrhaging child, returning a suffocated asthmatic to full health. Managing diabetic ketoacidosis. Or fighting acute lymphoblastic leukemia. *That* work was okay. But her time away from ICU patients was hard. Her time away from the ICU patients was a bad dream, complete dejection, a high-speed crash. She felt so despondent that, uncharacteristically, she thought of unloading her misery onto one of the residents now, Bob Kraselnik or Julie Roth. She'd even gotten the opening phrase ready: "I assume you have heard about the predicament?" She ended up saying nothing, of course.

At home, after work, she'd have her son's dinner sent over (Chinese was the most dependable)—letting James munch down *mu shu* alone by the television, while she'd go upstairs to seethe. Occasionally she didn't eat at all. She'd lie on her bed, smelling the MSG-thick sauces from across the house, blinking in epic anger and hearing the television's roar: its laugh tracks and explosions, its theme music, its uninterrupted chatter. The kitchen-tile coldness would still be on her—a reminder of hospital problems. Darlene was angry at St. Joe's, obviously. Darlene was angry at the judge, at her own colleagues, at herself for not speaking up sooner. Darlene was angry, in general. Darlene was angry at her mother for having made her feel guilty, for having been no more understanding in the end than anyone else. (Darlene hadn't talked with Alice in four days, a record.) Darlene was angry at her father. Darlene was angry at *the* father, Mr. Goldin, for his relaxed attitude toward the mother and the whole thing. Darlene was angry at life, for its broad unfairness. Darlene was still angry at Leo. (For a lot of things.) Darlene was angry at the press, for its dim-witted, maddening evenhandedness. Darlene was even angry at America—at American predictability, the relaxed standards in this society, etc., etc. It wasn't fair.

She was angry at herself for thinking these selfish thoughts, these graceless and vain concerns. Think about the baby! The poor baby who had to live in danger over there with that family.

Darlene had a sudden yearning to remember all Zack Goldin's features; she tried to call up his blunted chin and fat cheeks, his big eyes and fluffy head; she'd wanted above all not to forget—but she hadn't been able to summon more than an impression of the plump, senseless wonder that all babies show the doctor. In her brain, Zack Goldin had lined up behind the hundred other kids she saw every week, and he'd disappeared.

"But so," the med student Anne Maxson was saying now, "how do you *treat* DKA?"

"Well, you've got to have several treatment objectives," Darlene said. She decided it would be condescending to mention volume resuscitation again, and also to point out the obvious step of dealing with the precipitant event.

Now her cell phone went off—chirping the ring tone she'd chosen in a rare attempt at irony, "Edelweiss."

"In the first hour of treatment," Darlene said, "take care of volume resuscitation and confirm that it's DKA with lab tests. *After* you deal with the precipitant event, of course."

"Um, are you going to get that?" Sachs asked, meaning Darlene's chirping pocket.

No, she was not going to get it.

"So, what about fluids and stuff?" said the med student.

"Isotonic sodium chloride solution bolus, twenty milliliter eye-vee over an hour," said Darlene. There was so much that she knew! She had at one time been renowned, in this place filled with so many knowers, for knowing—for knowing and knowing.

"You also have to administer glucose," Julie Roth said. "Right, Dr. Stokes?"

"No. Not unless, during rehydration, serum glucose falls under three hundred milligrams."

Zack Goldin's chubby face did appear in Darlene's thoughts now, bold and full-lipped and kind of blotchy-cheeked—she was pretty sure that that had been him. But, as she peeked down now at her current patient, the blue-eyed toddler Chris Shepherd, Darlene had to admit: She may have conflated Zack with this or any number of other babies.

Her phone, which had quit ringing at least, now gave a solitary beep. Which meant Berg had left a message.

"What causes this condition?" the med student was asking.

"Negligence on a caregiver's part may be a cause," Darlene said. "You can't rule out negligence of a caregiver." And the residents immediately dealt out glances among themselves like playing cards. Even Julie Roth winked a look of sly derision: Dr. Stokes, the Don Quixote of negligent caregivers.

Darlene noticed all this, of course. Or was she herself just caught in the sickly glow of paranoia?

After finishing rounds (cases of seborrheic dermatitis, of bacterial sepsis, of diaphragmatic hernia, with Bob Kraselnik tongue-fucking these words out of all comprehending), Darlene excused herself. She told them she needed to check her phone messages. But she didn't. She had no intention of hearing what Peregrine Berg wanted to tell her. There was little point in listening anymore.

She walked with pep toward the elevator, past a tragedy-struck white family who talked in sniveling whispers. Darlene was headed to do something that she knew was probably stupid.

3

Intelligent Muhammad had had a feeling his daughter would fuck up.

Maybe he doubted that girls from the 'hood in general, or from his punk bloodline in particular, could hold influence in rich white hospitals. He admitted only to believing that he'd noticed something in *her*, an unlikability special to Darlene, that particularized her ruin for him.

Fuck her, he thought, but his heart wasn't in it.

It's funny: Even in the suburbs, even in *Great Neck*, you can find grubby pockets of 'hood. Poor people everywhere; folks always need somebody who'll clean their ICUs.

And so, Muhammad's apartment building—surburban in that it had flourishing trees nearby, and a potholeless street laid out before it—looked beat-up, an eight-story sloucher. Its north face appeared to have gotten a skin graft; the bricks there showed paler and older, fainter than the rest of auburn-colored 161 Handleman Avenue. Still, every residential building on this street was run-down in its way (barred windows, Snoopy bedsheets for curtains, streaks of water damage). And all around were the type of commercial barnacles that attached themselves to derelict neighborhoods: bail bondsmen, pawnshops, check cashers, fast-food chains, liquor stores, the same as Bushwick; same as everywhere.

Just want to keep my job, thought Muhammad, waiting in front of his lobby's elevator door, his face reflected in the webworked porthole. He was worried because St. Joe's knew he was related to Darlene. *I didn't go after some rich family, know what I'm saying?*

What the hell made her think she knew what went on—what passed for normal, in a Jewish family?

The elevator always took years to come, and rattled its chains before it like Father Time. Muhammad squandered half his daily commute waiting on that elevator. He lived on the third floor.

"Why you not in school?" he said to the only other person riding the piss-smelly elevator now: a long-haired, six-year-old Puerto Rican girl whose family lived down the hall. "You causing panic?" he asked, his try at avuncular.

She met his eyes with a face of confusion and slight regret.

"You a Hispanic causing panic? Where's your mommy, man?" If he'd had any candy, Muhammad would have given her most of it.

"So I'm not spoze'ta converse with people," she said, lowering her reluctant face. "Even if I recognize them."

When the elevator freed her, the girl walked, alone, down the indifferent hall. She scrabbled her key into her family's door, which had a wreath on it.

"Bet, bet," said Muhammad.

His apartment consisted of one 525-square-foot room, a mattress in the corner, the kitchen a tight linoleum square opposite the window. He had a TV and an easy chair in front of it, a future of national holidays spent alone.

It was better than prison.

Muhammad had started not disliking his job. He didn't mind helping people who helped people get healthy. He'd gotten offers to cheat, to break the law. Some young dude at work, Kurt was his name, had a "transaction" going: stolen Ativan and Flomax, a buyer in Glen Cove. It would've been easy money. Why'd Muhammad not get involved? This was a mystery even to him. Maybe he really did respect the idea that St. Joe's printed on a sign in the orderlies' changing room: *Helping People Who Help People Get Healthy.*

He grabbed a coffee mug from the sink now, sniffed it, filled it with tap water and felt sorry for his daughter. She'd gotten him the job, been pretty decent to him. She'd just almost never talked to him after, was all.

Muhammad's window gave onto a view of flaking green Dumpsters, which themselves were surrounded by garbage; some people couldn't be bothered to throw their shit *in* a Dumpster. Next to the window, he'd taped two newspaper articles to the wall, both of which were already yellowing. The first was entitled: "Hero Ex-Con Risked Taking Bullet, Turned Life Around"; the second was: "Vague Allegations Put Long Island Family in Jeopardy."

His feeling for his daughter, despite everything, was buoyed by thankfulness. All right, fuck her for not being nice to him, but he wouldn't have made it without her. He could admit that. *Yeah, I'm doing all right*, he thought with a chuckle. He had a clock on the night table next to his bed. Clocks meant something to him now; time existed again. There's no expressing how important it is, that feeling of time returning to a man. The past had never really been past when what had been the present was only nine years of empty, counted days, one dragging into the other. He had independence now, and with it choices. He might go to check out a movie tonight. He'd have to peep out *Newsday*, see what time the new *Spider-Man* was showing. Yeah, a movie be all right tonight.

And so here he came, Intelligent Muhammad, closing the front door behind him, having combed his hair, having put on his nice collared shirt. Every day he'd been free had pumped a little fuel in his tank, or at least sent him out into the world knowing which way he was headed—like tonight.

Yeah, he'd be okay. But what about Darlene? Hadn't she liked her job, or what? Muhammad wondered. Sometimes smart people were so damn stupid. Like just this week, for example: Why'd she have to go to that dude's office for?

Had she been *trying* to ruin herself?

4

JOSH HAD THOUGHT HIS EYES HAD LOST THEIR MIND.

Nine-oh-six on a Tuesday morning, at the edge of his office's front lot, just as he'd walked from his car to the paved walkway, an illegally parked Toyota Celica had opened its driver's-side door. A black woman had swung out toward him. She reminded Josh of Darlene, though he upbraided himself for thinking so. Not all black women look alike, you know. Still, he thought about Darlene a lot lately. Too much. He wouldn't have wanted to be that brainy. (Some kinds of intelligence seemed greasy diesel fuels that impeded almost as much as they propelled.) Whoa, wait a second. . . .

Dr. Stokes wore a hospital-green smock and clogs.

"Are you crazy?" Josh said, even before she reached him. "What are you *doing* here?" He sounded, in his own car, too intimate with this woman. Like an adulterer scolding a girlfriend for having barged in on his family dinner.

Dr. Stokes trudged right up to him, came to a halt, and smoothed her clothes in a parody of composure. "Mr. Goldin," she said, "I have to talk to you." She blinked and grimaced; her face was clinical.

Her nerves, however, had winded her. Her breathing came out rasped.

And neither did Josh look at all the cool, well-liked sales-man, winner of a court case against this woman; his handsome face paled. He was shaking his head. "I should have you arrested." This had seemed the thing to say, a movielike line, a smart person's threat—

Josh felt not just panic but also something close to nostalgia. A homesickness for everything that this woman jeopardized. But what *did* she jeopardize, exactly? Or rather, what did he feel nostalgic about? His son? Himself? His life? Didn't he have all these things back?

"You lost, lady," he said, lifting his chin. He'd sloughed off a little anxiety in the pleasure of enunciating those *l*'s. "You lost, lady. And we won."

Then a thought occurred to him: "Hold on a sec—you were waiting for me in your car? What is this?"

It was a sunny morning today, humid and blowing. There was some green on either side of the walkway, grass that the wind was moving in sections. Some stubble-chinned young business guy in jeans and a seersucker jacket walked past, then somebody else did, a skinny woman with a pinched face—both of them eyeballing Darlene as they went.

"Yes, I've been waiting for you." Her tone was still breathless, if quietly embarrassed.

"The Child Protective Services file," she said, "indicated where you worked."

"Uh-huh," he said.

Dr. Stokes's gaze shrank from his; her confidence wavered. She crinkled as if she'd given up trying to seem at all sane.

"You're going to tell me my wife is guilty," Josh said, "and my son's in danger, is that it?"

Dr. Stokes was perspiring. A frown greased her face. "Certainly, we, I mean our side, *my* side, did lose in court. Obviously."

"Obviously. Obviously is right you did."

"However, I think if you're focused on *that*, on the technicalities of winning and losing, you'll miss what's—"

But another thought had occurred to Josh, and he interrupted her:

"Does the hospital know? I mean that you showed up at my office? That you staked me out in your *car*?" He squinted into awareness: Her exploratory, begging look was recognizable—the keyed-up face of someone trying to sell an unsalable lemon.

"Maybe I should make a call, Doctor." Josh was smiling. "Get you fired. Or are you already fired?"

Darlene scratched her chin. In all her life, she'd never been impulsive, and almost never turned up anywhere that might have gotten her in trouble. *In trouble*—she even *thought* in goodie-two-shoes phrases. And she knew how this visit looked—how it *would* look. Again she tried to picture Zack Goldin and came up, again, with a litter of universal baby features.

"You could," she was saying, hands now folded in front of her. "You could do that."

She'd always had an elemental yearning to be right, which was only sharpened by all that had gone down, by the grindstone of scandal.

"What the fuck," Josh said, softly, a kind of dawdle while he figured what to do next. He could have just walked off, gone inside, abandoned her here. He really could have.

She said: "Mr. Goldin, I—"

This time, Josh's only interruption was to incline his head; it was enough. She shut up. Dr. Stokes had become a power structure toppled, a set of rules no one followed anymore.

And yet she was bending the corners of her mouth up in what actually may have been an inept smile.

What was it about these intellectuals, these brainiacs? This doctor didn't understand how to be *around* people. The way her wide-shouldered body looked built of lumps under her medical shirt; how she drooped her hips even standing still—she appeared loserish, right up to her baggy eyes. She might not be unattractive, but she didn't *do* anything with her looks. And now here she was, at his office: publicly a reverse racist, a woman who used a hospital for her own ends. It seemed obvious to him what a career demolisher this trip could be for her.

"I am a very good diagnostician," she said. "This is what I do."

She changed the heavy downward impression of her stance, rising into a nitpicking teacher's posture: a stab at dignity.

"Jesus Christ," Josh said. "You lost, Doctor. It's over." *I could just walk away right now.*

"Mr. Goldin, you guessed why I'm here. Well, you mentioned the word 'danger.' It's true. It's your son, your child, your responsibility. That's what we're talking about."

She'd composed all this on the drive over. She recited it now in a molasses voice whose condescension might be described as Al Goreish: "It's up to you to protect your child, to confront your wife, to *admit the possibility of truth*."

Josh took an automatic step back. He'd guessed she'd say something not unlike this, but he felt bowled over now it had actually been said. He blinked in the fast way of someone with grit in his eye.

Neither one talked at all. And Josh just stared. The phrase hung there hypnotically between them—*admit the possibility of truth*. Dr. Stokes still had this one live round, this one silver bullet to shoot off, after all.

The most disconcerting thing for Darlene was Josh's face, gaping like that, with his mouth open dumbly. Darlene wanted to say more, but she didn't know if he'd hear it, that's how bewildered he looked. The words made no difference: Being wrong was the purview of the law, and without the law she never could be right. There were only a few feet of walkway between them, and his nearness was something Darlene felt powerfully now. She also sensed Josh's private struggle not to lose his shit here, not to go off on her. And three more businesspeople, headed inside, walked around Darlene and Josh. But still nobody said anything to them, which seemed right. This was an intimate encounter. A bit of trash, the stray page of a newspaper, glided by, spinning in the breeze as it passed.

Josh's lips had puckered in thought. Even now he struck Darlene as a spotless example of good looks, his full and soft-seeming hair, his tallness, that Clinton squint. His Hugo Boss shirt wasn't tucked in and the sleeve cuffs were rolled. This may have been the first time Darlene really noticed the man's physical nobility. (She wasn't a woman to pick up on nonwork stuff during business hours.) His bluejeans were dark but had deliberate, pale abrasion lines branched horizontally across the upper thighs. Josh's grooming and beauty added to his whole air of being some hugely pampered thing in an abrupt stagger, a quality cruise ship lurching under unconceived-of storms.

At least it seemed, Darlene thought, that he wasn't going to spit in her face. Would he flare up, though?

Josh, in silence, closed his eyes. He took a fortifying breath that widened his torso. His face calmed, wiped of its contempt and worry. He had very little understanding, it seemed to her, of the potential of cruelty in the world.

And now he opened his eyes. This had all taken place in a second or two. Why hadn't he walked off? And then he did.

First, however, he made an odd move. He gave her a clown-wide smile and waved farewell, using only his fingers. "*Buh*-bye," he said—the last thing he'd ever tell Darlene—and he brushed past her. The quality cruise ship had righted itself; the quality cruise ship was walking off. She watched him going: the handsome *V* his back made, the spacious confidence of his stride. She couldn't believe it, or rather him. Such a man as Josh really *was* like a cruise ship: with his self-contentment, his comfort and ego, he functioned as a society unto himself, safe and complete off the shores of everyone else's concerns.

Maybe I shouldn't have been a clinician, Darlene found herself thinking. *Maybe I should have been a researcher, not dealing with people.*

She stood there, under the polished blue sky, with shivery knees; and everything in her chest felt knotted. *I'm disagreeable, a disagreeable woman. That's my downfall.*

Like a child, she kept on looking after the man who walked away from her. When she finally did turn back to the parking field's dead acreage, she saw a white golf cart, its yellow police light flashing, headed for her Celica. Darlene had parked in an illegal zone; this was the security guard.

She rushed to her car, giving her pursuer a moody nod, opening her door, and slumped into the driver's seat. Again she frowned at the idea of Josh, at his Taliban faith in the rightness of his own universe.

For a second, she didn't turn the key. Hands at ten and two on the wheel, she sat—eyes shut, mouth running off curses no one would hear. *Goddamn idiot!* Had she imagined Mr. Goldin would say, "You're right; my bad," and just smile? Why had she even come? She never understood how to handle her thoughts, those heavy and lame troublemakers. And yet there was nothing else to her—she was *all* thoughts. Well, no: There was her love for James. That was real. Her great hope was that in the middle of some night, while nobody was watching, the world could smarten up, lift out of its operative laziness, its juvenile habit of stupidity. The race was due for some evolution—a midnight upgrade. The thing was, she'd been too caught up these many years to know the sociable from the bothersome, the appropriate from its acid opposite. She'd lived in silence and exile, but she forgot the part about cunning.

And now, after this visit, Mr. Goldin would call his lawyer for sure, and the lawyer would call St. Joseph's administrators. Or a newspaper, even after the plea deal? And what could Darlene say? *Ooops?* A plump, tactless white hand—the security guard's—knocked on her car window. The guy stood here angry-eyed, flushed with exasperation. *"Let's get moving."*

Darlene, against her will, surprisingly, awfully, needed to duck her face. With the sunshine dazzling her windshield, with her hands clenched on the wheel, Darlene marveled at the everyday betrayals performed by one's own body, its arbitrary acts of upkeep. Because she'd started to cry.

The security guard leaned forward to look in her window, caught Darlene's turbulent face, and with the standard amount of human goodwill, he walked quickly off. Her chin was nestled into the body's perfect chin-holder—the collarbone. She couldn't remember having cried, not as an adult. *Is it*, she wondered, *the Goldin baby? Is that the whole reason for this crying?* When the hospital learned that she'd showed up here, she'd be finished at St. Joe's, really finished. Even now Darlene resented the dumb little pleasures she'd always gone without: the inexplicable kindness she imagined real friendship was. The baseline contact of all but the worst marriages. Even the ho-hum of some downtime.

And she pictured James. The son whose welfare she may have endangered in coming here, the son her schedule must have disappointed weekly. She considered his overenthusiastic hair, his thin chest, his strained look of nearsightedness and love, and the knotted feeling in her throat was loosened. He had a kind face—her kind son. Maybe there had been, before James, some gentle and thoughtful men in her family. And maybe James would bear his own gentle and thoughtful sons and grandsons. Why was it hard to accept that she, even poor she, was connected to the past and the present and the future through family? Darlene had always tried hard. In childhood, in school, at work, with her mother and James, even with love itself, she'd tried maybe too hard. She knew this. It's not easy to shake your personality; it follows you, in its old familiar clothes. But the world certainly wasn't going to change. So maybe Darlene would have to. She drove off with this thought opening locked doors in her head.

HAD SOMEONE BEEN watching Dr. Stokes at that moment, that person would have seen her hard moralizing expression waver and crack. The sun seems brightest when it lights up those who don't necessarily want to be seen.

In fact, there *was* someone there watching: Josh.

Standing under his building's lozenge of a canopy, Josh watched Darlene's somber profile pass. Her Toyota spurted into the exit lane and away. And he couldn't turn from the sight of that car shrinking into the nominal skyline, the supermarket architecture of polished offices that framed this business park.

"Hey, J. bro," said Soren Gantt, a market research VP who was passing by on his way into work. "How're you?" (Josh's status had only gone up after his court victory, his TV triumph.)

Josh didn't respond; Soren just looked at him, waiting for an answer, and then muttered into the building. Josh felt his own mood drop. He was in no hurry to get upstairs—to Doug Moscow's ass kissing or Alyssa's plagiarized smile. His understanding of even his own emotions (Darlene would have been surprised to hear) was shaking like a magnetic needle. Did he feel pity for that Dr. Stokes woman? Not really. He still hated her, sure. But his was a hate, an anger, confused by a sense of something on its way.

He needed just one look and that would do it. A glance to pacify himself, to confirm what he believed.

He drove home at lunch, puncturing the quiet noon of weekday suburbia; he was driving not to confront Dori, but simply to see her face. The children sprinkled on front lawns, the professional house-wives emerging from the manicurists' and the tanning salons, they didn't notice the confused white face driving past at fifty miles per hour. If Josh saw Dori with their son, if he saw her being the natu-rally good mother he knew she was, then he'd be sure that she was innocent and this would be all over, for good.

At the red light before Motts Cove Road he closed his eyes to calm himself. But immediately he snapped them open. Because maybe that was what nightmares were, fears that came true when the eyes were closed, then vanished in daylight hours.

He would just have to see her.

He had believed a man and his wife shared one existence, one life. That made this doubt intolerable. How do you wonder if that half of yourself is capable of the worst imaginable thing? You'd have to snap your life in pieces.

He trawled his pocket for the house key, opened the front door, and called out to her—"Dori?"—and she came right away, descend-ing the stairs with a quizzical face. He stayed where he was, on the front porch, as she arrived at the threshold, an inch closer to him in height than she would normally have been, because of the doorsill. She wore her Reggie Jackson T-shirt.

"What are you doing home, Mr. Goldin?"

He said only: "Where's Zack?"

Dori hesitated, deciding whether to respond until she got an answer of her own.

"Inside," she said, at length. It was a bright morning. She visored her eyes with her hand and something drew back in her expression. This brought up the feeling of an unpleasant memory, but he couldn't be sure what memory, exactly.

Is there a problem here? said her face. *Are you mad at me?* Her pretty mouth pinched, the tense forehead showed its unease.

"Is he all right?" Josh said.

She made a surprised face, tightened cheeks, squinched eyes. "What? *Zack?*"

"Yes," he said. He hadn't taken a step inside. "Zack."

"Of course. Yes, he's all right." She put her hands on her hips with a small squiggle of defiance. "Why?"

"Where's he now?"

Josh, who had lived as an unimaginative creature, a machine of happiness, had never in his life wanted so badly not to be a noticer, not to have seeing eyes. Dori was wiping at her cheek, slanting her head, looking away from him—all her little tells, her dead giveaways.

"What are you doing here?" she said. She swallowed. She turned her head slightly, to look at him sideways—as if to say: *What's up with you?* "Josh?"

They just stared at each other—but no silent conversation passed back and forth between their eyes, not anymore. The communication lines had been cut.

"What?" she said. "What is it?" Rising awareness hit her like an upwelling of sunlight, bringing clarity, bringing sharpness—awash as she'd been in the hazy optimism of her home. She knew what he was thinking. Neither of them was stupid.

"Josh," she said, and then, more serious sounding. "Mr. Goldin." With wide blue eyes narrowed and her face tilted in defensiveness, Dori was trying still to keep down all that had been buried. "What is this?"

"Dori," Josh said. His anxiety whipped around in him like a tornado. Structures in his mind kept toppling over. But he couldn't get himself to ask her.

Still, with his own features crumpling in self-disgust, he began to face it—he began to face it all. He'd been so trusting as to be a collaborator, a silent partner in this terrible guilt. He felt very afraid.

"Honey?" he said, in some last reflex of trust. He leaned back to take a good look at her, raising his brows and so her hopes.

"What?"

She thought about hoaxing up some transparent anger, shaking her head, even stomping out counterfeit *how dare you*s. Defensiveness had opened up something cruel in Dori: Josh looked idiotic to her now. The dumb grumble on his face, the sad eyes—he could be a little dense sometimes. He didn't understand. *No regrets.*

She leaned against the door and started into an everything-is-okay smile. He'd seen this look many times, its ease, its charlatan slyness.

And now he felt, having doubted her, like a total bastard, a terrible husband, the lowest piece of shit imaginable. He shook his head and inhaled through his nose. He dizzied and reddened—he churned and he wondered—but he didn't speak. Then the total bastard said: "You did it."

Dori's face jerked back. Her fleshy exquisite sad pink-glossed lips tightened, as if she'd heard a deafening crash and was now waiting in terror for the falling wreckage.

She lowered her face that would never again not wear its worry.

Josh eyed her with a wilted look. This moment lasted a short while that seemed very long.

She said something. His brain pawed at the meaning of what

she'd said, unable or unwilling to grasp it. Would they be able to continue their life—namely, to keep drawing everything that they needed from the well they'd made of each other for the rest of their days? But she spoke again, and this time he did hear it:

"I'm very safe," she said.

ACKNOWLEDGMENTS

I NEED TO thank a lot of people: Susannah Meadows, for her chronic encouragement and giant love and, most important, her invaluable editing; she's my secret weapon. And Jeff Giles, who—as he asked me to write here—believed even when I didn't. And, in particular, David Lipsky, for the remarkable amount of magnanimous and time-consuming and genius-level work he did. This book would be much, much worse without my having had access to his magic. Also, Brian Tart, the president of Dutton and of my career, a superb editor who has always had my back. The kind people at the John Simon Guggenheim Foundation—for their great munificence. And for their generous, much-needed help with medical research: doctors Andrea Truncali, Ken Feldman, Hal Strelnick and, finally, the catalyst for it all, Soren Gantt—who first told me a story about Munchausen. And Laurel Berger, another early, harsh reader. And Merrill Feitell, who gave me the title. My agents Andrew Wylie and especially the gifted, giving Sarah Chalfant—and also Sarah's miracle assistant Edward Orloff. My parents and my sister, Tracey. And my twin sons, who aren't born as I write this, but who'll be at least six months old by the time you read it.

ABOUT THE AUTHOR

Darin Strauss IS the author of the international bestseller *Chang and Eng*, and the *New York Times* Notable Book *The Real McCoy*, one of the New York Public Library's "25 Books to Remember of 2002." His work has been translated into fourteen languages, and he teaches writing at New York University, where he won a 2005 "Outstanding Dozen" teaching award. Also a screenwriter, Darin sold the rights to *Chang and Eng* to Disney and is currently adapting the novel for the screen with the actor Gary Oldman. Darin was awarded a 2006 Guggenheim Fellowship in fiction writing. He lives in Brooklyn, New York.